Shirley Heaton has lived in Yorkshire all her life and she enjoys quality time with her daughter, her son and her four grandchildren. At sixteen she began her career as a medical secretary, but some years later, with an urge to explore and fulfil her potential, she changed direction and entered the teaching profession, gaining a B.Sc. (Hons) and an M.A. before reaching senior status in a large comprehensive school. Having travelled extensively she has a wide knowledge of people and cultures and uses this together with her personal experiences in her writing. Shirley has previously written three novellas all of which have been published.

RELATIVE STRANGERS

Shirley Heaton

Shirley Heaton

RELATIVE STRANGERS

To my friends June & Carolyn

All my very best wishes
and
Happy Reading!

Shirley x

Vanguard Press

A CIP catalogue record for this title is
available from the British Library.

ISBN 978 1 84386 590 2

Vanguard Press is an imprint of
Pegasus Elliot MacKenzie Publishers Ltd.
www.pegasuspublishers.com

First Published in 2010
Vanguard Press
Sheraton House Castle Park
Cambridge England

Printed and bound in Great Britain

This book is for my daughter, Alison and my son, Philip
with much love.

Acknowledgements

With thanks to:

My best friend and daughter, Alison for her patience, time and enthusiasm in reading through my manuscripts, and giving me constructive criticism.

My friends June, Val, Joan, Elizabeth and Susan, members of the 'Baildon Scribblers' for their unstinting support, advice and encouragement;

Consultant Haematologist, Professor Liakat Parapia, who willingly gave his time and expertise to advise me on the medical aspects of my novel.

Prologue
October 1988

The baby stirred, her tiny nose twitched and a slight whimper emerged from those cherub lips. Like a hungry chick, she rocked her head from side to side searching for food, desperate to suckle on her mother's breast.

A flimsy shadow drifted across the child and a pair of shaking hands reached out, plucking the newborn from her cot and swaddling her. And as the faint sound of the baby's cries echoed around the side-ward, the intruder tiptoed into the corridor, crooking her little finger towards those tiny, puckered lips and gently slipping her knuckle into the infant's mouth. The baby sucked hard.

Afternoon visitors drifted into the ward and, although there were few people in the corridor, the walk seemed an endless stretch. The intruder quickened her pace but the child's more urgent cries pierced the atmosphere and tore through the place blotting out the familiar sounds of conversation, crêpe-soled shoes on polished tiles and creaking trolleys.

A white-coated woman leant over and peeked beneath the blanket. 'Bless!' she whispered and smiled. Startled, the intruder edged back, her heart pounding so heavily she could barely gain composure. But, realising it was an innocent gesture, she returned a weak smile, gripped the baby closer and hurried down the hospital steps. Her stomach churned vigorously as she looked back over her shoulder. *No one following!* The car was parked right beside the steps, ready. She opened the passenger door, fastened the child securely in the baby seat, and quickly made her getaway.

Part I

The Union
2007

Chapter 1
The Present - 2007

The more she tried to brush away the words that flooded her mind the more they drifted back. *Mama's test results.* Danielle's stomach gave a ragged flip. If only Mama had consulted the doctor earlier. But she'd ignored the tiny lump. And then it happened. The mastectomy. *Please, God, let her be in complete remission!* If the chemotherapy had done its job Mama could be home today.

Danielle rationalised, locking her worries away. She took a deep breath, a surge of optimism enveloping her, lifting her spirits. With her mother back home, it would mean she could finally take up her university place in Edinburgh come September.

Downstairs Papa was preparing coffee. 'Morning precious.' He turned his twinkling eyes on her, leant over and gave her a peck on each cheek.

Danielle gave him a squeeze. 'It's the big day today!'

She felt his arm slip around her shoulder and he remained quiet for a moment. When she looked up she noticed his features had softened and his voice dropped almost to a whisper. 'I'm sure Mama will be fine.' His look was eagerly expectant as he loosened his grip and turned back to the stove. 'And don't worry. I'll take care of her.' His voice was shaking now as he picked up the cafetière and set it down on a coaster beside a plate of croissants.

Danielle stole a furtive glance. His brow had furrowed and the twinkle had disappeared from his eyes. But without becoming emotional herself, she could think of no words to console him. She poured two cups of coffee and gave him a look of warm understanding, knowing deep down he was trying to make light of the situation for her sake, to relieve her of any responsibility.

Marcel brightened up. 'You must be looking forward to taking up your place in Edinburgh. And not before time.' He dwelt on his words, admitting to himself that Danielle had been his crutch throughout Marie's illness and, in truth, he didn't relish the thought that soon his daughter would be leaving. But on the positive side, running the business in Lille close to their home in Perenchies meant he was flexible.

He gazed across at her. She was such a beauty, just like Marie with that shiny chestnut hair cascading over her shoulders, those lovely brown eyes full of life, full of joy, and those faint dimples flirting in her cheeks. A smile sprang to his lips. He must stay positive for her sake, otherwise she would insist on staying home for yet another year before going to university. And that was the last thing he wanted.

'I could put in an application at Universite Pierre et Marie Curie in Paris.'

'What is the point, cherie?' Marcel was surprised at the suggestion. She must have read his mind.

'If they accept me I'll be closer at hand to help.'

He smiled good-naturedly and his gaze stayed level with hers. 'With your grades!' His statement was emphatic. He held out his hands and cocked his head proudly. 'Of course they would accept you. But you had your mind set on Edinburgh. And Mama insists you go.' He smiled. 'You know what! Her word is final.'

It was after nine when Danielle entered the clinic, a tiny flutter rippling inside her stomach. *What if the chemotherapy hasn't worked?* But she clamped down on that thought, completely dismissing it from her mind. All she was doing was torturing herself. She slapped a smile on her face but the tension refused to budge and her breathing quickened. Above all she wanted to remain strong for all of their sakes. And when she entered the ward Marie was sitting in an armchair, holding out her arms and smiling broadly. Bright-eyed, she nodded her head and confirmed the verdict. 'Clear.'

Danielle closed her eyes for a few seconds allowing the tension to drain from her body and when she opened them she searched her mother's face. 'Are you sure?' She took hold of her hands.

Marie nodded. 'I'm positive.'

Danielle let out a huge sigh, drew Mama towards her and smacked a kiss on each cheek. 'That's wonderful.' She held her mother at arm's length and squeezed her hands. 'Now, can I take you home?'

'Not so fast, darling.' Marie's eyes sparkled and she started to laugh. 'We must wait for Papa.'

'He went into work early. I'll pop outside and phone him, give him the good news.' Danielle turned and headed towards the door. 'He'll be ready to come and collect you.' Elated, she did a little skip down the corridor. She could hardly believe it. Mama had responded to the treatment.

As she rummaged in her bag for her mobile she began to relax. For the first time in ages, the knot inside her began to unravel. Mama was coming home, and Papa would make sure she wanted for nothing.

Amy tried to open her eyes but a shaft of blinding light pierced its way through the slit. Wincing slightly, she crammed them tight shut to block out the dazzle. Drastic or what! Her head was bouncing but she slid out of bed, fumbling her way towards the bathroom, hoping not to wake the sleeping Lucy. Then her mobile began to ring. Shit! She flinched. At bursting point, desperate for the loo, she ignored it. The mobile was bleeping when she came out. She peered at the time. Five to eleven. The message was from Mum. 'Your envelope's here. I'll ring back in ten minutes.' The envelope! The words trickled through Amy's brain and her stomach did a back flip as she perched on the edge of the bed. The A-Level results! Vacantly she clapped her hand on her forehead, setting off the heavy drum beat inside. Still in a daze, she lay back on the bed, trying to clarify the thoughts in that fuzzy mind of hers.

Aware it would be results week when they holidayed in Crete, it hadn't seemed to matter at the time. Malia was the in-place. It was Daddy's treat. Amy smirked. He'd always been a soft touch. If she couldn't squeeze the money out of him, she could sweet-talk Mummy into forking out. No kidding! They were putty in her hands.

Lucy, still half asleep, peered out from under the duvet like a little mole emerging from the winter's hibernation. 'Who was that?' she murmured.

Amy pulled a face and sat up. 'It was Mum. My results are through,' she offered woodenly.

Lucy's forehead crumpled into a heavy frown. 'Oh, God! I didn't realise what day it was. Better ring home.' She rolled over and struggled to drag herself out of bed. Slipping her silk robe around her shoulders, she padded across the room and plonked herself down heavily on the bed beside Amy. Stretching her arms in the air and yawning, she mumbled, 'We overdid it on the wine, didn't we?' She wiped her hand across her forehead and looked to Amy. But her words fell into a vacuum.

Amy, anxious to hear her results, wasn't really listening, and she jerked her head around, nodding absently. 'Mm.' She turned the phone over in her hand. 'Do I ring Mum or do I wait for her to ring me? Ten minutes could be more like half an hour.' She shook her shiny, blonde bob. 'I know. Seeing I'm running out of credit, I'll send her a text,' she continued brightly. 'It's cheaper.'

Within minutes, Amy answered her mother's call, and she sat listening to the ripping noise of the envelope being torn open. *Fingers crossed for good luck.* But luck shouldn't come into it. If her hard work hadn't paid off, she was fit for nothing but sweeping the streets. She smirked. As if! Her mind blanked for a moment and then she took a deep breath. 'Ready, Mum,' she confirmed, shuffling her bottom on the bed. 'Get it over with.'

'Here goes. Psychology and Biology As, English and General Studies Bs.'

'Yes!' Amy hollered, jumping up and forgetting about the bongo drum inside her head. 'That's awesome!' She stuck her thumb in the air. But after an awkward silence, she asked, 'Are you OK, Mum? You're not saying much.'

'I'm fine.' Amy could hear her mother drawing in breath and releasing it. *Wait for it*! 'It's just that you'll be leaving us soon,' she continued in pathetic tones.

'Oh, Mum, stop being pessimistic. It's a couple of hours' journey to uni, nothing more. So don't go on!' She smiled as she contemplated leaving Mum and Dad. They were so besotted with each other, there was no way they'd be lonely. She shook her head slowly, wishing they'd cut out that embarrassing business when her friends called at the house. They'd sit together on the sofa, Dad with his arm around Mum as though they were a couple of teenagers. *What are they like for God's sake? Why can't they do it in private? They've been married umpteen years and they're still lovey-dovey. It's disgusting.* And then the thought struck her. They still slept together. *They don't still do it, do they?* She shook her head absently. *Yuk, that's sick at their age.*

'Are you still there, darling?' Mum enquired, breaking into Amy's thoughts.

Amy let out a sigh. 'Yes, Mum. I just can't get over it.'

'How are you enjoying Crete?' She paused. 'You are taking care aren't you?'

'Mum! Don't you trust me?' Amy stifled a smirk, and Lucy rolled her eyes.

'It's not that, darling. It's the boys I don't trust.' She laughed – a nervous laugh.

'It's great, Mum.' Trying not to laugh herself, Amy slapped her hand over her mouth. Mum didn't know the half! And then, cutting the discussion short, she added, 'Thanks for ringing, Mum. See you next week. Love you!' She clicked off the phone and jumped up and down. 'Two As and two Bs. I'm on the Psychology course.'

'That's wicked. Now I need to find out if mine have come.' Lucy took a deep breath and rustled through her bag for the mobile phone.

James left the staff room, pushed open the swing door and slipped behind a rail of jeans. Peering over the top, he blinked. The store detective, Jeff, was holding a shoplifter firmly by the arm. He was pretty slick was Jeff. He could spot a glint in the eye a hundred metres away. James smirked. He certainly liked to make a meal of it, lingering near the till and holding on to the culprit whose face was a beacon glow. It looked as though Jeff was giving him the third degree. Typical!

When Jeff pushed the guy into the back room, James came from behind the rail and wandered casually over to the till. 'Not another shoplifter!'

'I'm afraid so,' the assistant manager replied vacantly, clipping a pair of combat trousers on to a hanger. 'It's laughable. They think they can get away with it.' He grinned and passed the trousers over to James. 'Here. Put these back.'

James replaced the trousers and looked at his watch. Eleven forty-five, and results day! The thought triggered a pang of doubt and his stomach did a nosedive. He needed straight As to get into law school. At the time of the exams he'd felt reasonably confident. But that confidence had seeped away after a couple of months.

He pulled his thoughts together as the manager walked past him. 'Another sorted,' he bragged brushing his hands together. 'Left the back way with the constable. We can do without that sort of publicity front of store.'

His assistant, still busy pricing jackets, replied. 'Don't agree with you there, Andy. If customers see them being hauled out by the police, it could be a deterrent.'

Andy, convinced he was always right, hunched his shoulders. 'Works both ways I suppose. But point taken, Darren.' Turning to James he changed the subject. 'I thought you were after an early lunch.'

'I am, but it's not twelve o'clock yet.'

Andy slapped him on the back. 'Get yourself off, mate.'

'Thanks, Andy,' he added, making his way to the staff room and returning minutes later wearing his jacket. 'See you tomorrow.'

Andy looked him up and down. 'I'll give you credit, James. You're always well turned out. I wish they were all like you.' He shook his head and threw a look of contempt in Nigel's direction. 'It would help if he'd put a comb through his hair.' His whisper was loud enough for Nigel to hear.

'The bed-head look's the fashion.' James grinned and took in the state of Andy, hair slicked back and parted with precision.

23

He was a bit of a geek in his ancient metal-rimmed specs. His spotty face did nothing to enhance his image, either.

As James turned to leave he gave Nigel a wicked grin. In response, Nigel pulled a silly face and ran his hands through his hair. Still smirking, James headed for the doors and looked back at Andy who still had that smug look on his face.

They were crowding around the huge notice board when James entered the hall. He smiled at the group of girls huddled in a corner. 'Hi, James,' they chorused and he waved. A couple of them blew him kisses. Edging his way forward to the front, he slid his finger down the list until he came to his name. He did a double take and then he re-focused, a smile ghosting across his face. There was no disputing it. Straight As.

After easing himself back through the mass of students, he crossed to the group of girls who had now been joined by some of the boys.

'How've you done?' one of them asked.

'Not bad,' he replied modestly, and smiled.

Several girls came towards him, overpowering him and giving him a group hug. But, grinning, he managed to extract himself as a leggy girl approached him, her long silky hair straightened to perfection. She stroked his cheek with her fingertips. 'Not bad? Who are you kidding?' she quipped, now plonking a kiss on his lips. 'I've seen your results. They're wicked, James.' She moved closer and hugged him. 'Now let's sort you out. You have your passport ready I take it.'

'Yes, Miss.' He tugged an imaginary forelock.

'It's not out of date is it?'

'No need to worry, Kate. Everything's under control. I'm ready. Clothes packed, the lot, thanks to Top Mum! She's not chuffed about the trip – thinks I'm still a little kid.' He laughed and shook his head. 'I keep on reminding her I'm eighteen end of August. But it doesn't sink in.'

Kate stifled a laugh. 'Tell me about it. I'm eighteen minus ten according to Dad. A week in Magaluf with the gang is too much for him to take. For God's sake, it's not a trip to Outer Mongolia! He seems to think we'll be up to no good.'

'Up to no good? What does he take us for?' James lifted his hand and gave Kate a high-five. 'If that's what he calls it, we could give it a try!'

Danielle's emotions ranged from excitement to apprehension. She had a constant nagging at the back of her mind, a pinprick of guilt at setting out for Edinburgh and leaving Mama. But Papa had said not to worry. He would look after her.

The flight was on time and once in Edinburgh, Danielle grabbed a taxi and headed for the university. The day was bright and remnants of the earlier mist were quickly dispersing as the sun peeped through a break in the clouds. And her spirits lifted when she approached the campus where the trees displayed beautiful russet shades, the fallen leaves in vivid bronze and flame carpeting the ground. The whole area was humming with students as she crossed a huge quadrangle.

Her accommodation was on the first floor of a purpose-built block where the corridor led to four student rooms, a lounge and a communal kitchen. Filled with excitement, she slipped her key in the lock and opened the door. The room was aglow with bright sunlight. She glanced around at the single bed and the desk and then checked out the shower room in the corner. It was small but adequate.

But then her concentration was broken by the sound of someone outside. She poked her head out into the corridor and spotted a fellow student locking the door to the room opposite. The student turned and Danielle took in the trendy blonde bob and the most vivid blue eyes she had ever seen.

'Hi there,' the student sang out.

Danielle was immediately impressed by her friendliness. 'Hi. I take it you're new too.' Her face softened into a smile.

'Yes. It's my first day.'

Danielle's face brightened and she pointed to her door. 'I'm Danni, room thirty-one.'

'Amy, thirty-four.' She rubbed her hands together and continued to smile. 'Fancy a drink? I'm meeting Rachel in the bar. She's in thirty-three.'

'I'd love to join you. Could you give me a couple of minutes?' Danielle was delighted she'd made such a promising start. 'I must ring Papa and let him know I'm here. You know what they're like!'

Amy laughed. 'Tell me about it!' And then she gave a puzzled look. 'Papa? I take it you're not English.'

'It doesn't take much working out does it? Not with an accent like mine. I'm from Lille in France.'

'But your English is brill!' Her voice was filled with admiration. 'I'll hang around.' She crossed the corridor and re-opened her door. 'See you in ten.'

The union bar was throbbing with students, the music blaring out as they slipped their way through the bodies to the far side of the bar. 'Rach meet Danni,' Amy chirped, taking the arm of a fellow student. 'Danni's in thirty-one. She's French.' She took a deep breath. 'Although to hear her accent you'd think she was one of us.'

Rachel turned and joined them. 'French? Oo la la!' she giggled.

Danielle lifted her hand and returned Rachel's high-five.

'I'm from Yorkshire.' Rachel rolled her eyes. 'Of course I know it's not as glamorous as being French.' She grinned. 'James is a Northerner too, but he hasn't turned up yet.' She glanced at her watch and avidly searched the bar area. 'You'll like him.'

'Like him? That's an understatement. She's got the hots.' Amy laughed and stabbed a finger in Rachel's direction.

'It's nothing like that.' Rachel began to protest but her face was touched with a pink flush, revealing the truth. 'Although I must admit he is gorgeous.'

'James and I are both from Manchester. Rach only met him at lunchtime, so she's been quick off the mark.' Amy slipped her hand on Rachel's shoulder. 'We're both studying Psychology. But James – he's the clever one – he's reading law.'

'Then I must meet this James, especially if he is a bit of a brain-box. I may need some help if I get stuck,' Danielle joked.

Amy leant on the bar. 'What are you having, Danni?'

'White wine, please,' Danielle replied. Then, straight-faced, she added, 'Preferably French. Chenin Blanc if they have it.'

'Who's the connoisseur?' Amy cracked, turning to Danielle. 'It'll be white wine full stop – house wine that is.'

Danielle chuckled. 'Only joking! All I need is a drink, preferably cold.'

'We'll pay for our own, shall we?' Rachel suggested. 'Let's start as we mean to go on. I don't know about you two but I'm skint.'

'Skint?' Danielle was puzzled.

'She means hard up, broke, short of money,' Amy explained.

Danielle laughed. 'I see. Then I agree. I am skint too.'

'By the way what's your course?'

'Medicine.' Danielle's reply was tentative. She hoped they wouldn't think she was some sort of egghead.

'Really,' Amy retorted, her blue eyes brilliantly alive. 'Then maybe between us we'll be able to put everyone to rights – body and soul.'

It was the following evening before James appeared. Tall with thick dark hair, a strong broad forehead and rich brown eyes, he was blessed with stunning good looks. And it didn't take him long to make an impression on Danielle.

After Amy had introduced them he leant forward and gave Danielle a peck on each cheek. 'Hello, Danni,' he pantomimed in dramatic tones, amusement lurking in his eyes and a cheeky grin on his face. He turned to the others and explained, 'I'm doing it the French way.'

'Any excuse!' Amy bantered.

Taken aback by his charm and lively nature, Danielle tried to appear nonchalant, but she found it hard to concentrate. There was something in the gentleness of his touch that had a strong emotional effect on her. Her pulse began to throb, her temple to pound, reactions she'd never experienced before.

But then he made a deliberate ploy of looking her up and down, giving her the once-over. 'So we've got a frog amongst us,' he joked.

'Do not call me that!' Eyes sparkling, Danielle retaliated, her natural exuberance bursting forth. She slapped him sharply on the back of the hand and laughed.

James grabbed her hand and pulled it enough to throw her off balance so she had to grip his shoulder. He held on to it, his eyes wide with excitement. He pulled her towards him and slipped his hands around her waist. She fought for composure and tried to tug herself free but his grip tightened and, momentarily, she was caught in his gaze, now hot and sensual. And this left her with the most bizarre and disturbing feeling. And then he let go of her. It wasn't surprising Rachel thought he was 'gorgeous'!

Amy chipped in. 'Come on you two. Stop star-gazing.'

Danielle shook herself, a rosy blush now spreading from her chin to her forehead. But she reprimanded herself. No way could she become involved. She wouldn't allow it. After the way her parents had supported her, her first priority was to study hard.

But James wasn't to be deterred. Whenever he was close she found it hard to stem those intense, powerful feelings that came over her. It wasn't easy trying to fend off his attentions and she just couldn't resist his invitational smile. That was why a few days later she weakened. They met at the bar where the band was making a valiant attempt at breaking the sound barrier, the beat pulsing so loudly she could barely hear James' words.

'Glad you could make it,' he offered, taking her hand and guiding her towards a table in the corner. 'What are you drinking?'

'How about white wine?' she replied, smiling and pitching her voice over the noise of the band. 'And before you say anything, I've been weaned on it.'

James shook his head. 'Not today, Danni! Let's be wicked and have a double vodka and coke,' he suggested. 'Let's celebrate the start of the new term and make it part of our induction.'

Danielle didn't take much persuading. She tipped her head to one side and giggled. 'Agreed.' She nodded. 'Why not?'

He grinned and as he headed for the bar Danielle glanced absently across the room at the students who were clutching bottles and dancing in front of the band. They were a happy lot. James returned, handed her a glass and looked at her quizzically. 'Why did you choose Edinburgh? Aren't there lots of unis in France offering medicine?'

A gentle smile creased her face. 'I'd heard Edinburgh was a top place. I wanted to improve my English too. And I would like to travel after I qualify.'

Returning her smile, he regarded her with fascination. 'Your English is fluent. I love your accent. Please don't try for absolute perfection.'

She laughed, her eyes lighting up even more. 'Why not?'

James leant forward, his smile brimming with sensual invitation as he whispered in her hair. 'You have such a sexy voice. I could listen to you all night.'

Danielle shook her head, a glow of pleasure warming inside her, her heart giving a hard knock against her ribs. 'Stop it. You will make me blush.'

One double vodka and coke turned out to be three or four, and by the time they were ready to leave, they were both tipsy. Then began the contest. And that's when it happened.

'Race you to the building over there.' Danielle threw out the challenge, nudging James and setting off before her words had registered with him. But when she reached the lawn in front of the building she was laughing so much she was out of control. She slipped on the damp grass and fell flat on her face. James deliberately fell on top of her and rolled her over on to her back. Danielle could barely catch her breath for giggling.

'Gotcha,' he claimed as they faced each other – a fraction too close for safety – his eyes probing hers for an uncomfortably long moment. And she weakened enough to let her gaze skim over his mouth. Tempting!

The minute his deep, dark eyes met hers she knew what was going to happen. A surge of anticipation and desire made her feel alive in a way she'd never felt before. His face relaxed, his eyes softened and his lips came down on hers. A thrill snapped through her like a whip and she savoured the long, deep kiss.

James lifted his head and took in the sensual smile lurking behind her luminous eyes, and his mouth plunged blindly into the next kiss. When he pulled himself away he shook his head.

'Sorry about that! It's not my usual style, but I couldn't help myself.' He lifted her hand and kissed it.

She could feel his lips, firm and strong against her skin. That fluttering excitement began again. But she didn't respond immediately. Hair tumbling about her face, she flicked it back over her shoulders. And, tearing her gaze away she pulled herself to her feet, brushed the backs of her jeans, and with a huge effort, tried to compose herself. She smiled and, to cover her embarrassment, quipped, 'What is your usual style?' her voice soft, almost musical.

'Can't divulge that,' he breathed thickly as he slid an arm protectively around her. 'I may have to use it on you some other time.'

She allowed her head to fall into the crook of his neck and shoulder, and closed her eyes. A perfect fit. But, pulling herself up sharp, she slipped from his grasp and, hoping to make light of it, wagged a finger. 'Then behave yourself in future,' she joked.

But somehow it wasn't easy for her to forget what had happened. The pull had been so inexorable that she hadn't been able to stop herself from responding to his kisses. That night, as she lay in her bed, she drifted into a dreamy state. His image was still as vivid as if he was standing right in front of her and, re-living that gentle kiss, ripples of emotion passed through her and a great surge of love filled her soul. It confirmed to her that, beyond all doubt, there was an immense pull between them. She was forced to admit to herself that she wanted him. But she tried to shake free the memory as she suddenly realised her only defence was to keep her distance.

Chapter 2
The Present – 2007

It was one evening in December after the students' Christmas meal in the refectory when the pains started. At first, Danielle was convinced she'd eaten something to upset her stomach. But the pain persisted and, after a sleepless night, she decided to have a word with Matron.

As she left the room Amy was in the corridor locking her door. 'You're looking a bit under the weather, Danni. Are you all right?'

Danielle clutched the small of her back and grimaced. 'I feel dreadful. I thought it was something I'd eaten at the Christmas lunch. I have the most horrendous pains.'

'It's not the dreaded lurgy is it?' Amy asked light-heartedly.

Danielle shook her head, her eyes shadowed with worry. 'It is nothing like that. I have had it before, but not as bad as this.'

Amy intervened. 'You ought to see Matron.'

'That is exactly what I've decided to do,' Danielle concluded.

Matron listened to her symptoms and gave her a brief check-up. 'From what you describe, this is no tummy bug,' she declared. 'I'd like you to see Dr Jennings.'

'Could it be gallstones or something like that, Matron?'

Matron laughed. 'The trouble with you medics is you're inclined to make your own diagnoses. You could be right, but I'm not prepared to speculate. Let's see what the doctor has to say.' She picked up the phone and dialled. But judging by her reactions, it was obvious the receptionist was giving off negative vibes. Danielle felt she'd pass out if she wasn't given something to ease the pain, and soon. She flopped into an easy chair opposite the desk and closed her eyes.

'My patient is in severe pain,' Matron stressed. 'I understand what you're saying, Maureen, but I must insist she's seen this morning.' Impatiently drumming her fingers on the desk, she waited. And then she smiled and replaced the telephone. 'Eleven o'clock, Danielle, and do be prompt. It's a busy morning for the doctor.'

Danielle sighed with relief. 'I will go early and wait.'

'Let me know the outcome,' Matron concluded as Danielle turned to leave.

By the time eleven o'clock came around, the pain was becoming almost unbearable. And it was fortunate things were running on time.

Dr Jennings ushered her into his room. 'I can see you're in pain. Do sit down my dear and tell me about it.'

Danielle explained her problem and, after a rigorous examination, he gave his diagnosis. 'I'm going to send you to hospital for tests. I don't think it is gallstones but I'm pretty sure you're right in suggesting it's renal. Could be a kidney infection or kidney stones, but I'd prefer the consultant to check things out.'

Danielle frowned. 'Is it serious?' Her voice was filled with anxiety.

The doctor smiled warmly. 'I'm hoping not, Danielle. All the signs tell me one of your kidneys is playing up. We'll know better once they start the tests.'

Danielle protested. 'But I am flying back to Lille next week for the Christmas holidays.'

'Don't worry. They'll probably have you sorted by then.'

But consultant, Dr Waxman, insisted Danielle be admitted. 'We need several tests including a biopsy. The sooner we get to the bottom of this, the sooner we can make a full diagnosis and decide what's best for you.'

Danielle's anxiety grew. 'But why a biopsy?'

Dr Waxman cleared his throat. 'The kidney is swollen. I have my suspicions there's some sort of tumour in there.'

Danielle's heart sank in her chest, but she tried to maintain a tight control of her emotions. 'A tumour?' She shook her head. 'Not malignant, I hope,' she added softly.

'I doubt it, but let's not speculate.'

But Danielle couldn't help but dwell on his words. It was scary. A tumour he'd told her, and that's exactly how things had started for Mama. Surely history wasn't about to repeat itself.

Now she knew there was no way she'd be out of hospital in time to fly back to Lille. But she didn't want to alarm her father. He would become anxious and, goodness knows, he had enough to worry about. During the last couple of weeks it seemed her mother wasn't pulling round as the doctors had hoped.

Danielle faked a lively tone when she rang and told him she wouldn't be home for Christmas. 'I am a bit off colour, Papa – a bug doing the rounds. But I do not want to pass anything on to Mama. I have lots of work to catch up on and some of the students are staying here over Christmas. I have decided to join them. I will try to get back home before the new term starts.' She knew she was being optimistic, especially after the number of lectures she'd already missed. She quickly changed the subject. 'How is Mama?'

'Holding her own. She was looking forward to seeing you – we both were. But I understand your reasoning. It is a wise decision. Take care, my precious.'

The tests dragged on until eventually Dr Waxman made his full diagnosis. 'The medication has eased the pain I know but the kidney is diseased.' He hesitated. 'I know it sounds drastic but I'd like to consult my colleague Mr Dexter. I think our best bet is to remove the kidney.' He paused once more and held up his hand. 'And before you say anything, the body can function quite efficiently on one kidney. But I'm sure you know that already.'

Things seemed to be going from bad to worse. 'I take it the biopsy results are back. Is it malignant?' she asked.

'As far as we can tell, no it isn't. But the tumour is quite large, and you'd be better off getting rid of it to avoid anything sinister in the future.' He opened the case notes once more. 'Mr Dexter will be here this afternoon. I realise this is a shock, but how do you feel about losing the kidney?'

Her breath caught in her throat. 'It seems I have no alternative. But I would like to talk it through with my father before I make the final decision.'

'Of course, my dear. Is he able to travel to Scotland?'

'It will be tricky because my mother is not well. But he will find a way.' She turned her face away, finding it hard to control her emotions. It was on Papa's shoulders once again. She would have done anything to save him from further anxiety. But she must fill him in on Dr Waxman's findings. She couldn't continue to string him along. He needed to know the truth.

Dr Waxman's diagnosis was confirmed by surgeon, Mr Dexter, who recommended excision of the kidney as soon as possible. 'But I'm sure you're aware there are one or two preparations we need to make beforehand.'

'My father will be here tomorrow. Maybe by the time he arrives, you will have done all your checks. The way I see it, once I've told him and we've talked it through, I'd like to get on with it.'

Marcel Dubois listened intently to his daughter's words and his face assumed an expression of gravity. He let out a deep sigh. 'You should have told me, cherie.'

Danielle gently interrupted him. 'I thought it might be something Dr Waxman could clear up quickly and I didn't want to involve you especially with Mama being ill.'

Marcel hunched his shoulders and held out his hands. 'But you are important to me too. I have told Mama nothing about your illness, especially now she's back in hospital.' His face creased with concern. 'It is true I am deceiving her, but I do not want to worry her.'

Danielle nodded and pulled herself up in the bed. 'I agree, Papa. But she'll need to know eventually.'

'Of course, but how could I explain when I'm not sure of the exact problem myself.' He sat down on the chair next to the bed, leaned forward and slid his arm protectively around her, kissing her lightly on the cheek. 'Now, treasure. Tell me all about it.'

Danielle opened her mouth to speak but, before she could explain, there was a light tap on the door and she looked up. It was Mr Dexter. He smiled and offered his hand to Marcel. 'You must be Danielle's father?'

Marcel stood up, nodded and shook the outstretched hand.

The surgeon perched on the edge of the bed. 'How much has your daughter told you, Mr Dubois?'

Marcel ran his hand through his dark, wavy hair. 'A brief explanation, nothing more.' He smiled. 'I'm hoping you can enlighten me.'

Danielle listened as Dexter outlined the problem. 'I can assure you it's the best way forward.'

Marcel wiped his hand across his brow. 'What can I say? It is very upsetting. But I agree. The operation must go ahead.'

Danielle turned to Mr Dexter. 'And now that Papa has agreed with me, I hope I'm pencilled in on your list.'

Dexter began to shake his head. 'I'm afraid it's not as straightforward as we thought, my dear,' he announced. 'We have a problem; one your father may be able to help us with.' He turned to face Danielle and continued. 'You have a rare blood type. I'm surprised you didn't know about it.'

Danielle frowned. 'But I've never been admitted to hospital before, nor had cause to have my blood checked.'

'I see.' Dexter nodded. 'It may be that you react well during the operation but, before we go ahead, I must be sure we obtain as close a blood match as possible. You may not need it, but I can't take any chances.' He paused and turned to the nurse. 'Get Dr Fry to come down would you, nurse. Tell him we're discussing Danielle Dubois. He'll need to bring the lab analysis with him.' As she left the ward, he turned his attention to Marcel. 'I've asked Dr Fry, the consultant haematologist, to come along. I think it might be better if he explained the situation.'

Marcel looked squarely into Dexter's face. 'What do you mean when you say I may be able to help?'

Dexter held up his hand. 'Bear with me, Mr Dubois. Dr Fry will explain what is meant by a rare blood type, and then we'll go on from there.'

Within minutes an elderly white-coated figure appeared, his gaze settling on Danielle. He smiled brightly. 'I take it we're checking out this young lady's details?'

Dexter nodded. 'That's right, Robert. Danielle is a first-year medical student. Mr Dubois here is her father.'

Dr Fry smiled warmly in Danielle's direction, offered his hand to Marcel and then he sat down. 'Let me explain –.'

Marcel intervened, the words rushing out. 'Are you saying my daughter's blood is so rare it might be difficult to match?'

'Let Dr Fry explain.' Dexter nodded towards his colleague. 'It is quite complex.' Danielle sensed the controlled impatience in the surgeon's voice.

Dr Fry took over. 'Let me explain what is meant by a rare blood type.' He folded his arms. 'Everyone has an ABO blood group. Most transfusions can be performed if the groups of the donor and the patient are compatible.'

Marcel nodded.

'But there's more to it than that,' he explained. 'It's the extra components, the antigens that make it rare.' He turned to Danielle. 'Let me try to clarify things for your father.' He moved his chair to face Marcel. 'Blood is inherited in the same way as eyes and hair colour. Everyone inherits two 'blood type' genes, one from the mother and one from the father. The combination of these two gives you your blood group. OK so far?'

'I see,' Marcel replied. 'Danielle's blood is made up of her parents' groupings.'

'That's right. But to complicate matters there are more than six hundred extra components we call antigens identifying the proteins found on an individual's red blood cells. There are some antigens that most people possess, but that others lack.'

Marcel mulled it over and a gleam of understanding lit his eyes. 'You mean they're missing from the blood?'

'Correct, that's the first possibility. The most common ones are missing. But there are also rare antigens that only a small percentage of the population possesses, that's the second possibility.' He hesitated. 'Now whether someone's blood lacks common antigens, or possesses the uncommon ones, the blood is categorised as being of a rare type.' He looked to Danielle and smiled.

Marcel stepped in quickly. 'But which one fits my daughter's blood type?'

Dr Fry pointed to the sheet. 'Danielle's blood cells possess rare antigens. It's imperative we obtain a close match of her blood before the operation can go ahead.'

Marcel shook his head. 'I understand, but what happens if rare blood cannot be found quickly? Surely it is possible to go ahead and transfuse, provided the group is the right one?'

Dr Fry nodded. 'On some occasions, yes it is. Sometimes this is the only option. But the medical complications can be very serious, even fatal,' he turned to Danielle. 'I'm sure you understand. A transfusion with some incompatibility in the blood can cause grave harm to a person who is already weakened. Your blood type is rhesus B negative and an exact match including the antigens is highly recommended. The next step is to find that match.'

Danielle sat up in bed more urgently now. 'How long is it likely to take?'

Dr Fry gave a heavy sigh. 'That's something I can't tell you. But we're already on to it.' He hesitated. 'There was a time when rare blood was frozen and stored. But that doesn't happen any more. In normal circumstances, the first step would be to take the patient's own blood and store it until it is required. It can be stored up to twenty-five days.' He turned to Marcel. 'But in Danielle's case we've discovered she's anaemic and, therefore, this is not possible. However these days, within the National Blood Service, records are kept of donors with rare blood types and these donors are called upon in times of emergency.'

Marcel gave an awkward smile. 'Then surely there is your solution.'

'It could be. As I said, we're already on to that.'

The muscles in Marcel's face relaxed and the anxiety seemed to seep away. 'So it should not be long before you find the blood?'

Dexter stood up. 'Let's hope not. Meanwhile Danielle must continue her bed rest until a match is found. She's being given medication to ease the pain until then.'

Dr Fry pushed his chair back. 'In addition to the donor service, it's our policy to test family members and try to find a match there. That could be the closest source.' He smiled. 'And this is where you come in, Mr Dubois.'

Danielle became uneasy. She turned to face Marcel. 'That could pose major problems, Papa.'

'I don't see why,' Dr Fry advanced. 'We would hope to be successful with our initial steps. Perhaps we could start with you.' He directed his comment to Marcel.

Danielle closed her eyes. 'You need to explain, Papa.' What her father was about to reveal was something she always refused to acknowledge, and certainly something he would normally be reluctant to divulge.

There was a long pause. Marcel looked at Danielle with evident dismay, and then he swallowed hard. 'Danielle is not my biological daughter. We gave her my surname when her mother came to live with me. Danielle was just a baby then.'

Doctor Fry took a deep breath and sighed. 'I see. It's obviously difficult for you to accept, and I do sympathise.' He drew his lips into a thin line. 'We've not made a very good start, but don't worry. Our next step is to check your wife's blood type.'

Marcel placed his hands over his face and his head drooped momentarily. 'That will not be possible,' he replied in a half-whisper. He lifted his head now and stared almost vacantly. 'Marie is not well. She is in hospital following a mastectomy.'

Dr Fry shook his head. 'You certainly have your hands full. I'm so sorry. But I agree, in view of the circumstances, it would be difficult in the case of your wife.' He became pensive. 'I hate to mention this but if you're not the biological father, we shall need to know who is.'

Marcel let out a heavy sigh. 'It's something Marie and I have never discussed. When Marie and her husband divorced, he never contacted her again, not even to gain access to Danielle. I found that rather strange, although Marie has never made an issue of it.'

'I know it's going to be painful bringing everything out into the open, but it is a matter of urgency you must understand.' The consultant's voice was tender.

Marcel cleared his throat. 'I realise that. Once I am back in Lille I'll explain our predicament to Marie, and I'll ask her about Danielle's father.' He hesitated. 'I find it so frustrating I cannot be the one to support Danielle. I love her dearly. I have been Papa to her since she was two years old.'

'There is no reason why you can't donate,' Dr Fry replied. 'Even though you're not Danielle's biological father, your blood may still match. It's not outside the realms of possibility.'

Danielle lay in bed with her eyes closed. 'Dr Fry is right. There may be a match.' She took Marcel's hand and squeezed it. 'Always remember you might not be my biological father but you are my real father. No one will ever replace you. I do not care who this guy is. He was nothing but a facilitator.'

As a young child, Danielle recalled asking her mother why her father had left when she was just a baby. *Didn't he want to be with me?* And always the same reply. *'We weren't getting along, darling. But that didn't mean he didn't want you. And you have Papa. He's your real father, and he loves you as much as I do. Would you want to swap Papa for someone you don't even know?'*

Danielle had to be satisfied with Mama's explanation. But occasionally as she grew older, thoughts of her biological father had fleetingly crossed her mind. What was his job? Was he a high flier? Did she look like him? And now, more importantly, did she have his blood type?

Marcel seemed to relax after Danielle's reassurances. He smiled and turned to the two consultants. 'You are right. There's no point getting upset about it when I could so easily donate my blood, if not for Danielle, for someone else in need.'

'I wish more people would respond in that way, Mr Dubois. I'll get Sister to sort it,' Dr Fry offered.

'That's fine.' Marcel smiled. 'But back to Marie. Originally I had decided not to tell her about Danielle's illness, not until after the operation, but now she'll need to know if I am to ask her about her ex.'

Danielle turned her attention to Dr Fry. 'Surely there is no rush, not for a couple of days or so,' she insisted. 'I've managed fine so far. Why not give Papa time to find the right moment to explain things to Mama?'

Dr Fry nodded. 'Point taken, my dear. But we don't want to hang around unnecessarily.'

'And the tumour's not getting any smaller,' Dexter stressed. 'You've said you want to get on with it, and so do I.'

Marcel shrugged his ample shoulders. 'I will see Marie first thing tomorrow morning and explain,' he promised.

Dr Fry continued. 'Meanwhile, we'll keep on checking at this end. Failing a close match, we'll carry out intensive screening. As a last resort, if no match is found locally, we'll contact other centres and check their registries.' He paused and his voice took on a note of optimism. 'On the positive side, it is possible to obtain the rarest of blood from anywhere in the world. But obviously this takes time.'

Marcel left the hospital and rushed back to the hotel. How he hated having to go through all this. But it had to be done. At all costs the blood must be made available.

His insides became agitated. He could hear the heavy throbbing in his head at the thought of someone else staking a claim on Danielle, a faceless man who would probably expect to meet her after all these years of neglect. Marcel wrung his hands together and frowned heavily. Danielle had always been his little girl and, although they weren't blood relatives, he felt she belonged to him. A flash of jealousy zipped through him. But he knew he must put his emotions aside. It was now a matter of urgency.

Part II

The Crisis
2008

Chapter 3
The Present – 2008

Marcel noticed Marie was sleeping as he was about to enter the ward. Sister approached and took his arm. 'I'm afraid she's had another setback, Mr Dubois. I'd prefer it if you didn't wake her. She needs the rest.'

He turned to face Sister, a bewildered expression in his eyes. 'But I thought she was gaining strength when I left the clinic on Friday.'

'Believe me, she appeared to be. But she had a relapse. Doctor's been to see her. The tests weren't quite as accurate as he'd hoped.' She shook her head. 'You see, certain cells in the body are capable of mimicking other cells, and this can often be confusing, even to the experts. But you know Marie better than I do,' she added, a smile touching the corners of her mouth. 'She's a battler, and I'm sure she'll pull through.' She hesitated and laid a hand on Marcel's shoulder. 'I must say, you look all in.'

Marcel wiped his brow, his nerves stretched tight now. 'I feel it.' Unsure as to what his next move would be he paused, and for a few moments he simply stood there. But, pulling his thoughts together, he cleared his throat. 'I'd like a word, Sister, in private.'

She gave an understanding smile and beckoned him to follow her. 'Of course. That's why I'm here. Come along down to the bay.' She pointed to a chair. 'Do sit down. Cup of tea? You look as though you could use one.'

'I would be grateful, Sister, thank you.' Marcel took the chair and within minutes she returned with the tea and sat down opposite, clasping her hands around the mug.

'I can see you're worried about your wife, but there's little more I can tell you.'

'But it's not only Marie. Our daughter is in hospital too.' It was painful to think about, but Marcel knew he must explain Danielle's condition to her.

'I see,' Sister shook her head. 'That's most unfortunate. Everything comes at once, doesn't it?' She patted his hand. 'But don't worry too much about your daughter. It's not uncommon for patients to live perfectly happily with one kidney.' She took a sip of her tea.

'My biggest problem is telling Marie about Danielle.' The words rushed out and anxiety tightened his mouth. 'She's already vulnerable. I don't want her to worry. I don't want her condition to worsen.'

Sister's face softened into a smile. 'You're right, but let's take this a step at a time.' She lowered her voice. 'Let's try to solve things without mentioning anything to Marie just yet. It would be a pity for her to become involved at this stage. I'd prefer not to unsettle her. She can always be told later, even after Danielle's operation.'

Marcel gave a sombre nod in agreement, knowing his real worry was the cloud over his family, a cloud that refused to disappear. 'It would be a relief. But that leads me to the problem of finding Marie's ex-husband. I desperately need to get in touch with him.' He explained about the rare blood type, sighing deeply and, with some embarrassment, continuing. 'It pains me to say this but, apart from Marie, he's Danielle's closest relative. How can I do that without consulting Marie?'

'Doesn't Danielle share his name?'

'She had Marie's name when she came to France. But then we gave her mine.'

'Is Lambert her husband's name? Could we make a start there?'

It wasn't easy touching on things that happened in the past before he'd even met Marie. 'Lambert is her maiden name. She reverted when they split.'

'How about checking Danielle's birth certificate or Marie's decree absolute? You could copy the father's details, and go on from there.'

Marcel ran his hand through his hair. 'That's not as easy as it sounds. Marie keeps her private documents in a locked box. I've never seen inside it. I've always trusted her. I've never had the need to pry. She was divorced when we met.' He hesitated and frowned. 'And I would have to ask her for the key which again means confronting her with the problem.'

'Let's try to remain optimistic and think this through carefully.' Sister folded her arms and, contemplating, bit her lip. She took a deep breath. 'Maybe the key is with her personal belongings. We sent everything back with you when we admitted her. Why not go through them? It's possible the key will be there.'

Marcel nodded. 'That would be a start.' He gave a weak smile and stood up to leave now feeling a little more positive about finding the key. 'Thank you for listening, Sister.'

'It's easier to share these things.' Sister patted his hand once more. 'I suggest you go home and start your search. Perhaps you could come back this evening. Your wife might feel a little brighter by then.'

Outside the air was clean and fresh, the afternoon warm and breezy. He tried to clear his mind of all the negative thoughts and concentrate on the positives. Marie would certainly have agreed with what he was about to do. With a newfound confidence, he determined that somehow he would gain access to the box.

Immediately he arrived at the house he went upstairs into the bedroom and began searching for the handbag he'd brought back from hospital the previous week. Was it a brown leather one? He'd been so on edge when he'd taken Marie back into hospital, he couldn't quite remember the colour, or where he'd put it. It wasn't in the wardrobe, but eventually he found it crammed into one of the dressing table drawers. He unzipped it at the top and rummaged inside. Unfortunately there was nothing in there other than the house keys and those for her car.

Having examined the metal box that was kept at the bottom of the wardrobe, he knew the key would be small. Perhaps she'd put it in one of her drawers, maybe underneath her underwear? But after a thorough search, nothing turned up. He sighed heavily. What next?

Needing a break and time to think things through, he dragged himself wearily downstairs, poured himself a glass of claret and stretched out on one of the sofas. He had to de-stress himself somehow before he resumed his search.

Ten minutes later he was back up there checking the shelves inside the wardrobe. There were maybe a dozen handbags stacked on two of the shelves, and he decided to look inside each one. But again nothing doing.

Changing tactics and, as a last resort, he felt inside the pockets of all the garments in the wardrobe. And this time he got lucky. The small key was in the pocket of Marie's chinchilla coat, one she hadn't worn since the publicity about animal rights.

Tentatively he turned the key in the lock of the metal box. Despite his earlier thoughts, he felt guilty. He shouldn't be doing this. It was a private box containing items belonging to Marie's past, things that didn't really concern him. But needs must!

As he carefully flicked through the documents he came across a passport and various letters and papers, but nothing he was looking for. He checked the passport. It was in the names of Alicia Marie and Danielle Jeanne Lambert. That was certainly her maiden name. He didn't bother to read the rest of the documents. He wasn't there to pry. His aim was to find either the decree or Danielle's birth certificate. But they were missing. That was strange. He would have considered both documents to be of importance. If they weren't in the box, where were they?

He was about to replace the documents when right at the bottom of the box he spotted an envelope. With a sense of expectancy mixed with apprehension he took it out and opened it. Inside was a wedding photograph showing Marie with her ex-husband on their wedding day. Marcel's stomach churned. A chill ran down his spine as he gazed at the two faces. They had once been happy and in love. What had happened for them to drift apart? Marie had never discussed her marriage, and he had never broached the subject. All he knew was that she was divorced.

He turned the photograph over to find stamped at the back of it details of the studio, J. Trusson & Son, 34-36 High Street, Charters Grange, Lancashire. His spirits lifted. That was a start. He'd check it out.

Marie's condition was stable but she was still sleeping when Marcel returned to the hospital that evening. Sister approached him. 'Did you come across the documents?'

Marcel shrugged. 'I am afraid not, but I did find a photograph with the name of the studio on the back. I am going up to Edinburgh to see Danielle tomorrow. I've decided to stop off in Manchester en route, call at the studio and check it out.'

Sister's eyes lit up. 'Good idea! It was lucky you found it.' She hesitated. 'But maybe they've already found a donor. Have you heard anything more?'

'Not yet. But I told them I'd be back later.' He turned to look through into the side ward. 'How is Marie?'

Sister gave a look of concern. 'Doctor came to see her this afternoon. It may be an infection, but we don't have the results as yet.' And then her voice became encouraging. 'She came round at four o'clock and we gave her a little tea, but she fell asleep again afterwards. It's the drugs you know. I told her you'd visited.' She smiled now. 'Why not get off? There's nothing to be gained by your staying here and watching over her whilst she's sleeping.'

Marcel was anxious about Marie's condition. His usually mild voice snapped. 'An infection you say?' He readied himself for an explanation.

But Sister had nothing more to add. 'That's right. But we just have to leave things to work themselves out.'

He regretted the way he'd responded and the sharpness of his tone. But surely she understood the effect all this was having, first Marie and now Danielle. It took him all his time to think straight. And before replying, he had to pause to collect his thoughts and calm himself.

'She may think I'm neglecting her if I leave. Perhaps I should stay, just for a few minutes, see if she wakes up.'

Sister took his arm. 'You have a very understanding wife. When I told her you'd called and had to leave, she said you probably had business to attend to.'

He smiled. It was kind of Sister to address Marie as his wife. They had lived together for a long time and had remained partners, but never married. And although they'd given Danielle his surname, he hadn't officially adopted her. He let his smile widen. 'I do have an early flight tomorrow morning.' It was as though he was trying to convince himself he should leave. 'I need a decent night's sleep – not that I'll get one. But at least I'll be resting.'

'Exactly. When your wife asks, I'll tell her you called again. So don't you fret.'

It was mid-morning by the time Marcel collected his overnight bag and stepped from the aircraft in Manchester. He wandered over to the taxi stand and asked to be taken to the high street in Charters Grange where, hopefully, he could visit the studio.

The driver looked at his watch. 'It's a fair run, sir. It's right on the outskirts. It'll take thirty, thirty-five minutes.'

Marcel nodded and slipped into the car seat. 'That's fine.' He closed the door. 'I'll need you to wait for me.'

The driver was right. They headed for the outskirts of Manchester and the harsh countryside. The wind picked up and the first fat drops of rain began to fall. Thunder shook the sky and the dark clouds burst open to pour out solid sheets of rain, giving the landscape an even more hostile appearance.

The rain had cleared and the sky was brilliantly blue when, thirty minutes later, they reached Charters Grange, a pretty little village almost hidden between the Pennines. The high street was easy to locate and as they drew up Marcel tapped the driver on the shoulder. 'I won't be long.'

The driver nodded and Marcel headed for the studio, which was right in the centre of the busy street. The doorbell tinkled as he entered, and an elderly woman came out from the back. 'Can I help you?'

Instinctively, Marcel took the photograph from his pocket. 'I do hope so. I need to identify the bridegroom.' He held it up. 'The photo is probably twenty years old, maybe more. But there is a number on the back. Do you still keep records?'

'Twenty years you say?' The woman shook her head. 'I'm afraid I can't help you there. My son took over the studio when my husband passed away. He cleared out a lot of the old records. We go back fifteen years, certainly not twenty. Sorry.'

Marcel's face took on a blank expression as disappointment engulfed him. His hopes fizzled away like a deflating balloon. In his desperation to identify the guy without having to involve Marie, the photograph had been his main source. But now, within seconds, he'd more or less been told it was a no-hoper.

But the woman's eyes warmed and she held out her hand. 'Perhaps if I look closely at the photo I might recognise someone on it.' Her voice was tinged with optimism.

Marcel handed it over and she studied it carefully. Then she slowly shook her head. 'I don't recognise either of them I'm afraid.'

His spirits sank even further and he put out his hand to retrieve the photo. But the woman held on to it. 'I take it you're not from round here.'

'I am from Lille in France. I need to contact the groom urgently.' He went on to explain the reason. 'Hopefully, once I have his name, I can trace his whereabouts.'

Mrs Trusson's eyes darted to the photograph. 'I could take a copy. When my son returns from the wedding shoot, I could ask him if he recognises the man.'

Marcel felt a rush in his bloodstream. That gave him hope. 'I would be grateful.' He was aware that maybe sometimes he worried too much instead of waiting for things to develop.

The woman nodded. 'It'll only take a couple of minutes.' She took the photograph into the back room, and on her return, she asked him for a contact number. 'I'll ring if anyone knows the groom. It would save you calling in again.'

'That is very kind of you,' Marcel concluded, writing down his mobile phone number and handing it to the woman.

The taxi driver headed for the airport where Marcel hadn't long to hang around for his flight to Edinburgh. And despite the short journey he was surprised he'd managed to relax and take a nap. The previous night his sleep had been erratic. A multitude of conflicting thoughts had tumbled in and out of prominence inside his head, keeping him awake. But he had decided during his restless night that, somehow or other, he would try to trace Marie's ex without involving her. And he felt fine now. Maybe his tenseness had been alleviated by Mrs Trusson's offer to keep in touch. It had certainly soothed his nerves to know someone was trying to help.

But it seemed he couldn't stop himself from dwelling on the 'what ifs'. As he set out to walk towards the hospital in Edinburgh he contemplated what might happen if Marie's ex could not be traced. He took the envelope from his pocket and pulled out the photograph. Marie appeared to be no more than nineteen or twenty at the time, but he'd guess the groom to be several years older. He stared vacantly at the photograph and his head began to throb. But he must remain optimistic. The headache had probably been brought on by nothing more than fatigue after his broken night's sleep.

Back to the problem. Supposing he located this guy and there was no match? Who would he approach next? He shook his head to clear that train of thought. Speculating wouldn't get him anywhere. In the hope his search would be fruitful and lead to a match, he closed his mind, locking away those thoughts. After all, failing a positive outcome, there was always the possibility that the clinic would come up with a listed donor. He winged a silent prayer. *Please, God, let me find someone soon.*

When Dr Fry gave him the news, Marcel was suddenly overwhelmed with it all. So far they had traced no one through local sources.

But why was he being so negative? It didn't help. He must make an effort to pick up Danielle's vibes and adopt a newfound resolve. After all she was the one waiting for the match, and yet he was the one down in the dumps.

Danielle tried to reassure him, her voice surprisingly controlled. 'Don't worry, Papa.' She smiled in anticipation. 'They are doing their best.' And as though to steer him away from dwelling on that particular issue, she swiftly changed the subject. 'How is Mama?'

'She is holding her own,' Marcel told her. It was not exactly a lie, but there was nothing to be gained in telling Danielle her mother's health had deteriorated. What was the use in her fretting? 'They are keeping her in for further observations, and that gives me peace of mind. She's in safe hands whilst she's in the clinic.' He felt no guilt in his deception. His only concern was to find a donor, and for Dexter to get on with the operation. Above all, he wanted to keep Danielle buoyant.

She maintained eye contact. 'Have you told her about my operation?'

Marcel averted his eyes and stared through the window, a look of distraction on his face. 'I decided not to. I thought it best to check things out first, tell her later when she comes home.'

'Perhaps that is the best way,' she replied gently. 'I don't want her feeling depressed about me.'

'I had a word with Sister at the clinic in Lille, and she thought it best if we tried to sort this out without involving Mama, for the time being that is. I know it is a sore point for both of us, but I am making headway into my search for your natural father.'

Danielle took his hand. 'I am sorry you have to go through this, Papa. It must be painful for you.' And then she looked perplexed. 'But what do you mean about making headway? How can you do that if Mama knows nothing about it?'

'I...,' he began, but to his relief, he was interrupted by a knock on the door. He turned to find a young man standing there.

'I assumed it was OK to visit.' The young man stepped into the ward, a broad smile on his handsome face.

Danielle's gaze switched to the doorway. 'James. How lovely to see you!' Her tone lightened immediately she saw him.

'I thought it might get me a few points.' He jokingly rolled his eyes and flashed a cheeky grin.

Danielle laughed and made her introductions. 'Papa, this is James, one of my friends from uni.' She nodded towards Marcel.

James stretched out his hand. 'Pleased to meet you, Mr Dubois.'

Marcel took it and gave him a firm handshake.

James continued. 'Sorry if I've disturbed you. I can't stay long. I wanted you to have these.' He brought a bouquet of roses from behind his back and gave them to Danielle, hovering over her and planting a peck on her cheek. 'I hope you like them.'

Her face pinked over with excitement and the blush accelerated. 'James, they're gorgeous! But you shouldn't have.'

Marcel looked bemused. He pondered. This was something he knew nothing about. He smiled to himself. But why should he know? He was being the over-protective father again. Danielle was old enough to choose her own friends. But she would need to watch out. The young man was far too handsome for his own good. Although Marcel had to admit he had a match in Danielle.

James grinned but Marcel's lively brown eyes missed nothing. It was clear from the young man's manner he adored Danielle.

'I wanted you to have them,' James insisted, his face cloaked in embarrassment. 'But how are you feeling?'

Danielle hitched herself up in the bed and pushed the strands of hair away from her temples. 'Better than I look lying here. The pain is under control, and now it's just a matter of waiting.'

His face creased with concern and a frown replaced his lively smile. 'But why do you have to wait?'

Not wanting to reveal the whole business of the blood typing and the search for Danielle's biological father, Marcel cut in. 'Just one or two extra checks.'

Danielle looked relieved.

'I see,' James replied, and Marcel suspected the lad didn't see, but knew he had to be satisfied with the answer he'd been given.

Hoping to steer James away from the reason for the delay, Marcel changed the subject. 'What are you studying, James?'

'Law. It's my first year.'

'Enjoying it?' Marcel continued.

'Very much,' James told him and, obviously anxious to chat to Danielle, he turned to her. 'We're all missing you. I take it Amy's already been to see you?'

'Yes, a couple of times. And she came with me when I was admitted.'

By this time, James appeared a little edgy. 'Sorry to be a pain, Danni but I must get back. Believe it or not I have an end-of-unit test tomorrow, and I need to cram in some last minute revision. I'll come again if that's OK.'

'I'd like that. And thanks for coming.' He took her hands and gave her another peck on the cheek. 'The op might be over and done with when you come again.'

'Let's hope so.' He turned to Marcel. 'Nice meeting you Mr Dubois.'

After James had left it was fortunate Danielle seemed to have forgotten her question about the search for her biological father. Marcel was relieved. He didn't relish the idea of explaining about the private document box or disclosing anything about the photograph. He certainly didn't want her to see it.

When the nurse entered the ward with Danielle's medication, Marcel took his cue to leave. He was anxious to get outside and switch on his mobile to check if there was any message from Mrs Trusson. 'Glad you're keeping optimistic, precious.' He clamped an arm around her shoulders and kissed her goodbye. 'I'll see you the day after tomorrow. And let's hope by then we have some good news.'

Her father had been gone less than ten minutes when Danielle shook her head. What was she thinking? He'd left and she'd forgotten to pursue the business of her natural father. She sighed. How she hated the term, natural father. The only father she'd ever recognise was Marcel. But now the more she thought about his words the more puzzled she became. If he hadn't told Mama about the search, how could he check anything out? He'd said he didn't know the man's name let alone his whereabouts.

Taking a deep breath Danielle lay back on the pillow. What was the point? She could go on forever puzzling it out, and she'd get no further. She let her body relax, having been told she must rest, and in particular she must not allow herself to become stressed. And she'd promised herself she would do exactly as she'd been told. With that in mind, she consciously brushed away all thoughts of her biological father.

But they were quickly replaced by thoughts of James. Her heart gave a flurry of joy. It wasn't the first time his image had drifted into her mind. His visit had certainly been unexpected. It was kind of him to bring the flowers. They were roses too. And what did roses signify? She smiled to herself. Papa must have thought there was something special between them. There was, of course. After all he was one of the gang. And she did have

59

feelings for him. But not in that way – at least she told herself not.

A twinge of disappointment stirred inside her. Although it wasn't what she wanted, once the operation was over and she was discharged from hospital she really must try to cool things. She shouldn't allow herself to be persuaded by James. That time they'd met in the bar had led to more than she'd intended. But it wouldn't happen again. There was no time for relationships. She had enough complications in her life. It was crucial she catch up on her studies, otherwise the Prof would likely refer her and recommend she retake the year. That had happened to one of the other students after an appendicectomy and six weeks' convalescence. And it wasn't only the extra work. She would need time to visit Mama in hospital. That was a huge undertaking in itself, flying to France to visit the clinic as often as she could.

But she would like to remain friends with James, even though she couldn't allow the relationship to develop into anything more serious. And there was Rachel to consider too. Right from the beginning Rachel had been sweet on James.

But why should her excuse be Rachel? Perhaps she was being overly sensible. When they were together the physical attraction between them was powerful. But there was something else too – a feeling of security. She sighed. She'd made a decision and that's the way she wanted it. No complications and enough space to attend to her own priorities.

Shortly after tea had been served, Amy appeared. 'Just missed it,' she joked, pointing to the empty cup and the shortbread biscuit left on the tray. 'You can't be so bad if you can sit here stuffing your face all day long.' She took Danielle's hands and popped a gentle kiss on her cheek.

Danielle laughed. 'I know. I'll end up like Madame Michelin if I'm not careful,' she bantered. 'There are chocolate biscuits in here.' She smiled brightly and opened the door to the locker. 'Feel free to join me.'

Amy placed her hands on her skinny hips and grinned back at Danielle. 'Thanks, but I'm trying to cut down. I have to watch the waistline you know.'

'You're joking.' Danielle grinned and took in Amy's figure, curves in the right places and a typical size eight.

Amy shook her head and, changed the subject. 'I see you have an admirer.'

Puzzled, Danielle frowned. 'An admirer? How do you mean?'

Amy pointed to the vase on the windowsill. 'The roses.'

Danielle's face eased into a tentative half-smile. 'Oh, those.' She paused. 'They are lovely you must agree,' she added, filling Amy in on James' visit.

Amy clapped her hands on her face and said jokingly, 'Better not tell Rach. It's *James this and James that* with her.' She hesitated before she continued. 'I've warned her if she doesn't get her mind on the course, she'll be left behind, she'll fail and then I'll be without one of my best buddies.'

With a quiet sigh Danielle hunched her knees under the bedclothes and wrapped her arms around them. There was no way she wanted to hurt Rachel. 'I don't want to cramp her style.'

'You can't force a relationship. I keep telling Rach that.' She looked to the windowsill once more. 'Judging by the roses, I take it you two could be an item.'

Danielle was put on the spot. She opened her mouth in denial only to choke on the words. 'No, it is not like that...' She hesitated, releasing the air and making herself relax. 'I have a feeling James would like us to be, you know, an item, but honestly it is not for me. I love him lots – I love you all – but I must put my studies first. I can't afford to get all dreamy over someone, not when I have missed so much of the course. I'll be lucky if they let me continue with the second years. So even if James would like us to be an item, I can't take him up on it.'

Amy's tone was soft but persuasive. 'As far as your studies are concerned, you have the brainpower to catch up. And what better place than in here? I bet you've learned lots already.'

Danielle laughed outright. 'Strangely enough you're right. I think I know everything there is to know about kidneys and blood types, so that's a start.'

'Seriously, Danni, life's about more than studying. Mum always used to say *work hard – play hard.* You work hard when you're back on track and you deserve some personal space, some time to relax and enjoy yourself. And you know what? James has confided in me. I know exactly how he feels about you. Let him down gently if that's what you decide.'

'I will, I promise.' And that was something she would have to worry about later.

When she looked to the door one of the nurses was standing there.

Amy stood up to leave and gave Danielle a hug. 'I'd better get off now. Remember what I said.' She waved goodbye. 'I'll see you again soon.'

The minute Amy left the ward, Danielle reflected on her words. She frowned thoughtfully. True enough James hoped they would become an item. Maybe they would, eventually. But not just yet.

As he walked down the hospital steps and headed for the car park, Marcel switched on his mobile. But he was disappointed. There had been neither calls nor messages. His mind flitted to Marie. His priority once he was back at the hotel would be to telephone Lille and enquire about her condition. But he didn't get a chance straight away. As he closed the door to his room a text came through from Mrs Trusson. And he felt a series of positive vibes as he picked up the telephone and dialled the studio number. Hopefully she had a lead for him.

The phone rang and rang. The studio would be closed but surely Mrs Trusson lived on the premises. He was about to ring off when she answered. 'Trussons.'

'Dubois here, Mrs Trusson. Sorry to ring after hours but I have just left hospital.'

'Don't worry about the time. I'm glad you've come back to me. Charles, my son, returned to the studio this afternoon and I showed him the photograph. He doesn't know anything about the bride, but he was at school with the groom. Knows him quite well. His name is Gary Croft. He lived just outside the village when he was a boy, but when he married he went to live somewhere in Manchester, closer to the city. Charles is not sure of his whereabouts but he suggests you try to locate him through the electoral register.'

Marcel held his breath. The earlier doubts which had flickered incessantly through his mind – doubts about ever finding the guy – quickly faded. 'That is wonderful news. The electoral register you say?'

Mrs Trusson continued. 'That's right. Meanwhile Charles will ask around. If you don't have any joy, perhaps you'd ring again in a couple of days' time.'

'You're a star, Mrs Trusson! That's an excellent start. Gary Croft, you say?'

'That's right. He'll be mid-forties by now, the same as my Charles. Good luck with your search. And do let us know the outcome. In any case, come back to us if you can't find Gary. I'm sure someone will remember where he went.'

Marcel couldn't wait to begin his search. 'I can't thank you enough. I'll certainly let you know what happens,' he concluded, thinking he must send the lady some flowers to thank her for her kindness.

Chapter 4
The Present – 2008

Aware of the feeling of guilt constantly chipping away at his conscience, Marcel hurried to the clinic in Lille. He blamed himself for not devoting more time to visiting Marie. And the deception didn't help. He couldn't go on for ever holding the truth from her and, determined to be positive, today he'd made a decision. It was time he told her about Danielle's condition, and the urgent need to trace her natural father. But as he entered the ward he bumped into Sister on the corridor and, judging by the look on her face, he knew it wasn't the right time to do so.

She approached him and spoke in a half whisper. 'I'm afraid your wife's not pulling round as well as we'd hoped, Mr Dubois. But doctor's put her on a different medication, so we'll have to wait and see how she reacts. She's awake if you'd like to go and see her now before she tires. But she mustn't be stressed!'

Marcel's immediate thoughts were for Marie's well-being and he tried not to show his frustration that, once again, his intentions to broach the subject of Danielle were quashed. He sighed deeply. 'I hope she pulls round soon.'

'Don't we all, Mr Dubois? The infection hasn't helped. But let's stay optimistic.'

'I'd psyched myself up to telling Marie about Danielle. But I take your point. Not today,' he promised, his voice now lacking any sign of energy. A state of permanent weariness seemed to be creeping over him, what with the regular trips to England, and the never-ending worry about his two loved ones.

But then he felt bad he'd voiced his disappointment and he decided to push any further thoughts away as being unworthy.

Sister nodded. 'I'm glad you agree. I can understand your dilemma, but leave it until tomorrow. We'll monitor her progress in the hope that she improves.' She smiled. 'But do go in. She's been looking forward to seeing you. I'm sure you can keep the story going about your business visits.'

Marcel tried to make light of it. 'Of course I will wait, Sister, although it's not easy keeping it from her.' He smiled. 'But you've got to give it to her. She's coping remarkably well.'

'Exactly. And let's try to keep it that way for as long as possible.'

Marie was propped up in bed when he entered the private ward. 'At last,' she murmured, arms outstretched, a little smile edging along her lips. 'Sorry I wasn't awake when you came.'

Marcel hugged her close. 'But you needed the rest, treasure. I was happy just to see you sleeping peacefully.' He gently released her and gazed into her eyes. 'I knew you would understand if I didn't wait around.'

Marie pulled him towards her. 'Of course,' she replied and he kissed her gently. 'You've heard from Danielle I take it?'

He took in a deep breath, hoping Marie wouldn't suspect there was anything wrong. 'I have. She was disappointed she couldn't visit.'

Marie squeezed his hands and closed her eyes. 'I don't want her interrupting the studies to come here.'

Marcel nodded but he was anxious to conclude the discussion. He wasn't comfortable covering up the truth. 'But what about you? How are you feeling?'

She smoothed her face with her hands and opened her eyes. 'A little better, but I've been tired these last few days.'

He took her hands and popped a gentle kiss on her forehead. 'Then let's hope, my love, that the new medication is working.'

She slipped down on the pillow and yawned. 'Once the pills kick in...' she started, but her voice faded and she closed her eyes. Within minutes she was breathing heavily, and Marcel knew it was time for him to leave. His priority now was to check out the electoral register and search for Gary Croft.

Priorities! He'd never been so pressurized.

No sooner had he closed his car door and switched on his mobile phone than he heard several bleeps. There were two messages, both from Mrs Trusson asking him to telephone the studio. His heart began to pound.

She answered the phone immediately he rang. 'I'm glad you've come back to me. Charles asked the lads at the rugby club about Gary Croft. One of them knows his exact address. Apparently Gary re-married shortly after divorcing his first wife.'

Marcel's thoughts were racing. The guy didn't waste much time, did he? But he decided not to comment on that fact. He didn't want to spoil his chances of finding Gary Croft by being overly critical, especially when the information had probably come from one of Croft's friends. 'I cannot tell you how relieved I am. Give me a minute and I will write the address down.'

Gary Croft lived in Elmfield, a tiny hamlet between Manchester and Liverpool. According to the source of information the house was detached, in its own grounds and, price-wise at the top end of the market. He had apparently done well for himself in recent years. But Marcel wasn't interested in either Croft's marital or his financial status.

'I will take a flight to Manchester first thing in the morning,' he offered. 'Fingers crossed for me. I am hoping we might find ourselves a donor.'

66

The minute he rang off he booked a flight and a hire car too. There was no knowing how far this place Elmfield was and he couldn't be messing about hiring taxis.

It was drizzling as the aircraft touched down in Manchester, but he didn't care about the weather. All he wanted was to pick up the hire car and make his way along the motorway to Elmfield and Gary Croft. The guy would probably be at work by the time Marcel arrived at the house, but if he could get in touch with someone, he could always leave a message.

Once off the motorway, the lanes became narrower, but Marcel wasn't easily fazed. He kept on looking for the sign Buckle Lane. But his task became more and more difficult when shrieking winds developed and the drizzle turned to heavy, slanting rain which furrowed across his windscreen. He switched on the wipers to double speed. And after searching the lanes for twenty minutes or more, it seemed he was completely lost. His search was becoming futile. He needed to talk to someone, check out the directions and get on the right tracks.

Eventually he came across the village sign for Castlemore and he continued for several hundred yards until he came to a small post office. He drew up and dashed inside.

'Lovely weather for ducks,' the postmaster clichéd. And when Marcel asked him directions for Elmfield, the guy confirmed that the place was miles away. 'You've taken a wrong turning, mate. Go back the way you came and when you see a sign marked *Westerton* turn right. It'll lead you directly into Elmfield.'

'Thank you for that,' Marcel began as the postmaster folded his arms, leant on the counter, and started to repeat the directions.

Marcel backed towards the door, sensing the guy wanted to chat. He clasped his fingers around the door handle ready to leave when the postmaster continued again. 'I take it you're looking for the Crofts' place?'

He turned the door handle. 'That is right. I am.'

The postmaster grinned. 'Be careful when you enter the drive. They have a couple of dogs. They're not exactly guard dogs, but they can be nasty. I know that to my cost. A parcel was dropped off here by mistake and, instead of returning it to the sorting office, I decided to take it up to them. One of the dogs nearly had my leg off.' The postmaster pulled a face and laughed out loud.

That's a put-off, Marcel thought to himself as he continued to back out through the doorway. He'd be here all day if he didn't make a move now. 'I will bear that in mind,' he replied, joining the postmaster in his laughter. 'Thank you for the help.'

Following the directions, Marcel eventually came to the huge open gates suspended on two stone pillars. He let the car trickle through the entrance and along the drive, pulling to a standstill in front of the door. Before leaving the car he checked around for the two dogs, and he decided they were either penned up somewhere, or inside the house. As he rang the bell he could hear barking and he desperately hoped the dogs wouldn't be let out. Eventually a middle-aged woman came to the door.

Marcel smiled. 'I am looking for Gary Croft,' he said. 'Is this the right house?'

The woman folded her arms. 'It is, but he's at work,' she informed him. 'Would you like a word with Mrs Croft?'

'If that is possible,' Marcel replied.

'Wait here,' she directed as she closed the door in his face.

After a few minutes, a glamorous woman in her early forties came to the door. 'Sorry about that. And you are…'

'My name is Marcel Dubois,' he was quick to intervene. 'Would it be possible for me to speak with Mr Croft? I have travelled all the way from Lille in France. It is urgent that I speak with him on a confidential matter.'

'I'm Gary's wife,' she told him. 'Can I be of help?'

This could be tricky, he thought to himself. 'I would prefer to speak with Mr Croft himself. But thank you for offering. When will he be back?'

The woman looked less than happy that Marcel hadn't opted to tell her what it was all about. A flush rose to her cheeks. 'I suppose if it's urgent I could get in touch with him at the office,' she offered. 'Come in will you whilst I ring?'

Marcel stepped inside and looked around at the huge entrance hall. He was directed to a chair by the older woman, whom he now assumed was the cleaning lady. Minutes later Mrs Croft walked through into the hall, a portable phone in her hand. 'Would you mind having a word with Gary? He's anxious to know what all this is about.'

Marcel took the phone from her and heard the man's voice at the other end.

'Mr Croft, my name is Marcel Dubois. I have travelled from Lille in France to speak with you. And before you ask, this is not a business matter. I am not trying to sell you anything; it is personal. I had hoped that perhaps I could have a word with you as soon as possible, preferably face to face and not over the telephone. It is a matter of urgency.'

Gary Croft asked if Marcel could make his way back into Manchester and offered for his wife to give directions to the offices in Quaker Street.

Marcel gave a sigh of relief. 'Thank you for agreeing to see me. I am on my way.'

The winds were dying down and the rain was spasmodic as Marcel left the Croft residence. He followed Mrs Croft's directions and set off back to the centre of Manchester. The city was bustling with traffic and, after following a one-way system twice around, eventually he came across a car park. He called in a newsagent's shop and bought a map of Manchester, stopping outside to look up the directions to Quaker Street. He turned in the right direction and set off, knowing he would have at least a ten minute walk to the offices. But that didn't bother him. He needed the time and the space to pull his thoughts together.

The office was based within a modern building. It was on the fifth floor, and Marcel, still feeling uptight, ignored the lift and took the steps. When he reached the fifth floor he stood in the corridor to recover his breathing and, after taking in a final gulp of air, he decided it was time he made a move. He opened the glass door, went through into the corridor and rang the bell at reception.

'I have an appointment with Mr Gary Croft,' he told the girl, and within seconds a tall man with a shock of fair hair came out from one of the offices to greet him.

'Pleased to meet you, Mr Dubois,' he said as he offered his hand. 'Come in and we can talk in private.' Marcel followed him. 'Do sit down,' Croft added, pointing to a seat. 'Now then Mr Dubois, what's all this about?'

Marcel found it difficult to find the right words, but he decided it was best to come straight out with it. 'This may sound strange, Mr Croft, but please bear with me. Your ex-wife is my partner. We live in France and have a daughter, Danielle, who is in urgent need of an operation. But she has a rare blood type and, before the final arrangements can be made, we need to find a blood donor with compatible blood.'

'I see,' Croft replied pensively. 'But how does that affect me?'

Marcel baulked. A lump came into his throat and he swallowed hard before he continued. 'When I say I have a daughter, that is not strictly true. I regard her as my own daughter but I believe you are actually Danielle's biological father.' His words had an underlying note of accusation.

Croft frowned and shook his head. 'Me? How does that come about, may I ask?'

'Your ex-wife already had Danielle when I met her. And when we decided to live together, I gave the child my name.'

Croft seemed to meditate for a moment or two. And then he placed the palms of his hands on his mouth and began to pace about the room. 'Oh, my God! Marie told me she was pregnant but, at the time, I thought she was playing for sympathy. To be honest, I didn't believe her.' The revelation literally rocked him.

'Playing for sympathy. How do you mean?'

Marcel pointed to the bride on the photograph.

'My wife, Marie Brechan as she was then, thought about nothing more than becoming pregnant. And she had so many false alarms. It never happened – or so I thought,' Croft informed him.

What's wrong with the man? Marcel thought to himself. 'Marie Brechan? But your name is Croft.'

Croft sat down at his desk and folded his arms. 'It does sound strange I'll give you that, but Marie chose to retain her maiden name. They all knew her as Brechan in the force.'

'The force?'

'She was a sergeant in the Manchester police force. Didn't she ever tell you that?'

'I understood she was from Liverpool. And, no she did not tell me about her job in the police force. It seems she did not tell me anything. But she must have had good reason not to,' Marcel insisted. 'It was obviously something she wanted to leave buried in the past. She certainly was not the furtive sort.'

'I agree,' Croft replied. 'She was always upfront.'

Marcel shook his head. 'But how and why did she change her name to Marie Lambert?'

'Marie Lambert? Ask me another,' Gary continued. 'We parted and I never heard from her again. Some time later I did try to trace her. There was no way I wanted to shirk my responsibilities if she had been pregnant, but I never found her. It was as though she'd disappeared off the face of the earth.'

Marcel stood up now and wandered over to the window, his back to Croft. 'It was not the face of the earth, Mr Croft. It was France. That is where we met.'

'But I assumed nothing came of it, the pregnancy I mean.'

Marcel was surprised Croft hadn't supported Marie when she'd told him she was pregnant. But since he didn't know the full story he assumed she'd disappeared before Croft had the chance. 'You were wrong. Danielle was born in 1988.' How they could have split so soon after Marie's announcement seemed rather strange to Marcel.

But Marcel wasn't there to question the guy's morals or to delve into Marie's past. He pulled his thoughts together. He must keep calm. He must not voice those thoughts. All he was there for was to persuade Croft to have a blood check.

'All I can assume is that she changed her name before she came to France, although why she should do that I have no idea.' He was becoming bemused by the whole issue. 'But back to Danielle. She has a diseased kidney which needs to be removed. We are desperate to find a blood donor, Mr Croft. The blood must be made available before the operation can go ahead. And you are our only hope. Would you be prepared to have a blood test to check if yours is compatible with Danielle's?'

'How do I know for certain Danielle is my daughter?' Croft replied, shaking his head, obviously still in shock at Marcel's revelation. 'Marie could have met up with someone else.'

'I realise I am making an assumption. But you can see the desperate state we are in.' Impatience shimmered through him.

'I suppose since you put it that way I've no alternative.' Croft slipped his jacket from the back of the chair and put it on. 'You know you could have told my wife. I don't keep secrets. She'll be extremely supportive.'

'But I was not aware of that at the time, otherwise I would have confided in her when I called at your house. The last thing I wanted was to,' he hesitated, 'drop you in it, if that is the right phrase to use.'

Croft smiled brightly. 'It is, and I understand your reasoning.' He shook his head. 'You wouldn't have dropped me in it. But you weren't to know.' He opened the door to the office and Marcel, unsure as to Croft's next move, followed him. And when they reached the outer door he turned to Marcel and with a wave of the hand said, 'Come on. Let's get it over with. There's no time like the present.'

Part III

The Evidence
1987 – 2007

Chapter 5
The Past – 20 years earlier – 1988

Gary Croft put down the phone and threw his pen on to the desk. It was like taking orders from the Badder Meinhof the way Marie made demands on him. All he wanted was some fun in his life, some laughter. Not this clinical thing she insisted on going through day after day. The time of the month, temperatures, timing this and timing that. OK, she wanted kids. He did too, but not at the expense of everything else.

He took his jacket from the back of his chair and tossed it over his shoulder. If she expected him to rush home and listen to her harping on, she could think again. He could forecast exactly what would happen. And after she'd given him the latest arrangements, she'd be back to the station, back on duty. Ten o'clock shift. He'd be sleeping alone – yet again.

And that wasn't the only thing that galled him. He'd always had a grouse about her name. Why couldn't she have taken his name when they married? But, oh no! She'd told him she couldn't possibly do that when they knew her by her maiden name down at the station. And why did it matter she asked him? She was an individual, not someone else's appendage! That was a laugh. He'd never intimated she was his appendage, never acted as though she was. He'd never been given the chance – more like the other way around!

Fair enough the money she earned as a sergeant in the police force was good. It was a damned sight more than he earned computer gazing. People claiming for this and that on their insurance, some making it up as they went along. Fucking cheats! He hated his job, but there was nothing else going. And why did she want kids so soon when she'd pushed her way up to sergeant? There was plenty of time for that, time to save, time to enjoy life.

The pros and cons of their life together continued to fizz through his head. Maybe he should stop toeing the line. Maybe he should show her he was an individual too!

The lift opened and he stepped out, walking across to the huge doorway where the outer steps provided shelter under the canopy. It was drizzling and the moist wind swept towards him and sprinkled a fine, damp spray over the skin on his arms. He stood there for a few minutes thinking things over. It might bring her to her senses if he made a stand. But what was his plan of action? He didn't fancy the cinema, and he wasn't one for sitting alone and having a meal in some fancy restaurant. So what?

A sudden darkness seemed to descend and as he looked up, the earlier smoky clouds drifting across the sky were turning to a black mass of rumbling fury. Suddenly they opened up, spilling their bulging weight to the earth below. And now the rain bounced on the pavement and collected in the gutters as flashes of lightning signalled the closeness of the storm.

How long would it last? With a growing look of exasperation on his face, he knew he couldn't stand there much longer, contemplating. But there didn't seem to be any let-up. It could go on for ages. And it was a fair distance to the car park. He'd be drenched before he even got there.

And then his eyes caught the flashing lights of the pole dancing club as he glanced up the street. Norris in the office had told him the food there was good and, of course, the entertainment was first class. It was on the corner, just metres away. A few seconds, that's all it would take for him to dash outside and reach the front door to the place.

Decision made. Why shouldn't he try it? If he got no fun at home, he'd make damned sure he got it elsewhere. To hell with the boredom of it all, the day-in day-out sameness of his life. He'd join the club, eat there and sample the entertainment. There was no need for her to find out where he'd been. Not that it mattered now that he'd made the decision to reserve a little independence for himself, too.

A frisson of excitement swept through him as he entered the place. He couldn't decide if it was the thrill of doing something different, or the challenge of deceiving her. He shook the rain from his shock of fair hair and brushed himself down.

It cost twenty pounds to join. So what? He had a hell of a lot of entertainment to make up for, and this was only the start. But when he was asked to sign the book at reception, his newborn courage disappeared. He entered a fictitious name and address. He couldn't have the wife sniffing around checking up on him.

Marie looked at the clock for the final time. He was late. He'd never done this before, so why had he started now? She'd have it out with him when he came back. He knew she was on duty at ten o'clock. Surely he wanted to see her before she left. She'd booked a week off work starting Saturday. It was the right time of the month. With luck, things should work out. She crossed her fingers hoping this time they'd be lucky. At least they'd be relaxed. The consultant had told her she was too strung up, too stressed out.

By nine thirty there was no sign of him. How dare he stay out so late? Unless, of course, something had happened to him. She'd not even thought about that. But no, someone would have called her had that been the case. She hoped it wasn't going to become a habit, this business of coming home late. He'd said they were busy at work but surely nine thirty was beyond the call of duty. She looked at the clock again. Nine thirty-five. That was it. She couldn't hang back any longer. Leaving a note for him, she locked the door and left.

The station was buzzing when she entered the locker room and changed into her uniform. Tall and attractive, she fastened her dark brown hair into a neat bun at the back and applied the minimum of lipstick, not that she needed cosmetics to enhance her natural beauty. A cacophony of sounds escaped from the duty room as an officer opened the door and closed it behind him. There was some sort of crisis out there by the noise they were making. Marie had the feeling it was going to be a busy night.

But Gary was still on her mind. It was neglectful of him not to contact her before she left. But she had to keep him sweet. She wanted everything to run smoothly next week.

The inspector was sitting at his desk tapping a pencil when she entered his room. He didn't look up. 'Brechan, you and O'Hara! I want you up at Planters Bank, pronto. Another attack. Check it out.' He used his words sparingly. 'Be careful. A member of the public reported someone screaming not far from the college, but she daren't approach.' He placed the pencil in a slim, plastic container and shuffled the papers on his desk. Then he stood up and gave a long, hard stare conveying the message, 'briefing over.'

Marie looked to Steve O'Hara, a constable new to the force. He'd been her partner for the last three weeks. He smiled.

'OK, Steve,' she called as she opened the door and he followed. 'You drive,' she added, knowing the responsibility of driving at high speed was the last thing she wanted. She found it difficult to keep her mind on the job.

'Right you are, Serg,' Steve replied as they stepped out into the cold night air. He slipped into the driving seat, drove along Cowling Road and parked the car.

A chill wind was blowing through the alleyway between the two college buildings as they stepped out. Marie shivered slightly and rubbed her hands together. The beat took them over the spare land past the college and up to Planters Bank. She stared ahead. Her mind still wasn't on the job. And then a faint cry triggered her thoughts to the task at hand. 'What was that?' She stopped and listened.

Steve pointed to the grassy area only fifty metres away. 'Sounded like a woman's voice.' He set off running and she followed, quickening her pace.

The grass was damp and slippery, and Marie detected a slight movement on the ground. Shining her torch in front of her and peering more closely, she brought into focus the shape of a young woman. She crouched down, and gasped as she stared at the massive wound on the woman's chest. It was bleeding profusely. 'We need back-up Steve. Quick as you can.'

In an effort to stem the bleeding, she took a clean handkerchief from her pocket and stuffed it over the wound. She lifted the skirt of the woman's dress and blotted the still oozing blood from her chest. But her actions were futile. There was nothing more she could do other than keep the woman warm and wait for the team to arrive. Slipping off her jacket and shivering, Marie covered the woman's bare legs, smoothed the hair from her forehead and tucked it gently behind her ears. 'What's your name?'

By now, the woman's eyes were glassy. 'Haley,' she whispered. 'My baby! I left her with a neighbour.'

A child left at home? Marie shook her head. 'We'll make sure she's safe.'

Shining her torch on the grass beside the woman she spotted a cheap plastic handbag. Opening it up, Marie picked out a wallet crammed with twenty-pound notes. Without counting them, she estimated there were at least three hundred pounds in there. Puzzled at the cheapness of the bag and the stash of notes inside, she frowned. But within seconds she realised the woman must be on the game. She was a prossie.

The fact that the money in the wallet did not appear to have been touched led Marie to conclude that the motive for the attack had not been robbery. She slid her hand into the bag once more and pulled out a small diary. The woman's name and address were written on the personal details page and, after delving deeper into the bag, she came across a small bunch of keys.

The clamouring sound in the background indicated the arrival of the ambulance. Another police car drew up beside it with a screech. A podgy, bespectacled guy came forward, knelt down and bent over the woman. 'Out of the way,' was his harsh command. Marie turned and saw it was the grumpy Doctor Livesey nudging her to one side. 'Breathing space!' And then he beckoned to the ambulance crew. 'Stretcher.'

Marie scrambled to her feet as the inspector came towards her breathing heavily. She told him what she knew and he pointed to the diary, taking it from her and flicking through it. 'Dates and times, Brechan. She's obviously on the game. Get back to the station and clean up. Check on the child.' He handed the diary back to her.

With a heavy sigh she moved away. The inspector had told her nothing she didn't already know. And then the anger started to bubble inside her chest. These women have kids and they don't know how to look after them.

Opening the small diary once more she shone a torch on it. *Haley Baxter* was the name inside and the address was *26 Melbourne Gardens*. The baby must be there being looked after by the neighbour.

Melbourne Gardens was deserted apart from a spindly dog wandering aimlessly. It spotted her and yapped. A pair of curtains flicked open and some busybody peered out. Rubbish littered the pavement and Marie carefully stepped between the debris, avoiding an empty coke can and what appeared to be a bundle of screwed-up, vinegar-sodden paper. That summed up the diet of the sort of people who lived in the area. And it seemed they'd never heard of litterbins.

She checked the numbers on the doors, and eventually twenty-six came into view. But she was stunned when she noticed that the house was in total darkness. Had the child been left in there alone? God, she hoped not.

Slightly more impressive than the other houses, this one was neat and tidy. The tiny garden boasted an array of evergreen plants, and the path had been swept clean. Although there was no light in the house, Marie knocked on the door, but she anticipated no reply. There was no sound coming from inside and, taking the bunch of keys, she tried them one by one, finally turning a brass-coloured one that clicked in the lock. The door swung open and she went inside.

There was a kind of cold, dank feel to the room even though it was clean. In the corner was a baby's carry-cot, the inner lining shining white in the darkness. It appeared to be empty. She switched on a lamp and looked again at the cot. She was right. There was no baby in there. The door in the corner led to the cellar steps and the tiny area at the top of them housed a sink and a water heater, nothing more. The door to the bedroom stairs which led directly from the living room was in the opposite corner. She made her way up and into the larger of the two bedrooms where there was a double bed and very little else. The other bedroom was empty.

Back downstairs, she crossed over to the sideboard and slid open the top drawer. Inside was a pile of neatly folded documents held together with a rubber band. Without releasing the band she flicked through them realising she would need more evidence to check on the identity of the injured woman at

Planters Bank. But there was no time to hang around. Her first priority was to find the baby and make sure the child was safe. She slipped the wad into her pocket and turned to leave.

There was a knock on the door as she reached for the handle and opened it. There on the doorstep stood an older woman. 'Oh,' she muttered, obviously taken aback. 'I didn't expect police to be in here. I thought Haley might be back. I have the bairn in my house next door.'

Marie looked down at the woman who stood a couple of steps up from the bottom. 'Haley, you mean,' she repeated. 'The woman who lives here?'

The neighbour nodded her head. 'Yes, Haley Baxter.'

'How old is the child?'

'Michelle?' The woman folded her arms. 'Three weeks.'

Marie continued her questioning. 'Where did Haley go tonight? Did she tell you?'

A heavy frown gathered on the woman's forehead. 'She had a date. Her regular fella. I said I'd look after the kid. She's usually back by half ten at the latest. Where the hell she's got to I don't know. ' She shook her head. 'She's not in trouble is she?'

Marie hesitated. 'She's had an accident I'm afraid. Are you able to hang on to the child?'

'An accident?' Obviously not prepared for the answer, she stood there open-mouthed.

Marie dropped the latch on the door. 'That's what I said. We're not sure how serious it is but it would help if you could see to the child until we get back to you.'

The woman paused for several seconds. 'What sort of accident?'

Marie could see the woman was prepared to pursue the matter to the nth degree. 'Sorry, I can't divulge more. We'll let you know when the doctor's examined her.'

The woman shook her head. 'Well, I suppose I'll have to hang on to the kid, but Keith'll be back soon.' She sighed. 'He won't be too happy, especially if she wakes up in the night and starts bawling.'

Marie began to close the door gently behind her. 'If you can't cope we'll take the child to the station. Social Services will sort things out.'

'What at this time of night?'

Marie was fast tiring of the woman's questions and her obvious reluctance to settle the matter. 'At this time of night, yes. Now can you hold on to her until morning or not?' She spat out the words.

'Leave her with me. I don't want the poor kid taken into care just because Haley's not well. She's been good to me, done my shopping and lent me money when I've been short.'

'Someone will be back in the morning Mrs…?'

'Whittingham, Susan.'

'Thanks, Susan. We'll be in touch.' She closed the door and listened to the woman's footsteps as she returned next door.

Marie drove back to the station. Surely Haley Baxter hadn't gone out on the game just three weeks after giving birth? And yet she had a wallet stuffed with money as though she'd been paid for services. But Susan Whittingham had said Haley had gone to meet her regular boyfriend. He was probably the father of the child. She should have asked the woman for his name. She'd slipped up there.

But she was tired. She had too much on her mind, and she was in no mood for this traipsing around, doing the mundane jobs. This was the sort of thing Steve should have been doing, not her. She'd much rather have been involved at the scene of the crime, doing something more active, something to keep her mind off things. But it was no good making up excuses. Someone would need to go back to the Whittingham house and find out the name of the guy. He could be the pimp for all she knew. Or maybe Haley had genuinely picked up a boyfriend. If that was the case, maybe he was the culprit.

She went through the possibilities in her mind. At first, she had thought the stabbing had been the work of a punter, someone who didn't want to be identified. But why hadn't he taken the money back? For all he knew some of the notes could bear his fingerprints. But if Haley was with the boyfriend, that threw a different light on the matter.

When the waitress came along in black mini dress and white apron, Gary ordered steak and fries, and a pint of beer. It was all a little pricey but he couldn't care less. Settling cosily in a corner he peered through the smoky atmosphere and the first dancer came out. It was then he made eye contact. He liked what he saw. She was tall, blonde, leggy and sumptuous, with glossy lips. But most of all she was disturbing. He had an immediate reaction.

Eventually she wandered over to him. 'Hi.' Her voice was throaty, husky. 'I'm Jan.'

And that was the start. She did her stuff, pouting, moving her hips enticingly, and bending over to reveal firm, creamy breasts. He'd never had it so good. By the time the show was over, he didn't feel up to leaving, and he hung around until the early hours. There was nothing to go home for, so why not stay? And by that time he'd had well over his quota of beer. But he felt well capable of driving back, provided he was careful not to be stopped by the police, or worse still that the sergeant didn't find out!

The club was about to close and now it was almost empty. The manager gave him the signal to leave just as Jan came out from behind the bar and headed towards him. He felt a stirring in his groin. And that was something he never got these days, not with Marie. She always failed to arouse him. It was always that clinical thing.

Without glancing behind him, he left the place. There was no use letting the manager see he was keen on Jan. He knew from what Norris had said that they weren't allowed to fraternise with the clientele. But he had that feeling in his bones that she fancied him. And he certainly fancied her.

He waited until they were outside, knowing she might refuse him. But that was the chance he was prepared to take. 'Need a lift home, Jan?' Marie wouldn't be home for hours. He'd be back at work before she hit the bed. And now that he was aroused, if he went straight home he'd only lie awake for most of the night.

His thoughts were cut short by her words. 'That would be nice, Gary,' she replied and she linked her arm through his as they set off towards the car park.

Her flat was at the seedier side of the city, but that didn't trouble him. He pulled up outside the place and she turned to him. 'Fancy a coffee?' He looked her in the eyes, trying to gauge her intentions. Her smile made it obvious he was welcome, and her reaction told him it was more than a coffee she was offering.

He was so excited the words seemed to get caught around his tongue. 'I'd love one, Jan,' he garbled. 'I could do with sobering up before I get back home.'

Jan was quick to reply. 'Before the wife gets her hands on you, you mean?' She laughed at her own comment.

Gary didn't want to think about his wife. 'Nothing like that,' he protested. In his present state, he felt no guilt, but no doubt he would by the time he got home.

Jan went into the kitchen and made the coffee whilst Gary sat there becoming more and more excited as he watched her bend down and take the milk from the fridge. She picked up the mugs and brought the coffee into the room. She sipped hers slowly and he took in those plump, juicy lips as she did so. And then she watched him watching her, his eyes now clouded with unmistakable desire.

The stirring started slow and deep inside him. And he knew he wanted her desperately.

Still maintaining eye contact she knelt before him and slid her hands over his knees. He became mesmerised as she massaged his thighs and pushed her hand over the thick bulge down the side of his leg. The excitement inside him accelerated. When her lips parted he closed his eyes in anticipation of the feel of her mouth on his. The long, deep kiss revealed the hunger and frustration within him.

Pulling herself slightly away, she began to unbutton her dress then, pushing herself to her feet, she let it slide down over her hips to reveal black lacy underwear. His gaze was fixed first on her feet before travelling swiftly up her legs and hovering at suspender level. And then taking in the shape of her it finally settled on her mouth.

His breathing became ragged as she unzipped his trousers and slid them to the floor before unbuttoning his shirt and slipping it off. He allowed her to take control and she gently eased him down on to the sofa. As he reached out, she straddled him and he stared as though in a trance, taking in her lovely face, vivid and clear above him. He fantasised about how her body would feel beneath his. He wanted her in every possible way.

Becoming more and more desperate, he drew her into his arms and crushed his mouth to hers. Need and desire surged through him. 'You know which buttons to push darling,' he whispered in a soft, unsteady breath.

Jan closed her eyes. All the passions she had suppressed, all the longings she had locked away burst free. Since her traumatic childhood she had kept a tight rein on her emotions, and full control over her body. But this was different. She had never known it was possible to need so much from any man. And somehow she knew that his needs were genuine too. She smiled. 'Exactly – you too,' she murmured as she felt herself succumbing to the temptation, to the magic of his fingers gently massaging her. Bombarded by sensations her body could not fully comprehend, she let herself float into a dreamy state, relishing those feelings and wanting them never to end.

Gary was too aroused to speak, he could only nod. He lifted her gently and slipped her body beneath his, needing to feel his flesh on hers. And then a fever rose inside him, rushing through his blood with a heat he couldn't control. He pushed himself inside her and myriad sensations crashed into passion. And at the height of it, he felt a series of violent shudders and he knew for sure her climax had coincided with his. They were left breathless, speechless. And then a feeling of lethargy settled over him, infusing his body with sheer joy and satisfaction.

It was more than he could ever have imagined. And that was only the start. His night with Jan was sheer ecstasy. She was all he'd ever dreamed of, sexy, warm, exceptionally pleasurable and a gymnast under the sheets. And before he left her, he gathered her close and kissed her smiling mouth tenderly. From that moment on he knew he was in trouble. He knew he would never be able to give her up.

It was six o'clock when he arrived home, just in time to shower and dress ready for work before Marie left her shift at seven. If he went in early, he could flex off at four thirty, hoping he could make up for his night away and talk his way out of things.

There was one thing for certain, he must see Jan again. But, thinking about it, not just yet. He couldn't afford to be greedy. He'd had a night of sheer ecstasy and he couldn't wait to repeat it. And when he dreamily brought her image into mind he realised the wonderful sensations had turned into a passion and that passion seemed to be turning into love.

It was obvious he'd already been and gone when Marie arrived home the following morning. But it was strange he hadn't made contact with her. He usually phoned and let her know what was happening. And as she climbed into bed, she noticed it didn't appear to have been slept in. She'd changed the sheets the previous day and they were still in pristine condition with not a crease to be seen. That was strange. *What the hell has he been up to?* The words floated through Marie's mind. She tossed and turned, unable to sleep. She'd tackle him when he got back from work, but she'd have to be wary, diplomatic too. It was no good spoiling things for the week off she'd booked.

But all Gary could think about was Jan and their antics the previous night. Could he afford to go to the club again? No, he'd better give it a miss. He didn't want any arguments with Marie. She was one tough cookie and once he got himself into a disagreement with her, she was always the victor. It was her police training. She was the officer and he was the victim – usually being cross-examined. But he wouldn't put up with that tonight. He'd soft-soap her, tell her he was late back and that he'd fallen asleep on the sofa. He knew she couldn't afford to upset him. She needed his maleness to make things happen.

Hands on hips, Marie tackled him as soon as he walked through the door. 'And what happened to you last night?' With a smidgen of suspicion in her eyes she stared, poker-faced.

'Don't ask,' he replied woodenly. 'I never want a day like that again!' he lied, as he felt that whisper of pleasure when he recalled the wonderful time he had with Jan.

Marie came towards him, arms outstretched. 'Poor love. What happened?' She kissed him on the lips and started to stroke his face with both hands. But it was too late for that. She didn't arouse him in the least. She never did these days. Somehow she'd become so absorbed in getting herself pregnant, there seemed to be no love in the act at all. It was merely sex for procreation.

And another thing. She made him feel inferior. This had started when she was promoted to sergeant. And he didn't like it. She didn't seem feminine any longer. She was like one of the guys with those male comments and gestures. He shook his head. He must maintain his stance.

'We had a crisis in the office. Someone made a crashing mistake and paid out thousands of pounds to a client whose claim was null and void. We had to stay behind and sort it.' He came out with the pack of lies he'd fabricated in his head on his way home. He slipped his arms around her and drew her to him. Now that he'd convinced himself he was telling the truth, he looked into her eyes with pure innocence.

'You must have been uncomfortable on the sofa, love. But don't worry. We'll be sleeping together all of next week.' She snuggled closer and patted his head.

Who the hell did she think he was, patting his head? A child! She treated him like one. He seethed inside, but he smiled outwardly. He could put up with that for the week. She was on the middle shift when she went back after her week off, which meant she'd be leaving for work at two o'clock in the afternoon, and wouldn't be back until after ten. Next week he could see Jan again before she left for the club.

On their week off he spent hours in bed with Marie. Normally that would have suited him. But not any more. The only way he could put up with Marie's advances was to close his eyes and make believe she was Jan.

But he didn't have to make believe for much longer. After the week off, Marie thought they were totally loved-up. She was in a better mood than she had been for weeks. Whatever he did now, she'd swallow his excuses. But they weren't needed. When she went back to work on the middle shift he took advantage. He called in on Jan before she headed for the club and they spent a couple of pleasurable hours in bed together. He was home just after ten and he told Marie he'd eaten out at the pub, which had often happened in the past when she was on middle shift. He hadn't eaten at all but he did call at the pub on his way back. His story needed to sound authentic, and that accounted for his beery breath.

But that no longer fazed her. It was as though something had happened to instil some calmness into her. What it was, Gary had no idea.

Chapter 6
The Past – 1988

Jan kissed Gary soundly on the lips, and she felt a warmth shimmer through her. He was her man, the one she'd been waiting for since she was a child. But what a childhood! The minute her mind slipped into the past, she recalled the horror of it, and an icy cold shiver replaced that warming glow. Her past was something she would never reveal to Gary.

She'd been twelve years old when her father had first taken her. He'd threatened the worst if she told anyone, especially Mum. But Janine was sure Mum knew what was happening and opted to turn a blind eye. The fact that she drank herself into a stupor on gin was proof enough that she didn't want Dad pawing her around. And she always managed to be out of the way when he came home reeking of booze. That made two of them, Mum and Dad, drinking a pathway to oblivion. So why couldn't they have satisfied each other?

Once Janine was sixteen she left school and foolishly thought by then the abuse would stop, that she'd be old enough to tell him straight. But it didn't work like that, and she was bitter. Mum could have put up with him, played him along, even if only to protect her daughter. But instead she allowed it to go on happening to Janine.

Dad would come home after a night at the club and start. He was rough in his handling, he was repulsive and Janine was terrified. It was wrong, she knew that, and it was so painful she thought she was going to die. On top of that was the shame of it.

She felt dirty, she felt nauseous. And when he continued to abuse her she threatened to report him to the police. But she didn't carry it through, knowing the best way was to clear off out of it.

It was early one morning when she grabbed a holdall from under the bed and packed the few clothes she possessed. It was time to leave, and she tiptoed down the stairs, letting herself out through the front door. The only money she had was her week's wage from her job at the shop. Usually she'd have to pay her board and be left with a pittance, but she wasn't going to stay around to pay for anyone's habits.

She needed to get as far away as she could and her sights were set on London. From what she'd heard, it was the best place to go. There were so many people there she'd be lost in the crowds. They'd never find her.

A sense of relief came over her during the bus ride to the railway station. She'd finally left it all behind her. But once she reached the platform and stood waiting for the train she dithered. Could she do it? Could she cope alone? It was either that or back to the abuse.

Decision made. She swallowed hard, took the chance and boarded the train. But throughout the journey her heart was pounding inside her chest, and she felt that at any moment she would burst into tears. What would she do when she arrived in London? She had to admit to herself that she was scared.

It turned out her question was academic. Once on the underground she was soon swallowed up in the gangs of homeless. And after ferreting through the rubble and finding herself a cardboard box for the night, she settled down. But within minutes Tracey, a streetwise girl, took a particular interest in her, and when Janine, desperate to off-load her fears, confided in the girl about her father's abuse, Tracey was sympathetic and fussed around her like a broody hen. 'Don't worry. It'll never happen again! I'll look after you.'

Tracey stuck to her word, but unbeknown to Janine it was for the girl's own ends. Janine wasn't to know Tracey was a drug addict and fed her habit using the money she made from shoplifting and selling on. And if Janine wanted to stay with Tracey, she too would be expected to do her share to contribute.

By the time she was seventeen, Janine realised the majority of her life had been spent being used by others. And after a narrow escape from arrest, she made her final decision to leave. Tracey had taken a blouse and been spotted by the store detective who followed her to the door. But she'd craftily passed the blouse on to Janine who'd walked casually from the shop with it tucked under her jacket.

Outside in the street, Tracey joined her. 'You were brill, Jan. You're getting to be a proper little professional.' But Janine turned away, mortified, knowing the game would have to stop. If she didn't split from Tracey, she was sure to end up in prison. Having kept herself sane and resisted the drugs constantly on offer, at last she knew she could fend for herself, she was a free spirit, she was independent.

The train to Manchester was on time and, once there, Janine headed for the job centre. And that's when she met Rob. He was hanging about outside. 'Looking for a job?' he asked, slipping his arm around her shoulder. 'How about working for me?'

Dumbfounded at his brashness, Janine shrugged his arm away and raked her angry eyes over him. She was no longer anyone's puppet. 'You can stop that for a start.' She brushed her shoulder.

'It's not what you think,' he protested. 'As I said, how about working for me?'

She stared him directly in the face. She hadn't gone through her London experiences without being able to stand up for herself. 'It depends what's on offer,' she challenged.

He gave a casual smile. 'It's legit, love, believe me.'

She must stay in control otherwise she could be at his mercy. 'Legit. How do you mean it's legit?'

'Ever heard of pole dancing? That's all there is to it. Nothing more. No favours.' He shook his head. 'Come and check it out. You've nothing to lose.'

'Where have I heard that phrase before?' she bantered.

'Honest, love. You'd be perfect.' And Rob continued in persuasive mode. 'You've got just the figure. I could get one of the others to show you the ropes and, as soon as you've cracked it, you could start. It's good money, especially with the tips,' he explained. 'But there's one very important house rule. No hanky-panky, and no going off with the punters.'

Still on her guard, Janine offered him a weak smile. 'I suppose I could give it a try,' she replied. Janine condescended to go along to the club and watch, but only out of curiosity she told herself.

And that was the start of it. Rob was right. It was only dancing after all. OK it might be suggestive, but nothing more.

By the time she was eighteen she was fully experienced. She had her own flat and, although it was in a rather run-down area of the city, it was home to her. For the first time in her life she felt she was doing something for herself and nobody else.

Her luck was definitely in the day she met Gary. Sure, he was married. So what? That didn't faze her. And when it came to this one, something clicked the moment they met. She was uncompromising. She meant business and she would stop at nothing to have him for her own. In her heart she knew she'd met her soul mate.

Marie reflected on their week together. It had turned out to be all she'd hoped for. And once she was back at work she felt completely de-stressed and ready for anything. With luck she'd conceived. Goodness knows they'd been at it all week! Gary had been Mr Virility. Surely their attempts couldn't fail?

She went into the bathroom and stared hard at the cardboard box on the edge of the bath, reflecting on the number of pregnancy checks she'd completed, and the number of negative results. She hesitated before she picked it up, took out the foil package and carried out the test, staring hard at the plastic stick. As the lines appeared she became mesmerised. It couldn't be right. Wide-eyed she stared again. This had never happened before. The test was positive.

At first she just couldn't believe it. But when she realised what it meant, she was so elated she could have raced outside and performed a little jig down the garden path. After their week of sheer bliss, she had hoped for a positive result, and now it had become reality. That smug feeling began to take over. She was bursting to tell Gary, let him into her little secret, but she wouldn't tell him, not until after her appointment with the doctor. It was better to wait for his confirmation, just to be on the safe side.

The news was good. 'You'll be delighted to know you're pregnant, Marie. The IVF treatment we discussed earlier this year is no longer necessary.'

At first, Marie seemed not to comprehend; she'd had so many false alarms in the past. 'Are you sure, Doctor?'

The doctor smiled easily, looked down at his notes and nodded. 'But just a few words of warning. Don't get too excited. Take it easy. Go home and let your husband know. I'm sure he'll be delighted too.'

Her spirits were high. It had happened at last. Gary was going to be a proud father. She smiled to herself all the way home from the surgery and almost did that little skip up the garden path. But when she opened the door and entered the hall he was standing there as though he'd been waiting for her. She knew there was something amiss as soon as she noticed the way his shoulders stiffened. Had he lost his job?

But she stopped herself from further conjecture. It was best to let him have his say before she told him about the baby. Whatever was upsetting him, she was sure the good news would perk him up.

His cough was a nervous one. His mouth tightened and she noticed the confusion in his eyes. Unable to meet her eyes, he looked away. Then he came out with it. 'Sorry love, I've something to confess.' She stared as he squeezed his eyes shut and noticed his body tense as he leant back on the wall. And then he opened his eyes and, turning his head, he stared out through the window. As though in a trance, he lifted his hand and splayed it on the glass, pressing hard and leaving a ghost of a shadow.

Marie didn't pick up on the tension at first. She was still euphoric about the baby. There was nothing he could do to disconcert her. She laughed. 'Don't say you've been a naughty boy,' she joked. 'Pubbing and clubbing behind my back.'

But his hands were shaking now and his voice seemed strangled. 'I'm not joking, Marie. I'm being serious.' He held his breath before he continued. 'I've met someone else.' The words ran off his tongue as though he'd rehearsed them. And then he exhaled, obviously relieved to have made his confession.

Marie's stomach nose-dived. 'How do you mean you've met someone else?' she asked crisply, biting off each separate word. Was she hearing things? Surely he wasn't coming up with some sick joke.

'Believe me, I wasn't looking for anyone,' he admitted. 'It just happened.' His words were more fluent now. He was getting into his stride.

At first his statement rendered her speechless, disbelieving. And then, as she tried to reconcile the situation, a multitude of conflicting thoughts flittered through her mind. For several seconds there was complete silence. 'Hang on. Just let me get this straight. You mean you've met another woman?' She laughed. He was joking, she was sure of that. She told her body to relax.

Still unwilling to meet her gaze, he continued to explain. 'You've been on duty so often recently when I've come back home.' His words had a defensive edge to them. 'Surely you can't expect me to live the life of a monk?'

Her teeth bit into her lower lip. She shook her head in bewilderment, colour seeping swiftly to her cheeks. 'The life of a monk? How dare you? I took a week off in May so that we could be together. I was very much under the impression you enjoyed our togetherness.' It took a moment or two for her eyes to focus on his. Immediately they darkened with confusion and shock. And then a screen of rage ripped across her vision. 'You've got a nerve! I hope you're not trying to blame me for what's happened. And as for the job, how come you told your mates how proud you were when I was promoted to sergeant? I suppose that was a load of claptrap as well.' She could feel the palpitations in her chest now, and she folded her arms as though to cover up her hurt.

'Not at all, Marie. You've got it wrong. I was proud. But I didn't expect you to change. It's OK you taking a week off when it suits you.' He'd been brave enough to confess and now it seemed his confidence was rising. 'Everything's so clinical these days. There's never any excitement, never any romance. What's happened to all that? All you think about is having a kid.'

She remained stubbornly silent for a minute or so, and now she could see by the look on his face that he was squirming inside. 'I thought that was what you wanted too. I wasn't aware the excitement or the romance was missing.' The doctor had suggested she took it easy. What was happening was exactly the opposite. She tried to steel herself. After all that's what she'd been taught as part of her training – not to become too emotional. But this was personal. It wasn't about some other body. 'Why didn't you talk it through with me?' Her heart began to pound wildly. 'I suppose when we had that week together you were faking it.'

He stood his ground now. 'You're wrong there. We had a marvellous week together. I started to think everything had changed, that we were getting back to the way we used to be. But afterwards all you could do was talk about what might happen,' he lied. 'We've been through it time and time again in the past. I'm sick of hearing about it. Let's face it, nothing ever comes of it. And after that week, you never came near me, not even a kiss or a cuddle.'

'My God, we're getting the full analysis now,' she shot back, her voice vibrating. She took a deep breath and narrowed her eyes. 'Who is this other woman anyway?'

'Her name's Jan. I met her at a club.'

Shocked, Marie recoiled. And then she pursed her lips. 'A strip club, I suppose.' She folded her arms as though in total resignation and tried to contain her emotions. 'If that's the sort of woman you're after then good luck.'

Gary stretched forward to take her hands but she stepped back and pushed him away. 'I'd like us to part amicably, Marie. There's no need for any animosity.'

Disgusted, Marie spun round. The news had set her over the edge. 'Animosity?' she shouted. 'You've got to be fucking joking. Don't you worry! I'll find her. She'll soon see whether there's any animosity or not.'

'Please, Marie, don't use that sort of language,' he begged. 'And you're not to go near her. She's pregnant with my child.'

Marie gasped loudly and turned towards him, her brown eyes the size of marbles. 'Then that makes two of us,' she ranted, discharging her venom. 'Where does your loyalty lie, tell me that you fucking swine?'

He smirked. 'Come off it, Marie. You're having me on. You'd never get pregnant if we stuck at it like rabbits for the next ten years.'

Frenzied now, she screamed. That was the worst insult he could have hurled at her. Tears began to well up in her eyes and her shoulders began to shake. But, determined to have her breakdown in private, she pulled open the bathroom door.

Gary moved towards her again. 'But Marie…,' he began.

Marie slammed the door and locked it behind her. 'Pack your bags and go!' she yelled between sobs. 'I never want to see you again.'

'There's no need for the histrionics, Marie. It's not like you at all. Let's talk rationally. Come on, love. Come out.'

'How do you mean it's not like me? You've no idea what I'm like. You only think you have. I've always been here for you. I've always been the strong one. But not any more. I mean what I say. Get out of my life and never come back!'

She clamped up. She'd been so elated at the good news and now all she felt was emptiness. How could he do this to her? And why couldn't he believe her when she told him she was pregnant? Did he regard her as some sterile old maid?

Whatever happened she would never take him back. Not after his affair with some slapper, and not after he'd come out with those nasty, insensitive words. Her heart felt as though someone had trampled all over it. She felt battered from the inside out. She pulled a blanket from the airing cupboard, lay on the floor and crawled under it. She clung to the edge of the blanket, her hands tensed.

It was twenty minutes later when she heard the door slam and then there was silence. But, knowing how he worked, she didn't leave the bathroom straight away. He was probably still in there.

Eventually when she opened the door he had gone. And now she must pull herself together. She splashed her face with cold water, changed out of her uniform and applied a little make-up, hoping no one would know she'd been crying. She must keep up her image. She slipped her coat on and locked the door behind her. Whether he believed her or not, she was pregnant. And if he didn't want their baby, she certainly did. She hadn't gone through all that planning for nothing. He'd left, and that was the end of it. The first thing she needed to do was change the locks. If he wanted to split that was the first step. She'd never have him in the house again.

'I feel like fucking crap,' Gary admitted to Jan as he slumped on the sofa next to her. He rubbed his temples hoping to smooth away the tension.

Jan snuggled closer to him. 'Don't let it get you down, love,' she murmured sympathetically. 'It's over with. You've got it off your chest. And we've got the baby to look forward to.'

Gary closed his eyes and shook his head. 'But she says she's pregnant too. Not that I believe her. She's just saying that to get my sympathy. But I'll have to sweeten her up or else the shit will hit the fucking fan. I'll go this afternoon. She might have come round by then. And she's not on shift until this evening.'

Jan sat up and turned to face him. 'Do be careful, Gary. I don't want any trouble.'

Gary kissed her on the forehead. 'Don't worry. I'll keep it calm.'

But Gary was gob-smacked when he realised the locks on the doors had been changed. What about all his stuff, his clothes and his personal possessions? She'd really taken up the dagger to him. But, knowing she was in there, he knocked until his knuckles were sore. And now what more could he do? He couldn't very well call the police!

The next best thing was to phone her. But his ploy didn't work. Each time the answering service had been switched on.

After a few days he was fast running out of clothes to wear. But he wasn't prepared to give up easily. He'd go round again and try to gain entrance. But as he drew up outside the house he noticed two suitcases on the doorstep with a note attached.

Your clothes. Don't trouble me again.
You can communicate through my solicitor.

So it really was the end. At least he had his clothes. But there were other things he needed, documents and personal items. He supposed he'd have to negotiate through her solicitor to collect those. It seemed he could never win. She was the victor again. And he never knew what she might have ditched. His guitar never appeared, the one he was playing at the police club party when they'd first met. He'd enjoyed the times when he and Kevin Osborne did the clubs a couple of evenings a week. But that was knocked on the head once Marie made it to sergeant. Irrespective of whether he enjoyed it or not, she didn't want him playing the clubs. They could manage very well thank you on their joint wages. At the time, he was still besotted, and he'd have done anything to please her. But later he regretted giving it all up. Kevin wasn't best pleased either. Gary had let him down big time, and to rub salt in the wound, Kevin had since taken on another partner and they were big on the concert scene these days.

Gary didn't stop calling at the house, at first to check if she had any more of his stuff. But his conscience kept on telling him he should make sure she was all right. After all she had said she was pregnant and he always had that niggling feeling he should have found out whether she was being truthful or not, or if she'd said it to make him feel bad after he'd told her about Jan.

He never saw Marie again. His divorce turned out to be expensive but it was swift. She'd taken a female solicitor. She would, wouldn't she? That fitted the bill. Powerful women! They all stick together. And there was certainly no need for Marie's animosity towards him. He'd begged her to part amicably, but no, she'd no intention of doing it that way.

If Marie was pregnant, Gary never discovered the truth. That was something he still felt guilty about. He'd heard rumours she'd left the police force, but he couldn't believe that to be true. After all, she lived and breathed the force. His guess was that she'd moved to another area, another force.

Once Jan's baby was on the way, Gary knew he'd have to go all out to make sure he earned enough money to support the three of them. Marie's money had been a huge boost to the family income, and he'd taken a few steps down since they'd parted. Jan had given up the job at the club and instead she worked in a little coffee shop not far away from her flat. Both were happier now, but her job didn't generate much income, a little 'pin money', nothing more.

Gary settled down and, now that he was more content, he threw himself into the job. His new allegiance to the company was quickly noted, and when a vacancy came up, Gary was sent for.

'You seem to have a more positive attitude to the job recently, Croft. We've been most impressed,' the managing director told him. 'I was particularly intrigued by your investigation into the Brocklehurst fraud. You did the right thing to delve. But I could never understand how you got on to it.'

'It was one of the partners at the company, Guy Lassiter. I happened to be chatting to a colleague, Ron Lister, at Bentley's. Apparently some years earlier Lassiter had been a partner with a company in Liverpool and they'd made a massive claim through Bentley's in similar circumstances. They were paid out and then they stopped trading. After what Ron had told me, I was suspicious, and that's when I sent someone over to check it out. Lassister and his partner had started trading under the name, Brocklehurst.'

'So I believe. Now I gather you know why we've sent for you, Gary?'

'I realise there's a vacant post, but I thought it was on the cards for Maurice.'

'Nothing is ever on the cards,' the managing director emphasised. 'I'd like to offer you the post of assistant manager. What do you say?'

Gary whistled through his teeth. 'I'm staggered. I didn't expect it, but I'm confident I can do it. And thank you very much. I won't disappoint you.'

When he returned to the office he didn't mention his promotion to any of the others, especially Maurice. The thing to do was leave the bosses to make the announcement. And the rise in salary would mean that within the next six months they could save the extra cash towards a deposit on a house. He'd been disappointed they hadn't been able to do that earlier, but he was still waiting for his half share of the proceeds of the house he and Marie had bought. No doubt the cheque had reached his solicitors and they were hanging on to it, gaining interest at his expense.

Why on earth Marie couldn't have been more understanding and gone for a quick, inexpensive divorce he would never know. Women! He felt he'd never understand them. But with Jan it didn't seem to matter. She was all he ever wanted, warm, loving and supportive.

Chapter 7
The Present – 2008

Marcel followed Gary Croft outside into the car park. 'There are two hospitals in the area. We could try either one,' Gary pondered. 'But I fancy Murray Park is the nearest,' he concluded as he opened the door to his Audi.

Marcel slipped into the passenger seat beside him, his expression eagerly expectant. 'Thanks for agreeing, Mr Croft. I'm glad I've found you. Danielle means the world to me and I'd do anything for her safety.'

Croft turned to him. 'Let's cut the formalities. Call me Gary. You don't mind if I call you Marcel I take it?'

'Not at all,' Marcel replied, thinking the guy wasn't the ogre he'd expected.

Gary turned the key in the ignition. 'And you don't have to be grateful. It's my responsibility. If Danielle is my daughter, it's the least I can do. And even if she's not my daughter, I wouldn't let you down. After all I'm doing it for Marie's sake too.'

They headed for Accident and Emergency which, according to Gary, was the only way to get immediate attention. And when Triage Sister called them over, Marcel was impressed by Gary's confident approach as he talked his way through the situation and explained the dilemma to her.

She looked puzzled at his request. 'It's rather unusual, Mr Croft. In normal circumstances we would need a letter from your GP,' she explained officiously.

Gary chipped in. 'But time is precious, Sister. My daughter needs an operation as a matter of urgency.'

Sister relented. 'OK, I'm prepared to turn a blind eye. Go to haematology. I'll give them a buzz, explain why you're here and let them know you're on your way.'

Gary led the way as they followed the arrows to haematology and it was several minutes before a young staff nurse came out to attend to him. She took the card from Gary whilst Marcel sat down in the corridor. 'Sister has explained the situation, Mr Croft. But I'm afraid you'll need to give us a ring tomorrow if you need a complete analysis. We can't tell you today. Doctor Hussain's in charge and he's away for the afternoon.'

Marcel fished in his pocket and passed a slip of paper over to the nurse. 'This is the blood type that is needed. We were hoping you could let us know straight away,' he stressed. 'It is urgent.'

'Sorry Mr…?'

Marcel stood up now. 'Dubois, Marcel Dubois. We are desperate to get this over with. Mr Croft's daughter – my stepdaughter – is in urgent need of an operation. It cannot go ahead without finding a match.'

She took the slip of paper and shook her head. 'I understand your dilemma, Mr Dubois. But as I said, there's nothing we can do until tomorrow morning. I'll copy this and let you have it back. And don't worry. As soon as Dr Hussain is on duty I'll ask him to give it priority.' She beckoned to Gary. 'Right Mr Croft, let's get on with it.'

Gary was in and out of the lab within five minutes and ready to leave the department. 'I've left contact numbers with them. They'll be in touch as soon as they know. Having said that I guess they'll know well before this Hussain guy comes back on duty. But you know what it's like, they have to follow procedure.'

'That's right. He probably oversees the results,' Marcel echoed as he joined Gary and they set off back down the corridor. The door was closing behind them when he heard a call from the nurse.

'You didn't give me the name of the hospital in Edinburgh, Mr Dubois, or the consultant.' She advanced towards them. 'Whether we find a match or not, we'll need to contact them immediately we've done the analysis, let them know one way or the other.'

Marcel approached her. 'The hospital is in Edinburgh, nurse. It is the Deansgate Royal,' Marcel replied. 'I have the number here,' he offered, slipping his hand into his jacket pocket. 'The haematologist involved is Dr Fry.'

'Thank you for that. But don't worry about phone numbers. We have them all to hand. It was the name of the hospital I needed and the consultant.' She took out from her apron pocket the piece of paper containing the blood analysis. 'Here you go, I've copied this,' she said, handing it back to Marcel who folded the paper and put it away.

Gary turned to the nurse. 'You will let me know the minute you find out, won't you, nurse?'

'Of course, the very minute!' she echoed.

Gary dropped Marcel off at the car park in the centre of Manchester where he picked up his hire car. It had been an exhausting day and all he wanted now was to get back to the hotel, telephone the clinic and ask about Marie. And, having negotiated his way back there, he sprawled out on the bed and picked up the phone.

Sister sounded lively. 'You'll be pleased to hear your wife seems to be perking up now she's on the new medication.'

Marcel sighed and he felt his body relax. 'That is such a relief.'

Sister continued. 'I don't suppose you've had any joy with your search?'

Marcel told her briefly about Gary Croft and their visit to the hospital.

'That's wonderful news, Mr Dubois. I'll light a candle for you.' She paused. 'You'll be carrying on to Edinburgh I take it first thing in the morning?'

Marcel slid further down on the bed. 'Yes I will, Sister. They are doing their best to find a match, and including a regional search too. I'm anxious to know if they have found a donor yet. Despite the check on Gary Croft, we cannot rely on a positive outcome. But we can hope.'

'I'm sure they've pulled out all the stops,' she replied brightly. 'But get a good night's sleep tonight and see what tomorrow brings. And don't worry about your wife. We're taking good care of her.'

'Thank you for your support, Sister. I will be in touch.' Marcel replaced the phone and immediately picked it up again. He dialled the Deansgate Royal and asked to speak to Doctor Fry. But when the consultant answered the phone, Marcel could tell by his tone there was nothing to report. Again he was disappointed. The regional search had generated no match.

Dr Fry explained. 'We're finding this more difficult than we'd anticipated. It's becoming a little drawn out. But I am hoping the father's type will be a match. Meanwhile, we'll keep on with our search.'

'How about international centres?' Marcel asked him. 'Would it be possible to contact them?'

'We've already made contact. We're going all out, believe me.'

Aware that the international service was the last avenue open to them, Marcel's anxiety returned. He was about to replace the phone on the hook when he had a final request. 'By the way Dr Fry, Danielle is not aware that we have found her father. I would like to keep it that way until after the operation.'

'I understand. Let's wait and see what comes of it.'

The following morning after breakfast he was about to leave his hotel room when the phone rang. It was Gary Croft. Marcel held his breath.

'Sorry to disappoint you Marcel, but Dr Hussain from Murray Park has been in touch. He tells me there's no point checking the antigens. I'm A neg and Danielle is B neg. Apparently both the red blood cells and the plasma of those two groups are totally incompatible. I don't understand all this medical jargon, but that's what they told me. I wrote it down so that I'd remember. They're contacting Deansgate Royal direct to give them the result.'

Marcel was riveted to the spot. An ice-cold current streamed through his body and a low groan escaped from his throat. He was about to reply but the words dried up, and his heart seemed to twist in his chest. Another blow. The tiny beam of hope that had bolstered him when he finally located Gary Croft was now dissipating, draining away at a rapid rate. It was back to square one. He closed his eyes momentarily and let out a sigh. But then he pulled himself together. 'Thanks for letting me know, Gary. Another disappointment. But we tried.'

It was as though Gary sensed Marcel's state of emotion. 'Keep your pecker up. I'm sure something'll turn up soon. You will let me know what happens, won't you?'

Marcel paused momentarily. So far Gary hadn't asked to see Danielle, and he hoped it would stay that way. 'Of course I will. And thank you for agreeing to help,' he added, holding his breath and quickly ringing off.

Later that day when he arrived at the Deansgate Royal, he called in to see Dr Fry before he visited Danielle.

'I realise how disappointed you must be at the test results, Mr Dubois. But there was no point continuing further with Mr Croft's blood analysis. There was nothing to be gained. You see, in addition to the antigens covering red cells, blood also contains lots of tiny antibodies in the plasma – antibodies are the body's natural defence against foreign antibodies. Mr Croft's blood is group A, which contains antibodies ready to attack group B cells. And that's why group A blood must never be given to a group B person and vice versa,' he stressed.

Marcel shook his head. 'It is all so complicated,' he breathed.

'You're right there. It is complicated. I'd be the first to admit that. And I hope you understand. But we don't want to rush into anything just yet. As a last resort we could use the group B and get as close as we can with the antigens.' He smiled reassuringly and patted Marcel on the shoulder. 'We'll find it eventually, believe you me. We just need a little more time. And as far as Mr Dexter's concerned Danielle is fine, provided they monitor her condition on a regular basis.'

Marcel turned to leave. 'Thanks for the reassurance Dr Fry. At least it is a relief to know things are not deteriorating. I will keep in touch.'

'Not so fast, Mr Dubois. There's something else puzzling me.' He picked up the sheaf of papers from his desk and looked at them. 'Are you sure Mr Croft is Danielle's father?'

Danielle sat up in bed. Papa was due to arrive at any time and she needed to tidy herself up before he came. She ran the comb through her hair and, as she gazed in the mirror her thoughts turned to her biological father. She wondered what he looked like. Was she like him? She had Mama's brown eyes and dark hair, but that was all. Mama was much taller than she was. Perhaps her father was not so tall.

Desperate to find out what was going on, she was determined to ask Papa what progress he'd made with his search. And she hadn't long to wait. Seconds later Marcel appeared in the doorway, reached across and hugged her. 'How are you feeling, treasure?'

Danielle smiled. 'I am glad you are here, Papa. I am fine, but I am bored just hanging around in here day after day.'

Her father sat down. 'I understand, my love, but all we can do is wait.'

Danielle sighed. She mustn't keep on moaning to Papa. He had enough on his plate with Mama in hospital. 'I know. You are right. But how is Mama?' she asked.

'Just about the same, although according to Sister, she is perking up.'

Danielle pulled herself up in the bed. 'Does she know about me yet?'

Marcel shuffled uncomfortably on the chair. 'I have managed to keep it from her so far. But how long I can go on avoiding the issue, I do not know.'

Danielle was silent for several seconds as she contemplated broaching the question, painful as it was to both of them.

Marcel filled the gap. 'Anything wrong, treasure?'

Danielle pulled a face. 'Nothing is wrong, Papa, but I have been meaning to ask you how are things going with the search for that man, you know, Mama's ex?' She hated even thinking about the guy, let alone referring to him as her father.

Marcel grimaced but, fortunately for him, Danielle didn't notice the guilt flicking over his face. 'I found some information at home and I thought it would lead me to him. But I was wrong on that score.'

Danielle was curious. 'How do you mean you found some information, Papa?'

He looked away and answered stiffly. 'It was a photograph. I thought the guy on it was a relative and I traced him. He agreed to have his blood type checked. But it came to nothing in the end.'

Danielle overlooked the comments about the relative, took his hands and recognised his discomfort. 'I see,' she replied, thinking *Poor old Papa. He must be exhausted.* 'Do not worry. You did your best.' She squeezed his hands. 'You must be worn out. Why not take a rest? Stay back in Lille for a couple of days with Mama. I will be fine here, and I am sure they will let you know the minute they find a match.'

Marcel put on a smile. 'I am tired with all the travelling, but I must keep myself involved.'

Danielle folded her arms and leant back on the pillow. 'But what comes next, Papa?' she asked him.

Marcel swallowed hard. 'I will have to tell Mama. As a last resort we may discover she has other relatives.' His voice was thin and desolate.

Danielle frowned. 'But she has none as far as we know.'

Marcel lightened up. 'There may be cousins somewhere. But leave it with me and I will do what I think is best.'

Danielle took a deep breath. 'Do be careful not to upset her.'

'No need to worry. I will be diplomatic.' He smiled and leant towards her, kissing her lightly on the cheeks. 'I must go now. See you soon, cherie.'

He waved goodbye and strode along the corridor. It was wrong of him not to disclose the full truth about Gary Croft to Danielle. But the comment from Dr Fry had stunned him. He'd thought for certain that Croft was Danielle's father, although he had to admit Danielle didn't bear any resemblance to the guy.

Croft was tall with blond hair and blue eyes. Danielle had dark hair and brown eyes like her mother. He realised Dr Fry was being diplomatic, but was there genuinely some doubt as to the paternity?

Marcel took a deep breath. It was time he told Marie. He could hold out no longer. He'd done nothing but screw up the courage, hoping things would happen more swiftly. And then of course, Sister had advised against it. But now that she'd told him Marie was perking up, perhaps he could put her fully in the picture and, hopefully, obtain fresh leads. He had to do something. Everything was at a standstill. More than anything he'd hated lying both to Marie and to Danielle. That wasn't his way. Each time Marie asked about Danielle he squirmed, hoping he wouldn't slip up and come out with the truth. And goodness knows, Danielle had asked plenty of questions but he'd skirted around the issue on each occasion.

Maybe he would take up Danielle's suggestion and leave it a couple of days before he visited her again in Edinburgh. He had neglected Marie and, now that he had made up his mind to tell her about Danielle, he needed time to break it to her as gently as possible. And, once he'd explained, he would need to stay with her, to support and reassure her.

But when Marcel arrived at the clinic in Lille there was chaos in the corridor.

Sister flew past him. 'Sit down, Mr Dubois,' she called out. 'We're in the middle of a crisis. Staff nurse will fill you in,' she added.

Normally Sister would call him into the office and tell him how things were going with Marie. But, puzzled that he'd been relegated to sitting in the corridor, his eyes followed Sister as she disappeared into a side ward. And then his gaze became fixed on the opening. It was Marie's ward she'd entered.

A sudden surge of anxiety seemed to kick-start him, and he jumped up from his chair in the corridor, frowning heavily. What was going on? He dashed down the corridor and stood uneasily in the doorway of the ward. There was a mass of complex equipment beside the bed and it seemed one of the doctors and Sister were trying to revive Marie. Marcel stepped closer as Sister turned round to face him, a heavy frown on her forehead. 'Stand back, Mr Dubois,' she ordered. 'I'm afraid your wife has had a relapse.' Her voice was sharp and filled with authority.

Marcel's shoulders stiffened. He felt his throat working up the questions he wanted to ask, but the words became tangled around each other. As though rooted to the spot, he felt unable to string the words together. But he couldn't stand there blocking the way. Now shaking, he backed towards the doorway and left them to continue. He sent up a silent prayer. *Please don't let her die.*

But it appeared things were worsening. He didn't quite understand exactly what was happening but Sister asked him to leave the ward. And now Staff Nurse had joined them, so any explanation would have to wait.

He didn't move far but stood outside and listened from the corridor. And then he was alerted by a rattling sound as two nurses ran towards him at full speed pushing the crash trolley towards Marie's ward. They closed the door behind them and all Marcel could hear were thumping sounds and a female voice counting.

He could bear it no longer. He carefully opened the door and entered. 'What is happening, Sister? You must tell me.'

Sister didn't turn around. 'I think we're losing her,' she murmured.

Horrified Marcel stared at the scene before him. Huge waves of fear permeated his body. There was nothing he could do, nothing he could say. He rubbed his face with his hands and tried to stem the tears that were welling up. She couldn't die. She couldn't leave him! And then Danielle came to the forefront of his mind. She would be devastated. If anything did happen to Marie, he might never find out the truth about Danielle's true biological father. The haematologist had hinted it might not be Croft.

Marcel was desperate now. But what could he do?

The team continued desperately to revive Marie. And for a passing moment, she opened her eyes, at first unfocused and glassy with sedatives. Marcel was transfixed by the agony he saw in her face. Even so, he fleetingly toyed with the idea of asking her that vital name. And then she seemed to rally. Strangely her face took on a sort of calmness. Now was the time.

His hands felt so leaden he couldn't even clasp them around hers. But then he bent over her and pulled her head gently to his chest. 'Marie, please tell me the name of Danielle's father. She is ill, my darling. I would not ask but we need to know his name for her sake.'

He heard her voice vibrating. 'I don't know…' She took a deep breath. Her voice began to trail away. 'You, Marcel.'

Marcel was desperate to learn the answer to his question, but he was losing his darling Marie. What more could he say?

'I love you, Marcel,' she whispered. 'Please let me go.' And when she slipped back on to the pillow he realised she was not afraid to die.

In his heart, Marcel knew her fight for life was coming to an end and he realised he'd left it too late to receive an answer to his question. Minutes later, all activity stopped.

The doctor turned to face him. 'It's no use,' he whispered. 'We can do no more. She'd been coping well with the cancer but I'm afraid the infection proved too heavy a burden for her body.'

Sister came towards Marcel and with a look of despair she spoke in gentle tones. 'She's gone, I'm afraid. Sorry I neglected you but I couldn't afford to leave her.'

Marcel nodded. He couldn't speak. He stepped forward and, although he'd seen it happen, he was filled with disbelief. And then his words came out in protest. 'But you said she was getting better.' He felt his veins flooding with ice as he stared at the bed. Slowly he approached Marie and took her hands. He lifted them to his face and pressed them against his skin. He could smell the essence of her, and he breathed in the sweet fragrance. And then he pulled himself upright and froze. Seconds passed before he continued. 'I do not understand,' he muttered as now he bent over her and touched her face. And then he kissed her lips before turning to Sister. Tears began to steal down his cheeks and he felt his knees about to give way beneath him.

Sister gently eased him away. 'Come along. I'll make you a cup of tea.' She led him to the nurses' bay and made sure he was seated. But once he hit the chair, he seemed to collapse. And then he buried his face in his hands and cried.

Danielle awoke feeling as though something was stuck in her throat. The dryness in her mouth prevented the lump she was trying to swallow from disappearing. Her head felt like a rubber ball being bounced on the pillow. And then she remembered why they'd prescribed the sedatives. Her stomach began its agitation when the realisation dawned. She hadn't seen Mama since November and already it was January. But she would never see her again. She'd never feel Mama's arm around her shoulder, comforting her like when she was a little girl. She'd never again hear that lovely, melodious voice in its broken French singing to her. Mama was gone forever.

'It is not true,' she cried in disbelief, 'it cannot be,' she whispered, her throat now closing up as she choked on the words.

'I'm sorry my dear.' Mr Dexter took her hand. 'I'm afraid it is true.'

Danielle tried to lift her body to sit up in bed, but it was as though she was glued to the mattress. She continued to strain and Sister gently eased her head back down on to the pillow. 'I must go home,' Danielle cried. 'You cannot stop me.'

Mr Dexter intervened. 'But I can't allow you to travel to France. I daren't risk it, Danielle. Your condition is stable at present. I can't afford any infections and I don't know how much longer we can continue with this holding phase. The growth has changed very little. Let's keep it that way.' He patted her hand.

'But I must go,' she insisted, holding back hot tears of frustration, and trying to pull herself up out of the bed. 'I must see Mama before she is gone forever,' she cried, weeping now and taking in gulps of air whilst trying to control her sobs.

Marcel intervened. 'Mama would not have wanted you to take any chances, treasure,' he told her as he stroked her forehead and tried to remain calm himself. He swallowed hard. 'I know how you feel, but Mr Dexter is right.'

It took a massive effort to open her eyes. They were swollen and they felt like they were sealed. Her eyelids flickered. They felt dry and gritty. Her head began to pound again and she realised they'd given her the extra drugs to keep her under control. They were afraid she'd take matters into her own hands and leave. And she would have.

She felt herself drifting again. But she wouldn't let go. Her mind was filled with questions that tumbled over and over, and she seemed unable to stop and concentrate on clarifying her thoughts.

It took the full force of her strength to pull herself round from losing consciousness. She thought of Mama and tried to bring the image of her into focus.

'Danielle, cherie, Mama is at peace now,' Marcel whispered, his own emotions almost at breaking point. 'We could not let her suffer any more.' He wiped the tears from Danielle's face with his fingertips, his own eyes damp and shiny.

Her eyes became glassy and were filled with anxiety. The light penetrated through a tiny gap as she managed to open them slightly. 'I want to die too. I cannot take any more, Papa, and I do not want to live without her.' The sedatives had almost taken over completely.

Marcel cleared his throat and, in an attempt to subdue his rising emotions, he begged, 'Do not say that, treasure.' He shook his head and his voice softened. 'You are all I have left. I love you dearly. I cannot live without you either. You must not say things like that.'

Everything was becoming hazier, and the world around her was moving so slowly now that things were almost at a standstill. Danielle could hear Papa but it seemed he was far away, somewhere in the distance. But his words began to register.

She shifted uncomfortably in the bed and again she drifted, now unable to hold on to a single thought. And then she curled into a ball.

Marcel took her hands and tucked them under the covers. He wiped a tear from his eye wondering if Danielle would ever forgive him for agreeing with Mr Dexter that she should not travel to France for the funeral.

Chapter 8
The Present – 2008

Marcel knew he could cope no longer, searching for relatives and coming up against so many obstacles. And then there was the funeral to arrange. Time could never dim or heal his pain and his mind just couldn't deal with everything that was pressing down on him. He no longer seemed to possess the energy to fight this battle. Eyes blank and lifeless, he flopped down in the armchair, buried his head in his hands and cried.

But it was no good. He must get a grip on himself. He'd lost Marie and he'd no intention of slacking as far as his daughter's health was concerned. He didn't want to lose her too. He needed help. He shook his head and hastily wiped away the tears.

Pulling himself up from the armchair, he began to pace the confines of the lounge. He focused his mind on the situation and began to weigh up the facts. Still they had no lead as far as the blood match was concerned. This triggered thoughts of Gary Croft. Dr Fry's comment had puzzled him. Maybe Croft wasn't Danielle's biological father after all. But who was?

He stared out of the window, his gaze fixed on the garden outside, his hands clutched onto the sill. He felt his back teeth clench. He was so keyed up he was practically on the edge of mental turmoil. And then his mind went completely blank.

Sinking back down in the armchair, he took a deep breath and tried to concentrate. Marie had never mentioned another man in her life. And she certainly wasn't the type to sleep around. But it was imperative he found the guy quickly. The blood service weren't getting far with their search. Something must be done. And soon.

It was then he remembered a business contact, Anton Le Bon, who had employed an apparent whiz kid to investigate a problem at his factory. That was it. A private investigator. It had to be the solution, the most efficient way to find a donor. If he hired this top-notch PI, maybe he would carry out all the spadework?

Knowing it was crucial, he slipped on his jacket and, once at the office, he leafed through the trade directory for the number. He dialled.

'Anton, I can't explain over the phone, but I need the services of a private investigator as a matter of urgency. I seem to recall you employed someone last year to solve a problem in your factory?'

'That's right. It was Pierre Clarisse. He's a bright young thing. Don't be put off by his age. He's mid-twenties and fresh out of the police force. He was a graduate and made it to sergeant, but decided he wanted to do his own thing. If you have a problem, he's sure to solve it. He comes highly recommended and he's pretty sharp – gets on with things. Whether he'll be available immediately is another matter. I'll give you his number.'

Marcel felt a sense of relief. All he needed was someone to share his problem, someone to help. 'He sounds exactly the sort of guy I need.'

'Then let's hope he's free,' Anton replied. 'He's a busy guy, always in demand.'

But that didn't faze Marcel. 'I'll take the chance. I'll give him a ring,' he said, taking down the number and replacing the receiver. And when he rang Pierre Clarisse five minutes later he explained the urgency of the situation. 'You can see how desperate I am to find a blood donor for my daughter. It could be a matter of life or death, and I mean that quite literally.' He held his breath.

'I understand, Mr Dubois, and you're lucky. I've just completed a job,' Pierre told him. 'Will you be in this afternoon?'

Marcel's optimism returned. 'I'll be in mid-afternoon. What time were you thinking?'

'Some time after three,' Pierre replied.

Marcel couldn't have been more relieved. 'That's fine. I'm with the funeral director until two thirty. I'll be back by then. I do hope you can help.'

'I'll do my best, Mr Dubois. See you at three.'

When Pierre turned up promptly at three o'clock, Marcel understood what Anton meant by not being put off. He was tall, broad-shouldered and had more than his share of good looks and charm. And once he had the full gist of what was required, he asked Marcel for Marie's private box. 'That seems to me to be the best place to start.'

Marcel was taken aback. 'But I've gone through the box several times. There's nothing in there except some bits and pieces Marie obviously kept for their sentimental value.'

But Pierre was insistent. 'I'd still like to take a look,' he declared. 'Perhaps you could bring it down for me.'

Marcel went upstairs and, before taking the metal box out from its place at the bottom of the wardrobe, he stared vacantly at it as though in a trance. Then he bent down, inserted the key and opened it up. His stomach lurched. The last time he did that he felt as though he was being furtive, as though he was about to pry into Marie's past. And that's exactly what he was doing yet again, even though it no longer mattered. Marie was gone. He swallowed hard to prevent his emotions from spilling over, knowing that, if she'd still been alive, she would expect him to do all he could to help Danielle.

He closed the wardrobe doors and took the box downstairs, handing it to Pierre who immediately tipped the contents on to the table and flicked through the documents. He picked out a couple and opened them up. 'My first thing is to check the birth certificates and then the passport.'

Marcel protested. 'There's neither a birth certificate for Danielle nor Marie's decree absolute. I've already checked. There is a passport and it's perfectly legitimate. It's in the names of Alicia Marie and Danielle Jeanne Lambert. Marie told me her parents had never used Alicia. They'd always referred to her as Marie and it stuck.'

Pierre smiled. 'Stop fretting, Marcel. Leave it with me. I know exactly what I'm doing' he insisted as he checked the personal documents. 'They seem to be in order.'

He spread the remaining contents out on the table. And then spotting a pink ribbon encased in a tiny plastic band, he picked it up. The band was folded in two and was sticking to a plastic wallet containing another document, itself attached by a paper clip to a photograph. It was half-hidden. First he glanced at the photograph, one of Marie when she was younger, but it didn't appear to be of any importance in his search. And then he peered at the faded writing on the tiny band. It was difficult to make out but on the white strip tucked inside the band was a number, 876423 (F).

Marcel sat there stone-faced. Surely that was nothing of significance? Perhaps he'd done the wrong thing hiring Pierre? 'I think that's just something she kept as a sort of souvenir,' he commented. 'I don't know what it is.'

'But I do, Marcel. It's a hospital tag, one they put on a baby's wrist as soon as it's born. This shows the baby was a girl and here is the child's hospital number,' he said pointing to the details on the strip. 'You say Danielle was born in the north of England somewhere?'

Marcel doubted that the ribbon would be of any help but he gave Pierre the information he needed. 'Marie came from Manchester. At least she was in the police force there. I'd always believed she was from Liverpool. But Gary Croft, her ex, told me otherwise. But why do you ask?'

'That's where I propose to start. Maybe if I check this out I can discover more about Marie and Danielle. Hopefully the name of the father will be registered on the hospital documents once I can gain access to the patient file. It's a long shot but it's worth a try.'

Pierre Clarisse rubbed his finger lightly over the raised impression on the plastic wristband. The name of the company was *Jacobs* and when he checked with directory enquiries he was informed they were still trading in Leeds. On arrival at the factory, he discovered they were in the business of manufacturing hospital supplies.

He entered the main office and rang the bell. 'I'd like to speak to someone dealing with identification tags,' he told the receptionist.

'What sort of identification tags?' the girl asked him. 'There are staff tags to pin on to uniforms and also patient bands. Some are on card, others in plastic. We have two different sections.'

Pierre realised the girl was right. 'I see,' he replied. 'Sorry, I didn't make myself clear. It's the person in charge of patient wristbands, plastic ones, I need to see.'

He took a seat and waited a few minutes before a man in his early thirties came out to meet him. He held out his hand. 'Simon Jacobs. Can I help you?' he asked.

Pierre took his hand and shook it. 'Pierre Clarisse,' he replied. 'I'm hoping you can, Mr Jacobs.' He showed the tiny wristband to Jacobs. 'I'm searching for information on behalf of a client whose daughter is seriously ill. I'm actually looking to identify someone, a child born at one of the hospitals in the north,' he told Jacobs. 'I need to find out the source of this band in order to identify the child who was given that number, and subsequently the hospital records,' he said, pointing to the white slip inside the band. 'I can't go into a detailed explanation, but let me tell you it's a matter of urgency. I need to find out the exact parentage of the child.'

Jacobs shook his head. 'This particular band became obsolete almost twenty years ago. The bands available these days have a much more secure fastening and need to be cut to release them from the wrist. You see, shortly after we'd introduced them we had a number of complaints. The fastenings were coming loose. That wasn't too bad with adults, unless they were going down for an op that is, but with babies the hospital staff couldn't afford any slip-ups, as you can well imagine. The one you have here is from that early batch. This particular one's still intact, but as you see,' he added, taking the band from Pierre, 'it doesn't take much to pull it apart.' He pulled gently and the press-stud opened up.

Pierre inspected the tag once more. 'I see what you mean,' he replied. 'But how long was this particular brand on the market?'

Jacobs placed his hand on his mouth and contemplated. 'Obviously I was just a lad at the time, but I can remember the controversy quite clearly. Dad gave us a running commentary every day. I believe we ran it for just six months, as a trial.'

'Six months you say. Was that in 1988?'

'Hang on. I'll ask Fred Wilkinson. He's been in the department since he left school.' He laughed. 'Sometimes the workers know more about the company than I do myself, even though I was born and bred into it.'

Jacobs was back within minutes. 'You guessed right. 1988 from July to December.'

Pierre pushed his luck further. 'I don't suppose you know how many hospitals took it on?'

Jacobs whistled through his teeth. 'Now you're asking. It's a long time ago Mr Clarisse. But, we had so much trouble, Dad will remember it clearly.' He drew his lips into a thin line. 'He's taken early retirement. He's in Florida just now at our holiday villa.'

Disappointed, Pierre frowned. 'That's a blow. I was hoping to start my investigation immediately.'

Jacobs smiled reassuringly. 'Don't worry Mr Clarisse. Hang on a few minutes and I'll give him a bell.'

Pierre was surprised at the response. 'You'll call him in Florida? I'd appreciate that.'

Jacobs set off towards the door. 'It's the least I can do in the circumstances. Sit yourself down. I'll be back in a few minutes.'

Pierre sat in the waiting room whilst Mr Jacobs went off to phone his father. And within a couple of minutes he was back, much quicker than Pierre had anticipated. 'Just our luck. Dad's out fishing for the morning. I've spoken to Mum and she's positive one of the places was Chadwick Infirmary in Liverpool. She's convinced there were only two hospitals trialling the band. After we received the complaints we took it off the market and replaced it with the new type. Why not check on Chadwick and let me know whether or not you have any joy there? As soon as Dad returns to the villa, Mum says she'll get him to ring me.'

Pierre was impressed at the way Jacobs was putting himself out to help. *Treat someone with respect and they'll bend over backwards* was Pierre's motto. 'Good idea. I'm grateful for your help. I'll leave for Liverpool straight away and ring you as soon as I've checked it out. I am trying to minimise on time. Every second counts as you probably appreciate.'

Jacobs handed the tag back to Pierre. 'I'm sure it does. You can rely on me. I'll get the information to you as soon as I can. If there's anything else I can help you with, you only have to ask.' He held out his hand and Pierre took it.

'Thank you, Mr Jacobs. What you've told me is spot on, exactly what I was looking for,' he replied.

Jacobs shook his hand and concluded, 'Good luck!'

It was almost a couple of hours' run to Chadwick Infirmary. Pierre drew to a stop in the hospital car park and was about to leave his car when he realised he had no coins for the machine. He let out a huge sigh. He didn't need this. He quickly scribbled a note, stuck it to his windscreen, dashed inside and asked for change at reception. He didn't relish the thought of his car being wheel-clamped whilst he was inside making his enquiries.

'We don't usually give change,' the receptionist told him sulkily.

'But this is a matter of urgency, dear,' he replied. 'I'd very much appreciate your co-operation,' he added, giving her a smile meant to devastate.

Once he'd placed his ticket on the windscreen of his car, he dashed up the steps and entered the hospital again. 'I'm safely parked now,' he said, smiling. 'I hope you can help me. I need to speak to the person in charge of records, please.'

The girl on reception now smiled sweetly and picked up the telephone, asking someone to come through to reception.

A middle-aged woman came out from the back office. 'Can I be of help?' she asked.

Pierre held out his hand. 'My name is Pierre Clarisse.' The woman stared at his hand but failed to reach out and shake it. 'I'm investigating a paternity case. I'm anxious to find out if this was one of your wristbands,' he said, holding up the band. 'It's almost twenty years since the child was born, but it's crucial I find out her exact identity and where she was born.' He handed over the band. 'I need to discover the identity of the father in order to obtain a blood match. The child is obviously now an adult, but needs the match as a matter of urgency before a serious operation can take place. Any information you can give me would be appreciated.'

'I'll do my best, Mr Clarisse,' the woman replied, a patronising smile touching her lips. 'I am in charge of the archives as well as up-to-date records here at Chadwick,' she told him, carefully scrutinising the band. She paused and shook her head. 'I'm sorry I can't help you on this occasion. The number on this band is not compatible with our system. You see ours always start with a two for the maternity unit and for paediatrics,' the woman told him as she flicked over the pages of a huge tome. 'That was the case when I was just an office girl here.' She gave a sickly smile and nodded. 'And it still continues. I'm afraid it's not one of ours.'

'That's a blow,' Pierre replied. 'But thanks for checking,' he concluded as he set off back to the car park and peered at his watch. His business had been over and done with so quickly he'd barely given Jacobs time to speak with his father.

It might be an idea if he went for lunch at one of the nearby cafés. He could telephone the company later to ask if there was any news. There was no point moving far away in case the other hospital issued with the bands was also in Liverpool.

It was after two o'clock when Pierre contacted Mr Jacobs.

'I'm glad you've rung back. I've spoken to Dad. The only other hospital to be issued with the bands was Murray Park in Manchester. How did it go in Liverpool?'

Pierre slipped into the driving seat of his car. 'Nothing doing, I'm afraid. Their numbering system doesn't tie in with the band. But thanks for the information. It's certainly narrowed my search.'

'Do let me know the outcome.'

He fastened his seat belt. 'Of course, Mr Jacobs and, once again, thanks.'

Pierre's enquiry at Murray Park was not as straightforward as he'd hoped. For a start he seemed to have been referred to some incompetent porter in charge of the archives housed downstairs in the basement. The man was elderly and obviously used to sitting on his backside all day doing nothing. He looked up, folded his newspaper and tucked it underneath his chair.

'I can't let you see anything without a docket from the office,' the old guy told Pierre. 'Up two flights and turn right.'

'But I've just made my enquiry there. They didn't offer me any form of identification. And it is a matter of urgency,' Pierre informed him. 'The child this wristband belonged to needs to be identified.'

'Sorry but rules are rules. Don't want to lose my job, sir.'

Furious at being sent back upstairs and wasting time, Pierre set off taking the steps two at a time. And when he arrived at reception he had to wait to see the records manager.

'Mr Ferncliffe's right,' the manager said, referring to the porter. 'Sorry about that. It's purely my fault although, strictly speaking, the archives are only available to the medical profession unless, as in your case, there's a special dispensation. I should come down with you and supervise or at least have given you a signed slip, which I overlooked. I'm trying to clear a backlog of work at present and I'm really under pressure but I'm sure Mr Ferncliffe knows what he's doing,' he explained.

Back down in the archives, Pierre approached the porter once more. 'Here's the slip. Can we get on with it now?'

'Hold your horses, young man. I'm doing my best,' he said as he set off, tottering along the aisles between the records, most of which were encased in brown cardboard wallets. Judging by the amount of dust on the shelves as he pulled out the dividers, it was obvious they hadn't been disturbed for many a year.

The way the old guy went about it, Pierre had the impression he was unsure of himself. He was looking at records in a random fashion and didn't seem to know just where to start. Pierre wanted to take matters in his own hands. But he stopped himself from interfering. He'd already crossed the old guy when he'd arrived without the slip. He didn't want to make matters worse. Eventually by a stroke of luck they came to the section for the second half of 1988. 'But isn't maternity separate from the rest of the records?' Clarisse enquired.

The old man looked at him and shook his head. 'Now you're asking me something. My job is to give the staff what they need. But I must admit they usually come in here and find their own records.'

'Then have you any objection to my helping you find this one?' Pierre asked him in the gentlest of tones. He didn't want the old guy thinking he was taking over.

'Help yourself,' he offered, and he watched as Pierre flicked through the wallets. He soon got the hang of the system and when he came to the maternity section, he pulled out the wallet marked with the exact number he was looking for. 'This is it,' he declared, a note of triumph in his voice.

'There's a little room over there if you want to sit and look through it,' the old man told him, pointing to a dingy little place in the corner.

'Thanks. That would be handy,' he replied, trailing behind the guy whose pace wasn't exactly rapid.

The porter opened the door and switched on a light. 'Take your time. There's no rush. I'm here all day.'

Pierre emptied the contents of the wallet onto the table and fingered through them. There were only three cards enclosed.

The first contained the number and sex of the child and the name of the mother, but not the name of the father. The second contained medical information, most of which was gobbledegook to him, and the third was a discharge sheet.

He stared at the first card and his eyes were drawn to the name of the mother. Paula Grimshaw. He picked up the wristband once more and checked the number against the wallet. He'd certainly picked up the correct wallet. The number matched. How come the mother was Paula Grimshaw when, as far as they knew, it was Danielle's wristband and the mother's name should have been Marie Brechan? Pierre shook his head in absolute astonishment when finally he looked at the discharge sheet. The mother, this Grimshaw woman, had absconded and abandoned her baby. The final note told him that the child, who had been christened Rosie by the nurses, had been transferred to paediatrics. Days later she had been abducted.

Abducted? Pierre couldn't believe it. Once more he looked at the name on the band. This was astonishing. Now he might never find Danielle's wristband, especially if it went by mistake with this Rosie Grimshaw, the child who'd been abducted. In view of what Simon Jacobs had told him about the faulty wristbands, it looked as though there had been a mix-up and that Danielle had been given another child's band and vice versa. Pierre made a note of the details he needed to track the mother down and, returning to the porter, he said, 'I'll replace this where I found it, shall I? It's been very useful,' he acknowledged.

'Thanks, mate,' the porter replied and he continued to read his newspaper.

But as Pierre made his way back to the aisle from which he'd taken the wallet, he turned the corner and slipped the wallet into his briefcase. This could come in useful as evidence, and surely no one else was going to need it now.

The advert in the paper read:

Pierre Clarisse urgently needs to contact Paula Grimshaw on a confidential matter.

Pierre included his mobile telephone number and announced he would accept a call at any time, day or night.

His next step was to contact Manchester police and ask if they knew anything more about the baby who'd been kidnapped in 1988. Had they found the child?

'It was a strange business,' the sergeant told him as he looked up the case in police records. 'The search was a futile one. The baby was never seen again, nor was the mother. What kind of people are they? I tell you things never cease to amaze me in this business.'

When Pierre told him the gist of the case in which he was involved, the sergeant went through to have a word with the inspector who offered to pass the information about Paula Grimshaw on to the media. They would request that the woman come forward as a matter of urgency.

Pierre continued his investigations and contacted the head office of Social Securities. But they were adamant their records showed only the registered details of an Alicia Marie Lambert who had died twenty-one years earlier. She'd been in her seventies when she passed away.

One of the clerks at the Home Office advised him the Lambert passport belonging to Marie was not on record there. It was obviously forged.

Pierre was not surprised at the revelation. He'd had his suspicions. But now the mystery was deepening. What sort of a woman was Marie to have been in possession of a forged document? And how could he tell Marcel all that when the poor guy was grieving for his wife? But did he have an alternative?

Whilst Pierre had turned up lots of detailed information, his only lead was Paula Grimshaw, someone who, in his mind, bore no relationship to the case he was trying to solve. It was as though the name had been plucked out of the air. But all he could do now was wait. If she didn't come forward, he would need to try a different ploy.

Chapter 9
The Present – 2008

Each time Marcel broke the sad news of Marie's death his emotions were in turmoil. But the sooner everyone knew, the sooner he could get on with his own grieving. And with this in mind, he decided to go along to Gary Croft's office instead of ringing him first. It was quicker that way. When he entered the office Gary was in a lively mood. 'How are things, Marcel?' he asked, offering his hand. 'Any joy?'

Marcel took it and tried to remain calm, but he found it difficult to control his feelings. 'Things could not be worse,' he murmured, almost choking on the words.

Gary looked at him for a long moment. 'What is it?' He frowned. 'Judging by the look on your face, I can see it must be bad news. It's not Danielle is it? I hope she hasn't taken a turn for the worse.'

Marcel shook his head. 'No, it is not Danielle. She is fine.' He paused.

Gary intervened. 'I take it they haven't come across a match.'

Marcel took a deep breath. 'No, not yet. But that is not why I am here.' He swallowed hard. 'It is bad news I'm afraid.' He stared into space before slowly and painfully coming out with the words, words he hardly believed for himself. 'Marie passed away two days ago. The funeral is on Friday.'

The words seemed slow to register. Gary's frown deepened. 'Passed away?' He turned to Marcel. 'I'd no idea she was so ill.'

Marcel's eyes were blank now. 'Nor had I,' he confessed.

Gary wrung his hands and shook his head. 'You must be out of your mind with worry. What with Danielle's illness and now this. I'm deeply sorry, Marcel. I'm stunned too. She was so young, and she always kept herself fit and healthy.'

Marcel's brown eyes were glossy now, and he tried to flick away the stray tear steeling down his face. 'She did, but she could not beat it.'

'Unfortunately not.' Gary stood up and pushed his chair under the desk. 'Is there anything I can do for you?' He clamped an arm around Marcel's shoulder.

Marcel shook his head. 'Not really. But I felt you needed to know.'

'Of course, and I'm grateful to you for that.' Gary paused and then he sat down again, obviously dwelling on his private thoughts. 'Jan will be devastated.' He took a deep breath and sighed. 'I must confess, despite the fact that Jan and I are blissfully happy, we've always had that flash of guilt at the way things went when Marie and I split.' He wiped his hand across his face and there was silence. Seconds later he leaned over to look at his diary on the desk. 'I'm sorry we can't attend the funeral. I have a very important board meeting on Friday. It's crucial I attend.'

'I did not expect you to come all the way to France, although it is kind of you to consider it. But do not feel guilty about what happened. Marie and I were very much in love.' The tears were more profuse now and Marcel brushed them from his cheeks. He turned, walked towards the door and took a deep breath, trying to curb his emotions. 'I must get back now and visit Danielle. You can imagine how distressed she is.'

'I can indeed.' Gary followed him to the door. 'Keep in touch, Marcel. And I hope you soon find a donor for Danielle.'

'Me too,' Marcel murmured as he stepped out into the corridor. He turned to face Gary. 'Danielle has been hysterical since I told her, and it is so difficult trying to keep her calm.' He shook his head in an effort to clear his mind. 'The trouble is I have so much to do, people to tell, arrangements to make.' He set off towards the outer door.

'I feel for you, Marcel, but do take care,' Gary called after him.

As Marcel reached the street outside, questions about Marie's past flooded his mind. He felt hurt that she had not told him about the change of surname, or about her job in Manchester. Surely being an officer in the police force was something to be proud of, unless she didn't want to be identified at Marie Brechan. But why would that be?

He closed his mind to those thoughts. If he didn't stop dwelling on things, his brain would become even more befuddled. He told himself firmly that, since he had no way of solving the mystery, he should cast all thoughts to the back of his mind until Clarisse came up with an explanation.

He sighed as he left for the airport. And his mind froze on one isolated thought. Despite what had happened in the past, Marie would always be *his* Marie. And, whatever the outcome, she would always stand out as the love of his life. No one could ever take that away from him.

But what had happened after Marie and Gary had divorced? That remained a mystery. And when Dr Fry had suggested Gary might not be Danielle's biological father, Marcel just couldn't perceive there might have been someone else in Marie's life. At first he had thought it would be an idea for Croft to take a DNA test, but seeing his blood type didn't match and there was some doubt as to parentage, Marcel decided it wasn't necessary. It would only complicate matters.

A knot of panic stuck in the back of his throat. How long was it going to be before they found a donor, and even more importantly, how long could Danielle's stability last?

Pierre gave Marcel an update on his progress with the wristband. 'I had access to the hospital records at Murray Park. But brace yourself, Marcel. I discovered the wristband didn't belong to Danielle after all. It matched up with the child of a woman called Paula Grimshaw.'

Marcel was overcome and his back stiffened. 'Paula Grimshaw? Who is the woman? And how can you say the wristband belonged to some other child? Surely it was Danielle's? He stared vacantly and then realised he'd addressed Pierre in an accusatory way. 'Sorry to be so sharp, but what you have just told me came as a shock.'

'I understand, Marcel. We automatically assumed the band belonged to Danielle, but it seems there might have been a mix-up.' He softened his tone and continued. 'But we can't speculate. Not until I meet the Grimshaw woman and talk to her.'

Marcel turned to face the window, his back to Pierre. 'Marie seems to be getting a great deal of flak one way or another,' he protested. 'The photograph did not generate anything much, other than the guy she married, and now the wristband seems not to be helping us.'

'Bear me out, Marcel. You know what Simon Jacobs told me. These particular bands opened up very easily. Perhaps that's what happened. The bands came off and were placed on the wrists of the wrong babies.'

Marcel murmured a reply. 'Mm. I suppose that could have happened.'

Pierre continued. 'We can't delve any deeper without finding the woman. My first priority yesterday was to put an ad in the newspaper asking her to contact me. If and when she comes forward, I'll hopefully find out what happened, and ask if there was any possibility of a mix-up with the bands and, as a result, the babies.'

Marcel shook his head and sighed. 'But the woman has to turn up before you can check that out,' he replied sullenly. 'It could be days, weeks, even months, if at all.' He spun round to face Pierre. 'Why not check the hospital records for Marie and Danielle?'

'That would be difficult until we find out more. We would need dates and a hospital reference number to go on. And we don't know if Marie was admitted to Murray Park. I suppose eventually we may have to pursue that line, but let's check out the Grimshaw woman first. We can only hope she comes forward soon. I'm banking on it, Marcel. We need to know how Marie came to possess the wrong wristband.' Clarisse slipped the band from his pocket and held it up. 'The way I see it, we have two options. Either Danielle is Marie's child, or she is the child of the elusive Paula Grimshaw. If Danielle is Marie's child as we've always thought she was, I can only assume the wristbands have been mixed up in hospital.'

Marcel moved across the room and sat down, distraught, and trying to control his shaking body. 'How much more of this I can take?'

'Let me do the worrying, Marcel. My first task is to find Paula Grimshaw. The police have put an appeal on TV and radio. Surely if she doesn't see the item in the newspaper, she'll listen to the news. Failing that, a friend or neighbour would surely prompt her if she's not heard the appeal.'

'But will she turn herself in?' It was obvious Marcel had his doubts about the woman.

'Your guess is as good as mine, but let's try to be optimistic,' Pierre replied as he slipped the wedding photograph from his jacket pocket. He looked away and Marcel could sense he was about to come out with something that might be embarrassing. 'I know this is painful, Marcel but we also need to check out Marie's background in Manchester and her job with the police force.'

'I was expecting that, Pierre. And, believe me, it is painful.' He paused. 'But it is no good asking Croft to fill us in. He said he had no idea what happened after they split. And that is the crucial time of course. Will you ask at the station if anyone remembers Marie? It is a long time ago, almost twenty years.'

Pierre continued. 'If she was a sergeant she must have been there a year or two. Surely someone will recognise her. First thing tomorrow I'll go straight back there and make enquiries. I'll ask if anyone knew about her pregnancy and if so the name of the nearest hospital. If it was Murray Park, maybe there was a mix-up, especially in view of what we know about the wristbands. She could have picked up her own baby who may have been wearing the wrong wristband.'

'She could also have picked up the wrong baby.' Marcel gave a heavy sigh and shook his head. 'The wrong wristband, the wrong baby – whatever!' he stressed, a frown once more developing on his forehead. 'It could be catastrophic, Pierre. If Danielle is not Marie's daughter, then whose daughter is she? And how are we ever going to find a match?'

Pierre's words were calming. 'I'm sure Marie would have known her own baby. Let's not make assumptions.' But when Pierre looked to Marcel for his reaction, he realised he was pre-occupied with his own thoughts. And it suddenly occurred to Pierre just how insensitive he was being, getting excited about the prospect of revealing the whole of Marie's past – some of which could infer criminal involvement – and Marcel hadn't even buried his wife yet. With that in mind, he decided not to mention the fact that Paula Grimshaw had abandoned her child or that the child had been abducted. That would only pile on more suspicion and worry. 'Sorry, Marcel. I realise this is hurtful to you. But all I'm concerned about is obtaining the match for Danielle.'

Marcel seemed to pull himself round. 'Of course, Pierre, that is why I employed you. You have done well finding the hospital and identifying the child. We must hope the media can get this woman Paula Grimshaw to come to our aid.' But then he squeezed his eyes tight shut and sighed. When he opened them again, he grimaced. 'I just do not believe what is happening. I do not know what will turn up next.' There was a tremor in his tone. His mood kept on flipping from positive to negative.

But he reprimanded himself for allowing such a negative stance. Then bracing himself, a state of calm took over. 'It is such a mystery, Pierre. But I agree you must pursue these things in your own thorough way. I really am grateful, even though I may not seem to be. The fact is I am still very shocked at losing Marie, and it is so frustrating not being able to find a donor for my daughter, especially when I know both Danielle and the surgeon want to get on with the operation.'

Pierre was up early the following morning and ready to make a start. With luck the central police station would not be too busy at that time of the day and it should be easier to get someone to talk to him about Marie Brechan. But when he asked for the sergeant he'd spoken to previously, it turned out the officer was on late shift. It was when he explained to the duty sergeant he needed to discuss one of their ex-officers that he was shown into the inspector's room.

'Thanks for putting out the search for Paula Grimshaw, Inspector. I haven't heard anything yet but I am hoping word will filter through to her, and that she'll come forward eventually.' He paused. 'But now I have another problem concerning the same case. I need some information on an ex-police sergeant, Marie Brechan. She was an officer at this station in the eighties. I know it's a long time ago, but it's important I find out some details about her.'

'I can't say I remember the officer, Mr Clarisse, but fill me in on the details and maybe I can pull something out from our records.'

Clarisse went on to explain about the link between Marie Brechan and Paula Grimshaw. The inspector listened intently. 'When my sergeant put me in the picture yesterday it sounded reasonably straightforward, but now I can see how things have become quite complex. I take it once you get hold of the background on Brechan, you may be able to tie it all together?'

Pierre leant forward, elbows on the desk. 'That's right, although when I started to check out some of her personal documents things didn't add up. I became suspicious. But it's very difficult involving her partner, Mr Dubois. Unfortunately Marie died only a few days ago, and now he's in mourning. The funeral is two days away, and I'd like to find out as much as I can without troubling him until after the funeral. I've checked out the passport we found in the private box belonging to Marie and I'm afraid it's a forgery. Who it belongs to and where she obtained it, I have no idea.'

'I can see you're up against it. But let's start by asking if anyone here remembers Brechan. We'll go on from there. I have a sergeant in his late thirties who works in personnel records, another who's in charge of case files. If Brechan was of a similar age, then maybe someone here worked with her. Give me a minute and I'll ask around.'

The inspector left Pierre alone in the room, and after a few minutes he returned with a uniformed sergeant. 'Sergeant Steven O'Hara,' the inspector announced to Pierre, turning to O'Hara and introducing Pierre. 'Mr Clarisse, ex-AGENT DE POLICE in Lille, is a PI working for a French client.' They shook hands and the inspector continued. 'Steve here tells me he was Brechan's partner during the early part of his career with the force. Perhaps if you give him the facts he may be able to help.'

Clarisse related Marcel's story about his meeting with Gary Croft and the reason why.

O'Hara whistled through his teeth. 'Takes some believing. That's not the sort of thing I would have expected of Marie.' He shook his head, a look of dismay mantling his features. 'She was one of the best. Taught me a lot. I was disappointed when she left. But she couldn't cope after the illness. She retired through ill health.' O'Hara paused. 'I certainly know the guy, Croft,' he confirmed. 'I met him a number of times before his split with Marie, mainly at staff functions. Seemed a nice enough guy. I was amazed when they divorced. I thought they were rock solid. But you never can tell.'

'Apparently not, sergeant,' Pierre replied. He then repeated the story about the passport and how it had been found in Marie's possession in France. 'Can you throw any light on that? Do you recall Marie being pregnant?'

The sergeant shook his head. 'If she was, she never told us here at the station. All we knew about was her illness. And we put that down to depression after Croft left her.'

Pierre continued to delve. 'Would you check through her records and tell me where she lived? I could, of course, get the information from Croft – via Mr Dubois – but this way it's more expedient. My next step would then be to contact the local GPs surgeries and make enquiries about a possible pregnancy.'

O'Hara quickly intervened. 'I don't need to check the records. I know exactly where she lived. It was one of the semis on Grantley Avenue, can't remember what number but I could take you to it. Of course they sold it when they split. I remember seeing the 'For Sale' sign outside. I've no idea where Marie went to afterwards.'

'Grantley Avenue you say?'

'That's right,' O'Hara said as he stood up. 'Give me a minute and I'll check out the local surgeries.'

This was exactly the sort of help Pierre needed. 'It's a good place to start if you could do that for me. I'll check out the practices and find out which one she used.'

The inspector leaned forward. 'You might come up against the patient confidentiality ruling,' he warned. 'Have you considered that?'

'I had but I'll try to talk my way through it, even if only to pick up one or two clues,' Pierre assured him. 'I need to know if Marie Brechan really was pregnant and that being the case where the baby was delivered. Surely if I stress the urgency of my search, someone will give.'

'Let's hope so,' the inspector replied. 'But they can be sticklers when it comes to giving out patient details. I know that from my own experience.'

O'Hara returned to the room. 'Here's the list. There are three practices in that area. And, by the way, there's a maternity home nearby too, St Mary's. They take in all the straightforward cases, but if there are complications, then it would be Grange General. If you've no success with the GPs, you could try those two places.'

'Good idea.' Clarisse stood up to leave. He reached across and shook hands with the two. 'Thanks for your help.'

'Don't mention it. Anything more we can do to help, just get back to us,' the inspector offered. 'Either way I'd like you to let us know how things go, Mr Clarisse.'

'Of course, Inspector,' Pierre replied as he left the office, realising the case was far more complicated than he'd first envisaged. But he enjoyed a challenge, and if it meant digging deep he was more than ever determined to get to the truth.

Chapter 10
The Present – 2008

The funeral took place two days later and the weather was as depressing as the occasion. A silent, diaphanous mist swirled around the little churchyard in Perenchies on the outskirts of Lille. The whole scene was highly emotional, a day Marcel would never forget, his dark brown eyes huge pools of sadness as he thanked his friends and colleagues for their support. He shivered and walked slowly back to the car which was waiting to take him to the reception.

His thoughts turned to Danielle. Denied the opportunity to attend her mother's funeral, what must she be feeling? But there'd been no alternative. And now he'd lost Marie he must try to concentrate his mind completely on Danielle.

Despite the emotional setback, he managed to get through the rest of the day, the reception and then his journey back home. He knew he needed to return to Edinburgh pretty quickly but he decided to stay back in Perenchies that night and start afresh in the morning. But he must telephone Pierre and make arrangements to meet. It was also imperative he book a flight to Manchester.

When Marcel contacted the hospital in Edinburgh, still no compatible donor had been found. Fortunately, according to the sister on duty, Danielle had had a quiet day and she was holding her own. 'Tell Danielle I have phoned will you Sister, and give her my love? I am taking a flight tomorrow and I will be there to visit in the afternoon.'

'I'll do that, Mr Dubois. And you take care,' she replied.

Marcel's eyes glistened when he thought about Danielle lying there in the hospital bed awaiting her fate. Marie had never been told of her daughter's illness, and perhaps it was as well. And then his stomach churned heavily at the thought of the information Pierre had turned up about Marie. How much should he disclose to Danielle?

He gave a deep sigh. For the time being he would reveal nothing other than the fact that they were trying to locate a suitable donor. The time to consider putting Danielle in the picture would be after she'd had the operation and was fully recovered.

After a broken night's sleep, Marcel was up by six o'clock and, having packed a small holdall, he left for the airport. He had arranged to meet Pierre at ten and fly up to Edinburgh at midday to visit Danielle.

Pierre was waiting in the arrivals lounge after Marcel had passed through customs. 'Let's have a coffee and talk things through,' he suggested. 'I'll update you before you get off and visit Danielle.'

'You have not confirmed who the father is yet, I take it?' Marcel asked tentatively.

Pierre folded his hands on the table. 'I'm afraid not, Marcel, nor have we clarified who the mother is.'

Marcel put his head in his hands. It was difficult for him to believe this was really happening. 'It is all becoming so convoluted, Pierre.'

But Pierre was optimistic. 'At least we seem to be getting at the truth quicker than I'd expected.'

Marcel looked up and then he turned his head away, silent.

'Don't you agree?'

'Of course I agree.' Marcel's jaw tightened. 'Marie's past does not faze me. I'm more concerned about finding a donor for Danielle.'

Pierre could sense Marcel was uptight. He patted his arm. 'Absolutely, and that's why I'm here. Leave the worrying to me, Marcel. I have the list of GPs in the area where Marie was living before she left for France. As soon as you leave, that's my plan, to visit them and find out as much as I can.'

Marcel perked up. 'Although some of the stuff you dug up is not exactly what I wanted to hear, at least we seem to be getting closer to the truth now that you have begun to establish the background to Marie's earlier life.'

'Exactly,' Pierre concurred. 'And if it's any consolation, Marcel, I had excellent reports from the sergeant who worked with Marie when he started with the force. He was a constable in those days and wet behind the ears, but he said she taught him a lot and that he'd missed her when she left.'

Marcel relaxed. What would his life have been without Marie? Empty! But he still had Danielle. 'I am glad you've told me that, Pierre. It does at least compensate for some of the things you have discovered, and for Marie's actions in those early days. I am certainly not prepared to make any judgements. For one thing we still do not have the full picture.'

'That's right, Marcel, so take solace in that.'

Pierre entered the waiting room to the Benson and Partners' surgery.

'Can I help you?' the receptionist asked him.

Pierre smiled brightly. 'I would like to make an appointment to see one of the doctors,' he replied. 'My name is Pierre Clarisse. And before you ask, I'm neither a patient nor a sales rep.'

'I didn't think you were with an accent like that.' She beamed a smile back at him. 'That being the case, tell me what it's about.'

Pierre continued. 'I'm trying – as a matter of urgency – to check the details of a woman by the name of Marie Brechan. She may or may not have been a patient of yours. She left the area twenty years ago, in 1988 I believe. I know it's way back, but if she was not on your list, I don't need to see anyone.'

The receptionist shook her head. 'As you say, Mr Clarisse, it is a long time ago. And of course there is the matter of patient confidentiality. But I can tell you Marie Brechan was a patient here. I knew her well. I'm afraid Dr Benson will most likely refuse to discuss the case. He is very strict about patient rights.'

Somehow Pierre had to get through to the woman. Maybe shock tactics would help. 'If I were to tell you Marie Brechan died in France last week and we're searching for a blood donor for her daughter, would that change the situation?'

The woman's eyes opened wide. 'Marie died last week?' she repeated, a shocked tone to her voice. 'But we were at school together. She was only in her forties.'

'Exactly,' Clarisse confirmed.

The woman picked up the phone. 'Sit down Mr Clarisse. I'll ring through to doctor.'

Pierre backed away and, as soon as the receptionist replaced the receiver, she beckoned him to the counter. 'Doctor will see you at eleven thirty but he can't guarantee giving you the information you need. Would you care to come back?'

'Certainly. And thanks for your help.'

It was a stroke of luck that Pierre had chosen that particular surgery as his first port of call. At least he now knew that if he didn't manage to find out from the GP what had happened, he could visit the local maternity home and the hospital to check things out there.

At eleven twenty-five Clarisse returned. Ten minutes later he was sitting in the consulting room where Doctor Benson opened up the buff folder handed to him by the receptionist. 'I'm surprised they've managed to turn these up,' he said, pointing to the folder. 'Would you care to fill me in on the details Mr Clarisse? Then I'll see what I can do for you.'

Pierre stressed the urgency of the situation and of the need to find Danielle's father. But he explained that it was proving difficult without establishing the true identity of the mother.

The doctor consulted the notes. 'I remember the case clearly. Mrs Brechan was pregnant in 1988. She had been anxious to conceive for some time and we did consider IVF treatment. I can tell you she was elated when I confirmed she was pregnant. And as far as I know, the father of her child was her husband, Gary Croft.' He ran his finger down the card. 'Her blood group was the same as Danielle's, B negative, which could, of course, be coincidental, although it's unlikely.' He slipped the cards back into the folder. 'After that we lost track of her. She never visited the practice again. We sent several letters asking her to attend the surgery for check-ups, but the letters were returned to the practice. She'd apparently left the area.'

'That's given me something to go on. At least it's established that Marie Brechan was one of your patients and that she was pregnant in 1988.'

'She certainly was, Mr Clarisse. Good luck with your search. I do hope you find a suitable donor before much longer.'

So Marie had been pregnant and the doctor seemed adamant Gary Croft was the father of the child. But, in view of Dr Fry's comment, this was most confusing.

His next visit was to St Mary's but the place was no longer a maternity home but a home for the elderly. The matron knew little about its previous use.

'Who are the new owners of the home? Can you tell me that?' Pierre asked.

'The Wolowski Group, Mr Clarisse. They're based in the south of England. I can give you the telephone number if that's of any help.'

Pierre took out his notebook. 'That would be useful. At least I can contact them and ask who previously owned the place. It could have belonged to the local authority I suppose. But thanks for that,' he offered as he wrote down the contact number.

But before getting in touch with the people in the south, Clarisse decided his next visit would be to Grange General. And that was when the task became less than straightforward. The administrator told him she did not have access to the archives. And in any case, she would be unable to discuss any patient with Clarisse without someone in the medical profession putting in a request. 'And even if I was able to check it out, it would be foolish of me to pass anything over to a non-resident.'

Pierre smiled. 'I can't see why my nationality should make a difference. I am working closely with the police on a particularly urgent case,' he insisted. 'If you could point me in the right direction, maybe Inspector Bayliss would vouch for me.'

'Sorry Mr Clarisse, but I have no idea where the records might be stored. For all I know they may have been taken by the trust secretary and stowed away at head office. This is my first year as administrator.' She paused. 'I could ring through and ask if you like.'

'I'd be grateful if you would,' Pierre replied.

The woman was trying to be helpful, and he didn't care how many years she'd been administrator, all he wanted was a contact number. And when she came off the phone she told him the records were, in fact, stored at head office.

'Would you mind letting me know the address and the name of the secretary there? I could approach them direct and not trouble you any further,' he offered.

She was adamant. 'Certainly I can do that for you, but they won't disclose anything, I'm sure of that.'

The head office turned out to be in the centre of Manchester, and when Pierre finally got to see the secretary, he was told the records had been computerised. 'But it's the policy of the trust not to reveal patient information other than to members of the medical profession.' The man clasped his hands on the desk. 'Now you tell me the information is urgent, and that the police are co-operating closely with you. Maybe if you ask the inspector to contact me, I could look into the file and give him the information?'

That was a compromise. 'That's fine by me, provided I find out as quickly as possible what happened in the case of Mrs Brechan, assuming she was admitted to the Grange General in the first place. According to the GP it would be some time during September 1988 when the child was born.'

The secretary shook his head. 'What I can't understand is that if she had a local GP, the hospital would have written to him and informed him of the birth. But leave it with me. As soon as I hear from the inspector I'll check it out.'

Pierre called in at the station on his way back. He needed to ask the inspector if he would vouch for the case and telephone the Grange General Trust office with a request for the information on Marie Brechan.

'Just as I thought,' the inspector said. 'I'm surprised they're letting me in on the information. But seeing that's what they suggest, I'll ring immediately,' he offered, smoothing out the sheet of paper Clarisse had passed on to him and dialling the number.

Clarisse was unable to make out the gist of the exact conversation but he gathered Inspector Bayliss was being given permission to gain access to the patient file. At last he was getting somewhere. And when the inspector replaced the receiver, he turned to Clarisse and said, 'Success Mr Clarisse. If I write out an authority on official notepaper, they'll be prepared to reveal the contents of the file.'

Sergeant Steven O'Hara was puzzled. He would never in a million years have believed that Marie Brechan could have done such a thing, changing her name and fleeing the country. But how on earth had she come up with the passport? When the French guy had told him the names, Marie and Danielle Lambert, he wrote them down and somehow or other they seemed to ring a bell with him.

He spent the day sorting through case files, making references and providing information, but at the back of his mind were those two names. And then a vivid picture began to emerge in his mind. It was one of Marie leaning over the woman who'd been stabbed at Planters Bank. He'd been new to the force at the time and that had been either the second or third case he'd shared with Marie as his partner. Together they had been the officers on duty that night. But what was the name of the woman?

Another hour slipped by before he remembered. The woman was Haley Baxter. And he seemed to recall Marie mentioning something about documents she'd taken from the Baxter woman's drawer the night she'd been up there to check on the woman's baby. At the time Marie had confided in him, telling him she was curious to know who the passport belonged to. It was in the names of Alicia Marie and Danielle Jeanne Lambert. She had told him she intended passing them over to the inspector when she arrived back at the station. But if the documents were intended for Haley Baxter, the woman who'd been murdered, maybe since her child had been left orphaned it was the Baxter baby Marie had taken to France with her. That is of course assuming Marie wasn't pregnant when she split with Gary, and that Danielle wasn't her own child.

Now that he had a lead, he went through the archives to check out the case file, hoping to find some reference to the documents containing the Lambert names. But he was disappointed. The stabbing had been reported and an investigation had commenced but then, as usually happened once they'd got their teeth into something, CID had insisted they take over. Just his luck!

But he wasn't to be deterred. He knew the sergeant in charge of records at CID and he decided to give him a ring.

'Off the top of my head I don't remember the case, Steve, but sure, I'll dig it out. Why don't you come over and look at it for yourself? It's a long time ago.'

O'Hara left a constable in charge of the office and went across to CID. The sergeant there had already taken out the file.

He spread the papers out on the desk in front of him. 'I've read these through and it's all come back to me. It was a complicated affair,' he told O'Hara. 'The woman was obviously a prostitute but she hadn't been on the game the night she was murdered. The culprit was an illegal immigrant, Boris Miladinovic. He was from Romania if I remember rightly. Anyway he was a pimp for several of the girls, and he was apparently Haley Baxter's boyfriend, although what sort of boyfriend he was God only knows!'

O'Hara picked up the sheaf of papers and ran his finger down the top one. 'Boris Miladinovic you say. There must have been an argument if he was the one who murdered her.'

The sergeant nodded. 'According to the evidence, that's exactly what happened. He was into the business of forgery.

He'd prepared the documents, the passport and the birth certificate, and he wanted Baxter to move abroad with him because the police already had wind of his activities.'

O'Hara looked up from the papers. 'And he was definitely the one who murdered Baxter?'

'Without doubt. He confessed eventually.'

O'Hara frowned. 'And what was the motive?'

The sergeant took the file from O'Hara and flicked through it. 'Here it is,' he said, pointing. 'After he'd prepared the documents for Baxter, passport, birth certificates and so on for her and the child, Baxter refused to leave the country. She went out that night to meet him. They'd been to a pub and they'd argued. The pub landlord was witness to it. And then on their way home Miladinovic lost his temper and knifed her.'

Now it all became clear to O'Hara. 'So those were the documents Marie hung on to. She intended handing them in, but what with the split with her hubby and her illness, she obviously never got round to doing it. And then they became useful.'

The sergeant closed the file. 'You must be right. They were certainly never found by us. The team couldn't weigh up whether Miladinovic had already prepared them, or if he was about to do so. His English was pretty poor according to the records. But we knew he was into forgery.'

'How did you come across him?'

The CID sergeant looked down at a slip of paper on his desk. 'It was the woman next door, Susan Whittingham who gave us the lead. You may want to speak to her. I've written her address down for you,' he offered, handing Steve the slip of paper. 'She knew he was called Boris and she gave us an excellent description both of the guy and his car. It wasn't difficult after that to flush him out. He was in the ghetto area where most of the illegals are. We checked his prints and they matched those on Baxter's handbag. Later of course one of the constables found the knife. He'd thrown it away hurriedly when a passer-by spotted what was happening. It hadn't been wiped. And that stitched it up for Miladinovic. He's still in Durham as far as I can tell from the records.'

O'Hara looked at the piece of paper. 'Thanks for checking through the record. It's given me a lot to think about.' He paused. 'Is there any chance I could borrow the file?'

'Go ahead. But let me have it back when you've finished.'

'Certainly, but I'd like to make a few notes before I return it. I don't want to slip up and give the wrong information. It's been useful talking to you, Mike.' He pondered and then he took a deep breath. 'Keep this under your hat. It's not official business. I'm checking up on a child by the name of Danielle Lambert. She was taken to France, we thought by her mother. But now it's anyone's guess as to who the mother might be.' He gave the sergeant the details of the case.

The CID sergeant smiled. 'I see. That's the name of the kid on the forged passport, the one Miladinovic prepared.'

O'Hara slipped the file under his arm. 'That's right and now it makes sense. It's obvious Marie never handed in the documents. As I said, she was having trouble around that time with her old man. They later divorced and she left the force.' He put his hand on the door handle ready to leave and then he turned back. 'But it occurs to me I need to check on the Baxter child. What happened to her, do you remember?'

The sergeant pointed to the file. 'It's all in there,' he offered. 'As far as I recall she was taken into care.'

O'Hara tapped his finger on the file. 'I'll check it out. But if that's the case, maybe Danielle isn't Baxter's child as I suspected.'

The sergeant shook his head. 'I wouldn't rule it out. We only have details of the crime itself in the records. Perhaps this Mrs Whittingham still lives in the area. Why not call and see her? She might know exactly what happened to the child. I'm sure she could fill you in.'

'I may do that. But I need to find out if a donor's been found before I start making more enquiries. And, of course, I'll need to be discreet. The inspector has no idea I've been checking around. If anything turns up though I will let him know. I'll also let the Frenchman in on it. He's not a bad sort, and he seems to have his head screwed on – for a frog that is.' They both laughed.

Sergeant O'Hara left the office and wandered back, his mind now full of possible scenarios. Could it be that the Baxter child was Danielle, and that Marie had secretly adopted her? She had certainly been very concerned about the child at the time. But that was something he definitely needed to check out.

Susan Whittingham was still living in Melbourne Gardens when Steve O'Hara paid a visit. He took out his police ID and showed it to her. 'I'm looking for a Susan Whittingham,' he said.

'What for might I ask?' she replied as her eyes narrowed with suspicion.

'Don't worry Mrs Whittingham, you're not in trouble. But I need your help.' O'Hara beamed at the woman and climbed to the top step. 'I'd like a word about Haley Baxter. I believe she was your next-door neighbour before she was tragically killed.'

'That's right,' the woman muttered guardedly.

'Would you mind if I stepped inside for five minutes, Susan?' O'Hara asked, his hand now on the door. 'There are one or two things you might be able to help me with.'

Susan nodded warily and opened the door wider.

He stepped inside. 'That's better,' he declared as he wiped his feet on the doormat. 'Now Haley Baxter had a small child, a daughter I believe. She was only a few weeks old when her mother was murdered. What was her name?'

156

'Michelle,' she offered.

'And do you have any idea what happened to the child?'

Susan Whittingham frowned. 'I looked after her the first day but then I couldn't manage, so they took her into care. I think she went to foster parents at first.' She looked away and continued without maintaining eye contact. 'I did try to keep a check on things in the first couple of weeks – I felt responsible for her in some way – but then I lost track.' She turned to face him. 'I do know the little one picked up some sort of virus and was admitted to hospital. After that I didn't hear any more. But I've a feeling she was adopted. That's what they were talking about the last time I spoke to them.'

'The Social Services you mean?'

'That's right.'

'Which hospital was she admitted to, Susan? Do you remember?'

'Murray Park, of course, but as I say, I heard nothing more.' She folded her arms. 'Why are you asking all these questions? It's nearly twenty years since Haley was murdered. The kid'll be late teens by now. She might even be married.'

'That's right, Susan. It's just that there seems to have been a mix-up and we're trying to track down the mother of a teenager who's ill.' He turned to open the door. He'd found out what he needed to know and there was no mileage in continuing the conversation. 'Thanks for your help, Susan. The information will be very useful.'

He stepped outside and Susan Whittingham hung on to the door. 'What's up with the teenager?'

Steve shook his head and continued down the steps. 'It's a long story, Susan. I can't explain just now.'

'If there's anything else, Sergeant, anything at all, I'll try to help,' she called after him, a smug look on her face.

O'Hara smiled to himself, knowing he had that winning way with the women he interviewed. Not that he was a womaniser, but he hadn't been in the force for twenty-odd years without knowing how to handle them.

He set off back to the station now vividly recalling Marie's concern for the child at the time of the murder. Was Danielle really Michelle Baxter? It was at times like this he wished he was back out there at grass roots level. He needed to check up on this Michelle Baxter, but whether the inspector would relieve him to make further enquiries was another matter.

Chapter 11
The Present – 2008

Pierre travelled back to the centre of Manchester with the inspector's written authority. Hopefully, he would find out once and for all if Marie Brechan's child was delivered at Grange General and if her baby had been involved in the mix-up at Murray Park.

There were three people in the waiting room when Pierre arrived at the trust's head office. The woman on reception took the authority slip from him. 'I'm afraid the trust secretary will be a while, Mr Clarisse.' She lowered her voice. 'Unless of course he agrees to see you before the others.' She nodded towards the three people sitting waiting. 'I'll see what I can do,' she mouthed.

Five minutes later, to the obvious annoyance of the people waiting, Pierre was ushered into the trust secretary's office. The secretary leant over and shook hands with Pierre. 'Mr Clarisse, I have news for you. I decided to consult the case notes for myself in anticipation of the authority from the police inspector. You're going to be disappointed I'm afraid. Mrs Brechan lost the baby at fourteen weeks.'

Pierre was puzzled. He frowned. 'Then why didn't the GP know what had happened?' he enquired.

'He did,' the secretary confirmed. 'At least he should have known. Here's a copy of the letter informing the practice,' he said, pointing to the item on the computer.

Pierre stretched across and looked at the document on the screen. 'Then it's obvious the letter was mislaid, either that or one of the girls at the surgery filed it in the wrong place.'

'It sometimes happens, I'm afraid.'

Pierre nodded. 'I'm sure it does. But what you've told me now confirms that Danielle was definitely not Marie's child.'

The secretary closed the case file and turned to Pierre. 'I'm sorry the notes were of little help,' he offered.

'But they were. At least it's eliminated that possibility. It's back to the drawing board I'm afraid. But thank you for allowing us to check out the information.'

Pierre decided Marcel should be told immediately and, not relishing the job of telling him Marie was not Danielle's mother, he took a deep breath before picking up the phone and relating the outcome of his Grange General search. 'At least now we know there wasn't a mix-up between Marie's baby and someone else's. Marie never had a child.' He hesitated. 'And you know what that means don't you, Marcel?'

Marcel's flat voice conveyed his feelings. 'I do, Pierre. Danielle is someone else's child.' There was a long pause. 'But what do we do now?'

'Wait for the Grimshaw woman to come forward, that's all we can do.'

Marcel sighed. 'Things are getting worse. Will we ever find a donor for Danielle?'

Pierre tried to keep him buoyant. His voice was light and his response positive. 'I'm sure we will. But let's give it a couple of days. Surely word will have filtered through to the woman by then. Failing that, I'll need to ask Inspector Bayliss to make a stronger plea, to let the public know just how urgent it is the woman comes forward. Surely if she doesn't come voluntarily, someone will have information about her.'

'You'd expect so. I will try to be patient, Pierre.'

Pierre replaced the phone on the hook. He decided to call in at the station again and let the inspector know of his latest findings. He owed it to them, it was the least he could do. And maybe he could press the inspector into sending a more urgent message out through the media.

The inspector referred him to Sergeant O'Hara. 'He's been checking up on the names, Alicia Marie and Danielle Jeanne Lambert. He thinks he has the solution to that one. I'll call him in, Mr Clarisse. Perhaps he can give you another lead.'

Pierre was surprised to learn O'Hara had been making enquiries into an old case, something that had happened almost twenty years ago. O'Hara placed the file on the desk and related the main details of the Baxter case. 'The names seemed to ring a bell. And I couldn't get them out of my mind. Then I suddenly remembered Marie telling me about some documents she'd picked up.'

Pierre clasped his hands together on the desk. 'Are you telling me one of the documents is the passport I have in my possession, the one taken from Marie's box?'

O'Hara nodded. 'I assume so. They were neither passed on to us nor to CID. Marie must have kept them, probably inadvertently. But you say you didn't find the birth certificates. Perhaps they'll turn up eventually.'

'Whether they do or not, I've now discovered Danielle was not Marie's child. Marie had a miscarriage.'

O'Hara gave a heavy sigh. 'I don't believe it.' He shook his head. 'But that's another possibility eliminated.' O'Hara looked down at the file. 'What has come to light is that Haley Baxter's child was taken into care. And then she suffered some sort of virus and was admitted to Murray Park.' He placed a paper on the inspector's desk and pointed. 'That's the name of the child, Michelle Baxter and the hospital was Murray Park. I was going to check it out for myself, but the inspector feels it's your place to do so.' His tone was indicative of his disappointment at having to pass his investigations on to Clarisse.

Pierre picked up the paper and frowned. 'I take it you're intimating that Danielle could be the Baxter woman's child?'

'That's right. At the time, Marie was concerned about the child. There is a slim chance Michelle could have been taken to France as Danielle. You have the pink wristband belonging to Paula Grimshaw's baby. Maybe the mix-up arose between Michelle Baxter and Grimshaw's child.'

Pierre stood up to leave. 'I must check out the Baxter child. That means going to Murray Park again and searching the archives, which in turn means dealing with the old guy in charge.' He smiled. 'I'll need to butter him up to get the information.'

O'Hara laughed. 'The things we have to do!' He smiled broadly and nodded his head. And then his forehead puckered, a puzzled look replacing the smile. 'But surely Michelle Baxter would be in a paediatric ward. Wasn't Grimshaw's child stolen from a maternity ward?' the inspector asked.

'No. She was moved to paediatrics a week after the mother abandoned her. She was later snatched from that ward,' Pierre confirmed as he opened the door. 'I'll let you know the outcome once I've tried my luck with the old guy again.'

'All the best,' Steve O'Hara called after him. 'Let's hope you get some joy this time.'

Pierre felt he was going around in circles, visiting first one hospital and then another. But he decided to make a start by calling on Social Services to establish what had happened to Michelle Baxter after she'd been taken into care.

The granite-faced young woman he was referred to maintained a deadpan front throughout their discussion. 'We can't tell you anything, Mr Clarisse, other than that Michelle was adopted. It would be totally unprofessional of us to reveal the details of the adoptive parents, but rest assured Michelle had a very happy childhood.'

Pierre shrugged, frustration building up inside him. Red tape again. When would someone come out with the simple truth? 'Unless you give me some sort of lead, my trip to the hospital will be futile. She was only a few weeks old when she was admitted to Murray Park. I gather she'd picked up some sort of virus. That's what I was told by Haley Baxter's neighbour. Is that correct?'

The woman was insistent and remained noncommittal. 'As I said, Mr Clarisse, we cannot reveal details about either the child or the parents.'

Pierre gave her a look of disdain. What sort of people are they? The woman was probably in her early twenties. What did she know about families? What authority did she have to be turning him away like that? If he didn't get any joy through his enquiries at the hospital he'd go back to Social Services and ask for the manager.

The old guy in archives at Murray Park recognised him. 'I see you're still here, sir. I'd have thought you'd have been back in France by now.'

Pierre remembered his name, and suspected he would be flattered by that. 'I'm still working on the case, Mr Ferncliffe,' he replied. 'We desperately need a lead to help us find the parents of the girl I told you about. I found the information you brought up for me the last time very useful,' he added, knowing a little extra buttering would go a long way. 'But now I need to make another search. It's about a small child who was admitted to the paediatric ward in 1988. I'm hoping you can help me again.'

The old guy gave an obsequious smile and slid from his chair, setting out towards the same aisle as before. 'Same year, you say?' he asked.

'That's right.'

'The other was maternity wasn't it?' he whispered.

'It was but we found an extra file in paediatrics,' Clarisse whispered back.

'Can you find paediatrics?' Mr Ferncliffe continued now in a half whisper. 'I know I can rely on you not to make an issue if I let you search through yourself.'

Pierre continued with this clandestine conversation, lowering his voice. 'That's great, Mr Ferncliffe. Thanks a lot. I'll show you what I've taken out if I find anything.'

Mr Ferncliffe rubbed his hands together and set off back to his cubicle, leaving Pierre to check out the files. And it didn't take long for him to find paediatrics. Sure enough the file marked 'Michelle Baxter' was near the beginning. He took it out and returned to the old guy's cubicle. 'Is it OK if I check this out?'

'You know where to go, sir,' he replied and pointed to the dingy office.

Pierre stared at the number on the wallet, 876467. He took a small notebook from his pocket and flicked through the pages until he came to the number of the wristband found in Marie's box. It was 876423. The registrations were just forty-four numbers apart, which would account for the patients admitted to the hospital and registered between Danielle's birth and Michelle's admission to the paediatric ward.

He slipped the contents from the cardboard wallet and began to read the first sheet. Michelle had been admitted to ward four from Thorpe House, which was apparently the children's home. She was in Murray Park for over a week and then discharged back into care once she was well again. Pierre was not surprised when he checked the dates. What the information did confirm was that the Grimshaw child and Michelle Baxter were in the same ward at the same time. But how could he check whether or not there'd been a mix-up in the bands?

Now that he'd picked up this additional evidence, there was nothing for it but to pursue both leads, although until Paula Grimshaw came forward they were at a standstill on that score. Perhaps he should go back to Social Services and ask for the manager, put her in the picture and hope to obtain more information? But then it occurred to him that the mix-up could have happened between any of the children who were in the ward at the same time. Just because Marie had been involved in the Baxter case didn't mean she'd taken Michelle.

But Pierre wasn't prepared to let it go. He could go on forever postulating. Surely it was more than coincidental that both children were there at the same time. And whilst there seemed no connection between Marie and the Grimshaw child, there certainly was a link between Marie and Paula Baxter.

He was about to slip the contents back into the wallet when he glanced at the medical notes. The language and the symbols were incomprehensible to him, but then something caught his eye. There was a small circle at the top right-hand corner of the medical card. It was of a fresher, lighter colour than the rest, as though something had been stuck onto the notes when the wallet was new, and then fallen off. Pierre tipped up the wallet and a small yellow paper disc fell out. His eyes opened wide. On it was printed the child's blood group – *'A positive'*.

That stitched it up. Danielle was not Michelle Baxter. Michelle's blood group was A Positive, not B negative. But Pierre decided to call on Steve O'Hara again to look at Haley Baxter's file. If there was some means of checking her DNA then the parentage could be established one way or the other. Assuming Haley Baxter was Michelle's mother and not

Danielle's, then there had been no mix-up. All he could do now was wait patiently for Paula Grimshaw to come forward when, hopefully, they could finally get at the truth.

Joanna Harlow listened to the six o'clock news as she peeled the potatoes and popped them into a pan. Tonight it was one of Wayne's favourites, sausage and mash. Normally he'd be home by six but tonight he was working overtime and wasn't due back until after seven. She smiled to herself knowing she'd hit lucky when she met Wayne all those years ago. He was good at his job and, now that there were just the two of them at home, his overtime pay allowed them to buy those little extras.

Once the vegetables were prepared, Joanna went through to the utility room, moved the washer programme on from 'rinse and hold' to 'spin' and returned to the kitchen, taking the sausages from the fridge and placing them on a plate next to the hob. Now everything was ready to cook.

With almost an hour to spare before Wayne was back, she went up to the bedroom and changed into a jog suit before returning to the kitchen to empty the washer, tip the clothes into the dryer and set it going.

It was then she thought she heard a familiar name. But the announcement was competing with the noise of the dryer and she didn't quite catch it. All she picked up was that it was something to do with an appeal by the police for a woman to come forward. She had a feeling the name of the woman was Paula Grimshaw. Her stomach lurched – as it always did when that name came to mind.

But she reasoned to herself that the name wasn't so unusual, especially in the north of England. Maybe there was more than one Paula Grimshaw. Whether or not that was the case, she must find out what the announcement was all about before she started to concern herself, and there was nothing for it but to switch on TV and check it out on one of the news channels.

It was well after six now and she dashed into the lounge and picked up the control, hoping she hadn't missed the item. When she flicked on to BBC, one of the presenters was discussing the policy in Iraq with a Member of Parliament. Joanna flicked over to the ITV channel and realised it was the regional news. Within seconds, sure enough, the item she'd half heard on the radio came up. Her gaze swept to the screen and rested on the presenter who was making an urgent appeal for a Mrs Paula Grimshaw to come forward. Joanna slumped down on the sofa.

Her eyes still fixed on the screen, she took a deep breath and released it slowly, hoping to clear her mind and think rationally. She had heard the name correctly. The search was for the mother of a young woman, who needed blood of a rare type, to come forward. The mother could be a suitable donor.

The announcement hit Joanna immediately and, heart pounding, she sat bolt upright on the sofa. If anyone knew about Paula Grimshaw, she did. And she couldn't ignore the fact that she could help them in their search.

Wringing her hands together, she thought about what she might do next. But she felt so uptight now she couldn't make the decision without talking it through with Wayne. It would have to wait until he returned from work.

She wrapped her arms around her slim body and lay back on the sofa, closing her eyes. She shivered. Paula Grimshaw! The name echoed in her brain. And then the memories began to flood back.

Chapter 12
The Past – 1988

Joanna Harlow's mind drifted. Of course she was Joanna Falconer then. She flinched as the memories flooded back.

It all began when she was eighteen. Joanna remembered it clearly. They were at Rick's parents' place. His mum and dad had gone off on a short break to London. It was the first time Rick and Joanna had been alone together. The lights in the lounge were turned off, and the bright flashes from the television screen shone on to Rick's face, revealing his adoration for Joanna.

'Feel what you do to me,' he murmured, taking her hand and pressing it against his chest. 'You're gorgeous,' he added as she lifted her hand and felt the heavy thump of his heart. And as her eyes met his she detected the sincerity of his words. He gently took her face in his hands and leant towards her, kissing her with the lightest of pressure. A delicious feeling of warmth streamed through her body, something she hadn't experienced before. It was wonderful. She wanted more.

She pushed up against him and he slipped his arms around her. He began to kiss her neck, and then her shoulders, working his way down until she thought she was going to go wild with ecstasy. He slipped off her blouse and then her bra. And she let him do that. She couldn't help herself. But, even though she felt hypnotised by him, she knew what would happen if she didn't maintain some control.

And then she began pushing Rick away. 'No, Rick. We can't, not without, you know – protection.'

'Just this once, Jo,' he begged. 'You want it as much as me. Don't spoil it.'

That was it. 'Just this once' had its own significance. The next thing she knew, she was pregnant.

It was a Friday morning just before she left for work. Her period was twenty-four days late and, willing it to start, she'd counted each day with dread, marking it down on a slip of paper she kept hidden under her knickers in her underwear drawer. She sighed. It wasn't as though she could talk it through with anyone, share her problem. Her mind began to race, as though she was reading a book at high speed. Future events tumbled into her mind, events she was sure she wasn't ready to face. Not that she didn't want a baby with Rick. She adored him. But it was too soon. She needed to finish her studies at college and earn enough money to save for the future. She didn't want it like this.

She opened her handbag and took out the carton, flicking up the cardboard lid and peeking inside. There it was – the pregnancy test she'd bought the previous day at the chemist. Not the local place. The last thing she wanted was nosey Miss Marshall telling Mum what Joanna had bought. She'd been all the way into town to buy it.

When both Mum and Dad had finished in the bathroom, she tiptoed along the landing, locking herself inside there to carry out the test. Just as she'd opened the plastic packet inside the carton and started to read the directions, a voice made her jump. It was Mum.

'Come on, love. Breakfast is ready.'

'I'll only be five minutes,' Joanna called out in reply.

'Well hurry. It's going cold.'

Joanna sat on the edge of the lavatory bowl and held the stick between her legs. Her stomach was riddled with butterflies. When she had finished, she brought the stick out in front of her and glanced back at the instructions. They read: *The test will indicate positive when the line turns blue and the plus sign appears.*

Joanna couldn't believe her eyes. The line had turned blue. No two ways about it. She was pregnant.

Mum would go spare. She'd rant and rave – after all there was the family's reputation to consider. And God knows what Dad would say!

But, for now, casting all thoughts of her parents from her mind, Joanna tried to console herself that it had happened, and that she and Rick were obviously destined to spend the rest of their lives together. She knew she must talk to him pretty quickly. She dressed and went downstairs to breakfast.

'Morning, love.' Her mother, bright and breezy as usual, smiled warmly. 'Scrambled eggs?' she added.

Joanna's stomach churned. 'Just the toast, Mum,' she replied, slapping a smile on her face. What with the test result and that sickly feeling she'd had for the last couple of days, scrambled eggs were the last thing she needed that morning. 'I'm leaving early this morning. We've a rush job on at the office.'

'Fair enough, love. But you need a good breakfast to start the day.'

'I know that, Mum, but not today,' Joanna insisted. 'The toast will be fine.'

Once she reached the office, the toast came back, straight down the toilet. She closed her eyes, and her stomach started to lurch violently. But it wasn't only the toast playing havoc. It was her emotions. She wasn't ready for this. And it looked as though her morning sickness had started. She'd never felt so nauseous.

But there was one thing for certain. She'd have to keep her problem hidden from her mother. And her colleagues at the office, too.

As soon as she left work later that afternoon she was determined to contact Rick and arrange to meet him that evening. But by the time she'd telephoned the plumber's workshop where the men congregated at the end of the day, there was no reply. She'd left it too late. She sighed. Whatever happened he'd have to admit the baby was his and he'd have to take responsibility too. After that they could plan their next steps and decide what would happen in the future.

Going straight home wasn't an option now. Mum would be fussing and making the evening meal, and the very thought of food still gave her that sickly feeling in her stomach. But hopefully it would pass. Didn't they say it was morning sickness pregnant women suffered? Surely not all-day sickness!

There was a Lytham bus standing in at the station when she arrived, and seeing that confirmed her earlier decision. The best thing to do was to go straight to Rick's place. If he wasn't back yet, his mother would surely know where he was.

By the time she reached the house it was ten to six. She pressed hard on the front door bell and his mother opened the door. 'Joanna, love. Come in.' Rick's mother shuffled along the carpet in her furry slippers. Joanna followed her through, wondering why the woman had let herself go. She was forty-two years old and already she moved around like an old granny. But she would be a granny pretty soon, wouldn't she?

That very thought started the agitation in Joanna's stomach once more. But she must try to control her feelings.

She spotted Rick's working boots in the kitchen and asked, 'Is Rick back yet?'

Mrs Stevens folded her arms. 'He's been and gone, love. Came back at half four, showered and dressed up. Out by five.

Said he'd something on. I thought you might have known where he'd gone.'

That was strange. He usually told her if he'd anything on. 'He didn't say anything. But don't worry Mrs Stevens. I'm sure it must have been something important. I'll catch him later.'

Mrs Stevens smiled. 'Will you stay for a bit of tea, love?'

The very thought brought back that nauseous feeling. 'Thanks, but I just called in on the off chance. Mum will have dinner ready for me. I'll get back if you don't mind.'

As she walked through the hall to the front door, Mrs Stevens turned to her. 'That's fine by me. I'll tell our Richard you've called, shall I?'

It was unusual for Joanna to call at the house. The last thing she wanted was for his mother to make a big deal out of it. He'd realise it was something important, and she didn't want to raise his suspicions. 'There's no need, Mrs Stevens. Don't bother him. He's obviously got other, more important things on his mind.' But inside she knew nothing could be more important than the child she was carrying.

Once back home the strong aroma of fish drifted towards her as she opened the door. But she knew she must try to maintain control otherwise Mum would sense there was something amiss. Stuffing her hand over her mouth, she lingered in the downstairs cloakroom, removed her coat and hung it up. Fortunately by now the nausea had disappeared. She washed her hands and went through to the kitchen.

'You're not usually this late, love.' Kim Falconer dished out a salmon fillet, new potatoes and garden peas. Before Joanna had the time to make up an excuse for not eating the meal, Mum continued. 'There you go. Just the way you like it. A nice, healthy meal.' She took the plate into the dining room and Joanna followed. And then Mum stood beside her and poured a trickle of hollandaise sauce over the fish. 'Enjoy it, love,' she added and moved back into the kitchen.

Joanna looked at the meal. Mum certainly knew how to look after her. It was a healthy option and she must try to eat it. It wouldn't do to feel sick on an empty stomach. But she hoped she could get it down before Mum noticed any signs of nausea.

Her parents were watching one of the soaps in the lounge when she went through into the hall. Maybe Rick would be back home by this time. She picked up the phone and rang his mobile. But there was no reply. That was strange. Wherever he was he'd deliberately switched off his mobile.

It was something Rick had always thought about, emigrating, getting right away and starting afresh. One of his mates had done exactly that and managed to get a well-paid job with prospects. And there was nothing for him here now that he'd completed his apprenticeship, nothing but the day-to-day grind, head under someone's sink detecting a leak or worse still, working outside on water pipes in the bitter cold.

Rick's first appointment was with a Canadian representative in Manchester. He didn't bother to tell Joanna. It was one evening when she was at her keep fit class. And it would be better if he told her after both interviews when he would be in a better position to make a decision. The guy who interviewed him seemed impressed at Rick's progress and his excellent results from college.

'There are a number of jobs in the North East that would suit your CV. A couple of them have excellent prospects too.'

When the interview was complete Rick was taken into a studio where, together with several more applicants, he watched a film. He was impressed and he promised to get back to the rep once he'd made up his mind.

But Australia was really the place he fancied. His Aunt Dorothy had gone out there just after she married Uncle Jim. Well, they weren't really his aunt and uncle. Aunt Dorothy was his gran's sister. They'd be knocking on now. Maybe in their sixties. But it would be a start if he could stay with them until he got himself established.

The representative was enthusiastic. 'You'll soon find your feet, I can promise you that. And there are lots of opportunities for plumbers, especially with your sort of background, a full apprenticeship and qualifications under your belt. They're pretty thin on the ground in Australia.'

Rick developed a feeling of optimism. Of course he had mentioned neither appointment to Joanna. There was no doubt about it she'd have put him off going. And he wanted to see for himself what was on offer. Obviously he'd like Joanna to go with him, but the trouble was that she hadn't finished her training at college. She had another year of the secretarial course to complete. If they wouldn't take her now, perhaps she could join him as soon as she qualified. Hopefully she'd be taken up with the idea, although he had to acknowledge that she did seem to be a bit of a clinger with her parents.

But it was up to her now. He'd made up his mind. There wasn't a great deal for him to stay back for. His mother had this new man in her life. And what a knobhead he was. Rick couldn't stand him. He could see right through the guy. Of course his mother was blinkered. She was too stupid to realise all he wanted was his feet under the table and a warm bed at night. He was on to a good number. And he was bone-idle. Never did a thing around the house. But his mother had been so flattered to have someone fancy her after his dad had disappeared years ago, that she was unaware of his ulterior motives.

Rick had been no more than eight years old when his father had sloped off with some fancy piece. And since then his mother

174

had cried the poor tale, feeling sorry for herself, at times neglecting her son. Eventually Rick became sick of it. And now it was even worse with this two-faced git on the scene.

'What do you think?' The Australian representative, anxious to know if Rick was genuinely interested, broke into his thoughts.

'I like what I hear.' Rick gave his honest opinion. 'And I'm sure I could stay with relatives in Perth. What are the chances of getting work on the west coast?'

'Better than the east just at present.' He flicked through his papers and handed a sheaf to Rick. 'Look through these. Go home and think about it, Richard. Discuss it with your parents. Come back and see me again when you decide to go ahead. Believe me you've nothing to lose and everything to gain.'

Rick was full of it when he arrived back home. His mother broke down and cried. But he could tell they were crocodile tears, and through her blubbering she had the cheek to say she was disappointed after all she'd done for him. That was a joke. He'd more or less had to fend for himself since he was eight years old. But Rick could have kicked his stepfather into outer space when he saw the glib look on his face.

Despite their reactions, the more Rick thought about it, the more his excitement accelerated. But then his stomach did a nose dive. He'd have to break it to Joanna, and the sooner the better. Whether she'd be elated too was anyone's guess.

Marie was reluctant to confide in her colleagues about the split with Gary. First she needed to pull herself round and, more importantly, allow herself to gain the strength to accept what had happened. Although she was elated about the baby, Gary's leaving her had been unexpected and she was still suffering the trauma.

But she never did confide in her colleagues at the station. And by the time she was five months pregnant, the worst happened. It was during the middle of the night when she awoke with terrible cramps in her stomach. Aware it was something drastic, she eventually rang for an ambulance.

With a great deal of effort, she managed to struggle to the door and turn the key to unlock it. The ambulance was there within minutes. Some of the tension drained from her body as she felt herself being lifted onto a stretcher and carried to the ambulance. And then the questions began. But she didn't want their questions. She wanted them to save her baby. Her brain refused to accept what was happening and the screams inside her head became cacophonous with the loud blare of the ambulance siren.

Everything happened so quickly at the hospital. She was rushed through Casualty into a large brightly lit room. And then came the most excruciating pains. She felt as though she'd been drained of her lifeblood. It was then she realised it was over.

'I'm sorry,' the doctor began. Marie tried to pull herself up. She rolled sideways and her body folded in on itself, her head drooping on to her chest. She didn't hear the rest. She'd lost the child, a precious daughter. Despair tore through her.

Once back home, Marie was dying inside at the loss of her child, and she tried, without success, to cover it up on the outside. But she found herself unable to concentrate. She'd sit mesmerised, staring into space, her eyes glazed and anguished. Her colleagues visited and, by this time, they'd discovered Gary had left. They knew at the station she'd been ill, but they never found out the truth, that she'd been pregnant and miscarried. And for some time she was so stressed she couldn't go back to work. When she eventually returned she couldn't cope.

'Don't you think you should take more time off, Brechan? You're not firing on all cylinders. And you know full well it won't do. Have a word with the doc. He'll get you sorted,' Inspector Trent suggested, his statement containing not an ounce of empathy. Not that Marie wanted it. All she needed was time to get over the trauma of everything that had happened within the space of the last three months.

The police doctor was reluctant for her to return to work. Her sick leave became extended. Having lost the strength to take control, it was obvious she could never go back to the station. Weeks later she retired on grounds of ill health. She spent hours sitting in a chair, her face white and strained, head in hands, wallowing in self-pity. She was empty. There was nothing left to look forward to after losing first her husband and now her baby.

Joanna took a deep breath. 'I'm pregnant, Rick. I did the test. It was positive.'

'What? After the once?'

'That's all it takes, Rick.' She felt the blood rush to her face, and she stared up at him, her eyes wet and shining. He'd have to support her. The child was his and he'd have to admit to it. Rick didn't reply immediately and Joanna started to panic. 'You've got to support me Rick. The baby's yours and you know it.' Joanna was at her wits' end now. She'd never expected this.

Rick frowned. 'But it's messing up all my plans Jo.'

Joanna couldn't believe what she was hearing. 'I feel sorry for you and your plans. Surely I come first.'

'I've been to see the reps and I've more or less made arrangements to leave the country, but I haven't decided yet whether it's Canada or Australia. Get rid of the baby and come with me, Jo.'

'You've got to be joking. How could you be so callous? I wouldn't dream of doing that.' She folded her arms and sat in silence, thinking surely he'd come round to her way of thinking.

'And I've no intention of coming with you. Mum and Dad would be heartbroken.'

Rick shot back at her. 'But it doesn't matter if I'm heartbroken, does it?'

'Don't come it. After all, you've decided to go with or without me. You didn't even ask me to come to the interviews with you. You did it all behind my back.' Joanna shook her head and gulped in air.

'You know why, don't you? Because you've reacted just the way I thought you would. I'd never have made it to the centres, let alone had interviews,' Rick countered.

Realising he was right in what he was saying Joanna knew he was now getting the better of her. She pouted and fluttered her eyelashes. And then her eyes began to glisten. 'I can't see why you want to go all that way.'

Rick took her hands. 'For the opportunities, Jo. I'm in a dead-end job here. I'll never be able to start my own business. I could never raise the capital.' He squeezed her hands. 'Come with me,' he pleaded. 'We can still have the baby. No one will know you're pregnant when we leave.'

Joanna's hurt changed to a choking anger. 'You're talking out of the back of your head. How could you possibly support the three of us? You don't even have a job to go to,' she maintained.

Rick took her shoulders and turned her towards him. 'I've more or less been promised I'll get a job straight away, either country.' He let go and took another drink of beer. And then he slipped his arm around her shoulder and pulled her towards him. 'We could get married over there. There's no reason why anyone should know. When it's born you could tell your mum it was premature.'

Joanna began to sob. 'I don't know where you get your ideas from. You know I can't go. You've got to face up to it, Rick. You can't go over there and leave me.'

He dabbed the tears from her face with his handkerchief. 'I'm sorry, love. But I've made up my mind,' he persisted. 'Come with me and everything will be fine.'

Joanna could tell he meant what he was saying. She panicked. 'Surely you can postpone your decision until after the baby? And then we can start afresh, especially if we get married. We'll manage. Mum could look after the baby whilst I finish my final year at college. Come on, Rick. Say you'll stay.'

He slipped his arm from her shoulder and placed his fist on the table. 'I know your tricks,' he said. 'I'll stay back here, you'll have the kid, and then you know I'd never leave you once it's born.' He took a deep breath. 'That's it, Jo. Either you get rid of it and come with me, or we go together and you have the baby over there. I can't say fairer than that.'

Joanna was heartbroken when she realised Rick meant every word he'd said. She mulled his words over in her mind. He was leaving the country and he'd asked her to go with him. But she'd refused. He was leaving her just when she needed him most. But she was adamant. She would have to choose between Rick and her parents.

There was no way she'd agree to go with him. If it was more important for him to leave than it was to stand by her, he obviously didn't love her.

That was as much as she could take. Tears streaming down her face, she rushed out of the pub. Going abroad wasn't an option. She'd never be able to tell Mum and Dad she was leaving, especially to live at the other side of the world.

Fully expecting Rick to come after her, she kept on turning to look back, but he didn't appear. Perhaps if she told his mother about the baby, she would persuade Rick to come to his senses.

But Joanna realised that Rick would begin to despise her and tell her she'd spoilt his chances if his mother intervened. And she'd rather be on her own than let that happen. Now the tears began to flow. But her mind was made up. Let him go. If he wasn't prepared to stand by her, she'd support herself.

All the way back home her mind was in a whirl. And once she'd climbed into bed and had another little weep, she made up her mind. She'd try to get a job in Manchester. If she moved over there, no one would know about the baby. And when the time came, she could have the baby in one of the hospitals there. It was obvious she wouldn't be able to keep it. She wouldn't want Mum and Dad to know anything about it. She'd have to put it up for adoption.

Rick contacted her once or twice before he left and tried to talk it through again with her. But she'd made up her mind. It was OK Rick saying most countries were easily accessible these days, but that wasn't the point. She didn't fancy going all that way. Full stop!

After thinking it through, Joanna felt sure her prospective move to Manchester was a sound idea. She wouldn't see her parents for some time. But she would have to keep in touch by phone. The last thing she wanted was for them to see her once the bump started to show. And when it was over and done with she could go back there.

After all it was her nineteenth birthday in November. Mum and Dad would be sure to throw a party for her, just as they had every year since she was one year old.

Rick was staggered when he learnt Joanna was pregnant. But she couldn't expect him to go back on things. He was twenty-one years old and ready to take up the challenge. An opportunity like this might never come around again. But she refused to pick up on any of his suggestions. What more could he do?

His head was buzzing with the thought of what might happen if he stayed here in England. He'd not only be stuck with the dead-end job but he'd be saddled with a wife and child too. He'd never get away.

The guy at the centre had promised to contact him again with any definite offers of job interviews. After an answerphone message, Rick called in to see the rep.

'Once we fix you up with a flight, we can arrange a series of interview dates for you – that's if you're still interested,' the Australian representative advised him.

'I'm definitely game,' Rick replied. 'I'll phone my relatives to confirm when I'll be arriving.'

'I take it you're travelling alone, Richard. I have it on your application that you're not married.'

Rick looked down at his hands. 'That's right. If my girlfriend had agreed to come along, she would obviously have contacted you for an interview. But we've agreed to part amicably,' he replied, knowing this wasn't exactly true, but it would have been amicable had she agreed.

After a couple of days, appointments came through for job interviews. And that sealed it for Rick. The arrangements were made. And although he genuinely wanted Joanna to leave with him, each time he rang she refused to discuss it. And the more he pleaded with her the more adamant she became that she would never leave England.

In the end he left without her.

Chapter 13
The Past – 1988

It was the pressure from Gary's solicitor to sell the house that was getting to Marie. Her initial response – *to hell with him, let him rough it with his hussy* – was a natural reaction but, deep down, she came to despise the house. And even though she had an icy thirst for revenge, she could no longer live happily in the place she'd once shared with Gary.

Decision made. He could have his money and, for all she cared, he could go to the other side of the world with the tart he was shacked up with.

The hassle of the divorce over, Marie moved into a little terraced house not far away. Having settled in she seemed to snap into an interim phase of reasoning. Her life with the force had been active, and this sitting at home doing nothing but mope was not her way of handling the situation. Life must go on and, unless she channelled her efforts into some other activity, she would never be completely rid of the depression. She needed to gather her strength to carry on, and her solution was to apply for a job that didn't require her to think on her feet. But it seemed both her breakdown and her premature retirement from the police force were holding her back when she sent in applications.

It would have been easy to allow the frustration to get her down, but she was strong, and determined not to let things overwhelm her again. She kept on applying and taking the negative responses in her stride.

After spotting an advert for a salesperson at Cromptons, a large store in the city, she reasoned this could be the sort of job she was suited to. It would allow her to meet people and hopefully help her recovery by taking her mind off recent events, especially the loss of her baby. She posted the application and was surprised when, a couple of days later, she received a letter asking her to go for interview.

Several heads turned in her direction as she entered the waiting room. What chance did she have against her fellow-interviewees? They were mainly women, but there was a solitary man sitting on the opposite side of the room. She sat next to him and he smiled.

Eventually the human resources manager invited her into his office. 'Do sit down Mrs Brechan. Have you had any experience at all in selling?' he asked.

Here it comes – totally unsuitable for their precious job!

'Not in sales, but I've had a great deal of experience dealing with members of the public. I'm sure I can apply myself to the job if I'm given a chance.' She gave a positive explanation, hoping he would be impressed by her willingness.

'What was your previous job?' *It was obvious he hadn't even read her CV.*

'I was a sergeant in the police force until recently.'

He regarded her searchingly. 'And you want to change direction and work as a sales person? That's unusual – and it surprises me. The pay for this job is certainly not on a par. Why did you leave?'

There was no point covering up the truth. 'I'd been ill, and when I returned to work, I found it very stressful.'

The manager leant with his elbows on the desk and studied her CV. He was frank in his comment. 'I don't believe the salesperson's job is for you, Mrs Brechan.'

Marie caught her breath as disappointment descended. 'Maybe if you gave me a trial I could show you I'm quite capable,' she replied. It was exactly what she'd been expecting, to be turned down yet again. But she didn't intend giving in easily.

'It's not as straightforward as that. There are several attributes to consider.'

Marie took a deep sigh and made to get up and leave.

'Not so fast, Mrs Brechan,' the manager continued. 'I haven't finished yet. Do sit down. When I talk about attributes, what I mean is that you're obviously suited to a different sort of job.'

Marie was not sure what he was getting at, but she held her breath and waited.

He continued. 'It's rather fortuitous that you've called today.' He smiled and picked up a clutch of papers from the corner of his desk. 'Yesterday I had to dismiss our store detective. Unfortunately he was hand in glove with several shoplifters who were apparently paying him commission to allow them access.' He shook his head.

She couldn't help laughing. In all her experience she'd never heard anything so infantile. 'What a stupid scam,' she offered. 'Surely he realised he'd be found out. Didn't he know anything about stocktaking or accountability?'

'Exactly, you've hit the nail on the head – apparently not.' The manager lifted his elbows from the desk and clasped his hands. 'I can offer you that job. It's slightly more money than the salesperson's job and you obviously have the requisite skills.' He looked to her for a response but before she had the chance, he continued. 'And I don't think there'll be anything too stressful there. We certainly need someone who's vigilant, who can spot a potential thief and catch him in the act.'

At this Marie perked up. 'I can certainly do that. And I must say the job is more in line with my experience.' She smiled. 'I'd appreciate the challenge if you're willing to give me the go ahead,' she said, now convinced that once she threw herself into a full-time job, she could overcome the depression completely.

The manager stood up and offered his hand. 'Then that's settled. Is next Monday OK? Eight thirty sharp.'

Her spirits rose. She felt better than she had for some time. She could still keep her hand in, but without the added responsibility that came with working for the force. 'That's wonderful,' she replied.

'Then it's been my lucky day,' he joked.

Marie smiled back. 'Mine too!' she said and, although she would never get over losing the baby, thoughts of Gary and the trollop he'd gone off with were already fading.

On her first visit to Manchester Joanna was disappointed there were no jobs available. She checked in at every agency but there was nothing suitable. It was two weeks later on a return visit that she managed an interview for a clerical job in a large advertising agency. The money wasn't brilliant, and she considered the job beneath her, but she couldn't afford to be choosy. A job was a job at the end of the day. And she needed the money desperately now that she had to fend for herself.

The bed-sit she took was shabby but comfortable enough. And the first thing she bought herself was small TV set. She didn't intend getting to know anyone personally. That would have complicated things. All she'd planned was to relax and stay in each evening watching TV.

During the first couple of months she went back and visited her parents at weekends and after that, even though the lump didn't show, she was reluctant to arouse any suspicions. Once she'd stopped her weekend routine, she telephoned her parents at least twice a week. And when her mother suggested she pop over and visit, Joanna found it difficult putting her off.

'I'm working weekends, Mum. We have a rush job on, and I've promised to help out. I don't want to let them down. They're considering making the post permanent.'

'Permanent? But I thought you were there as part of your college course, love, on an exchange to give you additional experience didn't they say?'

That was the trouble when you invented a story. You had to stick to it or manage to give it a different slant if you were caught out. 'That's right, Mum. Don't worry. I will be back. What they mean by permanent is that instead of it being on a weekly basis, according to their needs, it'll be on a monthly basis. Do you see what I mean?'

'I see,' her mother replied vaguely, obviously not understanding what Joanna was trying to convey to her. 'But are you sure it's nothing to do with Rick leaving, love?' She sounded a little dubious.

Joanna flinched at the comment. 'How do you mean, Mum?' she asked.

'Well, your father and I have the feeling you're trying to escape. We know you thought a lot about Rick, but he's gone now. And I must say I thought it was a selfish thing to do, leaving you like that.'

Joanna lightened her voice. 'Mum, don't worry. I never wanted to leave the country. How do you think I'd feel if I had to leave you two? And I'm over Rick now, I have been for months. It doesn't bother me any more,' she lied. 'I've made lots of new friends here in Manchester.'

She heard her mother's heavy sigh at the other end of the line. 'Well good riddance to him, that's what I say. And I know what you mean about leaving us. We wouldn't have wanted you to go either. As long as you're happy, love. But don't overdo it. I'm sure there's no need to work weekends. Don't let them make a mug of you.'

Joanna smiled. She'd talked herself through. 'I won't, Mum. But the money comes in handy, and the shopping's good here in Manchester.'

Her mother laughed. 'I know what you're like when it comes to hitting the shops. There's no dragging you away. Do take care though, love,' she added in serious tone. 'You will be back for your birthday won't you? Dad and I want to arrange something special for you.'

Joanna whooped. 'You don't think I'd miss that do you, Mum?' she added realising that, according to her calculations, the baby was due early October which would give her the chance to be back by then.

By the time the end of August came around Joanna was feeling tired. She'd had no summer holiday, not even a break from it all. It was then she decided to hand in her notice at the advertising agency and maybe take on a part-time job, something nearby. She was due some respite after spending so much time on her feet, taking reports from one department to another. She felt so worn out she could hardly drag her body out of bed each morning.

The part-time job never came about. It was less than a week later when the pains started. She felt the cramps in her stomach, forcing her to bend over, clutch at her middle and hiss out breaths until it subsided. Surely it couldn't be the baby!

She stuck it out for half an hour before she realised the pains were never going to subside. It frightened her. What should she do? She didn't want to ring for an ambulance and let anyone know where she lived. But if she rang for a taxi it wouldn't take long to get to hospital, and there was a stand across the road. And in any case, a taxi would probably get her there more quickly than an ambulance.

The taxi was at the door in less than five minutes and Joanna held her breath and slipped into the back seat. Minutes later she was forced to stifle her cries when the pains became more severe. But she managed to steel herself. The last thing she wanted was to let on to the taxi driver she'd started in labour. It would scare him off.

She took deep breaths between the pains and, as they drew close to the hospital, she asked him to drop her at the gates, telling him she was visiting a relative. She paid the guy, waited until he'd disappeared and then struggled the fifty yards to the entrance.

Once in Casualty she let herself relax and her waters broke as the nurse asked her name. It was on the tip of her tongue to give herself away, but she'd decided some time ago that if she gave a false name, perhaps no one would ever find out. And it came to her in a flash. She announced herself as Paula without thinking about the future and eventually signing adoption papers.

The nurse was jovial and tried to chivvy her along. 'Here we go,' she said as she helped Joanna into a wheelchair. The delivery room was buzzing with noise as they wheeled her in. 'Up here,' directed one of the midwives as she patted the trolley mattress. The nurse helped her up, called out 'Good luck!' and left.

'Now, let's have a look at you, Paula,' the midwife said in gentle tones. 'Deep breathing. Don't push yet.'

The other mothers in the delivery room seemed to know what the midwives meant by 'deep breathing' and 'panting', but Joanna was totally ignorant as to what was expected of her or when. She hadn't been to classes. After all, she had no partner and the others would be either taking their husbands with them or talking about them. More to the point, anonymity was of paramount importance.

The contractions were coming in rapid succession now, shuddering down her spine, shooting across her insides and clawing viciously.

'Hold it, hold it. Deep breaths again, Paula,' the midwife insisted.

But how could she stop herself from bearing down and pushing the baby out? And in between the painful spasms, Joanna's mind drifted. More than anything she wanted Mum. How could she have let this happen? She should have confided in Mum. Mum would have known what to do. Another pain. 'Oh my God,' she called out and, as the tension gripped her, she felt as though she was going to die. 'I can't do it!'

'Of course you can, love. Hold on. It'll soon be over.'

Joanna winced. Within seconds there was another contraction, which seemed to last for ages. She cried out, 'It's coming!' And this time she simply couldn't hold on.

The midwife took hold of her hand. 'Push now,' she directed. 'Come on, love. Do your best. It won't be long.'

Another couple of pushes and the baby made its debut, immediately bawling its head off. 'That's the way,' the midwife whispered as she gently patted the child. 'Good clear passages. That's what we want.'

Joanna felt her body relax as the young nurse wiped the baby's face. Smiling down at Joanna she said, 'Well done, Paula. It's a girl, five pounds three. You'd better think of a name,' she added and laughed. 'Unless you already have one in mind.'

Joanna shook her head as a warm bundle was thrust into her arms. She brought the tiny, squirming body to her chest and looked down at the screwed-up face, reddened with the effort of pushing herself into the world. She contemplated the nurse's words. Think of a name? She intended doing no such thing. If she became attached to the baby, she'd never let her go. She couldn't keep her. Rick had gone off and left, and he wasn't about to come back, baby or no baby. And her parents knew nothing about it. Nor were they ever likely to.

Within minutes the baby was taken from her. 'You need to rest now, Paula. I'll clean baby up,' the young nurse told her, 'and then you can see her again in a while. Sister will want you to try breast-feeding.'

Breast-feeding! Joanna couldn't cope with that.

The baby wouldn't stop crying and eventually one of the nurses brought in a bottle, handing it to Joanna. 'Try this,' she said. 'But give the breast-feeding another try later today, Paula. I'm sure once things start to flow you'll be fine.' But Joanna didn't want things to flow. She didn't want to start anything she couldn't finish.

Sleep never came that night. Her mind was a jumble of thoughts, of the baby, of Rick, of her parents and most importantly what her next move would be. She hadn't mentioned anything yet about adoption. It just hadn't seemed appropriate when everyone wanted her to act the 'earth mother' and breast-feed her child.

'You need plenty of nourishment, Paula, and then we'll try the breast-feeding again, shall we?' Sister suggested.

But that was out of the question for Joanna. She had other plans.

As Joanna lay in the hospital bed, her task complete, her mind became saturated with thoughts of a possible escape. She must get away somehow. And what better time than early morning when, hopefully, she could slip out unobtrusively whilst the night staff, due off shift, would be chin-wagging with the day staff.

She pulled herself up in the bed. 'I'd like a bath if that's all right Sister, before I have breakfast?' She smiled. 'I'll take care, promise. I need to ease my body.'

'Good idea, Paula. But don't lock the door,' she insisted. 'It's a ruling we have in case anything goes wrong. We may need to get in there.'

As she glanced around the ward, Joanna noticed the other mothers were too busy cooing over their babies to notice what she was about to do. Furtively collecting her few clothes and small holdall, she scrunched them together, covered them with a towel and stuffed the bundle under her arm. After closing the bathroom door behind her, she turned on the tap to its full extent and let the water gush out noisily. But she didn't get into the bath. Instead she slipped on her outdoor clothes and crammed her nightwear and toiletries into the bag. It didn't take long.

She turned off the tap and opened the bathroom door, peeking out. The corridor was clear. With a heavy beat drumming noisily in her chest, she tiptoed out of the bathroom. Gently closing the door behind her, she walked quickly and purposefully down the corridor into the main entrance hall. Once at the outer steps, she put on a spurt, gulping in cold draughts of air as she ran, racing through the car park and out of the grounds, flagging down the first taxi she saw.

'City centre please.' She slipped quickly into the back, trying to regain her breath and hoping the driver wouldn't notice her state of exhaustion. Running from the hospital after giving birth to her baby only a day earlier was bound to have that effect. But what was her alternative?

The city centre was buzzing with people. She pulled up the hood on her jacket, dreading meeting up with someone she knew and, as she furtively glanced around her, the heavy beat began to hammer loudly in her chest once more.

There was a bus in the bay when she crossed over to the station and it was a relief to rest her feet and legs even for the ten minutes it took to reach her stop on the outskirts of the city. And now her mind was bursting with plans for the future. There were two alternatives. Obviously she could get right away now, once she'd been back to the flat and packed her things but she decided against that option. There could be a search, and they'd be looking for someone small with short, fair hair. That meant there was a chance she might be spotted. And besides she wasn't ready yet to go back to her parents' place in Blackpool. Self-composure must come first and a boost in her confidence. And above all she needed to rest a while. That meant she must stay put. .

Before she even considered leaving Manchester she must alter her appearance, change her fair hair to a dark brown shade. That would help in her disguise. And with that in mind, she called at the chemists on the parade and bought a hair dye before hurrying across the road to the flat.

Very soon she must clear her things, leave the flat and get right away from the city. But not today. She needed to lie low for at least a week.

The main item on local TV that evening concerned an abandoned baby. The mother, Paula Grimshaw, was small and fair, possibly seventeen or eighteen. As they drew in the camera to take a close-up shot of one of the nurses holding the baby, Joanna looked away. *Don't show me*, she mumbled to herself, knowing if she started to feel the slightest remorse at this stage, her plans would be scuppered. The presenter stressed that the mother would be in need of medical care and should turn herself in to the police immediately. They would say that wouldn't they? Anything to get her back there! But the deed was done. She hadn't bonded with the baby and, from now on, the child was someone else's responsibility.

Exhausted with the effort made she lay on the sofa. Tomorrow she would colour her hair. But for tonight she needed to rest.

Jan and Gary put all their efforts into the new house. By this time Jan was seven months pregnant but she continued to work at the shop, despite Gary's pleas for her to retire and put her feet up. And for the first time in years, Gary felt settled. He knew he'd done the right thing when he'd met Jan and they'd decided to make a home together. He was blissfully happy. The day he met her had been the best day of his life, and he was determined never to look back.

From time to time, he thought about Marie, but then he always tried to cover up his guilt and tell himself it was her own fault they'd parted. He had heard from someone on the force that she'd left. But that took some believing. It wasn't like her to give up her precious job, although he certainly hadn't seen anything of her since she'd sold the house. But perhaps she'd changed. Maybe when she considered what he'd told her, about the way she'd been treating him, she'd come to her senses, realising life with the force wasn't everything.

But hadn't they all changed? When he considered his own actions, he knew he paid far more attention to Jan than he'd ever paid to Marie. Sometimes, when those thoughts kicked in, he really did suffer pangs of guilt. But don't they say 'six of one and half a dozen...?' That's the way he looked at it. He wouldn't have wandered off with Jan had his relationship with Marie been sound.

At the start of December Jan finally gave up her job at the shop. But it seemed she couldn't sit still for long. She always had to be doing something. And they were having breakfast when she came out with it. 'I'm going down to the shopping centre today,' she told Gary. 'I need one or two extras for the baby.'

Gary huffed. 'That's ridiculous,' he replied. 'You're certainly not going alone.'

She smiled, chucking him under the chin playfully. 'I'm fine,' she insisted.

Gary was on the phone to the office before she had the time to slip on her coat and leave. He arranged to take the morning off. If she needed to visit the shopping centre then he would go with her. He couldn't risk letting her go without him.

They parked up and he took her hand. She was so precious to him. He needed to look after her. As they headed for the door, it started. She placed her hand on her tummy. 'I felt a bit of a twinge just then, Gary.' She giggled. 'I think the baby might have started.'

Gary panicked. 'A twinge?' he repeated. 'Come on, love, let's get back home and ring the hospital,' he added, hoping he wouldn't be involved when the time came for the baby to be born.

Jan continued to giggle. 'They told me at the hospital it could be hours after the start of the twinges, especially with a first,' she reassured him. 'It may even be tomorrow, or the day after that. I'll be fine. Let's do a quick shop and then we'll get back.'

But Jan was wrong. She didn't have hours to go. They'd barely entered the place when the pains became stronger and she clung on to Gary each time they started. 'I think I might have misjudged things,' she told him, her face now a mask of concern. 'They're getting worse.'

There was a public phone box just inside the entrance, but Gary wasn't about to leave her alone, not even for a couple of minutes. His only solution was to ask a passer-by to ring for an ambulance. And within minutes they were on their way to the hospital.

Much to Gary's amazement, their baby was born before they arrived. And the birth of their child appeared to shake him even more than it had Jan. The whole business was too much for him. He hadn't intended being there during the birth. But what choice did he have? By the time they'd reached the hospital he was exhausted – but elated too.

It was six days later when Joanna decided the time had come. Things seemed to have died down on the hospital front. She fleetingly wondered what had happened to the child. Her stomach gave a nervous twitch. With all the publicity someone somewhere would want to adopt her child. And why not if it made them happy?

After applying an ample amount of mousse to her hair, she picked up the dryer and straightened out the natural curl into a dark brown medium length bob with a side fringe. She looked in the mirror. That was better. No one would ever recognise her as Paula Grimshaw now. Feeling a little more rested and ready to go, she went into the estate agents and paid her final rent on the flat.

'I'm sorry to give you short notice but something's cropped up. I have to leave,' she told the clerk. 'If you'd care to inspect the property I'd like to collect my bond some time tomorrow morning,' she urged. 'I'm sure everything's in order. It shouldn't take you long.'

'You'll need to forfeit some of your bond. You haven't given us the requisite month's notice. We could have let the flat to someone else had we known.'

'I see. But I can't stay on.'

'Then someone will come to the flat tomorrow. We'll bring your account. You will be in, I take it?'

'In the morning, yes. But I'm leaving the area in the afternoon.'

'You're leaving Manchester for good?'

'That's right. I've been promoted. It's an offer I can't refuse,' she lied.

'Good for you. We'll see you tomorrow then. If you give me your new address we could post your money on.'

'I don't have the exact address until I arrive, and I would prefer to collect it tomorrow. I really do need the cash. I'll have furniture to buy for my new apartment once it's established where I'm going to be staying.'

'That's fine. We can give you cash. You'll have to sign for it of course.'

Joanna left the office, intending giving an illegible signature. She must sever every connection with Manchester before she returned to Blackpool.

There was a crowd waiting for the train when she arrived at the station, but she pushed forward and managed to get a seat. And once the train pulled away she felt as though she'd been released from a straightjacket. She breathed a heavy sigh. Ordeal over! She'd done it.

The train picked up speed and started to wend its way through the countryside, its rhythm regular. She stared through the carriage window at fields of cows and horses, and anglers sitting patiently on the banks of the river. Despite the long, hot summer, after a wet autumn the rich, green pastures were fresh again. And the peace and tranquillity of the countryside gave her an immense feeling of relief. It was over. She'd beaten them. They'd never find her now.

But the feeling of elation didn't last. The sound of a baby's cry coming from the next carriage brought her right back to reality. A feeling of guilt enveloped her. What she had done was wrong. But at the time she felt she had no alternative.

This was not the first time she'd felt remorse. At the sound of the cries the guilt she'd experienced when she'd abandoned her own flesh and blood, returned. Her mind had been set on passing on the blame. After all, the child wasn't wholly her responsibility. The child was Rick's flesh and blood too. And with that in mind, she'd managed to shake the guilt right away. But the guilt was back now, and she would have to steel herself. She must blank everything about the baby from her mind.

She frowned and sighed deeply. Would this feeling ever go away? Or would she spend the rest of her life racked with guilt?

Chapter 14
The Present – 2008

Danielle refused to allow the young nurse to draw back the curtains in the ward. 'I want to stay in the dark,' she mumbled. 'I don't want the light streaming in. It hurts my eyes.' That wasn't the reason at all. She closed her eyes and shuddered. There was such an enormous void inside her. Someone was missing from her life – and that someone was Mama. She turned on to her side with her back to the door, hoping anyone visiting would get the hint she didn't want to see them. Tears began to stream down her face, and her mind seemed to drop a gear.

She fluttered her eyelids and the image of Papa seemed to emerge before her. Her sobs became louder. Papa was relying on her. He loved her. And *he* hadn't abandoned *her*. Yet *he'd* lost Mama too. She felt a rush in her bloodstream. This is no way to behave. She must be strong, for herself and for Papa.

Swallowing, and struggling for reason, she began to pull herself together. She'd lost Mama but she didn't want to lose Papa too. Hauling herself up in bed, she slipped her legs out, and plodded across the floor to the window, drawing back the curtains. Just as she climbed back into bed, Mr Dexter appeared at the door.

He sat down beside her and took her hand in his, patting it gently. 'I won't ask how you're feeling, my dear. There's not much point. I know things are dragging, but we must be patient.' He smiled.

Danielle returned a tremulous smile. 'But it is so boring hanging around in here. There is only so much I can do to catch up on my studies, and only when I can focus my mind. It is not easy. When I think of Mama I become depressed. And I cannot seem to claw my way out of it.' Her voice faltered. 'Is there any chance I could have a few days away, go back to France and stay with Papa? And then I could visit Mama's grave.' Tears started to steal down her cheeks and she flicked them away. She must try for control. Crying was something she could do in private.

'I realise how much you must be grieving for your mother, Danielle, how precious she was to you. You have my deepest sympathy. Your mother was too young to go like that. But grieving is something you can neither rush nor hide. You have to let it out. And it has to take its time.' He patted her hand. 'Sorry, my dear, but I can't let you return to France, although I do feel it would be better if you had some company of your own age.' He placed his hand on his forehead. 'Let me think this through,' he said, taking a moment to contemplate. And then he relaxed and smiled. 'Maybe we could allow you out for a few days, but we must monitor your progress. You seem to have regained some of your strength but you're still anaemic. Having said that, I think you could cope, provided you take care and continue with the medication,' he stressed. 'It's crucial your condition doesn't deteriorate. Once a donor is found, we need to get on with the job.'

His words seemed to perk her up. That might be what she needed to alleviate her depression. 'I would appreciate that, Mr Dexter. But please try to see it my way. I was devastated that I could not go to Mama's funeral. And until I see the grave, I cannot think of her as having gone. But I suppose I do need someone to talk to.' She looked into his eyes. 'I promise to do exactly what you say.'

'I certainly don't want you left on your own in student accommodation. Is there anyone who could be with you?'

Danielle's heart sank. Anxiety filled her eyes. 'Only Papa and he is in France. Please, please, let me return to France for a while?' she begged.

'I'm sorry, Danielle. As I've explained it's out of the question travelling such a distance. The only way I'll agree to discharge you is if there's someone here in Scotland you can stay with,' he continued. 'Perhaps if I had a word with your matron in halls she could think of a solution.'

Danielle took a moment to compose herself. 'It would give me a boost seeing my friends. I think it would lift my spirits too, help me take my mind off things. Please, please try your best!'

He smiled and started to back away, palms raised. 'OK, OK. Don't rush me,' he joked. 'I'll give Matron a buzz; see if anything can be arranged. But don't bank on it. I'll be back this afternoon after my clinic,' he promised.

Optimism surged and gave her a temporary lift from the depression. She could hardly wait for his return in the afternoon. Time seemed to drag, but she'd stuck it out so far and she wasn't about to let a couple more hours faze her.

When he returned in the afternoon she was delighted. Things turned out much better than she'd ever expected. James and Amy trailed in behind him as Mr Dexter shook his head and threw up his hands. 'Talk about press-ganged!' He smiled. 'It's contrary to our usual arrangements but, together with Matron, these two have promised to look after you.' He stepped back and the two came forward, planting kisses on Danielle's cheeks.

'How about that then,' James exclaimed, a wide grin spreading across his lively face. 'You're to do exactly as we say, otherwise you're back in here, pronto.'

'Up to your tricks again, James,' Danielle bantered, suppressing a giggle.

'Don't worry,' Amy promised. 'I'll be there to keep an eye on you – as well as him,' she said pointing to James. She winked.

Mr Dexter intervened. 'In all seriousness, Danielle, you really must take care. You know the score. You'll be in Matron's charge during the daytime but that doesn't mean you can't move about. I'm not expecting bed rest all the time, but what I do insist is that you rest in the evenings, after dinner.'

'You mean I can actually walk about the place?'

'That's right. There's nothing wrong with your legs is there?' he added, a grin on his face. 'The last thing I want is for you to tire yourself.' He paused. 'I suggest you put in a normal day attending lectures whenever you feel up to it, have your meal in the evening with your fellow students, but afterwards I would like you to rest. Continue with the medication as before, and if you feel unwell or even slightly under the weather, ask Matron to contact me immediately.'

It was such a relief! She'd suddenly gone from the depths of depression to a mixture of exhilaration and anxiety. Hopefully she was doing the right thing. But she was confident her condition wouldn't deteriorate, at least not through her own negligence. She smiled eagerly. 'Has anyone spoken to my tutors? Do they know the score?'

'They don't know you're returning, but Matron will sort things. Just do what you can and be sensible.'

A gentle surge of excitement whispered inside her. She couldn't wait to shower and dress ready to leave. 'I would be foolish not to do as you ask. After all, it is in my own interests to stay as strong as possible.' She reached out and took his hand. 'I cannot thank you enough,' she added. 'I will contact Papa and let him know. I am sure he will be relieved you have agreed to discharge me for a little while. Perhaps he could have a few days respite at home whilst I am back at uni.'

As Mr Dexter left the three of them to make their arrangements, Amy put her arm around Danielle's shoulder. 'Don't rush around,' she stressed. 'We've plenty of time to get your things together.'

Danielle's brown eyes gleamed. 'I am perfectly all right, Amy. I do not stay in bed all the time even in here. I wander about quite a lot. I am sure Sister and the nurses will be glad to get me from under their feet.' She laughed.

After showering and dressing, Danielle said goodbye to the staff in the ward.

'Behave yourself.' Sister smiled as she gave Danielle her medication and final instructions whilst Amy sped down the corridor and went outside to collect her car. James picked up the holdall and took Danielle's hand. A feeling of warmth flowed through her, and her heart began to thump loudly. She took a deep breath, telling herself, as she always did, that she couldn't afford to become involved. Her studies must come first. She was already so far behind it would be a miracle if she ever caught up again.

Once they reached the front entrance she gently shook her hand free. Amy was there waiting, the car engine running. Danielle slipped into the back seat and James snuggled beside her, taking her hand and squeezing it. 'It's good to have you back,' he confessed, popping a kiss on her cheek. 'And don't worry, we'll look after you.' He turned to face her and they studied one another intently. Her stomach flipped. He was doing it again. But she didn't want to hurt him by freeing her hand. She sat there, gritted her teeth and tried not to let those warm feelings wash over her. But it wasn't easy.

Matron was at the door to greet her when they arrived. 'You're looking well, love, I'll say that for you. You need to keep your strength up and continue with the iron,' she stressed, wagging a finger jokingly. 'Have a meal in the refectory with your friends and come back here for a little while this evening. And don't get over-excited.' She stepped inside the room and Danielle followed. 'I'm not off duty until eight. You can rest here, and then whoever is in charge tonight will take you back to your room. We've managed a truckle bed for Amy. She's going to stay with you nights, except when I'm on duty, and then you'll stay here.' She slipped her arm around Danielle's shoulder. 'But let's hope it's not for long. I gather they're going all out to find a donor.'

Danielle nodded. She'd been so excited to be let loose that the matter of a donor had temporarily slipped her mind. 'Yes, and the sooner the better. All I want is to get the operation over with and get on with my life again. So much has happened whilst I have been cooped up in there.'

Matron took her hand. 'I know. I was sorry to hear about your mum, love. We were all thinking about you.'

Sensing the genuine concern in Matron's tone, Danielle's eyes glistened. 'Thank you, Matron. That is very kind of you.'

Matron squeezed her shoulders and slipped her arm away. 'I'll see you after the meal. Look after her you two,' she added, pointing to Amy and James.

'Don't worry. She's precious to us too,' James replied, and his comment brought a reluctant smile from Danielle. It was clear that he adored her but the way he was behaving it was too much for comfort.

Just before afternoon break they headed for the common room. 'I wanted to get here before the rush,' Amy said. 'It gives us time to find somewhere to sit before the others turn up. We can do without you being jostled about.' She laughed.

Minutes later Rafina, one of the medical students approached. 'It's so good to see you, Danielle. Have you had the op already?' She gave Danielle a hug.

Danielle gave a weak smile. 'Unfortunately not,' she replied. 'We are still waiting for a donor.'

'You must be really special,' she said, laughing, 'if your blood type is so rare.'

Danielle jokingly preened herself. 'I certainly am special,' she confirmed, her soft laughter infectious. But she had no intention of revealing anything about her parentage. No one at university, not even Matron, had been told of the search for her biological father. And Danielle wanted to keep it that way.

After a bombardment of questions, and lots of information from the medical students about how the course was progressing, Danielle felt exhausted. By the time the thirty-minute break came to an end, she was ready to leave. 'I would like a little rest before dinner,' she told Amy and James.

'We'll take you back to Matron and collect you about six for the meal,' James offered.

Matron came out from her room in the medical bay. 'I'm glad you're being sensible, Danielle. People talking at you can be as tiring as physical activity.' She led Danielle into the side room. 'Close your eyes for a while, love. Even if you don't sleep, you'll be relaxing.'

'I would like a shower before I go to the refectory, Matron. Would you mind waking me if I do fall asleep?'

'Don't worry. I'll give you a call at five.'

'Thanks,' Danielle replied as she slipped off her shoes and climbed on to the bed.

With time to herself, her thoughts reverted to Mama, and secret tears began to flow. Danielle couldn't shake the thoughts from her mind, and she struggled to relax and drift into a light sleep. And when eventually sleep did come, she dreamt about Mama. But it was a pleasant dream, of the times when Danielle was a child and Mama had worked in the café where she'd met Marcel.

When she came round, she was in a far more relaxed state, contemplating the years of joy and love Mama had given her. And she drew strength from the knowledge that Mama would be forever with her, in her memories, and in her heart.

Amy stayed with her the first two evenings. The room was so small, especially now it contained the additional truckle bed, they both sprawled out on Danielle's bed chatting. But the following evening when Amy had an extra tutorial, she asked James if he would stay with Danielle until she returned.

James was affectionate towards Danielle, and he provided a broad and comfortable shoulder, literally and emotionally, especially when thoughts of Mama came to mind. He wrapped his arm around her and she cuddled up to his chest.

An anxious expression on her face, Danielle explained how much she missed Mama, and James listened attentively, offering soothing words. He seemed aware of her need to snap out of her depression, steering the conversation away, relating an amusing incident when Prof Warren tripped up and landed on his back with the waste bin stuck on the end of his foot. Danielle started to giggle and then she collapsed in irrepressible laughter. 'You're an idiot, James. Stop it,' she mouthed. 'Don't tell me any more.'

James looked at her, wide-eyed with amusement. 'I'm glad you can see the funny side.' He took hold of her hands and his smile faded, his eyes darkened and were filled with a look of adoration. As he pulled her closer and skimmed his thumb over her lips, Danielle linked her hands together around his neck. His gaze was square on now, and she felt a flutter in her chest as he bent his head towards her. She felt her mouth go dry and her heart begin to thud loudly.

'Hi you two. It's only me,' came a call. Startled out of their tender kiss, the voice was followed by a loud knock on the door.

Danielle tore herself away from James as the door opened and Amy came in, a mischievous smirk on her face. 'Thought I'd better knock.' She turned to Danielle. 'Not that you'd be getting up to much when James here promised to look after you.' She winked.

'Chance would be a fine thing,' he retaliated.

Danielle felt a kind of disappointment float through her. But she shook herself. It was just as well it had happened that way.

James struggled to pull himself together. He would never have believed after splitting up with Kate at the end of their holiday in Magaluf, that he could have met someone as special as Danielle. There was something about her that made him feel comfortable when they were together, so much so that he felt an almost overpowering emotional hold over her, a feeling of belonging. She sparked off such intense feelings in him, a need to be close, a need to be intimate. He had the definite urge to hold her close and especially to kiss her. At times Danielle seemed reluctant to let herself go and James was of the impression the depth of his feelings were disproportionate to hers, although he was sure she was drawn towards him too.

When his lips had hovered close to hers, he'd felt a mixture of excitement and exhilaration. Then Amy burst in on them and his instant reaction was one of annoyance. But he couldn't afford to let his emotions get the better of him, not in front of Amy. After all, what she was doing was in Danielle's best interests.

He covered his annoyance and, in jest, slid his arm around Danielle, pulling her close. 'Isn't this part of taking care of her?' he asked, a cheeky grin developing as he plonked a gentle kiss on her cheek.

'Somehow I think you've misunderstood, James,' Amy replied, laughing.

'I think he is trying for the father-figure,' Danielle chipped in, and James smiled, realising that was her way of covering for him.

'That's right,' he said as he stood up to leave. 'See you tomorrow,' he added as he opened the door. 'Hope you manage to get off to sleep OK,' he concluded, wishing he was the one staying there and looking after her during the night.

Once Danielle became involved with her studies she realised why she'd chosen to read medicine in the first place, and she began to pick up the threads and enjoy the course. But after a few days she started to tire, a premature reaction in her opinion seeing she'd made a positive effort not to pressurise herself. Hadn't she promised Mr Dexter she would not go down that road? It would be foolish, knowing it was imperative she remained fit and healthy before the operation.

James called to collect her that morning and she begged off going to lectures, citing a headache. But it was more than a simple headache. Tiny beads of perspiration were gathering on her forehead, and that certainly was not a normal side effect. A squeezing pain mushroomed across her back when she lifted herself up from the bed and she winced. What on earth was going on? She began to worry, realising she must contact Matron at the hospital bay as quickly as possible. Rolling herself carefully from the bed, she lurched across to the desk and snatched the internal phone. 'I'm not feeling well, Matron.'

Matron interjected. 'Is there anyone there with you?'

'Not at the moment.' She paused, knowing she'd never make it to the sick bay on her own. 'Could you possibly come over, Matron?'

Danielle heard the panic in Matron's voice. 'It's obvious you're more than off colour,' she offered and, minutes later, catching her breath after rushing across to Danielle's room, she burst in, her face plum red and etched in worry. 'What are your symptoms?'

'I have an excruciating pain in my back.' She hesitated. 'I think I have a temperature too,' she admitted reluctantly.

'We need to get you back to Deansgate. Mr Dexter's going to be none too happy if he thinks we've neglected you.'

'No one has neglected me. I have been really careful and everyone has been so supportive – you certainly have, my friends too.'

'I'm not happy Danielle. You shouldn't be having pain like that when you're on medication to prevent any pain and to keep things stable.' She took Danielle's temperature and smoothed her brow. 'It's higher than I would like. I'm going to ring the ward and make sure your bed is available before we send for an ambulance.' And then she smiled. 'Having said that, they might not want a nuisance like you back, causing them so much extra work,' she joked.

Danielle smiled back, but the smile failed to reach her eyes. She was so keyed up she could barely think straight as she struggled to bear the pain in her back. But she must thank Matron. 'It's been great getting away from Deansgate, Matron. It's only been a few days but it was so good to have a change of scenery, and meet up with all my friends.'

'I'm glad you've felt the benefit. And don't worry about the others. I'll let them know what's happened,' Matron said as Danielle climbed into the ambulance and said her goodbye.

Sister settled Danielle back into her ward. 'Mr Kollitsis, the registrar is not on duty until later this afternoon, but Dr Swallow the new houseman will come and see you. He's read your case notes and he's really keen to check you out.'

'It sounds as though I am something of a freak the way you say that, Sister.'

Sister laughed. 'Not at all, love. You know what these new doctors are like. They think they can spot something neither the registrar nor the consultant has detected.' They both laughed. 'Having said that, I must say sometimes they can.'

'I suppose that'll be me some day, if I ever complete the course,' Danielle replied flippantly. But inside she was worried. What had caused the pain? Other than attending the lectures she'd done nothing out of the ordinary.

'We need Mr Dexter to take a look at her, Sister,' Dr Swallow reported after he'd completed a thorough examination. 'Did you say he was at his private rooms today?'

'Yes,' Sister told him, 'and he'll have a list of patients to see. But you're right. We can't wait for the registrar. We'll go direct to Mr Dexter. He'll give us instruction until he's able to get here himself.'

Dr Swallow tapped his fingers on the desk. 'I'm confident it's nothing to do with Danielle being allowed back to university. And I'm convinced it's not a progression of the disease – it's some sort of infection.'

'That had crossed my mind,' Sister replied, as she fluffed up the pillow behind Danielle and straightened the bed covers.

Mr Dexter was at Deansgate by mid-afternoon. 'Now what have you been up to, young lady?' he asked, a frown developing on his forehead.

'Nothing out of the ordinary – promise,' Danielle replied.

'Then let's take a look at you.' He placed the stethoscope on her chest. 'The houseman seems to think it's an infection you've picked up,' he said as he began his examination, 'and I'm inclined to agree with him,' he smirked, 'which I'm sure he'll be delighted to hear. That'll be a feather in Swallow's cap!' He paused and grinned. 'Pardon the pun.' He turned to address Sister. 'It is possible she picked it up here before she left the ward. Keep her isolated, Sister, and watch out for anyone else having the same symptoms.' He turned to Danielle. 'Don't worry. These things happen,' he told her, hesitating before he continued. 'But we need to nip this in the bud – smartish. I can't afford for you to pick up anything else. I'll give you a course of antibiotics, but then we'll need to wait a few days until after the course is complete before we even consider carrying out the operation.'

Danielle shrugged her shoulders. 'Does that mean if a donor comes along I'll have to wait?' she asked.

'I'm afraid so. But we're only talking about another ten days at the most.' His face softened into a smile. 'Don't look so glum. It's as well we knew about this. And I don't think the tumour's increased in size, which is a bonus at least.'

But nothing was a bonus to Danielle. All she wanted was to get on with things, to get the operation over with and return to uni as soon as possible.

Chapter 15
The Present – 2008

Wayne was later than Joanna had anticipated. It was almost half past seven by the time he returned from work. For a moment her heart stopped beating when she heard the garage door opening, the revving of the car engine and the door banging to a close. What she dreaded most was telling him she'd abandoned her baby. What would he think of her?

He was whistling as he walked through into the lounge. 'Sorry I'm late, love,' he said bending over her on the sofa and plonking a kiss on her cheek. 'The boss mislaid the safe key and we had to help him find it. It was obvious he didn't want anyone leaving the building until it was found.' He slipped off his jacket and put it over the back of a chair. 'You're looking a bit pale, Jo. There's nothing wrong is there?'

'Sit down, Wayne,' she said, patting the sofa beside her. 'There's something I must tell you. I've been keeping it to myself all these years, but I must confess. I can't hold out any longer.'

Wayne laughed. 'It can't be that serious, unless you've been married before and forgotten to mention in.' He grinned and took her hand in his. 'Come on love. I can see it's worrying you. Get it off your chest.'

Joanna looked him in the eyes. 'It's not easy, Wayne,' she admitted and she gave a heavy sigh. 'When I was eighteen, I became pregnant. Rick, my boyfriend, was twenty-one and he'd made arrangements to go abroad. He wanted me to go with him.

But, of course, I couldn't leave Mum and Dad.' She shook her head. 'I was scared and I didn't know what to do. Eventually he left the country and I went to Manchester.' She drew in breath. 'I had the baby there, a little girl.' The moment the words came out of her mouth she felt a sense of relief that her guilty secret was out.

Wayne's face was wreathed with concern. 'Where is she now?'

Anxiety rose inside her. 'Bear me out, Wayne. It was a foolish thing to do but I was so scared about what Mum and Dad would say, I left the hospital and the baby behind.'

Wayne stood up, his brow heavily furrowed as he started to pace the room. 'You mean that was it?'

She pressed her fingers on her temples and her face was mottled pink. 'That's right. But that's not all. I was so worried when I was admitted that I gave a false name. I told them I was called Paula Grimshaw. I went back home and then it happened. The baby was kidnapped from the hospital.'

Wayne recoiled, at first unwilling to look at her. 'Bloody hell! Kidnapped?' He shook his head. 'I can't believe all this has happened. It's just a series of disasters.'

The room was claustrophobic now and the walls seemed to be drawing in on her. A rush of heat surged through her. 'I can't either, Wayne. But it did happen. To this day I still feel guilty and ashamed of what I did. And I've always wondered what happened to my baby. The police never found her.'

Wayne sat down beside her and she sank into his arms, burying her sobs against his shirt. 'You poor love. You were just a kid. Why didn't you tell me all this before?'

She shook her head and wiped the tears from her face. 'I intended to, but like everything else I kept putting it off. I was so ashamed. And then this evening when I came home from work I heard it on the news. The police are asking a Mrs Paula

Grimshaw to come forward. Apparently a student needs a blood donor urgently. It's a rare blood type they're looking for. I'm worried, love. I think the student is my daughter who was kidnapped all those years ago.' Joanna began to sob again uncontrollably. 'What am I going to do, Wayne?'

He pulled a tissue from a box and dabbed her eyes. Pushing her to arm's length he looked her squarely in the eyes. 'Let's face up to it and get the facts straight. They want Paula Grimshaw because they think she might be the student's mother. She might have compatible blood, right?'

'Yes,' she murmured.

He took her hands and pulled her to her feet. 'Come on, love. Let's get down there. I'm not judging you. It all happened before we met and it's nothing to do with me. It was a foolish thing to do, but you've had years of agony to realise that.' He led her out of the lounge and through into the hall. 'Now's the time to make up for the events of all those years ago. Get your coat. Let's go.'

Pierre held back his annoyance at the inspector when Joanna made an appearance at the station. There was no gentle approach, no empathy. He was straight to the point and immediately accusatory. 'What were you thinking? What you did was criminal.'

Wayne jumped in. 'You may think so, Inspector, but she was just a kid,' he urged. 'And she has made an appearance, which you must agree takes guts. It was after six o'clock when she heard the news, and here she is, ready and willing to co-operate. So why don't we get on with it instead of you giving us a lecture?'

The inspector was taken aback by Wayne's confrontation. 'What you don't seem to understand is that this situation would not have arisen had your wife not abandoned the child in the first place.'

Wayne was in no mood for this. 'What's done is done. We can't change the past,' he stressed.

The inspector refrained from making any further comment and, before Wayne could step in once more, he continued. 'I'm handing you over to Mr Clarisse here,' he said, directing his comment at Joanna and ignoring Wayne. 'He's in charge of the investigation.' He leant back in his chair. 'They'll be no charges you'll be relieved to hear, Mrs Harlow. It's a long time ago and Danielle's father is anxious to find a donor. He's not laying the blame at anyone's doorstep, but I wanted you to know the severity of the crime.'

Joanna ignored his words about the 'crime' she was supposed to have committed. But the comments about Danielle's father had stirred up emotions within her, and her thoughts turned to Rick. 'Her father? How do you mean?'

'Her stepfather.'

Wayne jumped up from his chair. 'What about the girl's mother? Wouldn't you say kidnapping Joanna's baby by the so-called mother was a serious crime, Inspector?' he implored.

Pierre wanted to put a stop to this negative, knuckle-wrapping technique. It wasn't the best way to get information, and surely the inspector knew it. But he held back, knowing these guys were promoted to a nice, comfy position in their plush offices, and in no time they seemed to have forgotten the skills of real policing. They were more interested in dictating policy and administrating, which was a pity when they were promoted because they were good officers. It was the same in France, and it was one of the reasons Pierre had left the force himself.

He bit his tongue. It was no use irritating the guy when all he was doing was asserting himself, establishing his authority.

Pierre asked Joanna and her husband to follow him into an interview room where Joanna gave him every last detail as to what happened all those years ago. And eventually he closed his notepad, slipped his pen into his jacket pocket and looked up. His gaze swept to Joanna. 'The main purpose of our request is to check your blood type, Mrs Harlow. There's no mileage in getting carried away with the ins and outs of things. We can talk that through later.' He stood up. 'After what you've told me, I have reason to believe you are the mother of Danielle Dubois, Mrs Harlow. Would you be willing to take a blood test?' He watched for her reaction.

Her face had lost its tension now that she'd confessed everything to Pierre. 'Of course I would. That's the reason I'm here after all, not to be given a lecture by the inspector.'

Pierre took his jacket from the back of the chair and slipped it on. 'Sorry about that,' he said. 'But I too have to tread very carefully with the police, otherwise I wouldn't get the information I desperately need. After all, it was through them I was able to locate you.'

The interview with the Harlows over, Pierre left them. His next task was to try and check out Haley Baxter's blood group, just to make sure she was the mother of Michelle and that there hadn't been a mix-up in bands. When he asked the duty sergeant if Steve O'Hara was still around, the sergeant laughed. 'He's one of the nine-to-fivers now. And it's already knocking on,' he pointed out, glancing at his watch. 'Unless he's doing overtime.' But when he returned he confirmed O'Hara had left. 'It'll have to be tomorrow I'm afraid.'

'Then I'll come back some time after nine in the morning.'

The sergeant hesitated. 'That's fine, unless of course there's anything I can do?'

Pierre leant on the counter. 'I doubt it. It's regarding an old case – going back twenty years or so.'

'You're right. If that's what you're after it's definitely Steve's department, records and archives.'

Pierre left the station and wandered back to his car. At least the Grimshaw woman had come forward. If he could prove there was a match between Haley Baxter and her daughter Michelle, then hopefully Grimshaw was Danielle's biological mother.

It was pretty straightforward to check out Baxter's details the following day. O'Hara was confident. 'We had to check things out at the time to make sure the blood on the knife was hers. It was, of course. But we had skin and hair samples too, some of them taken from Miladinovic. I could have Baxter's DNA checked. We'll soon know if there's any link.'

Pierre couldn't believe his luck. 'Would you give me a ring as soon as you know?'

'I certainly will, Pierre. We'll soon get through the elimination process. It's amazing what can be done these days,' he said proudly, and Pierre reckoned O'Hara was enjoying his comeback as an investigative copper.

Chapter 16
The Past – 1988

Marie threw herself into the job. The shoplifters tried it on but they didn't find it easy, not with Marie on the case. Word spread like a bushfire in a forest. This Marie woman had an eagle eye. Attempts at shoplifting at the store dwindled.

But one day events led to a change of direction in her life. She'd been chatting to one of the girls on cosmetics when she spotted a woman taking costume jewellery from a display. Marie made eye contact with the woman who, aware she was being followed, made for the door. She started to run, but Marie was too quick for her and she grabbed the woman by the collar, dragging her back inside the store.

'And where do you think you're going with that?' she asked, pointing to a newspaper under the woman's arm. She'd seen the woman slipping the jewellery in between the pages as she ran. But the woman was so nervous she let the newspaper slip to the floor. The jewellery slid out.

'Pick it up,' Marie ordered, and the woman obeyed without uttering a word. Taking the jewellery and the newspaper from her, she marched the woman through the store to the offices at the back and directed her to sit down opposite the store manager. 'There you are, sir, another who thought there was nothing to it.' She poured out the jewellery, folded the newspaper and tucked it under her arm.

Compared with her job at the station solving 'real' crime, this sort of thing was child's play.

After the manager contacted the police, Marie was relieved when neither of the constables on duty, a couple of young, fresh-faced lads, didn't recognise her. She didn't want the gang down at the station knowing about her new job, not yet anyway. They'd obviously find out some time, but for now she wanted to get on without the wise cracks.

The manager clasped his hands and leant his elbows on the desk. 'You're a credit to us. That's three this week.'

But his words had little effect on her. She smiled. If only he knew how easy it was.

It was her break time when she left the office and she was ready for a cup of tea. The newspaper was still tucked under her arm as she climbed the stairs to the canteen and poured herself a drink. She sat down at a table, opened up the newspaper and spread it out in front of her. It was then she saw a particular news item, one that sent her mind into a frenzy of tangled thoughts. She took a deep breath to clear her mind and concentrate before she began to formulate a daring plan.

Joanna stepped off the train but before she left for home she went into the waiting room, tidied her hair and freshened her lipstick. Now bright and bubbly, she walked back to her parents' place thinking what a shock they would have when they saw she'd coloured her hair. But that was nothing compared with the shock they would have had if she'd taken home a newborn child.

'Joanna, darling, you look really sophisticated with your new hair colour. But whatever made you do it?' Joanna couldn't make out whether Mum was genuinely impressed or not.

'There was a special offer at the hairdressers close to the office,' Joanna lied. 'I'm glad you like it.'

Her father looked up from the newspaper he was reading and narrowed his eyes. 'I don't,' he chipped in.

'Don't be so old-fashioned, Ron. I think it's really attractive,' Mrs Falconer concluded, pulling a face at her husband as he turned back to the newspaper. Joanna grinned.

'It's lovely to have you back with us,' her mother admitted.

'I'd come to the end of my time with them in Manchester. And enough was enough.'

Ron Falconer flicked on the TV switch. There was another announcement about a recently abandoned child. Joanna's stomach churned.

'That's terrible, isn't it, love.' Mrs Falconer pointed to the screen and directed the words at her daughter. 'Fancy, I can't imagine anyone running off and leaving a newborn baby, can you? I expect everyone was talking about it in Manchester, weren't they?'

'Can't say I heard anything about it, Mum. I've been far too busy to be watching the news,' Joanna replied, quickly changing the subject. She smiled. 'But now I'm back, I need to get in touch with them at the office. I'll pop back in there tomorrow and see if my job's still available.' The minute she uttered the words, she knew she'd made a mistake. Her face pinked over. She hoped Mum hadn't noticed.

Mrs Falconer, annoyed at her husband once she realised her daughter had no interest in the news item, said, 'Turn it off, Ron. We don't want to see any more.' She folded her arms and sat next to Joanna on the sofa. 'Now then, love. How do you mean see if your job's still available? You still have the job haven't you? I thought the work in Manchester was some sort of extra experience. How come you need to see them about getting your job back?'

'Strictly speaking I should still have my job, Mum. But to tell you the truth, I had an argument with them in Manchester. I'd had enough. They kept on pushing and pushing,' she said. Her lips twitched. 'And then I walked out.'

'Oh dear! That's not like you, Joanna. But I'm glad you stuck up for yourself.'

'Don't worry, Mum. If they don't take me back there are plenty of other jobs on offer.' She got up. 'Let me take my things upstairs and put them away. What time's dinner?'

'It'll be ready about half past. I'll give you a call, love,' her mother replied, her voice tinged with delight at the return of her daughter.

Leaving the hospital and the baby behind didn't really hit Joanna again until she was back in her own bedroom. There had been the crying child in the next carriage and for a few seconds she had felt some kind of remorse. But now that she was back home and she'd left everything behind, it freaked her out. How could she have done such a thing? How could she have abandoned her own child? She lifted her flat, dull eyes and looked at herself in the mirror. She recoiled, took a deep breath and then she hugged her arms about herself. There was one thing for certain, she wasn't about to give herself in. Not after what she'd gone through already. She'd achieved what she'd set out to do, and there was no use being chicken now that it was over.

Marie peered at the newspaper and then she did a retake. It was when she spotted the headline:

Mother abandons baby

that her plan started to take shape. The mother had apparently absconded from Murray Park Hospital only hours after giving birth. If she didn't give herself up within the next few days, the baby would be taken away by Social Services and found a foster home.

Marie's first reaction was one of rage. The world was an unfair place. Desperately sad that she'd lost her own baby, she was unable to comprehend how someone, whose child had been safely delivered, could abandon the tiny, defenceless soul.

After that, one thought triggered another, and the seeds of her plan began to develop. The idea that the baby could be hers, a child to call her own, was prominent in her mind. After the miscarriage, desperation had set in, and she didn't see why she couldn't replace her own child with the unwanted one.

The idea attacked her brain and became firmly entrenched, making her more and more anxious, more and more determined. She must have the child. It was then she began to tell herself the little girl was rightfully hers. And that became the challenge. Her confidence soared. She could walk into the paediatric ward and take the child. But she checked her thoughts and sanity intervened. Surely she couldn't do that? And if she did, how could she possibly get away with it?

When the pendulum swung in the opposite direction, euphoria took over. She was on a high! She could do it! There was nothing impossible in Marie's book. Surely it was better than sending the baby into care? She smiled to herself. She hadn't moved up the ranks in the police force without any nous, without using her skills – and lots of bottle. If anyone could snatch the child, she was convinced she could. But would it work? She'd make damned sure it worked!

The plan must be put into action right away. Another couple of days and the baby would definitely be taken into care. Then it would be too late.

Marie knew the hospital inside out. She'd been there many times when on duty with the force. And as soon as her shift at Cromptons was over, she went straight to the hospital to suss things out. The child had apparently been admitted to one of the two paediatric wards days after the mother had cleared off. Marie checked out the one mentioned in the newspaper, just to make sure it was the right one. She needed to know exactly where to go. It was not far from the front entrance, and it would be pretty straightforward to walk in, take the child and then disappear.

The nurses had named the baby Rosie. And Marie hadn't gone far down the corridor when she spotted a side ward containing several cots. Of course they'd be kept near to the nurses' station. And then she spotted it. 'Rosie Grimshaw' was the name at the bottom of the cot. Her heart tumbled with excitement. She took a deep breath and walked away. She didn't want to be spotted before she was ready to make her move.

It was the business of obtaining the uniform that became tricky. But not to be fazed, she made her way to the laundry where a group of women were busy talking.

'Now then ladies,' she said, her tone tinged with authority. 'I need a change of uniform quickly. One of my elderly ladies has been sick all over me. I've had to change into mufti.' She walked over to the shelves and pulled out what she thought would be the appropriate size.

The women quickly dispersed, leaving one of them to deal with Marie. 'Not that shelf, Sister,' she said. 'Those are all named. These are the spares. Size twelve?' she asked.

'That's right,' Marie claimed, taking the uniform from the woman and calmly walking away.

Her mind now set on the task ahead, Marie began putting things into perspective. Where would she go once she had the child in her possession? She couldn't stay in her little terraced house, the one she'd bought after her divorce from Gary. Most of the people in the same street were elderly and they spent much of their time gazing out of the window. She didn't want them seeing the baby. That meant she must get right away from Manchester, somewhere she'd be swallowed up in the crowds and hopefully not be noticed.

The names of nearby cities and towns darted quickly through her mind. And then she came up with it – Liverpool. You couldn't get a much bigger city, and it was close to the docks where lots of seafaring people came and went. The place was infiltrated with strangers. Why should she be any different? She'd be a stranger there, too.

She rang Cromptons and spoke to the manager in human resources. 'Sorry I won't be in today. The depression's back. I just can't cope when I'm like this. I'm seeing my doctor this evening. I'll let you know how things go.'

'I'm sorry you're off colour, Marie,' the manager replied tactfully. 'Do keep in touch and let us know how you're getting on. You're the best store detective we've had here at Cromptons. We don't want to lose you.'

But Marie knew better. Once the plan was complete, she'd kick the job into touch. If anything went wrong, she was keeping her options open. She could still return to the store claiming she was much better and ready to start work again. Step one completed. That was easy enough.

Minutes later she left for Liverpool and there she walked the streets calling in at every estate agent she came across. Eventually she managed to rent a furnished ground floor flat in a huge block. It was in one of the run-down suburbs, an area she was unfamiliar with, and when she drove there she parked the car on spare land, realising why the flat was so cheap. There were one or two shady-looking characters hanging about, obviously unemployed, and as she walked away from the car several teenagers appeared, obviously truanting and up to no good. Her first instinct was to confront them, check out why they weren't at school, but she was no longer in the force, and it was no business of hers. She would have to take her chance like everyone else and hope they didn't set about vandalising her car.

Taking the key from her bag, she stepped inside the entrance, which was littered with rubbish. The flat was on the ground floor to one side of the stairs. Poised, ready to open the door, she looked around her. The place was filthy. Feeling tense and ill at ease, she managed to ignore all of that and enter the flat. It had obviously been empty for some time. Dark patches were evident around the metal windows where the damp had dried out, but Marie reasoned she would only be there for a short time and she could put up with that. The kitchen was ill equipped and the lounge area was sparsely furnished but she could bring a few things over the next time she called back at the house. That was another job on her list.

The teenagers seemed suspiciously close to her car when she glanced through the window before leaving the property. She locked the door and purposefully headed across the road where she'd parked it. The gang cleared off sharpish the minute they saw her. She could only hope they'd done nothing to the car that would jeopardise her chances of getting back to Manchester.

All appeared to be well apart from a deep scratch down the side of the driver's door. But that didn't worry her. All she wanted was to get on with things, especially now that she'd managed to get somewhere to live, a place she could occupy in anonymity. But if she wanted true anonymity she'd need to acquire false documents, and that was a tall order even for someone of her astuteness.

It was then she remembered the papers she'd taken from the drawer in Haley Baxter's house only months ago. She recalled her conversation with the boss when she returned to work after her week at home with Gary.

'The woman we found at Planter's Bank, Haley Baxter. How is she?' Marie had asked the inspector.

'Dead.' His words were flat and unemotional. He shook his head. 'She'd no chance. Murdered by a client no doubt.'

'Dead? Murdered?'

'That's what I said, Brechan.'

'But what about the child?'

'I've no idea. Where was it?'

'It's a she.' Marie corrected him, her voice tinged with disapproval. 'And she was with a neighbour.'

'Ring Social and let them know. They'll deal with things from now on.'

'How's the enquiry going?'

'It's not.' The inspector scratched his head. 'CID's picked it up. End of story.'

At the time her mind had been focused on her possible pregnancy and, of course, her split from Gary. In the knowledge they were now off the Baxter case, she forgot about the documents and they were never handed in. She'd put them in her jacket pocket the night she left Baxter's house and then popped them in a drawer when she arrived home. She had told Steve about them but they must have slipped his mind, too. It was only later, once she'd left the force, and after all the upheaval of the divorce, that she found them.

It was fate that she'd kept them and, once back in Manchester, Marie dashed into the house and took the wad from the drawer. She slipped off the rubber band and carefully turned the documents over in her hands. Amongst them was a passport. The photo on the passport was of Haley, and it was decidedly more flattering than when Marie had last seen her. But the name on the passport was Alicia Marie Lambert and there was an endorsement to include a baby by the name of Danielle Jeanne Lambert.

It was all coming back to her now. What would a woman like Haley have needed with a passport? It was obvious she was living on the breadline, so how was she expecting to travel abroad? And how come it showed Haley's photograph when it was in the name of Alicia Marie Lambert?

Marie hadn't quite understood at first. But then it came to her. She fingered the passport. Alicia Marie Lambert could have been Haley's working name. The passport looked genuine enough although Marie deduced that it was either forged, or it had been obtained with forged documents. Perhaps Haley was set to leave the country and ply her trade abroad. She must have been set up by someone, but who?

Marie's plan extended itself. The papers could be put to good use. The name Alicia didn't appeal to her but it was fortuitous one of the names was Marie. There was no reason why she couldn't opt to use the second Christian name, her own name; people did.

At first she thought it would be easy. Once she had the baby in her grasp, they could travel abroad to a place where no one knew them. But, having thought it through, it could certainly be tricky.

Marie's mind veered to the state of play at Murray Park Hospital. She switched on the TV set and checked the news. The child was still being kept in there. It was reported that the baby was already gaining weight and, if the mother did not come forward within the next few days, the child would be transferred into care, most likely with foster parents. Marie's stomach began to somersault. She must get on with it otherwise her plans would fall apart. Someone else could take on the baby.

Once things gained momentum, there was no stopping her. Now she had the place in Liverpool, all she needed to do was to take the child. There was no time to waste. For certain tomorrow she must carry out her plan. The flat wasn't one she'd have chosen but she'd make sure the baby was comfortable once they were in Liverpool.

There were lots of people around during visiting hours the following day. Marie entered the ward and boldly took Rosie Grimshaw from her cot. And once in the car, she drove from Manchester to Liverpool, her heart thudding in her chest throughout the journey. The baby whimpered once or twice but Marie kept on going. And once they were inside the flat she managed to calm her down.

After lighting the gas fire to make sure the place was warm, she prepared the baby's milk and fed her. The baby was no longer Rosie. Now she was Danielle. The little pushchair Marie had bought doubled up as a cot and once Danielle had been fed, Marie placed the child in there and watched her whilst she slept.

She's mine now, she told herself, *and no one will ever take her from me.*

Chapter 17
The past – 1988-1990

Reports in the media indicated it was a woman who'd taken the child. But the police had few clues to go on. All they knew what that she was tall, wore a nursing sister's uniform, but nothing more, and as the days passed their task became more and more difficult. They checked out the nursing staff and enquired if any of the sisters had recently resigned from a job at the hospital. But the results led them nowhere. And then they began to question relatives of members of staff, anyone who might be able to gain access to a uniform.

Nobody seemed to have a description of the woman's face or hair colouring – except Freda of course in the laundry. But she was too afraid to admit she'd passed over a uniform to someone she didn't know, someone without any identity. She was usually more thorough than that, but the woman who'd demanded the uniform seemed to have some authority. Freda assumed she was a new sister and, normally, she would have asked her for an ID check, but the group of laundrywomen were idling around and chatting. It was Freda's guilt at not getting on with her job that led her to hand the uniform over. But she was not about to let slip that she had actually spoken to the woman. And it was too late now to go to the police.

It was essential that Marie return to Manchester to put her house on the market. But, reluctant to be seen with Danielle, her only option was to leave the child outside in the car whilst she visited the estate agent. Luckily there was a space right in front of the office where she could keep a check on things. Her meeting with the agent was brief.

'I'm moving out of the district, and I need a quick sale. I can't afford to handle my bridging loan for much longer,' she related convincingly.

'We'll try our best. Having said that, we have a list of young people waiting for terraced houses,' he replied. 'Would it be convenient for me to view this afternoon?'

Now came the tricky bit. It was too risky for her to be seen with Danielle, which meant she couldn't possibly be at the house when the valuer arrived. 'Any time of the day would be fine, but I can't be there personally. I'm out of the district.'

The agent looked puzzled. 'It's rather unusual for the owner not to be present. All I can do is let you know my valuation over the phone.'

'That will suit me fine. Here's the key,' she offered, handing it over. 'I'll give you a ring tomorrow in case you have any questions about the house. When we've discussed your valuation, I'd like you to put it on the market straight away.' She hesitated. She'd need as much money as she could lay her hands on if she was to go abroad. 'I'll not be taking the furniture with me. Maybe any potential buyer would be interested.'

'The furniture is, of course, a separate issue. But I'll give you an approximate valuation. The sale of the furniture would obviously be negotiable.'

Everything ran smoothly after that which made the task much easier for Marie. She collected the very minimum of personal belongings from the house, only those things she could handle and, within the month the house was snapped up by a young couple, first-time buyers who were about to be married. The furniture was a bonus for them too. And by that time, Marie had officially sent in her resignation to Cromptons.

Now for the second part of her plan – but nothing too hasty, although she felt certain no one in the tenement knew much about her. The tenants were nothing but faceless humans entering and leaving the place. Hopefully she was the same to them.

But now she had to make sure there was a good likeness between herself and the woman on the passport. They both had brown eyes and Marie's hair was dark like Haley's, the only difference being that Haley's was shoulder length and wavy whilst Marie had always worn hers straight, loose when she was off duty, taken back when she was at work. But she'd always been good at styling her hair and once she'd experimented with a set of rollers she knew just how she could make herself look like Haley, alias Alicia Marie Lambert, the woman on the passport.

If the plan was to work she must go for a more or less exact likeness. Once she had perfected the style she took a long, hard look at herself in the mirror. The hairdo was not what she would have chosen, but she had to admit to herself that it did suit her, and it knocked at least five years off her age.

All she needed now was the money from the sale of the house. The sooner the people moved in and she received the proceeds, the sooner she could leave Liverpool and start a new life. She'd already reasoned that the easiest place would be France, and she had a good grasp of the language, enough for her to get by. It had come in useful when she and Gary had holidayed abroad, although he'd always been jealous. He probably felt belittled that he couldn't join in the conversation. But why hadn't he done something about it? His reaction was stupid when all she was doing was helping them get by in a foreign country. But he was like that.

She smiled to herself. She didn't care two hoots about Gary these days. He'd hurt her so much going off with the stripper woman that he'd killed any feelings she'd ever had for him stone dead.

Joanna did a valiant job of covering up her emotions, although privately the guilt and remorse never left her. She was gutted when she heard that her baby had been abducted, and she suffered a rapid weight loss at the thought of someone else claiming the child as her own. And, as she mulled over the sequence of events that had taken place since she and Rick had parted to her subsequent abandonment of the baby, the gnawing in her stomach continued, but what could she do? It was too late to confess she'd been the guilty one. There was nothing to be gained from a confession. And it wouldn't bring the child back. All she could hope was that the woman would be capable of giving her baby a good home and the love and care she needed.

But as the weeks passed Joanna withdrew into herself. Why had she done such a stupid thing? She hadn't thought it through properly and she'd panicked. She wanted the child back now. She wanted her desperately.

It was some weeks later when her best friend, Bev persuaded her to go clubbing. 'I don't know what's got into you, Jo. You've always enjoyed going out.'

'But it's just not my scene these days.'

'Give it a whirl, babe. Let's have some fun.'

Joanna curled up on her bed in the foetal position feeling sorry for herself. But, after she'd spoken to Bev she told herself she must snap out of this depression. All she was doing was fretting. If something could take her mind off the baby even for a short time, it would help. And despite her initial pessimism, once they arrived at the club Joanna became her old self again and began to enjoy the experience, but not without two or three vodka and tonics to boost her morale.

And then she met Wayne. They seemed to hit it off straight away. He was tall and dark and certainly hunky, a sportsman of some description. But she'd drunk so much vodka, she couldn't recall his sport.

The following morning didn't she know about it? Her head was thumping in loud and rapid rhythm. And the very thought of another drink made her want to throw up. Yuk! She never wanted to see another bottle of vodka as long as she lived. Fortunately it was Sunday, time to rest and hopefully pull herself round. And plenty of water was what she needed to subdue the hangover.

Bev rang her midmorning and came up with a suggestion. 'The two lads we met last night, Sam and whatshisname,' she chirped. 'They're playing rugby later this morning. They asked us to go and watch them, do you remember?'

Rugby? That was Wayne's game. Joanna remembered now. She groaned. How could she face getting out of bed, showering and going to a rugby match? 'Now that you mention it, yes I do. But I feel so fragile, Bev, and a rugby match. Honestly, I don't feel up to it.'

'Come on, Jo. Get yourself moving. The fresh air will clear your head and we could always have a couple of drinks at the Brown Cow after the match – you know, "hair of the dog".' She laughed.

'Well if you're pressing me…'

Bev rang off and Joanna replaced the receiver, now gently lifting her head from the pillow and slipping her legs out of bed. A shower was a must, and then she'd need to blow dry her hair. Having bleached out the colour she wore her hair shoulder length now, flicked out at the sides. She looked in the mirror. It was certainly an improvement on the way she looked when she returned from Manchester. Her thoughts brought back memories of the birth of her child. But she tried hard to blot out those images and to perk herself up ready to meet Bev.

There was a nip in the air as they stood outside, close to the touchline. Joanna shivered. But the freshness felt good and it helped to clear her head. The match was more interesting than she'd anticipated. Wayne scored twice. He was certainly the macho type, far different from Rick. But why was she still thinking about Rick? He was out of her life for good, now.

Wayne had managed the first team yet again. He was delighted. But what annoyed him was that his dad would be down at the club bragging as usual. Wayne wished he wouldn't. It always came back via the other lads. 'Our Wayne's done it again!' they'd say, mockingly quoting their own dads who had gone back home and poked fun. But there was nothing Wayne could do about it. He'd mentioned it umpteen times, but the bragging still continued.

The worst thing about it was that he didn't want Joanna to find out. He'd feel a fool if he heard the other lads making jokes about him. He'd met Joanna at Korkie's disco. Granted he was rather the worse for wear at the time but she was a lovely mover. He walked her home, or rather staggered home, and arranged to meet her the following day at the match.

When he reached the back door of his parents' house, he could hear them rowing again. They never seemed to do anything else. He was sick of it. The sooner he got himself away from there, the better.

Wayne was certainly not disappointed when he saw Joanna again on Sunday at the match. She wore a pair of slim-cut trousers and a skinny-rib sweater both of which enhanced her slim, curvy figure. He couldn't take his eyes off her. 'You look gorgeous,' he said. She was even lovelier than he'd remembered from the previous night.

Things began to hot up after that. It was only a month since they'd met but now he was seeing her two or three times a week.

And then it happened. Her parents went away to Benidorm and Joanna invited him to stay the night. His luck was in. He couldn't count the number of times he made love to her during the night but in the morning he was completely exhausted. She was as bright as a glowing star in the sky and when she challenged him again, he knew he'd need to keep up his fitness regime if this was to continue.

Joanna found going out with Wayne exciting. Thoughts of the baby and of her disappointment over Rick started to fade. And when after some weeks she discovered she was pregnant yet again, she wasn't upset, she wasn't scared. She was joyful. Her hands smoothed over her stomach. Now she had another life to consider and this time it would be different. She'd lost one baby through her own stupidity, and she wasn't about to lose another, especially when the father was here with her and, hopefully, not about to disappear as Rick had done. The tiny life inside her would be a new member of her family, a fresh start for her, and Wayne too, hopefully. It was as though she'd challenged herself to become pregnant again to make up for her past stupidity and subsequent loss. And this time who cared what her parents said about it? She certainly didn't.

And Wayne couldn't have shown more excitement when Joanna told him. It was not only the news of the baby that delighted him but also the fact that it was the best excuse yet for leaving his parents' place.

'I don't know what Mum and Dad are going to say,' Joanna confessed. 'They won't be happy about it, but it's happened. End of story.' Her smile was radiant. 'You are happy, aren't you, Wayne?'

'I'm over the moon, darling. And don't worry. I'll talk to them,' Wayne promised. 'Remember how I hit it off with your

Mum and Dad right from the start. I know they'll be disappointed we haven't waited, but we'll get by.'

Joanna's parents weren't exactly delighted at the news, but they liked Wayne and felt the two of them could make a go of it together. In particular, Mrs Falconer was relieved Joanna seemed to be completely over Rick. And now she'd met someone of whom they approved.

'He'll not leave you like Richard did,' her mother announced once she was alone with Joanna. She shook her head and pulled a face. 'Of course this is not the way your father and I would have wanted it, but we'll make the best of it. You're not showing yet so no one will know. We'd like you to have a white wedding at St Cuthbert's. What do you think?'

'Thanks for the vote of confidence, Mum. You're the best mum in the world,' she announced, giving her a hug. 'We won't let you down, promise.'

The mention of Rick set her thinking. It was only a matter of months since she'd abandoned her child. And here she was planning a wedding with yet another baby on the way. Her heart beat faster in her chest when she recollected the events of those few weeks. Where was the baby now, and the woman who'd taken her? Was she looking after the baby properly?

And then Joanna thought about Rick's new life in Australia. Good luck to him, she thought. It would never have worked even if she'd persuaded him to stay back in England. He'd always have had itchy feet, and there was no way she would traipse to the other side of the world for Rick or anyone else. She convinced herself she'd done the right thing in letting him go, but she would never forget the child she'd left behind. And she hoped the one she was expecting now would make up for her loss.

They hadn't much money between them but it was the opportunity Wayne needed to start afresh. 'I've found a flat to rent at the other end of Lytham,' he told her. 'It's not far from the main road and the bus stops.'

'I can't wait to see it, Wayne. Have they asked for a deposit?'

'I haven't said we'll have it yet, not until you see it, darling, and make the decision with me.'

Joanna agreed immediately. And that was it. They had somewhere to stay and now they had her parents' blessing.

They married at the church close to her home. Wayne's parents kicked up a fuss but what could they expect? Joanna was going on nineteen now and he was twenty. They didn't have a nest egg stored away; they hadn't anticipated marrying so soon, but they didn't care. Joanna knew that if they came up against financial difficulties, Mum and Dad would help out.

And after the birth of their baby, the pair couldn't have been happier. By that time Wayne had put in lots of overtime. 'I've been checking the building society account,' he told her. 'I think we've managed to save up enough money to pay the deposit on a small semi.'

'Wayne, that's wonderful. How about the one close to Mum and Dad's? We both liked it.' She held her breath, hoping he would agree.

'That suits me,' he told her. 'It's a smashing little place, in good nick too.' He liked her parents and the Falconers soon discovered they were lucky to have a son-in-law like him.

Marie stayed in the flat as much as possible during the daylight hours. It was dreary in there, but she took so much pleasure caring for baby Danielle that it didn't affect her. If she needed anything from the supermarket she'd go during the evenings when she was less likely to be seen.

It was on one such visit that Marie faced an ordeal she wished never to encounter again. Having driven her car into the underground car park, a police car drew up beside her as she was about to step out. She shrank back in her seat and took a furtive glance at the driver, a constable. Nothing fazed her at first. But then as he made to step out of the car, she realised the passenger door was being opened and who should step out but her old boss from Manchester, Inspector Trent. He was in full uniform and had obviously been promoted to Chief Inspector in Liverpool.

Wave after wave of fear shot through her making her head pound and her legs weak. How could this happen to her? Trent would be sure to recognise her even with the new hairdo. He may have been as subtle as a box of firecrackers, but he knew his job, he knew how to suss things out, hence the promotion. And what puzzled her was that it was unusual for someone of his rank to be there. But since he was newly appointed, maybe he was making a point that he could carry out the mundane tasks as well as the next man.

She shuddered. Once he recognised her he'd surely become suspicious, especially when he saw Danielle. They knew at the station she and Gary had divorced. Surely the news would have spread? Trent and the others would have known if she'd given birth to a child Danielle's age after she'd left the force. Momentarily she froze and sent up a silent plea. *Please, please don't let them take my baby.*

The two officers set out to walk towards her car. It would have been impossible for Trent to recognise her from such a distance but they were inches away when the constable tapped on her window. Her stomach threw itself into action, somersaults, back flips, the lot. The inspector hovered behind the constable, turning this way and that, obviously searching the car park for something.

Tentatively Marie opened the window, but only fractionally.

'How long have you been here?' the constable asked her.

'I've just driven in,' she replied, keeping her voice down. 'Why?'

'There's a man on the loose. Escaped this morning. He's been sighted entering the car park in a blue Ford Focus. Seen anything of the car?'

'Sorry, I haven't.'

'I take it you intended going to the supermarket.'

'That's right.'

'Better leave it until later, or call at another supermarket. Drive off slowly, love.'

Marie closed the window and pushed the lever into gear. Trent was still looking around, obviously leaving most of the legwork to the junior officer. He was probably there as a figurehead, nothing more.

What a relief! She was off and away before anyone else had the chance to recognise her. It was certainly time to leave the country after that little escapade.

And now, getting away to France with six-week-old Danielle was her only option. She needed to be absolutely sure she distanced herself from the police in England. She smirked. That was a bit of an anomaly since, as Sergeant Brechan, she could not have been closer to the police.

Chapter 18
The Past – 1988

Marcel Dubois entered Le Bistrot Bouvier and headed for the corner close to the window where he took his usual seat at a table marked 'reserved'. It was late afternoon and the place was filling more quickly than usual. But it was Friday and many of the workers finished mid-afternoon for the weekend.

Within minutes the manager, Henri Taupin had joined him. Marcel had known Henri since they attended the same college when Marcel was studying printing and Henri hospitality. 'Good afternoon my friend,' Henri said. 'And how are you feeling today?'

Marcel shrugged. 'Very much the same Henri.'

Henri bent his head towards Marcel's. 'Fancy a new challenge?' he whispered.

Marcel wasn't fazed. 'Depends what you mean by a new challenge,' he replied, his tone matter-of-fact.

Henri got up. 'When you've finished your wine, come into the back. There's something I'd like to discuss with you,' he explained, making his way back to the bar where he began to serve his customers.

Marcel had lived alone for three years now after his wife, Yvonne, had passed away. After a second bout of MS her health had sadly gone downhill and eventually it seemed she gave up the will to live. Marcel had been told the attack had been severe and that, unless something in the form of a miracle occurred, Yvonne had not long to live. He'd been expecting it to happen, and although he'd psyched himself up to cope after his loss, when it came to losing her, he found it difficult. They'd been close and were wonderful companions. Yvonne had supported him and helped him make business decisions. She was one bright and attractive lady. And he'd missed that wonderful smile and her eagerness to be involved in everything he did. Now he was desperately lonely, and it had become his ritual to visit the bistro every day, except weekends.

He sipped his wine, knowing that when he left the little restaurant he would drive back to his business in Lille, work until seven thirty, return to Le Bistrot Bouvier for his evening meal, leave for home, watch the news on TV and go to bed.

Henri had foolishly tried his hand at matchmaking. But it hadn't worked. The last one had been a waitress employed at the restaurant. She'd fussed around him every day when Marcel visited, and it was obvious she had a soft spot for him, even though it seemed it was Henri who was pulling the strings. Eventually, Henri got the message and never tried to 'fix things' again. It seemed he'd finally realised Marcel neither wanted nor needed a partner in his life, at least not yet. Marcel smiled to himself. Good old Henri. He'd tried.

Marcel's thoughts slipped back to the time they were at college together. He reflected. They were good times. And how they'd progressed since then. Henri now ran his own place here at the bistro, whilst Marcel had formed his own company, Dubois et Cie, ten years ago when he was twenty-six. And throughout the years, he and Henri had remained close friends.

Marcel poured the last drop of wine into his glass and drank it, picking up the carafe and returning it to the bar. 'I'm on my way, Henri. Did you want a word?' he called, curious to know what Henri had in mind. He hoped it wasn't another one of his attempts at matchmaking.

'Yes. Hang on Marcel. I have a proposition for you. Come through to the back.'

Marcel followed him through and they sat at a table at the far end of the kitchen. Henri folded his arms and leaned on the table.

'I don't know whether I mentioned it before but my partner Claude is retiring shortly. I appreciate you have the business in Lille, Marcel, but it seems to me you need a new challenge, something to give you a different focus. We've been friends all these years and I wondered how you would feel about coming in with me, as a business partner of course, no cheffing.' He laughed.

Marcel clapped his hand on his mouth. 'I hope not,' he replied, joining in the laughter.

'I realise your strengths lie in a different direction from mine. But, goodness knows you're in here every day. You may as well own part of it and share the profits.'

Marcel clasped his hands and settled them on the table, pondering on Henri's proposition before he replied. 'You've taken me by surprise, Henri. I don't know what to say.'

'The thing is I cannot afford to buy Claude out completely. I worry that he'll sell to some stranger, maybe someone who wants to change everything. With you, Marcel, I know we could discuss the running of the place and come to some mutual agreement. I can afford to buy half of his investment if you would be interested in putting in the other half. That would mean I would own seventy-five percent of the business, and you would own Claude's remaining twenty-five.' He paused and looked Marcel in the eyes. 'It would be a good investment, but I'll leave it with you. Think it over and let me know.'

Marcel perked up. It sounded interesting. 'I don't need to think it over, Henri. Let me see the figures and I'll make my decision based on those. I must say it sounds rather tempting, but

I wouldn't be a businessman if I didn't check the figures before I agreed.' He smiled and stood up to leave.

Henri stuck to his word and brought along the information he and Claude had prepared ready for the sale. Marcel glanced at the papers. 'You seem to have done well over the last twelve months. The profits are excellent. You've netted a much higher profit than Dubois et Cie. Count me in.'

Henri patted him on the back. 'Bravo,' he said. 'I'm delighted. You won't regret it, Marcel. It's completely different from your printing business, and there'll be a nice little profit in it for you.'

Marcel clapped his hands. 'That's what I like, a good investment.'

He drove home that night after his evening meal at the bistro. And for the first time in ages his outlook was positive. He liked the atmosphere in the restaurant and he looked forward to spending some of his time with Henri discussing the business and making plans for the future. As far as the printing business was concerned, he decided to ease himself away gradually and maybe delegate some of the work to Gerard.

After giving notice on the flat and packing the basic requirements, Marie planned to buy the extras once she was out of the country. Now that she had the money from the sale of the house and contents, there would be no financial problems, not for some time. But she must be careful to prepare herself for the airport. Her appearance must resemble the photo on the passport as closely as possible.

Heart pounding, Marie approached security and they helped her through with the pushchair. She smiled gratefully. Passport control glanced at her passport and waved her through. Luck was on her side. So far – easy-peasy!

Still with that feeling of unease, she boarded the aircraft. Danielle was quiet during the flight, and it was only when the plane touched down that she began to whimper. But nobody made a fuss. And it was with relief that she picked up her suitcase and pushchair from the carousel, hailed a cab and made her way to a four-star hotel, one she could afford now that she'd been paid out. She'd left England behind and now she was on French soil she felt more secure. Surely they wouldn't be looking for her here in France?

Once she'd established herself, she began to look for somewhere to rent and, eventually she decided on a cosy one-bedroomed cottage in a village on the outskirts of Lille.

The months passed by and at first she stayed home a lot of the time and enjoyed looking after baby Danielle. And when she did leave the cottage, she befriended many of the villagers and practised her French. There was nothing like a baby to bring people together. And after a time she knew she was accepted by the villagers, and she no longer suffered those feelings of paranoia that everyone was regarding her with suspicion.

Soon she was almost fluent in the language and by that time she realised she needed to bring in an income to supplement her equity from the sale of the house in England. But her major problem was Danielle. She didn't want to leave her, but she couldn't go on spending the money. Her police pension was paid into an account in Manchester, under her own name, Marie Brechan, and there was no way she could touch that without going back there. So that was a non-starter. Some day, when sufficient time had passed, maybe she would go back, but not for some years.

With a part-time job still in mind she took the pushchair into the village and sat down at a little café in the square where she met up with her neighbour, Justine Bougard. They passed the time of day as usual before Marie mentioned the job she'd had her eye on at Le Bistrot Bouvier in Lille.

'But what about your little girl?' Justine asked her.

'That's the problem, Justine. The job is only part-time but I'd love to take it. I'm slowly running out of money. But there's no crèche in the village. Do you know of one in any of the other villages nearby?'

'Forget that, Marie. How about if Danielle stayed with me? Claudette would love to have a little friend to play with.'

Marie couldn't believe her luck. 'That would be the answer to all my prayers. But are you sure, Justine?'

'Absolutely. She's a placid little soul and the two of them will be good company for one another.'

'That's wonderful. I'm delighted you've offered. And it would be a little income for you too. That way we can both benefit. I'll call in at the agency today in the hope that the job is still open.'

Marcel's day at work had been quiet and he'd left early knowing it was time he gave himself some space. He entered Le Bistrot Bouvier and took his usual seat in the corner, spreading his newspaper on the table before him and smoothing out the creases. The bar was noisier than usual. There were one or two holidaymakers in there laughing and generally enjoying themselves. And why shouldn't they?

As he looked across at them, he dwelt on his own situation. He supposed it was time he took a holiday himself. But what sort of a holiday would it be without a partner? Things had changed since he'd joined Henri and taken a quarter-share in the bistro. He acknowledged to himself that since he became involved with the restaurant his heart wasn't set on taking a holiday, not just yet.

Turning his attention back to the newspaper, he glanced at the headlines and then flicked over to the business section. The market had fallen drastically.

'What will it be, sir?' A voice broke into his thoughts, and Marcel was startled by the intrusion. He looked up. The waitress, a woman in her twenties, smiled down at him, her brown eyes twinkling. She was happy in her job. He could tell by the vibrancy she emitted. He'd never seen her before. But he liked what he saw.

He smiled back. 'It's no use saying *my usual,* is it? You're new aren't you?'

'Yes. I'm Marie. I started here today. And no, I wouldn't know what *your usual* is,' she laughed.

'Judging by your accent, you're obviously not French.'

'I'm English. But I do hope it doesn't stand out a mile. I have been trying so hard with my French.'

'It's good, believe me. How long have you been in France?'

'About sixteen, seventeen months.'

'You've done well. I hope you'll enjoy working here,' he said, so taken in by the woman, he'd forgotten all about his order.

She shook her head and smiled back at him. 'You said I wouldn't know what your *usual* is. Maybe you could tell me?'

'It would be an idea, wouldn't it?' He laughed. 'A small carafe of cabernet would go down a treat.'

Marcel spent the rest of his time watching Marie. Henri had told him there was to be a new waitress starting at the restaurant, but Marcel hadn't taken much notice. Henri certainly hadn't mentioned that she was English, or that she was so attractive. And it wasn't just her looks. There was something about her that made Marcel feel warm inside. A frisson of excitement sent his stomach into a flutter. And, although he couldn't concentrate on his newspaper, he kept on glancing at it. He didn't want her to see him looking.

She was there every day when he called after work. He looked out for her each time he entered the bar, and he had a feeling she looked out for him too. And then one day when he called in there were no customers at the bar. Marie brought his usual order. She placed the carafe on the table and he asked her to sit down.

She looked around. 'I suppose the boss won't mind, seeing there's no one else in here.' She smiled. 'But if anyone turns up I must go back behind the bar.'

Marcel was aware the new waitress had no idea he had an interest in the business, and he didn't want to spoil their little chat by informing her. Henri had been away on holiday for the last two weeks and he'd installed his assistant head chef, Jacques to take charge.

Marie sat down and clasped her hands in front of her. 'I take it this is your after-work treat, your relaxation time.'

'That's right. I've nothing to rush home for, and this gives me a chance to unwind.'

'You live alone, I take it.'

'Afraid so. My wife passed away some time ago.'

'I'm sorry to hear that, Marcel.'

The sadness returned as it always did when he thought about Yvonne's untimely death. But he forced himself to smile. 'And you? There's no doubt you have a man in your life.'

'Not any more. But I have a daughter, Danielle.'

'That's nice,' he replied, somehow relieved she hadn't a partner – he didn't know why. 'How old is Danielle?'

'She's eighteen months now. She's a real sweetie-pie,' Marie said proudly.

'I'm sure she must be if she's anything like you.' He paused and took Marie's hand. 'Do you ever get any time to yourself in the evenings? Perhaps I could take you out for a meal.'

Marie was taken aback. And then she smiled. 'That would be a treat for me. Danielle stays with Justine Bougard – she's my friend and neighbour – when I'm here. Occasionally she baby-sits in the evenings. But those are rare occasions. I could ask her if she'd mind. Any night in particular?'

'Saturday would be best, but if you can't manage that, any night except Thursday.'

'Leave it with me,' Marie replied, as she stood up to serve a customer who'd entered the bar. 'I'll get back to you.'

Marcel's heart gave a little skip. He hadn't felt like this for a long time. In a way he felt guilty. He felt he was betraying Yvonne. But surely he was entitled to some happiness. And he was sure Yvonne would have been pleased for him.

He picked up the empty carafe and made to go to the bar just as Henri appeared in the doorway.

'Marcel, my friend. Good to see you.'

'And you Henri. How was the holiday?'

'Very enjoyable, very relaxing,' Henri replied. 'Things have gone well I hope?'

'As far as I know, Henri, but I'm not in the business of interfering. Jacques would have come to me if there'd been any problems.'

Marcel could see out of his eye corner that Marie was giving them a strange look. Marcel turned to look at her. 'By the way, Henri. Marie is the new waitress you requested from the agency.'

Henri turned his head in her direction. 'I can see I didn't need to interview her.' He laughed. 'And I can see too that you've already introduced yourself, Marcel.'

'Not from a business point of view. But we have talked.' He turned to Marie. 'Marie, Henri Taupin, the real boss.'

Henri held out his hand. 'Good to meet you. How's it going?'

'I'm enjoying it M Taupin,' she replied, a puzzled look on her face. 'But I thought Jacques was the boss.'

'When I'm away, Jacques is the boss in the kitchen,' Henri told her. 'But you have another boss too.' He held his hand towards Marcel. 'Marcel Dubois is my business partner, Marie.'

Marcel rolled his eyes, and Marie gave a little smirk.

'He didn't tell me he was a partner in the restaurant,' she replied. 'I could have been complaining about the job or something like that.'

'But I wasn't trying to hide anything from you or trip you up. I just didn't want to spoil our informal little chats.'

'I forgive you, M Dubois,' Marie advanced in formal voice.

'Less of the formalities, Marie,' Henri insisted as he gave a sly wink in Marcel's direction. 'I'm Henri and he's Marcel,' he added, pointing to his partner.

Marie was delighted she'd been asked out. Marcel was such a gentleman. She had to admit to herself there was no spark there but surely it was personality that mattered. She'd been badly let down in the past and, after all, love wasn't everything. She smiled to herself. What was she thinking? For goodness' sake, it was only a dinner date! The guy hadn't asked her to marry him!

Saturday night was the first of many nights out. She was aware she was becoming very fond of Marcel, and it was obvious he adored her. It was two and a half months after they'd first met when Marcel came up with a proposition.

'We're spending a lot of time with each other and we seem to be getting on so well – I have a suggestion to make. Feel free to put me right, Marie if I've pre-empted the situation.' He paused and took Marie's hands in his. 'I think you know by now that I've fallen head over heels in love with you. I'm not sure how you feel about me, but I know we can grow together if we give it a chance.'

'Marcel, you're keeping me on tenterhooks. Come out with it'

'What I'm trying to say is that I'd like you and Danielle to move in with me. It makes sense. You wouldn't need to work at the bistro. You could stay back and look after Danielle, that's if you'd prefer it.' He paused for a long moment. 'The house is so big I'm rattling around in it. Please say you agree,' he begged, and then he continued before Marie had the chance to respond. 'I'd like us to marry at some time in the future – if you'll have me.'

Marie couldn't believe what she was hearing. 'That's a very generous offer, Marcel. But it's not a case of *if I'll have you*. You don't have to marry me just because you've invited me to stay with you. I'd be happy for us to live together as partners. I'd be loyal to you.' She paused. 'I don't know if I could make such a permanent commitment as marriage, not after what's happened in the past.'

'I understand, Marie. I know you had an unhappy marriage, and that's all I need to know. I'd love you to move in – on your own terms of course. We don't have to make it legal if you'd prefer not to. Surely we can trust one another?' He slipped his arm around her. 'But, once we're together, I would like Danielle to think of me as Papa. Yvonne and I never had children. She couldn't have coped after the illness. But I would never have let her know how disappointed I was. And now I feel it's time to move on.'

'Danielle has never had anyone to call Papa. And it's obvious she adores you, Marcel. I'm glad you feel that way. We could be one happy family.'

'My feelings exactly.'

One happy family! That's all Marie had ever yearned for. And at last here was the ideal opportunity. She couldn't believe how close she and Marcel had become. She'd met someone she was falling in love with, he'd asked her to join him and make his own life complete. What more could she wish for? It would make her life complete too, especially now that she had little Danielle. Earlier in her life she'd hankered after some security. She'd been desperate to feel that togetherness with her family around her. But it had never happened. Things had gone sour. And then, just before she'd left for France, she'd found the solution.

Reflecting on the past, Marie vowed never to tell Marcel what had happened. Fair enough, she would have to tell him something, but not the important details. She would never let him in on her secret. She was too guilt-ridden to disclose the true story to anyone. And she hoped Marcel would never find out by other means.

Although she'd never regretted her secret plans, or the resultant actions and sequence of events before she left for France, it wasn't something she was proud of. And Marcel was so kind and understanding, she didn't want to spoil things between them.

Her thoughts reverted to Marcel's offer. For as much as she'd enjoyed working at Le Bistrot Bouvier, she had missed being with Danielle. And now it would be possible for her to be with her child all of the time. Everything was falling into place. She couldn't have been more elated.

Part IV

The Solution
2008

Chapter 19
The Present – 2008

Pierre knew as soon as he heard Steve O'Hara's voice that the results of the DNA tests on Haley Baxter were through. He felt himself tense up. 'Any news?'

'There was no match with Danielle. Both Haley Baxter and her daughter Michelle are A positive and their DNAs match. So we can cancel Haley out of the equation. She wasn't Danielle's mother,' he announced. 'I'm almost certain now the Grimshaw woman is Danielle's mother.'

'She's in the next office, Steve. I'm in the middle of an interview. I'll let you know the outcome.'

Pierre switched off his mobile phone and returned to the interview room. 'Sorry about that, Mrs Harlow.'

'I've been thinking. How do I know for certain it was my baby the woman kidnapped, Mr Clarisse?' Joanna spat out the words and shook her head.

Pierre sat down and leant with his elbows on the desk. 'I checked out the case history at Murray Park. Your daughter was down as Rosie Grimshaw, the name the nurses gave her. We found her hospital number on a pink wristband in the mother's possession.'

'But she wasn't the mother.' Joanna reminded him crisply. 'Don't you think I've had years of pain and worry?' she added, 'and remorse. But I tried to shut my mind to it. It's been a nightmare not knowing what happened to my baby.'

'I understand how you must have felt, Mrs Harlow.' Pierre nodded gravely. 'But the fact of the matter is that your daughter now needs compatible blood to be made available before the surgeon can operate. That's our priority. She's been anaemic since she was admitted to hospital which makes it impossible for the haematologist to take her own blood and store it.'

'I realise the urgency. You don't have to spell it out. And I have been for the test haven't I?' Joanna was adamant. 'Surely I am entitled to know who stole my baby? I was eighteen at the time. I was in shock. I was frightened,' she continued, a flicker of regret in her gaze. 'I might have gone to the police and claimed the baby back once I'd come to my senses. But I didn't get the chance. Before I knew it, that woman had stolen her.' Patches of angry colour appeared on her cheeks. She had suffered enough indignity at the hands of the inspector and, although Pierre had taken a gentler approach, Joanna was desperate to know the truth.

Pierre tried to calm her. 'Don't worry, Mrs Harlow. I'm sure things will sort themselves out in the end. But we can't give you access to your daughter right now. I'm afraid the story is a sad one.'

A heavy frown gathered on her forehead. 'My daughter is all right, I take it? Nothing's happened to her? It's just that I would like to meet up with her.' She spoke more calmly now.

'That's not possible at present.' He hesitated. 'Marie, the woman who took your child died last week. As you will appreciate, Danielle is devastated. She was very much attached to her. Marie was in her mid-forties and no one expects a parent to die at that age. But these things happen. Obviously Danielle always thought Marie was her natural mother. She still does. Her stepfather has yet to tell her. And I'm sure you'll appreciate that will be very painful both for him and for Danielle.'

'Did the stepfather know Danielle had been kidnapped?'

'Not until a few days ago. It was a shock to him, too.'

Satisfied with the explanation, Joanna stood up to leave and followed Pierre to the car park.

Joanna had an anxious wait for the test results. Would they prove she was Danielle's mother, and would her blood be compatible with her daughter's? She went in alone, leaving Pierre in the waiting room.

The haematologist came out from the lab. 'We've analysed your blood but unfortunately it doesn't contain the rare antigens. However, we accepted your request for a DNA test and we'll let you know as soon as we have the results.'

Even though Joanna had been expecting a positive result, once she learnt the DNA test confirmed she was Danielle's biological mother, the news sent shockwaves through her. She gazed into space as though in a trance. And then she shook her head. 'I'm heart-broken, Wayne. Danielle is my baby and I felt sure I'd be the one to help her. What will happen to her now? I've worried all these years,' she whispered through a dry throat. 'For once, I thought I could make up for the past. But it's not to be. And now that I've found her all I want is to see her.'

'Calm down, love. All in good time. I'm sure Mr Clarisse is right. We can't start getting involved until Danielle's had the operation.'

When they eventually met up with Pierre again, he looked to them expectantly. 'How did it go?'

'I was disappointed my blood wasn't compatible,' Joanna told him. 'But the DNA tests prove I am Danielle's mother. When can I see her?'

'All in good time. As I said earlier Danielle doesn't even know yet that Marie was not her mother.' Pierre was emphatic in his reply.

'But surely you can tell me where she is,' Joanna insisted. 'I must see her.'

'At the present time, that wouldn't be possible. I can tell you that your daughter was brought up in France, and French is her first language. Marie was English, but Danielle's stepfather, Marcel, is a Frenchman.'

'Brought up in France? I'm not surprised the woman got away with it, taking my baby out of the country. Then I take it Danielle's in France now.'

'Mrs Harlow, I understand your need to find out about Danielle, but our priority is to continue with the search. Once a donor is found, the operation can take place and in time Mr Dubois will explain everything to his daughter.' He paused. 'Only then, once she knows the truth can you expect to meet up with her. Having said that, there is the chance Danielle will refuse to see you. She is now of age and entitled to choose for herself.'

'But don't I have a choice in the matter? I am her mother after all,' Joanna insisted, her voice heavy with sorrow.

'There's no point arguing the toss, love. It's all in the past. Let's wait and see. We must start building bridges now, not demolishing them.' Wayne slipped his arm around her shoulders.

Pierre sighed. 'We're going over the same ground again and again,' he reminded her, an edge of impatience in his voice. 'We really must get on with the search. I'm afraid there's nothing for it but to contact Danielle's biological father, that's if he can be traced.' He turned to Joanna. 'Do you know his whereabouts?'

Joanna flushed with embarrassment, making eye contact with Wayne. He gave a gentle nod, his way of telling her he agreed with whatever she needed to do.

'Rick was a qualified plumber and he left for Australia when I became pregnant.' She hunched her shoulders. 'I don't know exactly where he went. I assume he's still in Australia but we're talking nineteen years ago. He could be anywhere.' She shrugged non-committally.

'Then first of all let's start with his full name,' Pierre suggested.

Joanna bit her lip. 'It's Richard Barry Stevens.' Worried that she was digging up the past in front of Wayne, she wanted to refuse the guy, but she made a massive effort at self-control. This was something she could not avoid, something that was irrevocably bound up with their search for a compatible blood type for her daughter. 'I could tell you where his parents used to live. Whether or not they're still in the same house I've no idea.'

'That would be a start, Mrs Harlow. If they're not there, perhaps a neighbour would know their whereabouts.'

Joanna proceeded to fill Pierre in on the details of Rick's family, their names and their address.

'Thanks for co-operating,' Pierre said as he wrote down the details. 'I'll get off to Lytham and check this out straight away.'

'Don't thank me. It's the least I could do. But please let me know how things go. I have the full support of Wayne,' she added, turning to offer a weak smile to her husband. 'We'd like to know if you manage to contact Rick and what the outcome is.'

'I'll be in touch. But it is possible Mr Dubois will not tell Danielle that Marie was not her real mother until well after the operation,' Pierre informed them.

'I'm sorry I've carped on, Mr Clarisse. I do understand. But surely you understand how I feel, too? Now that everything's out in the open I'm desperate to tell Danielle how sorry I am for leaving her like that.' Her heart ached with so much grief that her mind was unable to encompass it all.

Wayne took her hand, rubbed the back of it and directed his gaze to Pierre. They exchanged glances of concern. 'I think we all understand how upset my wife feels.' Wayne resolutely turned his head towards Pierre. 'We'd be grateful for anything you can tell us, anything at all.'

Still with no donor available, Marcel was anxious for Pierre to fill him in on his latest investigations.

'A Mrs Joanna Harlow has come forward. And you might wonder what relevance the woman has in on our search for a donor but, after working closely with the police, I discovered Paula Grimshaw was a name the mother adopted at the time of the birth of her child.' Pierre gave him details of Joanna's confession, her reasons for abandoning her child. 'She was very remorseful.'

'I should hope she was remorseful.' Marcel's voice faltered. 'Look at the trouble she's caused.' His face became tight with anger.

Pierre, determined not to be drawn into the emotional aspects of the case, ignored his comment. 'We checked her blood but unfortunately it doesn't contain the rare antigens. However, the DNA test proves she is the mother and she has told me who the father is.'

'Then I hope he's available for the test?' Marcel's mouth pursed disapprovingly.

'That's where another complication arises, Marcel. Mrs Harlow thinks the father, a Richard Stevens, is still living in Australia. He left her in the lurch so to speak before Danielle was born.'

Marcel's face became drawn. 'But Marie has always claimed Danielle was her child,' he reminisced as though in disbelief. 'When all this came out I assumed she'd adopted Danielle.' His voice was strangled now.

'Exactly. That's what we all thought.'

Marcel slowly shook his head. 'How much more are we going to rake up?' His eyes began to glisten and his anger began to fade as he reflected. 'For Marie to have taken Danielle from the hospital, she must have been desperate for a child.'

'You're right, of course. And the baby had been abandoned. That obviously gave her the reason to give the child a home,' Pierre professed, wanting to humour Marcel rather than make him feel worse.

Marcel gave a huge sigh. 'But this doesn't change anything in my book. Marie was Marie.' He brushed a tear from his eye. 'We must find the father. You've done well Pierre in such a short time. But time is precious.'

'I'm already checking on the father. He left England in 1988 for Australia. I was given his parents' address in Lytham by Mrs Harlow, and I visited the house. A neighbour told me Richard Stevens' mother went out to Australia to join her son some years later. Apparently the man she was living with stole all her money and left her penniless.' He turned a strained smile towards Marcel. 'Fortunately Joanna Harlow also remembered Stevens was interviewed by an Australian representative and he was placed in a job. I've contacted that department and, as I speak, they're checking on his initial whereabouts.'

'That is a start,' Marcel admitted, now looking a little mollified.

'It is possible I'll need to go to Australia on the first available flight once I find out where Stevens is living. I know I could telephone when I receive his details, but it's too delicate a matter to discuss over the phone. The guy might not even admit he is Danielle's father, especially if he's now married with a family. He may not wish to divulge such information in front of his wife. It would be much better to talk to the man face to face and explain the situation. After all we're only asking for a check on his blood type. Obviously if there is a match we'd hope to take the matter further. I take it that'll be all right with you?'

'Of course it is. I don't care how much it costs. We can't afford to hang about. I would like to come with you, but I don't want to leave the country whilst Danielle is waiting for the operation. Get a ticket booked straight away, business class.' He paused. 'I can't keep Danielle guessing for much longer. But I'm not prepared to mention anything about her being abandoned and then kidnapped, not until after the operation. But I can't hold off much longer about her father. It's becoming embarrassing for the medical staff as well as for me. I must tell her we're in the process of locating him.'

When Pierre rang the Australian immigration office again he was told Rick Stevens had originally taken a job in Perth at Watkins and Son, Plumbers, a company regularly contracting their workers out to several large building companies. When he telephoned the company he discovered they had been taken over by a larger group. On consulting the company records, the general manager there confirmed Stevens had opted not to stay with the company after the takeover.

'It's a long time ago, Mr Clarisse, but I vaguely remember Stevens telling me he was moving to Darwin in the Northern Territory. The reason I remember Stevens in particular is that he was a good worker and we didn't want to lose him. But it was his choice. I've no idea which company he moved to.'

'Thanks for that. I'll make Darwin my first stop,' Pierre replied and he promptly booked a one-way ticket, knowing he would need to put in a great deal of leg-work to have any chance of locating Stevens. The guy could be anywhere by now.

Once packed and ready, he drove to the Charles de Gaulle airport in Paris where he picked up the flight, and from there, they touched down in Singapore before resuming the journey to Darwin.

Darwin was hot and humid as Pierre stepped from the aircraft. He slipped off his tie and undid the top button of his shirt. Fortunately the place was not as extensive as he'd imagined, and it was relatively straightforward for him to check out all the companies employing building trade workers, both in the centre of Darwin and on the outskirts. Eventually a plumbing foreman at Denzil and Company said he recalled Stevens.

'The POM, Stevens?' he laughed. 'Yes I do remember him. He wasn't with us for long, mate,' he informed Pierre. 'He didn't like the climate up here. Too much rain.' He chuckled. 'I don't know what some of them want. From what I've heard it rains all the time in England. But there you go,' he added. 'He moved down to Brisbane in Queensland, but not to a job in the building trade as far as I recall. I think he applied for a job selling vacuum cleaners of all things. I don't know why. There's good money in the building trade.' He shook his head. 'Mind you, I couldn't be certain that's the job he took. People have a habit of changing their minds, you know.'

Pierre smiled. 'That's true, but it should get me on track,' he replied as he left the office thinking what a futile trip this had been, although he had to acknowledge he would never have known Stevens had transferred to Brisbane had he not visited Denzil and Company. At least things were moving and he was beginning to follow the guy's tracks, even though so far he'd only caught up with the first seven years' of Stevens' stay in Australia.

Now came the tricky bit. The guy in Darwin had mentioned Stevens had applied for a job selling vacuum cleaners but he hadn't been sure. The obvious place to start was to contact companies selling electrical goods. Failing any success in that direction, Pierre had no idea where he would go next.

Unfortunately, Brisbane was a much larger city and more highly populated than Darwin. None of the companies he contacted had heard of Rick Stevens and, at the end of his search, he still had no clue as to the guy's whereabouts after leaving Darwin. Deeply disappointed, Pierre realised he was back to square one. What next? He certainly wasn't prepared to go back to England having failed to locate Stevens.

And then he had an idea. Perhaps if he contacted the local council he could find out if Stevens had been a taxpayer in Brisbane back in the nineties.

When Pierre reached the office, he caught the clerk absorbed in reading something she was holding under the desk. She hurriedly slipped it out of sight and looked up. 'Yes?' she mumbled, looking a little guilty at being caught with her head in a magazine.

'I'm trying to trace the whereabouts of someone who came over from England in the eighties,' Pierre explained. 'As far as I can gather he lived in Brisbane during the nineties. I need to check his whereabouts. His name is Richard Stevens. I wondered if you had any record of him.'

The woman seemed none too pleased at the request. 'I don't know if I'm allowed to give you information like that,' she replied sulkily.

'All I need to know is where the guy lived. He's done nothing wrong, but it's imperative that I locate him.'

'You're expecting me to check back all those years?' she remarked, her tone indicating she was very much put out by such a request.

'If that is possible,' Pierre replied in gentle tone, surprised by her negative attitude.

'Of course it's possible,' she muttered with a sigh, shaking her head.

'I would be grateful. Your finding the information for me could quite literally save a life. I'm searching for someone with a rare blood type,' he informed her, 'a relative of a nineteen-year-old student who is in dire need of that type before she can undergo an operation,' he continued, now spitting out the words slowly and precisely.

At this the woman looked a little shamefaced. 'I see,' she said, now avoiding eye contact with Pierre. 'You should have mentioned that in the first place.' Her tone was still brusque. She clicked on the mouse and eventually came up with an address on the outskirts of Brisbane. 'There was someone of that name living in Brisbane,' she told him. 'He stayed for almost three years, ninety-five to ninety-eight. Can't tell you what happened after that.'

'Thank you for your help,' Pierre replied a little obsequiously as he collected the scrap of paper on which the woman had written the address. All he could do now was visit the house and ask if they knew Stevens' intended destination after his move.

He studied the map and picked out the place, Redland Bay. It was a little way from the centre of Brisbane, thirty minutes or so at a guess. The roads were quiet and, once he found the street, he spotted the house at the end of a row of about a dozen. He parked up outside, followed the path to the front door and rang the bell.

After waiting a couple of minutes, there was no response. He rang the bell again, knowing there was definitely someone inside the house from the sound of footsteps. But it seemed obvious whoever was in there was reluctant to open the door. Perhaps they'd seen him walking up the garden path and assumed he was a salesman of some sort. He was about to leave when the inner door opened and a skinny arm reached out and locked the outer mesh door. A young boy of about seven was standing there peering through the mesh.

'Is your mother about?' Pierre asked him.

'She's out,' came the boy's terse reply.

'How about your father?'

'Work,' the boy replied sullenly. 'I'm not to open the door to strangers.'

'Sorry young man I realise that. I'm not asking you to open it.' Pierre smiled at the boy. 'Tell me, how long will your mother be before she's back home?'

'She's gone to the shopping centre.'

Pierre realised he would be lucky to gather anything further from the boy and he fully understood why. The boy was doing exactly what his mother had told him not to do. The child should not have been left in the house alone. But Pierre didn't want to alarm him further.

'I'll come back later,' he concluded and, as he turned to leave, a woman came scurrying up the path towards the front door.

'What have I told you about opening the door to strangers?' she shouted to the boy. And then she turned, giving Pierre an angry stare. 'What is it you want?' she blustered.

'Sorry to trouble you but I'm looking for a Rick Stevens who used to live here. It's several years ago now, but I am hoping someone will know his whereabouts.'

'Never heard of him,' the woman declared, shaking her head and continuing to glare, suspiciously now. 'The Jacksons were here before us.'

'Thanks for that,' Pierre replied. 'It is important I find him. I'll ask the neighbours.'

'Don't bother going next door. They only moved in a month ago and it wasn't anyone called Stevens before them.' It was obvious the woman was now making a show of trying to help him.

Pierre, still intent on calling on the rest of the neighbours, thanked her and left. He skipped the house next door and called at the one after that. 'Sorry we've only been here a couple of years ourselves,' the woman told him.

But at the next house he had more joy. 'I remember vaguely the family living at number one. There were three of them, the husband, his wife and a boy of about six. I think they went to the west coast, but I couldn't be sure.' The man pondered momentarily. 'I'll tell you who would know, the people at number nine. They seemed to be quite good friends with the Stevenses.' The man stepped out of the house and peered up the road. 'You're lucky. They're in. The car's in the drive.'

Pierre felt he might be getting somewhere now that at least someone in the street recalled Stevens. He opened the gate of number nine and set off up the drive. But before he reached the front door, it opened. A woman in her forties appeared on the doorstep.

'Looking for someone?' It was obvious word had gone around.

'Yes. I believe you knew the Stevens family. I'm looking for Rick.'

'He's not in trouble is he?' The woman frowned.

'Not at all. We think he has a relative in England whom he may be able to help.'

'His mother or someone like that you mean?' The woman was obviously curious, and at the same time quizzing him to see if he was genuine.

But Pierre knew Rick's mother had moved out to join them some years earlier. 'Sorry I can't discuss anything with you. It's confidential. And as far as his mother's concerned, doesn't she live with them?'

'Maybe she does,' the woman replied, aware now that Pierre had tumbled to her ruse. Her face took on a pink flush.

'Did they move far?' Pierre continued.

'Over to the west, Hilary's Boatyard. He took over a diving and watersports equipment business.' The woman sighed. 'They may as well have gone to the other side of the world as far as we were concerned. They were good friends of ours, but we haven't seen them since. Never asked us over there, not even a Christmas card,' she maintained bitterly.

'I'm grateful for your help,' Pierre said, edging away and not wishing to become involved in her complaint. Maybe Stevens had been glad to see the back of her he thought as he looked again at the woman's sour face.

After a five-hour flight, Pierre landed in Perth. There he took a taxi to Hilary's and booked in at the nearest hotel. Once he'd changed into casual trousers and short-sleeved shirt he went along to the main shopping area and looked around for Stevens' business. There were several shops selling the same sort of gear but none of them had the name Stevens outside. Maybe that wasn't the name of the shop.

Pierre decided he needed to call in and make enquiries. But it seemed no one was overly willing to reveal Stevens' whereabouts, that was until Pierre decided to change tack and call at a gift shop.

'Rick Stevens' place you say?' the proprietor repeated.

Pierre nodded.

'It's in the arcade across the road. *Top Deck* it's called.'

'Have they been here long?' Pierre asked him.

'Five years or more,' he replied. 'Nice couple. From what I gathered they came over from Brisbane,' he continued. 'Shop's doing well. He has some real modern gear in there. All the youngsters seem to like the place.'

'So that's why the other shops were reluctant to tell me where they were.' Pierre grinned.

The man laughed. 'There's a bit of competition around here, especially in that sort of gear. Some of the things they sell are real pricey, you know, fancy labels and all that?'

'I know what you mean,' Pierre replied, humouring the guy, whom it seemed could talk for Australia. And eventually, Pierre managed to drag himself away and cross the road as he headed for *Top Deck*, the Stevens' shop.

Chapter 20
The Present – 2008

Danielle quickly felt the benefit of the antibiotics. Once they kicked in the pain in her back disappeared and her temperature dropped to normal. But whilst she waited for a donor to come forward, time seemed to drag.

'Is it absolutely essential that you obtain the blood, Mr Dexter?' she asked him on his next visit. 'Surely a transfusion is not always essential.'

'You're right. It isn't. But in your case, we must be prepared. You're still slightly anaemic, otherwise we could have taken your own blood in gradual stages and used that if necessary. But you know that's not possible Danielle.'

She shook her head and sighed. 'I'm wasting so much time hanging around in here. I wish someone would turn up soon.'

A voice intervened. 'We may already be on track.' Marcel was standing in the doorway directing his words to Danielle. 'But I need a word with Mr Dexter first. I'll be back to see you, cherie and tell what's happening.' He turned to the surgeon. 'Have you a minute?'

Dexter smiled. 'Sure. Come along into Sister's office.'

Marcel thought it best if he told Dexter about Pierre's search in Australia before he had a confidential word with Danielle. He wasn't sure how she'd react.

Dexter demonstrated a modicum of relief when Marcel told him about the search in Australia. 'But we can't raise our hopes too high,' he warned. 'The nearest match would obviously be an identical twin but since we don't have that option, the next best thing would be a close relative. Mrs Harlow was reasonably close but she didn't quite fit the bill. Maybe the father will. We need to stay positive.'

'Has anything turned up from the transfusion service yet?'

'Dr Fry tells me there are three people on the list of donors who are fairly close. But I would prefer to wait just a little longer in the hope this Stevens guy is found. We can afford that. Danielle's condition certainly hasn't worsened.'

Feeling a little tentative now, Marcel left Sister's office and wandered down the corridor back to Danielle's room. Danielle had known since she was a small child that Marcel was not her biological father, and she had always insisted she never wanted to see the man. But now they were getting closer to a revelation, Marcel had no idea how she would feel. But he kept on telling himself it was only for Danielle's well being that the search was on. And the guy might even refuse to acknowledge that Danielle was his child.

'I'm back, treasure,' Marcel said as he appeared in the doorway of Danielle's ward. He crossed over to the bed and kissed her gently before releasing her and sitting on the chair next to the bed. He took her hand in his.

'There's something I must tell you. In a way it's good news and bad.' He paused and rubbed the back of her hand.

'Get on with it, Papa. Don't keep me in suspense.' She squeezed his hand gently.

'Here goes then,' he continued. 'The investigator I told you about, Pierre Clarisse, is in Australia searching for your father.' Marcel maintained eye contact, waiting to see the reaction from his daughter.

'Australia?'

'That's right. Your father apparently emigrated before you were even born.'

'That man, you mean.' Danielle spat out the words. 'Don't call him my father, Papa. I never want to meet him. I hope that's the bad news.' She shook her head and smiled as if the very mention of the guy meant nothing. 'Go on, Papa.'

'Neither of us could ever acknowledge him as your true father, so from our point of view, yes that is the bad news.' Marcel let out a huge sigh. 'But the good news is that Pierre phoned me last night. He thinks he's located the guy and he's on his way to see him. He's apparently somewhere on the west coast. Obviously Pierre wants to sit down and talk calmly with him. There's no mileage in confronting the guy in some accusatory way. Pierre has agreed to phone me back this evening and let me know the latest information.'

'But it's not to say the guy will volunteer to supply the blood even if there is a good match,' Danielle maintained solemnly.

'Agreed, but that's why Pierre wants to talk rationally, face-to-face. He's good with people, extremely diplomatic. I'm sure once he gets the guy on his own, he'll easily persuade him.'

'I'm glad you've told me that. No one could ever replace you. You will always be my Papa.' She hugged him and then lay back on the pillow. 'But I'm becoming very restless. I've reached the stage now where it doesn't matter to me who my father is. I just need the blood so that Mr Dexter can get on with it.'

'I appreciate that, cherie. It's frustrating for me too. But there are only certain times when Pierre can contact me. They're nine hours ahead over there in Perth. It has to be either early morning or late night. I can't just pick up the phone and talk to him.'

'Then let's pray that something will turn up soon.' Danielle leant over and kissed Marcel on the cheek. 'It hasn't been as bad as you thought, telling me, has it, Papa?'

'Not at all. And I've been to church and had a word with Father. I think the whole of the congregation in Perenchies is praying for us,' he replied, a smile touching the corners of his mouth.

But Marcel knew that was only the start. He dreaded to think what would happen when he told her about Marie and this woman Joanna Harlow.

Top Deck had a huge frontage with wonderful displays in the windows. Pierre entered to find several shoppers browsing. A woman he guessed to be in her forties was stocking one of the rails with bikinis, and a man of a similar age was serving at the counter. Pierre was aware he must choose the right time to speak to someone, preferably the guy at the counter.

He busied himself wandering around the shop and checking various items, all the time keeping an eye on the guy who, once he'd served the customer, moved over to Pierre. 'Can I help you, sir?'

'Pierre Clarisse,' he said, introducing himself and holding out his hand. 'I'm looking for Rick Stevens.' He handed over a business card.

The guy smiled. 'You've found him.' He took Pierre's hand and shook it. But when he looked at the card, his face became serious. 'What's all this about? Private investigator?' he added, lowering his tone.

'It's nothing to be alarmed about, Mr, Stevens, but I wondered if maybe we could have a word somewhere, in private?'

'Come through into the back, Mr...?' he looked at the card, 'Clarisse, is it?'

'It is. I'm based in France but I'm working from England at present.'

'Come through,' he repeated, turning to the woman who was stocking the bikinis on the rail. 'I'm through in the back if you need me, love.'

Pierre followed and Stevens pointed to a chair next to the window. Pierre sat down. Stevens perched on the edge of the table nearby.

'Right. Whatever you want to talk to me about, let's get on with it,' Stevens said briskly.

'It's rather a delicate matter, Mr Stevens. I don't want to put you on the spot but,' he hesitated, 'it's regarding a child you fathered nineteen years ago.'

Stevens slid down from the table and stood directly in front of Pierre as though to challenge the statement.

'Maybe this isn't the right place to discuss the matter?' Pierre was aware the guy was staggered at the news.

Stevens stood rigid as though he'd been sprayed with an ice gun. He didn't move for several seconds, and then his forehead became furrowed. He released a heavy sigh and looked Pierre directly in the eyes.

'They say things come back to haunt you, don't they? You're referring to Joanna Falconer's child, I take it?' He shook his head as though in disbelief.

'That's right,' Pierre confirmed. 'But there's more to it than talking paternity. I'm not here to make any claims on Joanna's behalf. As far as I'm concerned we can keep the matter purely between the two of us. It's about Joanna's daughter, Danielle – your daughter too of course. She's in hospital waiting for an operation to remove one of her kidneys. Unfortunately she's anaemic and it may be that she needs blood during or after the operation. It's a long and convoluted story, Mr Stevens and I'd like to fill you in on the details, but not here. My first priority is to ask if you would be prepared to have a blood test and, if there is a match, would you donate blood for Danielle?'

Stevens shook his head once more as though to clear it. 'This has all come as a shock, Mr Clarisse.' He looked to the door. 'It's something that happened so far in the past I've never told Liz about it. I was only a lad at the time. I didn't see the need to tell her. But now it looks as though she's got to find out, but not like this.'

'That's the point I'm making, Mr Stevens. But would you be willing to have the test?' He pressed the question again. 'That's all I need to know for now. We can discuss things in more detail in private and I can put you more fully in the picture, maybe later today or tomorrow.'

'As soon as I shut up shop today, I'll tell Liz. She needs to know. And then could you meet me at the place across the road, *The Drum and Monkey*, say seven thirty when I've had time to sort things out?'

'That's fine Mr Stevens. Thanks for accommodating me so quickly.'

'I'm not saying I'll do as you ask, not without more details, but at least I'm willing to talk it through with you.'

Rick Stevens and his wife were there when Clarisse returned to Hilary's Boatyard and entered *The Drum and Monkey*. Rick stood up and shook hands with Pierre. 'I'd like to introduce Liz to you. I've told her everything, so we can speak openly.'

Pierre extended his hand. 'Pleased to meet you Mrs Stevens. I know it's a lot to ask, especially coming out of the blue like this, but I am hoping your husband can help us.'

'I hope so too. I feel for the girl. We have a son, Brett. He's fifteen, and I know I'd be at my wits' end if he was the one waiting for a donor.' She smiled and Pierre knew instantly that the woman was genuinely concerned for Danielle.

Rick intervened. 'Let's cut the formalities. We'd prefer Rick and Liz,' he announced, smiling, the tension having

273

disappeared. And Pierre recognised the relief on his face now that everything was out in the open.

'Then do call me Pierre,' he replied, now optimistic that he might get somewhere once he'd filled them in on the details.

'Before we start, Pierre, have you eaten? We're about to get a bar snack. I don't know if you're interested. We've had a busy day. Haven't had time to eat. And Brett's out playing tennis so we don't have to worry about him.'

'A bar snack would suit me too,' Pierre replied as Rick handed him the menu.

Throughout the meal, Pierre filled them in with the details of how Joanna had absconded from hospital and Danielle had been kidnapped and taken to France.

'My God,' Rick exclaimed. 'I just can't believe it. It's like some work of fiction. I'm surprised at Joanna. I would never have thought she would abandon the baby.' He shook his head. 'I can't take it all in.' He turned to his wife. 'You know I did ask her to come to Australia with me, I begged her in fact. But she wouldn't have it. She was very close to her parents and she refused to leave them.' He took a deep breath. 'The opportunity was here waiting for me but all she wanted to do was stay back there and carry on as normal. But that wasn't for me. I suppose I was irresponsible to leave her, but she was so stubborn. And I wasn't prepared to spend the rest of my life in a mundane job, just because she wanted it her way.'

'I must say, Rick, I'm surprised you left her especially when she was pregnant. That's not like you at all.' Liz Stevens looked down at her hands.

Rick reached over and took her hand in his. 'Believe me, Liz, you're right. It's not like me. But I was a twenty-one-year-old wanting to get on with my life and take up any opportunity to better myself.'

'Did she not write to you once you arrived in Australia?' Liz asked him.

'Not once. I left my address with her, and I wrote to her from Perth and Darwin a number of times, asking her to join me, but she never replied. What more could I do?'

Pierre intervened. 'I realise this is hard for you both to take in, but I can't see any mileage in your making judgements on something that happened so long ago. After all Joanna was irresponsible too, but like you, Rick, she was young and she was naive.'

'I suppose I have gone off at a tangent,' Liz admitted and she squeezed her husband's hand. 'And if you had stayed back or brought her over here, we would never have been together.' She looked directly into Rick's eyes. 'You didn't have to tell me about this, Rick, but we don't keep secrets do we? And you wanted to come clean. Pierre is right. I have gone all judgemental, but it's been such a shock. Believe me I do feel upset about Danielle.' She folded her arms. 'Let's try to sort things out and do our best to help.

'Thanks, Liz. I agree. I ought to get off to the hospital and check out my blood type straight away. After all from what you've told us, Pierre, time is precious.'

The medical people in Perth were quick off the mark and the results were with them in hours. But unfortunately the antigens were not present in Rick's blood. He was disappointed. Liz was too.

'How about if we ask Brett if he's willing to have his blood checked? It could be that there is a match,' Liz suggested.

'Good thinking,' Rick replied as he turned to the haematologist. 'What do you say?'

'It's unlikely,' he told them, 'but there could be the remotest chance.'

'It's worth a shot. But what do we tell him?' Rick was obviously worried that Brett would judge him if he found out about Danielle.

'There's no need for your son to know the details,' the haematologist suggested. 'The person needing the blood is a relative in England. I'm sure a fifteen-year-old is not going to want any details.'

'You're right,' Liz declared. 'Let's get on with it.'

But Brett's blood type was no match. Both Rick and Liz were bitterly disappointed. 'There's nothing more we can do, I suppose,' Rick asked.

'I'm afraid…' Pierre hesitated. 'It might be an idea if you have a DNA check. And then we'll have proof one way or another on the paternity front.'

'I'll do that and let you know. I don't suppose I could get in touch with Danielle or her father, once it's established?'

'I think it best if you didn't for now. Danielle doesn't know about Joanna yet. She's still under the impression Marie was her biological mother. Marcel has a hard task on his hands once the operation is over and he has to reveal the truth to her.' Pierre got up to leave. 'I need to get in touch with the airline and book myself back on a flight as soon I can. Thank you for being so positive. I'll let you know how things go. If when Danielle discovers the truth about her parentage she wants to contact you then would you be agreeable to my giving her your address? It's entirely up to you, although of course these days she is entitled to search for her biological parents.'

'I don't know about Rick,' Liz replied, 'but she'd be welcome as far as I'm concerned.'

'Thanks, Liz. The same goes for me. You know you can't help but feel curious to know what she's like.'

'I can't go into any details, Rick, not until she knows the truth, but she's a very clever girl. She's studying to become a doctor.'

Rick gasped. 'Then one of us has passed on the brains.' He smiled. 'But Joanna was always the brainy one of the two of us. I suppose she's married now,' he asked tentatively, a slight look of guilt on his face.

'She has a husband and seems happily married. He was very supportive when they came to the station.'

'That's a relief. I feel better now. I wouldn't have liked to think I'd ruined her life completely by leaving her to face things on her own.'

Marcel was bitterly disappointed when Pierre gave him the results of his search. 'It takes some swallowing. Surely someone somewhere has the right type?'

'Absolutely. At least we've established through the DNA test that Stevens is Danielle's father.' He patted Marcel on the back. 'Let's try to stay optimistic. How about if we go along and see Dr Fry together, tell him the outcome and ask his advice? You never know, maybe something's turned up.'

'I know what you're saying, Pierre but it's not easy to remain positive after everything that's happened. I've barely had a minute to think about Marie since I lost her, what with the problem of the blood donor constantly on my mind.'

'I understand, Marcel. I've been amazed at the way you've kept yourself afloat and put on a front for Danielle's sake.'

'I've had no alternative,' Marcel explained. 'I need to keep her spirits up, at least until she's had the operation.' He sighed heavily. 'And the worst is to come. God knows how she's going to take it when I have to explain how Joanna Harlow ran off and abandoned her. And that Marie was not her real Mama but a woman who snatched her from the paediatric ward.'

They left in silence and headed for the hospital to see Dr Fry.

'We've just about exhausted our contacts. As far as I'm aware there are no more relatives. Neither Rick Stevens nor Joanna Harlow has brothers or sisters. There were definitely no other siblings. So what happens next?' Marcel asked him.

Dr Fry pointed to a couple of chairs. Marcel and Pierre sat down. 'It's difficult I know, but I think now's the time to make a move,' he suggested. 'I'll have a word with Mr Dexter. He too is becoming anxious. He'd like to get on with the operation as soon as possible. Apparently over the last couple of days there's been a slight increase in the size of the growth. Things in general seem to have deteriorated since Danielle picked up the infection.' He shook his head. 'It's a pity she was allowed to leave the hospital,' he muttered disapprovingly.

Marcel was alarmed. 'You say the growth is bigger? Why haven't I been told?'

'The results of the test came out only this morning, Mr Dubois. Dexter hasn't seen you today I take it? Apparently it's nothing to worry about unduly. But Dexter feels we've pushed matters far enough.'

'I'll go along now and have a word with him.' Marcel stood up ready to leave.

'You won't catch him yet, Mr Dubois. I'm afraid he's in theatre this morning,' Dr Fry explained. He turned to check out Danielle's case notes on his computer. 'But don't rush off. I mentioned earlier there are three donors in England who are reasonably close, but we've also come up with someone in Pennsylvania with a much closer match. In view of the disappointing family results, I think that's as close as we're going to get.' He consulted the computer again. 'There are several units available right now.' He turned away from the computer. 'Perhaps that's the solution.' He stood up obviously wanting to get on with arrangements. 'Have you spoken to Danielle about the results of your search in Australia?'

'I thought it best to tell you first. I don't want to depress her even more.'

'Leave it with me, Mr Dubois. I'll have a word with Dexter as soon as he comes out of theatre and, once I've spoken to him, I'll go along and talk to Danielle. Perhaps it would be better coming from me.'

'I don't mind telling my daughter her biological father doesn't match her blood type. But it would be better if we had something positive to tell her at the same time.'

'I couldn't agree more. I'll get back to you as soon as I've discussed the matter with Dexter. If the units in Pennsylvania are still available perhaps he'll pencil in Danielle's operation on next week's list.' He clicked off the computer programme and turned to face them. 'Give me a couple of hours to sort things. Could you hang around and visit Danielle later – after I've explained things to her? That would mean you wouldn't have to dodge her questions when she asks about the results of the test in Australia. I'll come back to you as soon as I have something concrete to report.'

'She'll be expecting me, but I take your point. It is a good idea. You have my mobile number. I'll wait for your call.'

Chapter 21
The Present – 2008

Tom Trench had been with the *Leeds Gazette* over ten years now and he'd done his fair share of snooping. He could wheedle his way in, come up with fairly successful answers to most of his questions, and pull out a scoop. The problem was that he was due for a front-pager but they'd been thin on the ground since the Willis case, and that had been a sordid one. But that was months ago now.

He'd heard the announcement on the news asking the Grimshaw woman to come forward as a matter of urgency. Apparently there was no offence involved but the police were anxious to interview her. How many times had he heard that before – *no offence involved!* They couldn't kid Tom. Vince in the print room had told him the item had been placed in the paper. *How the hell had he missed that?* But it wasn't inserted by the police. According to the front desk it was a French guy who'd placed it in there. Tom was curious. What was the link between the Grimshaw woman and this Frenchie?

He needed more information but what was his next move? And then his mind focused on Sergeant Rob Cox. They were squash team mates. Maybe if he bought Rob a couple of pints when they met up at the *Stansfield Arms* on Thursday, he could stand to pick up a few snippets. They were due to play Railston, and after the match would be a good time to chat. Meanwhile, he'd keep in touch with Vince. As soon he found out a name for the French guy, Tom would pick things up from there.

Thursday came and they lost the match. Rob, the team captain, was not in the best of moods when they arrived at the pub for the after-match tipple. At first, he was reluctant to divulge anything about the Grimshaw case. He was more interested in carrying out a post-mortem on the squash match. But Tom stuck at it and pursued the case, trying to pick up whatever he could from the sergeant's responses to his questions.

'What's all this about the Grimshaw woman, you know, the woman the police urgently need to interview? What's she done, Rob?'

Rob leaned on the bar. 'She's done nothing. It revolves around a young lass who needs to find a parent,' he offered, in brief. 'They think Grimshaw could lead them to the mother.' He took a swig of his beer. 'That's all I know, Tom. It's not my case.'

Tom didn't quite understand and, even though it wasn't Rob's case, he pushed him further. 'Needs to find a parent? How do you mean?'

Rob's reply was matter-of-fact. 'The girl needs rare blood, something to do with an operation.'

Disappointed at Rob's casual approach, Tom dug deeper. 'I see,' he replied. 'Was that all? I thought it might have been something more serious.'

Rob huffed. 'Don't you think that's serious enough?'

Tom pulled a face. 'It doesn't make much of a story even if they do find her.'

Rob scowled, revealing his impatience. 'Look here, Tom. I hope we're not going to talk shop all night. I'm not at the station now. And I fancied a game of darts. Give a guy a break will you?'

'Sorry mate. There hasn't been much doing recently. I thought I could pull off a scoop if I could talk to the woman.' He sighed heavily. 'But as I said, there doesn't seem much to go on.'

'Believe me, there's something of a mystery attached to it, but I can't discuss that with you just yet. Catch up with me later and maybe I can fill you in.' He pulled out the arrows from the dartboard.

A mystery? Something Rob couldn't reveal? If Rob wasn't prepared to help him solve the mystery he'd need to check things out for himself some other way.

It was a few days later when Tom engineered his way into bumping into Rob again. And he couldn't believe his luck. According to Rob the Grimshaw woman had been found. And that wasn't all. Rumour had it that she was the woman who'd abandoned her kid all those years ago. Tom had been working for the *Keighley Chronicle* at the time, but he remembered it vividly. They'd searched high and low for the young lass who'd gone off and left the baby in Murray Park Hospital. And then all hell was let loose when somebody went in there and snatched the child. The case had never been solved.

And now the police had interviewed Paula Grimshaw and, according to Rob, that wasn't her name at all, it was Joanna Harlow. But who'd taken the baby from the hospital in Manchester? If only he could set up a meet with this French guy, the one looking for the blood donor. It could be that he knew the name of the woman who'd taken the child. But, if he couldn't find that out, he could make a reasonable story out of the Harlow woman's confession. It might not be front-page stuff, but did it matter? It was a story. And it was a start. Maybe he could tie the rest in later.

The next step was to find out where she lived. And he could do that discretely enough. He'd had enough practice. The police had apparently finished with her now, and the guy who'd hired the French PI had asked them not to bring about any charges. All he wanted was a donor for his daughter. Well, he called her his daughter but how could he be the father? Tom was getting more excited by the minute.

Rob had mentioned something about Belmore, and that wasn't too far out of the city centre. Tom decided once he discovered where the Harlow woman lived he'd give her a ring, offer her something for the story.

There were over thirty Harlows in the directory, but Tom was patient, although it would help if he could find out from Rob the name of the woman's husband.

'I've no idea, Tom. There's nothing more I can tell you. And there's one thing for certain, I'm not about to look up the name of the guy in the case file and give it you on the QT, not after my brush with the inspector last year. There's no way I'm going to mucky my ticket again.'

'Brush with the inspector? What was all that about?'

'Come off it, Tom. No more I said. End of story!'

Danielle closed her eyes. The hospital bed felt hard beneath her body, and now she'd been refused permission to get up and wander about like she had been doing before. And as if that wasn't enough her stomach had started to swell, and that worried her. She envisaged the kidney pumping up like a balloon inside her. All she wanted was for Mr Dexter to get rid of it. The more these thoughts preyed on her mind, the more anxious she became. She turned over on to her side and closed her eyes, hoping to shake off the feeling of depression that was building up inside her.

At first her mind was engraved with a single thought – *I need Mama to help me through this ordeal.* But Mama wasn't there and never would be. Danielle flicked her eyelids to shake away the tears that were welling up. They began to steal down her cheeks and she tried to brush them away. And then several conflicting thoughts tippled through her mind and became entangled. The heartache and frustration inside her was driving her mad so much so that her head felt fit to burst.

In an effort to overcome the negative feelings, she sat up in bed, took a tissue and dried her face. Slipping a magazine from the locker, an issue she'd read over and over again, she absently turned the first page and stared vacantly. And then a sound penetrated her mind. She jumped visibly, drawing in a sharp breath.

'Can we come in?' came a chorus from the doorway. Danielle looked up. It was James and Amy. Danielle exhaled. She was becoming edgy these days. But, relieved it wasn't one of the nurses set to carry out yet another test, she pulled herself up in the bed and smiled.

'It's so good to see you.' She stretched out, leant forward and offered her cheek. James took her hands, pulled her close and planted a kiss there.

Amy gave her a big squeeze and then held her at arms length. 'It's taking long enough to find that donor, Danielle.'

Danielle tried to suppress her emotions. 'Tell me about it,' she shook her head. 'I'm beginning to think they'll never find anyone. It's been weeks now and still no luck.'

'But surely there's the whole world to go at,' James protested.

'Exactly. They're searching for someone in Australia just now,' Danielle told them, not mentioning that it was her biological father they were looking for. 'It's all so drawn out.'

James sat down on one of the bedside chairs and suddenly his brow furrowed.

'Something wrong, James?' Amy asked him.

'Nothing wrong, Amy. It's just an idea, one we haven't even considered before.' The frown disappeared and he smiled. 'How about if we ask the donor service to come into uni for donors? It didn't occur to me earlier, simply because you've mentioned how rare the blood type is. But it's worth a shot. I'd be willing to get involved for a start.'

'Me too,' Amy echoed. 'Who's in charge of that sort of thing?'

Danielle beamed. 'I know it's unlikely they'll find anyone, but it would be a miracle if they did. Dr Fry is the consultant haematologist,' she told them. 'He'd make all the necessary arrangements I'm sure. It's a brilliant idea but perhaps you'd prefer to wait until the Australian check is through? It shouldn't be long now.'

'There's nothing to be gained by waiting,' Amy stressed. 'We need to get on with it. Even if there's no match for your blood, we're sure to be of benefit to someone.'

'True,' Danielle admitted. 'After all as far as we know most of the students are young and healthy.'

'Exactly and there's no reason why some of the lecturers shouldn't offer to donate too.' James became even more enthusiastic. 'Come on Amy, we'll ask Sister how we can contact this Dr Fry, and see if he's available to see us – right now. The sooner we sort it the better.' They turned to leave, smiling back at Danielle. 'We'll be back, hopefully with good news, as soon as we've managed to pin him down.'

Dr Fry smiled and nodded his head. 'It's a sound idea, although many of the today's youngsters are already donors, especially students who see it as "a good cause". But I'll get on to the service right now and see what can be done.' He picked up the phone and pointed to the seats in front of his desk. 'Do sit down.'

They listened as Dr Fry explained the urgency of the situation to one of the senior officers and, as he replaced the phone, he turned to face them. 'You heard what I said. They've agreed to contact the bursar at the university – obviously they'll need permission. Assuming he agrees, someone will take posters and place them in the corridors. They aim to be available on campus the day after tomorrow.'

'Great,' Amy replied and then she glanced up at the doctor. 'But I'm sure Danielle wouldn't want to be identified as the one needing the blood type.'

'They'll be no mention of specific recipients. It'll be another trawl for donors as far as the students are concerned. And it goes without saying; strict confidentiality is always maintained. But I must have a word with Danielle herself. She'll need to give permission for us to tell the bursar what it's all about – in confidence of course – and of the reason for the transfusion service's attendance at such short notice.'

'Then let's hope something comes of it,' James replied.

When James and Amy left Dr Fry they returned to Danielle's ward. She was reading when they entered.

'Organised,' James told her, a smug look on his face. 'Barring the red tape, a couple of days and that's it. So let's hope there's someone out there who can help.'

'The silly thing is that no one thought about it before,' Amy confessed.

'Well, you've organised it now, and I can't tell you how grateful I am.' Danielle smiled and sent up a secret prayer. *Please let them find someone to help*, she begged.

Marcel was overjoyed when Dr Fry explained. 'I must say I'm really impressed. The kids have only known each other a term and here they are giving their full support.'

'Exactly, and we complain about today's youth. But when something like this happens they're out in force, showing their loyalties.'

'What do you reckon the chances are, Dr Fry?' Marcel asked.

The consultant pulled a face. 'Less than point nought-nought-one per cent,' he replied. 'The type really is extremely rare.'

'Then all we can do is wait for the outcome.'

'Absolutely. I've had a word with Mr Dexter. In view of the deterioration in Danielle's condition he's agreed to schedule the operation for a week Wednesday. I've been to see Danielle and told her the news. She's accepted the fact that the Australian contact was not a match.'

'How did she seem?'

'I was surprised how readily she accepted the news. But I think this was because her two friends had suggested the service visit the campus. I'm sure that helped.'

'Then I can go in and see her now.'

'You can, Mr Dubois. I think she'll be looking forward to telling you the news.' Dr Fry opened the door. 'By the way, I've checked on the Pennsylvania donor and the units are still available. The donor is ready and willing to become involved if more is needed, which is good news.' He picked up a copy e-mail from his desk and waved it in the air. 'Here's the reply from the States. They're pretty efficient over there.'

'How long does it take before you can obtain the units?'

'The time it takes for an aircraft to get here, plus road transport of course, and there again the service here is excellent.'

'Will you wait until the service has visited the university before you make arrangements for the units to be flown here?'

'Not necessarily. We'll need it here before Mr Dexter goes ahead. I don't hold out much hope of finding anyone within the university. It's merely another possible source that we can't afford to overlook.'

When Marcel left Dr Fry's office he called in to see Sister on Danielle's ward.

'I'm afraid Danielle is a little off colour today, Mr Dubois. Her temperature's up and she's worried about the excessive swelling, which doesn't help. Apparently Mr Dexter has made a decision to operate next week. All I can hope is that she keeps up her strength ready for the operation.'

'It's worrying,' Marcel replied, frowning. 'I thought it was too good to be true.'

'There's time yet. Her temperature could be down in a couple of days. But I hear what you're saying. The sooner we get this over with, the better.'

'It's all right for me to go in and see her, isn't it?' Marcel asked. 'There are things we need to discuss – nothing too serious.'

'That's fine, Mr Dubois. But try not to tire her. Half an hour at the most.'

'That suits me. I need to get back to my hotel. I've so much to organise. I've been away from the office for the last couple of weeks.'

'You must be worn out with it all. Do take care not to overdo it. Danielle will need you after the operation.' Sister folded her arms. 'I think she's been holding back since you lost your wife. She's been trying to maintain her strength for the operation. But she can't go on much longer. It's got to come out some time.'

'We'll grieve together once this is over. My feet have barely touched the ground since Marie died. The sooner this business is sorted, the better. And then perhaps Danielle and I can spend quality time together.'

'Good idea, at least for her convalescence. She won't be back at university for some time. You could catch up on things and, as you say, grieve together.'

Dr Fry couldn't get to the phone quickly enough. 'Mr Dubois, we've found a very close match amongst the students, closer than the woman in Pennsylvania.'

'I don't believe it,' Marcel replied as he struggled to take in the words. 'What does that mean?'

'It means we have enough for transfusion in the first instance, that's if it's necessary.'

'Then are you saying the operation can still go ahead as planned?'

'That's right.'

'And who is this person, this donor?'

'We're not told. Confidentiality must be maintained, unless of course the donor wishes to disclose his or her name. But it's so uncanny that there's someone with such a close match.'

'All I can say, Dr Fry is that it's a miracle. I'll certainly attend mass this evening and offer up my prayers.'

'You do that, Mr Dubois. We must all have faith.'

Marcel's spirits rose. The students had come up with the idea and it had been a stab in the dark. But the exercise was fruitful. Someone out there had a similar blood type to Danielle's which, as Dr Fry had said, was uncanny. But these miracles happen. And weren't they due for one after the ordeal of the last couple of months?

Before he left the hotel he telephoned Pierre and gave him the news.

'It looks as though our search could be over, Pierre. I've had a call from Dr Fry. They've found a donor.'

'That's wonderful news, Marcel. Perhaps I can get back to France now.'

'Of course, Pierre.'

'You will let me know how things go, won't you?'

'You'll be the first to know after all the work you've put in. Thanks to you we're starting with a clean slate. Danielle's parentage is no longer a mystery. It had to come out some time. Hopefully, we've no more shocks to come.' He sighed. 'I am worried of course. I will be until the operation is over and Danielle's health is back to normal.'

'But that's only natural. Good luck, Marcel.'

Tom Trench was still sniffing around for a front-pager when he bumped into Rob Cox again – accidentally on purpose. 'Any news on the Harlow case?' he asked.

'The woman's admitted absconding and leaving her child at Murray Park in Manchester. And the French guy you mentioned, the one who put the ad in the newspaper, he's a PI working for the girl's French stepfather. The mother is the one who kidnapped the child. She died a few weeks ago.'

Tom whistled through his teeth.

Rob continued. 'It was so long ago there are no charges. In fact the stepfather wants to keep the whole issue low profile. You can understand why, can't you?'

'Fancy that! I'd imagine the Harlow woman wants to keep things low profile too. But we'll see about that. What sort of person is she, abandoning a newborn child?'

'Exactly! But whatever you do, if you follow this lead don't mention my name.'

Tom tapped his nose. 'Mum's the word,' he replied and smirked. 'You don't want any more trouble do you?'

Rob glared. 'You can stop that or it's the last time I feed you any juicy snippets.'

'Only joking, Rob,' Tom insisted, wondering why he didn't keep his big mouth shut. But he smiled to himself as he left Rob in the pub car park. Had he finally hit the jackpot?

The next morning he sat in his car at the end of the road and rang Joanna Harlow from his mobile. 'I'd like to speak to Mrs Harlow please.'

'Speaking,' she replied.

'I wonder if I might have a word with you, Mrs Harlow. It could be worth your while.'

'What do you mean by that? Who are you?'

'I'm from the LEEDS GAZETTE. I wondered if we could run a story on you, you know, the human angle?'

'I don't know what you're talking about...' The phone clicked dead.

Blast! He'd cocked it up. He must be losing his touch.

He contemplated. Maybe the phone call had been a mistake. Maybe he should hang about there and hope for a face-to-face interview. A little surveillance wouldn't hurt. He'd wait until someone came out from the house, hopefully Joanna herself or the hubby maybe. The thought crossed his mind that the hubby might be more open to a bit of a back-hander. He felt sure he could persuade the editor to cough up. He'd get the truth out of someone whatever happened.

He rubbed his hands together and tried to get the circulation going. He wasn't a hot-blooded lad any longer bouncing with health. It was no joke this sitting about waiting for something to happen – anything would suit as long as he could come up with a story at the end of it. And he was so busy feeling sorry for himself he almost missed the guy walking down the garden path. In Tom's estimation he'd be mid forties. Now could he be the husband?

Tom decided to change tack. He'd follow the husband instead of pursuing the woman, assuming he was her husband. But not today. Cold and hungry, he'd had enough for now. He needed to get back to the office, warm himself through and get a bite to eat. And there was always tomorrow. He had a clear enough picture of the guy in his mind. He'd recognise him again. Perhaps if he got there early next morning he could wait until the husband came out of the house again and follow him.

It was seven o'clock when Tom took up his place at a spot where he was partially hidden on spare ground at the end of the road, the Harlow house still in view. At seven thirty a large, silver Volkswagen reversed down the drive and pulled out into the road. Tom switched on his car engine. He couldn't figure out who was driving. It would be a bonus if it was the woman herself.

Tom set off after the car, peering through the windscreen to figure out the sex of the person driving. When they stopped at a traffic light he took a closer look. It was just as he thought. He now knew for sure it was a man and, once they moved off from the lights, the guy put on speed. Tom put his foot down. He didn't want to lose him now that his luck was in.

The ring road was busy when Tom caught up with him. He hoped he could stay with the guy. It only took someone to slip in between them, slow him down and the guy could speed ahead out of sight. Fortunately, Tom managed to stay directly behind and, at the next roundabout the guy turned left, taking a minor road which led to a narrow track. Tom followed. This could be tricky!

The guy slowed down and approached a pair of large iron gates, which opened up before him. He continued through and waved to the security guard perched high above in a booth just inside the gates. Immediately the Volkswagen passed through, the gates closed behind him. Not wanting the guard to become suspicious, Tom turned around ready to leave, but before he did so he looked up and memorised the name of the company, J. Whiteley & Son Limited, Engineers.

He acknowledged it was going to be difficult latching on to Harlow, unless he could find out where the guy socialised. Was

292

there a particular pub or a club he frequented? And even though Tom had taken the name of the company, there was little mileage in returning and waiting for the guy to leave. All he could do was follow him home, and then what? Maybe it had been a futile journey. But the company name might come in useful later. It depended how things developed. But now he must think again.

Chapter 22
The Present – 2008

Now that a donor had been identified there was nothing to stop the operation from taking place. Afterwards when Danielle opened her eyes the grogginess made her head swim and all she wanted was to close her eyes again. Her hand was drawn to the padding covering the wound and she immediately felt the soreness. She winced.

'It's over,' Sister whispered as she bent over Danielle. 'We're on the home straight now.' The words echoed inside Danielle's head. *It's over – at last!* And Sister's words began to soothe that strange feeling of apprehension, helping the uneasiness to disappear.

Danielle opened her eyes once more and looked up. Mr Dexter was standing beside Sister. 'How are you feeling, my dear?'

'Fine,' she murmured putting on a brave smile. 'Did everything go to plan?'

'Absolutely,' he replied. 'And not before time!' He smiled in response, adding a lift to his voice. 'A few weeks' convalescence and you'll be good as new.'

'And the transfusion?' Danielle envisaged someone else's lifeblood rushing through her veins.

'For the time being it wasn't necessary.'

Danielle sighed. 'After waiting so long?' she whispered.

'That's right,' Dexter confirmed. 'But we had to take precautions.' He took her hand. 'We're leaving things to settle.'

He hesitated. 'We may need to transfuse later, dependant upon how things go. It is possible the presence of the diseased kidney was causing the anaemia, we're not absolutely sure. And now the kidney has been excised, the anaemia may disappear completely.' He patted her hand. 'At least we know the blood is available should we need it when the test results come through.'

Sister bent over to straighten her covers. 'Rest now before your visitors arrive,' she suggested, turning to leave the ward with the consultant.

The minute Danielle closed her eyes Papa arrived, his face still bathed in concern. 'Thank God it's over. Progress at last, treasure.' He gently kissed her cheek. 'How are you feeling?'

Danielle opened her eyes and smiled, a drowsy smile, as she felt a tiny surge of elation. She had crossed a thin, shaky line but now it was only a matter of time before she was up and about again. 'Better than I expected to feel.'

'I can't wait to take you home with me.'

'I know, Papa.' She turned her head towards him. 'Sister told me they didn't have to transfuse.'

'That's right. It's amazing after all the effort they put in to find a donor, and all the time you've waited. But it was worth it, cherie, just to know the match was available if it was needed.' Marcel sat down on the chair beside the bed. 'Take a little nap if you're tired. I'm happy just to sit here, knowing that everything's OK now.'

Neither of them spoke for a moment or two but somehow Danielle couldn't rest. An important question was floating about inside her head. 'Papa, can you find out who gave the blood? Even though I didn't need it, I'd like to thank whoever it was.'

'I don't think there's any chance of that. They usually remain anonymous.'

'That's a pity. I presume it was someone from uni,' she murmured as she closed her eyes again, hoping to recharge her system as she drifted off to sleep.

When she woke up her father had left. She stuck out her hand and clasped her fingers around the watch on the locker beside her. It was maybe a couple of hours since she'd closed her eyes. She slipped the watch back on top of the locker, and then she touched her fingers on the dressing covering the wound. The area was still very sore but the pain seemed to be lessening by the minute. She must try not to touch it or put on any pressure in that area. It shouldn't be long before they removed the padding and then, hopefully, it would quickly heal. So far so good.

When she was given permission to get out of bed and sit in an armchair, she knew she was on the mend. Maybe someone else would need the blood. She certainly felt she would make a full recovery without it.

Although she had missed several weeks at university, she'd had visits from one of the lecturers who'd given up time to give her private tuition once she'd shaken off the general anaesthetic. 'You may need to start at year one again,' he told her, 'but we'll see how things pan out once you're back with us.'

When he left the ward, Staff Nurse came in with Danielle's medication. 'Mr Dexter is delighted at the progress you've made so soon after the operation,' she claimed. 'You may be allowed to go home next week if it continues.'

Danielle's eyes lit up. 'That would be wonderful. Papa will be pleased. He'll pick me up as soon as I have permission and I'll return to France with him for a week or so.' She held out her hand for the glass of water and the pills.

'Steady on, love,' Staff Nurse replied. 'Don't build your hopes. Wait until your next blood check.' She shook her head. 'And you'll be at home a jolly sight longer than a week.'

'Well, whatever. But I can't wait to go back and be with Papa again.' She pondered. 'And it'll give me the chance to see Mama's grave and say my goodbyes.' She fluttered her eyelids and tried to lighten up. Although that devastating rawness inside had failed to ease, the tears had lessened. 'I've been patient so far,' she added, 'I'm sure a few more days won't make a great deal of difference. But I feel fine now. All I want is for things to get back to normal again.'

Staff Nurse slipped her arm around Danielle. 'You've been an ideal patient, love. In a way, we'll be sorry to see you go although we're delighted things have turned out so well.'

When Staff Nurse left the ward, Danielle put her feet on the footstool, shuffled about in the armchair until she was comfortable, sat back and relaxed. Sister had insisted she took a rest after the study she'd put in, and with that in mind Danielle decided to watch television, but it had to be something light. She flicked through the programmes, eventually choosing a game show she hadn't seen before. A contestant came out and started to choose box numbers. Danielle was puzzled. What a strange game. There are no questions to answer. It was pure luck.

Just as she became engrossed and was beginning to enjoy the programme, she was startled by a gentle tap on the door. James was standing there, a bunch of flowers in his hand. He walked over to Danielle, leant over and kissed her. 'Sorry I haven't been for a few days,' he offered. 'But I've been under so much pressure with the workload. What with end-tests and then visits to the courts, I haven't had a minute to spare.'

Danielle took the flowers. 'I'm so glad to see you, James. And don't worry. Come and sit down.' She pointed to the chair next to her locker. Gazing at the flowers, she said, 'They're lovely. But you shouldn't have.'

She made to place them on the locker but James reached out. 'Don't get up,' he insisted and immediately took them from her. 'I'll put them over here and ask the nurse for a vase when she comes in.' He pulled out the chair from beside the bed and sat close to Danielle. 'I didn't know how you'd be feeling. The last time I came you were out for the count most of the time I was here.' He smiled.

Danielle laughed. 'Oh dear. I do apologise. Hope I wasn't snoring,' she joked.

James joined in the laughter. 'That's not possible from someone as delicate and feminine as you,' he told her, his eyes conveying the love that flooded into him, swamping him completely. He took her hand and kissed it gently. 'You've no idea how I'm missing you.'

Danielle felt her heart skip as she blinked her tired eyes and locked them on to his. 'I've missed you too,' she told him, suddenly realising she was being a little forward in her response.

He slipped an arm around her, squeezing her shoulder gently and popping another kiss on her cheek before staring across at the television screen. 'I hope I'm not disturbing your viewing.'

'Not at all.' She picked up the control and turned the TV off. 'It was a case of something light, something to make me relax.'

'Well maybe I can make you relax,' he told her, grinning and snuggling up to her. And something in the gentleness of his tone touched her. His body was warm and inviting as she lay in the crook of his arm. As her hair tumbled over her face, James smoothed it back from her forehead and gently took hold of her chin before kissing her on the lips. A surge of emotion flooded every part of her and shudders of pleasure raced through her body. She quickly tucked away the urge to respond and offer her lips to him again. Her mind drifted. She knew beyond all doubt how she felt about him.

By this time the usual debate was raging in her head. Could she afford for this to develop? But she felt so comfortable in his arms, why shouldn't she give in?

When Sister came in to check her temperature, James took his arm away and eased himself back into his chair, now looking towards Danielle with a gentle, luminous gaze.

'Hope your temp's not up,' Sister joked giving James a meaningful look, 'or we may have to keep you in longer.'

Although Danielle found it hard to concentrate, she managed to reply. 'Don't say that, Sister. Staff tells me I'll be out of here within days.'

'Only if you behave,' Sister continued as she glanced once more in James' direction and winked.

By the time Sister had completed her checks the magic was broken.

'I hear you've had one of the tutors here to see you,' James offered.

'It was Doc Strachan. He's been three times so far. I'm really impressed. I think he realises how hard I worked before all this happened. He's hoping I'll catch up. But of course, none of us knows how long it'll be before I'm allowed back to uni.'

James gave her another squeeze. 'I do hope you manage to catch up, Danni. It's a hell of a job keeping on top, even with full-time attendance.'

'Tell me about it,' Danielle replied. 'But I'm not prepared to make myself ill again for the sake of an extra year. I don't mind starting afresh. What's another year?'

'Exactly, although I'm keen to start earning some money, and the sooner the better.'

'Me too, eventually. But that's the least of my worries for the time being.' She turned and looked once more at the flowers. 'They really are gorgeous. I'll get Staff to put them in water when she comes back.' She hesitated. 'By the way, I've been meaning to ask you; what happened with the National Blood Service? Did you ever find out whose blood type matched mine? I believe it was someone from uni.' She smiled. 'Of course they didn't have to transfuse after all that waiting, but wasn't it amazing that they found a compatible type after the trawl?'

'Absolutely. But we've no idea who the prospective donor might have been.'

Danielle was waiting for her father to arrive when James called in to say goodbye before she left for France. 'I'll miss you, Danni,' he said, taking her hands, leaning forward and kissing her. 'Don't stay away too long.'

Danielle laughed. 'I'm hoping to be back after the Easter holidays. That's if they'll let me.'

'I'm sure they will. You're looking fit already,' he added, slapping a cheeky grin on his face.

'Behave, James. Papa will be here soon,' Danielle replied, but she couldn't help but smile at his comment. He was such a fool with his light-hearted banter.

James looked to the door. 'OK. Got the message,' he said, still grinning as he stood up to leave.

'I'll be back soon,' Danielle promised. 'They can't keep a good girl down,' she clichéd, laughing. And as James left the ward, Danielle realised she'd now reached the stage where she couldn't deny him any longer. She was falling deeper and deeper in love with him.

They'd been back home in Perenchies only a few days when Marcel dropped the bombshell. Danielle just couldn't believe his words.

'I'm sorry to break it this way, treasure and I wish I didn't have to tell you, but during the search for a donor, Pierre discovered something about Mama that I know will upset you.'

'How do you mean, Papa?' His words set her stomach lurching. What did he mean by that?

Marcel coughed, a nervous cough. 'It's difficult to break it gently, treasure, but Mama was not your natural mother. Your real mother abandoned you and Mama wanted you so much that she took you from a hospital ward soon after you were born.'

'You mean I was someone else's baby and Mama stole me?'

Marcel nodded.

Danielle held her head in her hands and the words kept on rattling around inside. Tears pricked the backs of her eyes. How much more could she take? She'd accepted the fact many years ago that Papa was not her real father, and now he tells her Mama wasn't related either, and that some other woman had absconded, leaving her in the hospital only a day after she was born.

At first, the words wouldn't sink in. She shook her head. 'It's not true, it can't be.'

Marcel took her hands. 'It is true, cherie, but Mama was desperate and she loved you dearly.' He told her about Joanna and Rick.

And then, lost in a wilderness, those desperate feelings flooded over her and she couldn't seem to fight her way back. *I don't know who I am any more, except that I must be somebody nobody wanted.* She looked up. 'Why wasn't I told? Why did Mama hold out on me?' Danielle blurted out, burying her face in her hands.

'How could she tell you? She knew that what she had done was wrong. But she was desperate to have you. And then as you got older, she didn't want to lose you. If the authorities had found out they would have taken you away.' He shook his head. 'She didn't even tell me, treasure. I found out the hard way,' he insisted.

A rush of heat surged through her. 'But I wouldn't have left Mama, even if she'd told me. I wouldn't have gone with them. I would have kept on coming back. She's the only mother I've ever known and loved.' Danielle stood up and paced the room. 'And that Joanna woman. She didn't want me. Why else would she have left me there in the hospital? How could she do it? I wouldn't treat a dog like that. And the guy in Australia, the one who's supposed to be my father, he didn't want me either. He was a coward, scuttling off to the other side of the world as soon as the merest inkling of potential fatherhood surfaced. He was too scared to face up to things. He couldn't accept responsibility for me,' she ranted, knowing that whilst it wasn't Papa's fault that all this had happened in the past – before he'd even met Mama – she had to offload on to someone.

Marcel squeezed her hands. 'I agree, treasure. But look on the positive side. You were lucky it happened. Always remember, Mama wanted you. She wouldn't have put herself at risk otherwise.'

'I know what you're saying, Papa,' Danielle replied, immediately regretting her outburst. 'And I'm sorry to be pouring out my frustrations on you, but I feel so let down. And you're right. Mama would have done anything to have me.' She pondered. 'But maybe she felt sorry for me when she heard I'd been abandoned.'

Marcel's reply was brusque. 'Don't say that, Danielle. And stop feeling sorry for yourself.' He shook his head. 'How can you think such a thing when Mama risked both her job and her reputation? She could have been sent to prison if she'd been caught, all because she was desperate to keep you,' he added firmly.

'I know, I know. And, of course, I realise she wanted me, but you don't know how it feels to discover the truth after all these years.'

'I understand, treasure, but Mama would have told you eventually. Had she known you were ill, or that she, herself, had not long to live, the truth would have come out before she died. But she's gone to rest thinking what a happy family we were, so let's try to keep it that way.'

'You're right, Papa. But I need to get over this in my own way.'

They left the house in Perenchies and set out for the cemetery, travelling in complete silence, Marcel from time to time glancing sideways at his daughter. She had said she must see Mama's grave to convince herself once and for all that Mama was gone forever. Marcel's stomach churned. How would he ever get over losing Marie?

But he was worrying about his own feelings and that was selfish of him. At least he'd been there at the service to say his goodbyes to Marie. Danielle had been denied that opportunity, she'd been excluded from all that, and now she would need his support to get through the day's ordeal.

He took her hand as they entered the gates to the little churchyard and she gripped it tightly. Marcel was aware that her eyes had started to glisten, but they must get this over with. It was the only way. Danielle had talked of nothing more since she was discharged from Deansgate Royal.

Marcel went ahead and approached the grave. He turned to Danielle who was following closely behind him and pointed to the tombstone. 'I'm glad the stone is in place now. I hope you agree with the epitaph.'

Tears began to trickle, slowly at first, down Danielle's face as she knelt on the grass beside the grave. Her heart tumbled in her chest with love for Mama, and then her stomach began to churn violently. She would never see Mama again. She took a deep breath and tried to stop her emotions from getting the better of her. But it was useless. After placing the flowers on the earth in front of the tombstone, she fingered the words on the stone itself. 'They're exactly what I would have chosen, Papa.' She closed her eyes and now the tears began to flow. Clasping her hands together, she offered up a silent prayer, thanking God for sending Mama to care for her and asking that He keep her safe forever.

And then a state of calmness seemed to take over. She took out a tissue from her pocket and wiped the tears from her cheeks, opening her eyes now and staring at the tombstone. She gulped in air. 'It's sinking in now, Papa. But I'll never get over losing Mama.'

Marcel held out his hand to pull Danielle to her feet. He slipped his arm around her shoulders. 'Nor will I, cherie. But now we can grieve together.'

Danielle nodded as Marcel steered her away from the grave, back through the grounds and towards the door of the little church. They went inside, lit candles and knelt once more in prayer.

The sun was shining when they left the church and headed for the car park. They looked at each other and Marcel gave her a hug. 'Come on, treasure. Let's get back home and you can tell me all about your course at university.'

Danielle smiled. 'We haven't had the time for that, have we Papa? We've been caught up in too many other things. But, yes, I would like to talk things through with you. Whether they'll allow me back into second year, I don't know. But I don't mind staying down, if that's what's best for me.'

After three weeks with Papa in Perenchies, they travelled back to Edinburgh to see Mr Dexter for a follow-up appointment. 'We made it at last, Danielle,' the surgeon said, a smile on his face. 'And your progress has been remarkable. I can't tell you how delighted I am.'

'When can I go back to university, Mr Dexter?' Danielle rubbed her hands together in anticipation.

'I'd say another couple of weeks respite and then back to work. I must insist you monitor yourself whilst you're studying. Don't get too tired and overworked. Don't go gallivanting with the others,' he grinned, 'at least not for a while.'

'That's great. I'll contact my tutors and let them know.'

'Make another appointment to be seen in three months' time.' He took her hand and squeezed it. 'Do take care, my dear.'

They left the hospital and went into the city for lunch before heading for the university. 'I'll let them know I'll be back in a couple of weeks, Papa.' Danielle turned to him. 'You will be all right without me won't you?'

'Of course I will, treasure. I'll miss you, but it's not long to the end of summer term. And I've so much work to catch up at the office, I need the time to sort it.'

'That's great. If we both become engrossed in our work, maybe it will see us through, just until I'm back home again for the summer break.'

'Agreed. Let's try to keep strong. I'm sure that's what Mama would have wanted.'

Chapter 23
The Present – 2008

The request came unexpectedly, but Danielle agreed to see Joanna Harlow, more than anything to see what the woman was like and to tell her exactly what she thought about her.

'I know this is going to be an ordeal for you, treasure. Would you like me to come with you?' Marcel was anxious.

Danielle shook her head. She was strong now. The truth was out and she was prepared to face the consequences. On the surface she'd accommodated everything her father had told her and with the operation over, she was recovering well. For as much as her father had been her crutch throughout the ordeal, she no longer needed him to hold her hand. She could cope.

'I know you've always been there for me, Papa, and all you want to do is protect me. But this is something I must do on my own.'

Danielle was early and several people came and went as, stern-faced, she sat on a small sofa in the foyer of the hotel, her eyes fixed on the revolving door. All she wanted was to get on with it.

After ten minutes a woman entered and looked around. Danielle took in her features. Small and attractive with fair hair styled neatly in a pleat at the back, she couldn't possibly be Joanna. The two of them didn't appear to have a single physical characteristic in common. But Danielle began to have second thoughts when it became obvious the woman, anxiously twisting the edge of her scarf, was searching the foyer for someone. And then she spotted Danielle.

Danielle took a steadying breath, taking her time as she turned her head to study the woman. *She must be Joanna. But why that look? Stupid woman! And how can she be worried? She wouldn't have abandoned me in the first place if that was how she felt. What sort of person is she?* In that moment of realisation, it wasn't easy for her to cover those extreme emotions of resentment and anger.

The woman walked over to where Danielle was sitting and held out her hand. But Danielle shrugged and looked away, refusing to take it. *How dare she come along as though nothing had happened, trying to act as though she could possibly take the place of Mama, or at least what she imagined it would be like to take her place?*

'I take it you're Danielle. I'm Joanna.' She smiled and sat down on the sofa opposite. 'I can see this is going to be awkward for both of us.'

Danielle was determined to show the woman she didn't care. She frowned and leant back on the sofa. 'For you maybe, but not for me,' she insisted, her face now as pale as ice.

'I realise I don't deserve to see you, and that you will never acknowledge me to be your true mother, especially after what's happened. But I'd like to explain what it was like for me.' Her eyes glistened.

What it was like for her? How dare she? Now she's coming out with the sob story. Danielle continued to frown. *She's not even asked me how I am.*

'When I was abandoned by your father, Rick, I had to face the pregnancy on my own and I tried to be strong. But when I had a newborn child to take care of, a child no one knew anything about, I was frightened to go home and tell my parents.' She slowly shook her head, her eyes now wet with tears.

Danielle became straight faced, fury pounding in her chest and bitterness simmering inside her. 'Why didn't you confide in them? It would have been easier for you that way. Surely they would have understood.' She paused for a long moment, but the woman failed to respond.

As Danielle looked across at her, waiting for some comment, she made direct eye contact. But nothing. And her back went up the way the woman expected her to understand without any clear explanation. A curtain of rage ripped across her vision. 'What is it with you?' She felt herself flush with the built-up anger. 'I just don't understand. Rather than apologise to me for what you did, you try to make me feel sorry for you.' She let out a massive sigh and shook her head. 'Well, let me tell you this. You've taken the wrong approach as far as I'm concerned. I don't feel sorry for you, and I never will.' Her words were clipped.

Joanna shuffled nervously on the sofa. 'I didn't intend for you to feel sorry for me.' Her voice was thread-like. 'All I wanted was to tell you my side of the story. I know I'll never get over my guilt. And, yes, I realised afterwards my parents would have understood, but at the time I panicked.' She dabbed her eyes. 'And then when you disappeared from the hospital I was beside myself. Believe me, by that time I'd come round to thinking I should give myself up and claim you back. But my decision was too late. You'd disappeared.'

Danielle stared hard into the woman's eyes, her anger dissipating now. But her voice still had a bitter edge to it. She spat out the words. 'You'd come around to *thinking* you should claim me back. But you didn't did you? And thanks for asking me how *I* feel,' she countered, her tone wrapped in sarcasm. 'And thank God I did disappear. I've never felt so grateful for my parents than I do now that the truth has come out. I was lucky I had them to care for me and not you. Let me tell you, I've had love and devotion lavished on me since Mama took me to France and Papa joined us. No one can take that away from me.' She took a deep breath before she continued. 'And what you've told me is a weak excuse. You never wanted me. Not like Mama did. And now she's gone.' Danielle reined in her emotions. She didn't want the woman to know the depth of her grief over the loss of her mother. And her feelings towards this Joanna woman were becoming more and more venomous. *Why couldn't **you** have died instead of Mama?* For one irrational moment the words almost slipped out.

With a flicker of regret in her gaze, Joanna continued. 'But I did want you and I'm sorry you're looking at it like that. I understand how bitter you must feel.' She sighed, her confidence now restored. 'I wish we could have hit it off a little better on our first meeting, Danielle,' she stressed, acknowledging the futility of it all. She stood up to leave. 'Before I go, whether you acknowledge me or not, I want to tell you how very proud I am to have a daughter as lovely and as bright as you, and studying to be a doctor too.' She smiled now and patted Danielle's hand.

Danielle snatched her hand away. 'Don't ever refer to me as your daughter. I find that insulting.'

'You can't deny we have blood ties. You have my genes.' She opened her bag and took out a slip of paper. 'I hope you'll think things through, maybe give me some credit for the way you've turned out. And, remember, if at any time you need to talk, I'm always here for you.' She placed the slip of paper on the coffee table. 'My address and phone number.'

Always here for me? Danielle couldn't believe the stupidity of the woman. After all she hadn't been there at the most important time of Danielle's life – to care for her after she was born. *If I needed someone to talk to it certainly wouldn't be her!*

How could she ever think she could make it up to me? That's nothing but ironic!

It was certainly too late for any sort of reconciliation. Danielle was glad the woman had abandoned her. Had she not done so, she would have missed out on Mama and Papa. And that would have been catastrophic.

'How did it go, love?' Wayne stood in the hall as Joanna took off her coat.

'Not good, Wayne.' She turned away.

'How do you mean?'

'She didn't want to see me, and she certainly wouldn't acknowledge that I was her natural mother.' Joanna's face was drawn and her hands were shaking as she hung up her coat.

'But all this has come out of the blue for her. You've got to understand her side of it.' Wayne slipped his arm around her shoulders and gave her a peck on the cheek.

'I realise that. And I thought I'd made allowances. But obviously not.'

'I suppose you can't blame her for the way she's reacted.' Wayne squeezed her shoulders. 'You've made a start. What she needs is time to think things through.'

'It's not as simple as that. All she could do was criticise me for abandoning her. She wouldn't listen to reason.'

'As I said, give it a chance. She knows where you are.'

Joanna followed him into the lounge and sat down beside him on the sofa.

'I take your point, Wayne. We'll see how things go.' She hesitated, her face easing into a tentative half-smile. 'In a way I feel relieved I've met Danielle. She's healthy now the operation's over, and she's such a lovely-looking girl, talented too. She's studying medicine would you believe?'

'Then she is talented.' Returning her smile, he continued. 'But that seals it as far as I'm concerned. She's obviously working hard, so why upset the applecart at this early stage? You'll have the opportunity to contact her again once she's finished for the holidays, once she's relaxed. She'll have had time to think things through by then and maybe come to terms with it.'

'If there's anything we can do to help, Danni, you only have to ask.' Amy linked her arm through Danielle's. 'We're so glad you're back.'

'Thanks for that, Amy. I'm fine now. But I'll be spending most of my time trying to catch up on the work I've missed. And then, of course, we have the end of year exams in a couple of months' time. I'll need plenty of luck then.'

'If you need any help with revision, testing and things, let me know. I'm quite good at that.' Amy smiled warmly.

Danielle managed to collect all the notes she'd missed. Any problems she had understanding them, she consulted the tutors. Although she was fit and well now, she still followed Mr Dexter's advice, most nights staying back in her room to study rather than going down to the bar with the others.

Towards the end of term when she felt her health was just about back to normal and she was fully on track with her studies, James came along, initially to invite her to join them in the bar. 'How are you doing? Need any help? I'm a dab hand at medicine,' he joked.

'I so believe that,' Danielle bantered. 'I'm doing OK, but it's hard work.' She yawned. 'Sorry about that. I'm not yawning because I'm bored, but I think it's time for a rest.'

'Fancy a drink?'

'I do, but I can't face getting ready and going across to the bar.' She pulled a face and stretched, easing the tiredness from her spine.

'That's the reason I called, but we needn't go out if that's how you feel. I'll pop over there and grab us a bottle of wine. We'll relax and drink in tonight.'

Danielle pulled herself up and collected her books from the bed. 'That will suit me better, James. I'll get us a couple of glasses.'

Before slipping her books back on the shelf above her bed, she went into the shower room and glanced in the mirror. What a sight! Tendrils of hair had escaped from her ponytail. She took out the bobble, brushed her hair through and left it loose. It was much more comfortable that way. And then she realised her wine glasses were in the kitchen sink unwashed with the rest of the students' dirty dishes. After sorting through them she brought a couple of glasses back, washed and ready.

When James returned he confessed he'd had a lucky escape. 'Rachel came over and asked me to join them. But I came up with an excuse. I told her I needed to get on with some work and that the wine might help me along.' He laughed.

'But why didn't you tell the others you were here with me?' Danielle sat back on the bed and pushed one of the pillows behind her head.

'Because I didn't want to share you.' He opened the wine and poured out two glasses. 'Here's to exam success for both of us.' He sat on the edge of the bed, lifted his hand and reached over, clinking his glass against hers, his expression eagerly expectant.

Danielle tore her gaze away and avoided looking at him directly. That feeling had come over her again and ripples of emotion flooded every part of her body.

James seemed to sense her reaction. He became still and gazed into her eyes. 'I can't tell you how it feels to have you back. I don't know how I've managed to get through without you.' He took her glass from her and placed it with his own on the bedside table. Hitching himself up on the bed, he slid his body alongside hers and Danielle swivelled herself around to face him. She popped a pillow behind his head and he moved closer. His arms slipped around her and his mouth found hers. He kissed her gently on the lips. She urged herself to resist even though there was no doubt she'd completely lost her heart to him. But how was she supposed to think clearly when he looked at her with those rich mocha eyes so dark and intense, so focused? How could she resist when he made her feel like this? The pull was so strong that she had an overwhelming rush of sensations, and she confessed to herself that, since the day she set eyes on him, an irresistible feeling – of falling in love – had accompanied those sensations.

Her skin became alive now, each pore vibrating as her lips sought his hungrily. And it was all the encouragement he needed. When his mouth swooped down and claimed hers, she melted under the force of his lips and her head began to spin. Her heartbeat raced almost out of control as his hands gently caressed her.

The minute their bodies came together, she began to slip away. She felt the thunder of his heart against hers now, and he possessed her with all the urgency and feeling she so badly needed. It felt so good, so right. He made love to her with such tenderness she gave herself completely, knowing she would never want another man the way she wanted James. And their togetherness was bound up with a multitude of emotions and filled with ecstasy.

When it was over her hands slipped limply from his back and on to the bed. They gazed into each other's eyes, knowing that physically and spiritually they were meant for each other.

With a feeling almost of disbelief, James lay on his bed, the edges of his mouth creased in a smile of contentment and satisfaction. A shiver of excitement attacked him as he recalled the feel of Danielle's body in his arms, the soft expression in her glowing eyes. She was all he could think about. And for several minutes he went over and over in his mind what had happened, realising he must have started to fall in love with her the moment they'd first met. A bubble of joy floated about inside him and he gave a sigh of sheer happiness. Since she'd returned from France she was more strikingly beautiful than ever. He couldn't get her out of his mind. He loved her so much.

To think she had almost dismissed him, telling him she must concentrate on her studies, although she had always seemed to enjoy being with him. At times she'd shied away, and for most of the time all he wanted to do was kiss away the doubt and worry in those velvety brown eyes. But he had spent time agonising over whether or not he should pursue her when it seemed obvious she didn't share his enthusiasm.

That was before the nightmare of her illness and the death of her mother. In the end he knew he could never forsake her. He'd persevered. He'd been patient. And now he would have to take care not to overwhelm her. She needed space to continue with her studies, and she still needed to grieve for her mother.

All he wanted now was to be with her. And for her to respond to his affections.

Chapter 24
The Present – 2008

The grounds were milling with visitors. It was late June and the day of the Annual Summer Party. By this time Danielle was able to think about Mama without becoming too emotional, but she had not overcome her feelings towards Joanna. When her father had told her the truth about her parentage he had been sympathetic and he'd stressed the woman's predicament. 'Try not to be too hard on her. Try to be positive and understanding. After she abandoned you she did have second thoughts, she did come to her senses. Surely the woman has genuinely repented.'

But Danielle wouldn't listen. As far as she was concerned she'd been an unwanted child – end of story.

She pulled her thoughts together and, camera held ready, she concentrated on the task at hand. 'Amy you, James and Rachel first.'

'OK Danni.' Amy smiled as Danielle stood back. 'What a relief to get the first year over.'

'Stop talking and give me a smile.' Danielle flicked her hand at them and began to snap away.

'It's the first year over for you, too, Danni, but have you heard from the academic board? Are they passing you, or do you have to start afresh?' Amy looked concerned.

Danielle changed places with Amy and passed the camera to her for a second photograph. 'I'm not sure. I passed the end of year exam but I haven't caught up on all my assignment work. They still haven't come to a decision. I think the Prof would like me to start afresh. But Strachan and Willis are adamant I can cope. I'm sure I can. And they know me best. I rarely see the Prof. He's not usually on the scene until year two. But I don't mind either way.'

James slipped his arm around Danielle's waist and pulled her to him. She felt the closeness of his body and her heart seemed to ricochet in her chest. Amy clicked on the camera several times. 'There should be a good one amongst those,' she reckoned.

When the photo session was over, Danielle reluctantly released herself from James' grip. 'How do you feel now that the first year is over?'

'I'm more relieved than anything,' James admitted.

Amy rejoiced. 'Well I'm chuffed to bits. And Mum and Dad are over the moon. They think it's wicked. I'm the first one in the family, either side, to go to uni.' Her eyes lit up as she looked across the field at the couple walking towards her. 'And here they come,' she added, dashing ahead. 'Hi there,' she called, catching her mother's hands and giving her a hug before plonking a kiss on her father's cheek. 'Come on you two. I want you to meet the gang.' She beamed and pushed her way through the milling crowd.

Danielle took in the handsome couple, realising why Amy was so attractive. And then Amy turned to her. 'Danielle, I'd like you to meet Mum and Dad,' she said, as she took Danielle's hand and pulled her forward.

'This is Danielle, my best friend here,' she claimed as she made the introduction.

Amy's father took her hand. 'Pleased to meet you, Danielle. I take it you're not on the same course as Amy?'

'I'm reading medicine,' Danielle informed him.

'Yes, and she's missed a whole term and still managed to get through the first year. Who's the clever one?' Amy continued, chucking Danielle under the chin.

'That's not strictly true, Amy. I may need to repeat,' Danielle insisted.

'I can tell you now you won't need to repeat, Danni. You've worked so hard, despite everything.'

Frowning, Amy's mother intervened. 'Missed a whole term? I take it you were ill, Danielle.'

'That's right, but I'm fine now.'

'I hope it wasn't anything too serious, love.'

'I had a kidney removed.' Danielle realised it was no good beating about the bush. Amy would be bound to tell them.

'Goodness. That was rather extreme! But I must say you look as fit as a fiddle.'

'I am, and I feel fine now.'

'I suppose you took quite some time to convalesce, especially if you were absent for a whole term.'

Amy frowned and looked anxiously at her friend. 'Mum, I don't think Danielle wants to talk about it. There was a complication if you must know.' She turned to Danielle. 'You don't mind me telling them, do you Danni? And then it'll shut her up.' She grinned and her mother shook her head. 'But she had to wait ages for a blood donor, didn't you Danni?'

Danielle nodded.

'As you can see, Mum it all turned out fine in the end.' She turned and whispered to Danielle within her mother's earshot. 'Sorry about that. She's not only nosy, she's a born worrier too.' They both laughed and her mother joined in.

Amy turned to James. 'When Mum's finished the inquisition, James, perhaps I can introduce you, too?' She turned to her parents. 'This is James. Another best mate. He's from up north.'

'I think I might have met you before, James,' Amy's mother declared. 'Were you at Romney High with Amy?'

'You haven't met him before, Mum. And, no, he wasn't at Romney High. He was at the Boys' Grammar in Manchester.' Amy shook her head and turned to James. 'By the way, are your lot coming or what?'

'They said they were, but Dad had to pop into work first. Something urgent cropped up.'

Amy slipped between her two friends, linking Danielle with one arm and James with the other. 'Then we'll look forward to meeting them.' She smiled. 'Come on. Let's go over to the marquee. I could murder a glass of wine. I think we deserve one.'

Taut and strained, his face deeply etched in discomfort, Gary Croft stared into space. He was staggered. Hot blood raced around his body and settled on his cheeks and forehead. He ran his finger around his shirt collar. 'I don't believe it,' he whispered to Jan. They reached for a glass of wine from the table. 'Let's move away,' he murmured. 'We need to talk,' he added and, realising Amy and her friends had met up with more students who were busy chatting away, Gary took Jan's hand and they headed for the far side of the grounds.

He fanned his face with his hands and shook his head. The flush had disappeared and now his face was turning ashen. 'Are you thinking what I'm thinking?' he asked her.

Jan squeezed his hand. 'I am, love. I can't believe it. She's Marie's daughter, Danielle, isn't she, the one they thought was your daughter? I thought the name rang a bell as soon as I heard it,' she replied, a look of bewilderment on her face.

'Same here, but it didn't register at first.' Gary sucked in air and then released it. 'It's incredible.' He paused momentarily, collecting his thoughts. 'But it puzzles me. There was very little trace of a French accent. What did you think?'

'I agree. She sounded English.'

Gary smiled. 'I suppose she would be pretty fluent with her English, Marie being her mother. Having said that, Amy hardly let her get a word in, she's so excited.'

'Exactly. But what I can't understand is why we didn't know until now. We hadn't a clue.'

Gary took a sip of his wine. 'It's obvious when you think about it. Marcel Dubois didn't reveal anything about his daughter, whether she had a job, whether she was a student, nothing. So how could you tie her up with Amy, studying at the same university? And Amy never mentioned anything. But they're not on the same course are they? So you wouldn't expect her to.' He took another sip of the wine. 'Come to think about it, I did know the hospital was in Edinburgh, but I didn't link it up.' He put his hand over his mouth and gazed ahead vacantly. 'After all this time, she was right their under our noses.'

'And by the sound of it, she's a very bright girl.' Jan smiled. 'And she's a lovely girl too. Did they ever find out who the real mother was?'

'I don't know, love, and I'm certainly not going down that road. I wouldn't like the girl to get wind of the truth, Amy either.'

'I agree, Gary. It's our secret. Let's try and keep it that way.'

Tom Trench took a glass of wine from the tray and wandered through the grounds. It was like looking for a sprat in the ocean. He knew what the lad looked like but he wouldn't recognise the parents. His name was James. He was tall, dark-haired and good looking. But that would fit the description of many of the students wandering about the grounds. He checked the scribbled details in his notebook. His mind flittered from one idea to another. If only he could get the Harlow woman's angle, perhaps he could go along and see the girl, check out what she thought about it. There was quite a story to be had, the mother abandoning her child and then the kidnap. It had been something of a mystery for all those years and if he could get at the truth it really would be a scoop. Readers would certainly be curious after all this time.

His mind reverted to the incident several weeks ago. He'd been annoyed after following the husband to Whiteley's. That had been a complete waste of time. But he did eventually get some joy. After hanging around day after day, it was not until the following Monday morning Tom set eyes on a young man leaving the house, walking along the road into the main street and joining a bus queue. It would be pretty straightforward to follow the bus.

After parking on a double yellow, he hung back, hoping a traffic warden wouldn't approach and, on that occasion, he was lucky. When the bus drew up, the young man climbed aboard and Tom followed it to the train station. He hurriedly stuck his car in the station park, not bothering to take a ticket. He hadn't time to mess about. It was quite a job keeping up with the guy who was tall and moved in long, easy strides, as he made his way inside.

Almost completely out of breath, Tom gulped in air as he checked out the direction the guy was taking, and then glancing briefly at the departure board, he discovered the destination of the train on that particular platform. What happened now? He couldn't afford to lose sight of the guy, and yet it was a hell of a distance. Dammit! There was nothing else for it. He'd have to go the whole hog.

Hoping the train wasn't due out any minute he dashed over to the ticket office and paid the fare for the complete journey. Of course, the guy could be getting off the train anywhere. He wasn't necessarily going all the way. Still out of breath, Tom hurried over to the platform and pushed open the gate. The flag was poised to go up when he jumped aboard. As the train pulled out of the station, Tom sat down a few seats behind the guy and made himself comfortable.

Once the young man had settled down, he took a couple of hefty tomes from his backpack and started to read. It didn't look as though he'd be getting off the train in a hurry. Tom realised it could be a long ride.

The train chugged its way into the countryside towards the east coast. Tom was tired. He'd had a poor night's sleep and then the alarm had rung just as he'd nodded off again. He closed his eyes momentarily and the drone of the engine and the rhythm of the train were a comfort to him. But then a loud thud brought him back to the surface. The young man had dropped a thick file and out had slipped all the papers. Tom leant forward and peered hard but he couldn't quite make out the heading on top of one of the sheets. As the young man slipped the papers back into the file and closed it, Tom fixed his gaze on the words emblazoned on the front cover – *The University of Edinburgh*. Underneath was the name of the student, *James Harlow*. His luck was in. The woman had a son. That was all he needed to know. He got up ready to alight at the next stop.

Once at the office, it was fortuitous when Tom discovered the date of the forthcoming Annual Summer Party. Decision made. He would travel to Edinburgh and search out James Harlow. There'd be lots of people milling around and, with luck, the young man would be there with his parents. But did he know anything about his mother? Maybe not. It could make a juicy story!

Tom pulled his thoughts together. He was here now. His legs began to ache, trailing about searching for the young man.

And then he spotted him with a group of students and from what he could gather some of their parents. But Tom didn't want to jump in too quickly and spoil things. He'd played the waiting game so far and he wasn't about to act impulsively. There was nothing else for it. He'd have to hang around in the hope that the young man would move off on his own. He couldn't confront the whole gang, even though the Harlows themselves might be amongst the group. He would have welcomed an interview with Joanna herself, but softly, softly! He'd start with the son.

He soon realised he couldn't afford to drink any more wine otherwise he wouldn't be in a fit state to interview the lad. And it was an hour and a half later before James crossed the field towards what appeared to be student accommodation. This was the opportunity Tom had been waiting for. He followed James and stood outside the building until he came back out. Tom approached him.

'Excuse me. I'm looking for James Harlow.' He held out his hand. 'My name is Tom Trench.'

Looking slightly bewildered, James took his hand. 'I'm James Harlow. But how did you know that? More importantly what do you want?'

'I'm with the *Leeds Gazette*. I'd like a few words if you can spare the time.'

'But I'm from Manchester. The LEEDS GAZETTE won't be interested in my progress.' He smirked.

'It's not about your progress, James. It's about your mother.'

'About my mother? What the hell are you talking about?' James was puzzled. And then he became concerned. He didn't like the sound of this.

'You mean she never told you?'

James frowned and Tom began to suspect the son knew nothing about it. Had he jumped the gun? But he couldn't reverse things now. He'd have to come clean.

'Told me what?' James shook his head, 'What on earth are you talking about?' He started to move away.

'About her recent interview by the police.' Tom called after him.

'What are you on about? You've got the wrong person.'

'No, I haven't. Your mother is Joanna Harlow I take it.' James remained silent whilst Tom continued. 'Her child was kidnapped and taken to France. It was in all the papers at the time, 1988 it was.'

'You're making all this up!' James accused, but his legs seemed to turn to jelly and his heart began to pump.

'Not at all.' He paused. 'Are you telling me you didn't know?'

James nodded his head.

'I'm sorry to have sprung it on you like this, but I thought we might get something on the human angle.'

It was then a light gradually dawned in his head and suddenly the truth hit him right in the pit of his stomach. He was not an only child.

Tom rattled on excitedly. 'How do you feel about it?'

James stood rigid. Why hadn't they told him? He closed his eyes. It was too much to take in, all this business about his mother being interviewed by the police and her child being kidnapped and taken to France. He tuned the old man out. He didn't want to listen to his scandalous accusations. If that was the truth, then his parents had some explaining to do.

To Tom's dismay, James quickly turned and marched off towards the group he'd left a little while earlier. Tom's hopes of a front-pager began to dissipate. He'd cocked it up again!

'Mum, what are you doing over there?' Amy called. 'I've been looking all over the place for you.'

'We thought we'd leave you to have a little chinwag with your friends,' Jan replied. 'We've had a bit of exercise, a walk round the grounds.' She smiled at her daughter.

'Well come on now. James is looking for his Mum and Dad. He thinks they should be here by now. But they could be anywhere. We've arranged to meet in the marquee.'

'James, we're over here.' Amy waved wildly towards the other end of the marquee. James had his back to them and he was standing with a well-dressed couple, obviously his parents.

'Coming,' James hollered and he nudged his father. The couple turned and the woman beamed. They advanced towards the little group.

As they came closer, Danielle blinked. And then a cloud masked her face. She refocused. Was she seeing things? A cold shiver ran down her back and her veins began to fill with ice. The woman's smile disappeared too.

James proudly presented his parents to the little group and then he introduced each one individually. When it was Danielle's turn, the woman put on a false smile. 'Pleased to meet you.' She stretched out her hand. Danielle took it and the woman held on tight. She turned to James. 'You certainly know how to pick them, James. You never mentioned the girls in your life.'

'I don't tell you everything, Mum. But they are special to me.' The comment was aimed in Danielle's direction.

The woman's mouth dropped open and she let go of Danielle's hand as though it were diseased. Danielle knew exactly why. She turned to look at James, who was still regarding her with that look of adoration.

It all fell into place. To Danielle's horror, the truth shot into her brain and hit her like a juggernaut. The blood types, the potential donor – that was no coincidence. Everything pointed to one thing. She was crushed!

James collected his thoughts He had the right to know and a war was raging inside him between wanting to discover the truth and wanting to ignore it.

Wayne and Joanna saw the look on his face and they moved slightly away from the rest of the crowd as though they knew something was wrong. And from that, he could tell they knew. 'I need a word in private,' he growled, his eyes now cold.

His father took his arm. 'I know, son. Let's go to the car.' When they reached the car he stood beside it and his father clicked open the doors.

'I'm not stepping in there. I want to get to the bottom of this out in the open where I can see your faces.' He breathed heavily and then frowned. 'I've just been told by some reporter that you, Mother, have recently been interviewed by the police. You had a baby many years ago, and that baby was kidnapped. Is that true?'

His mother lifted her head, closed her eyes and bit her lip. 'Yes, it is.'

'Then how come I'm the last person to find out?' he retorted sharply.

She dithered. 'We were going to tell you after the exams,' she offered anxiously.

'After the exams? They've been over for weeks. We've had the results. We're finished for this year. I suppose you'd conveniently forgotten.' He spat out the words.

His father intervened. 'Now don't go upsetting your mother like that. She's been through the mill with all this. We wanted to wait until you were back home. We wanted to give you time to unwind before we told you.' He threw his arms in the air. 'This is what we didn't want.'

'I see. Leave it until Christmas. I might be relaxed enough by then,' he countered, his tone laced with irony.

'And what happened to that child? My brother or sister.'

'Danielle was taken to France.'

'Danielle?' James shook his head in disbelief. 'Danielle who?'

'Dubois.' Wayne intervened. 'But there's no way we're going to discuss the matter until you can be rational and speak to your mother in a civil manner. We're leaving now, going back to the hotel. You know where we are if you want to talk it through.' He went to the passenger door and opened it. 'Get in Joanna,' he directed and his wife stepped inside. As he slipped into the driving seat he continued. 'If you want to come back with us, get in the back. Otherwise you'll find out all about it when you can approach your mother with at least some understanding as to how she feels.'

James almost stopped breathing, blood slowly draining from his face. He was too full of grief, and his emotions were more volatile than he was used to feeling. His heart became a lump of iron and he stiffened as a surge of anger shot through him. And when he opened his mouth to retaliate, the words jammed tightly in his throat.

His heart almost came to a standstill now as sorrow broke over him. He couldn't bear to think about it. He loved Danielle, he cherished her, but now he knew he was about to suffer the worst agony that could have been inflicted on him. And all this time he hadn't known. In an instant he tried to reason it out in his mind. If Danielle was his mother's child and she'd been kidnapped, then Danielle must be his half-sister!

He was stunned. It was as though a volcano had suddenly erupted inside him. But it all made sense now. He should have known, especially after being called back by the Blood Service weeks earlier. The haematologist there had told him his blood

326

was of an extremely rare type and was needed for a patient requiring a transfusion. He asked if James would allow his name to be placed on a national donor list. James had agreed readily but he was anxious to know the name of the patient needing the blood. He suspected it might be Danielle. But he was told they never divulged the name of the potential recipient and that, since the search for donors was a national one, it could be for anyone in the country. 'Sometimes we set up a trawl to find a match for a particular patient, and end up with a type we've been combing the country for to save a completely different patient,' the doctor admitted. 'When someone like you turns up with a rare blood type, we think we've won the lottery! I'm not saying the more common types are not important. In a way they're even more so. After all, the majority of patients need those types, and we can never have too much.'

James had left the centre with Danielle on his mind, convinced they didn't have the same rare blood type. If they did, that would be uncanny. Amy had quizzed him and, convinced his type was not the same as Danielle's, he'd laughed it off and gone on jokingly about his celebrity status, nothing more.

But now he knew better.

What was he going to do now? He felt numb as he dragged his feet back to where the others were still gathered. He took in a deep breath and tried to compose himself.

'Is everything all right, James?' Amy asked.

'Fine. It's just Mum. She's developed a migraine.' He looked around. 'Where's Danni?'

'She's gone back to her room. She was feeling a little tired,' Amy replied, adding in a more hushed tone, 'I think she was disappointed her Dad couldn't come over for the party. But he had an important meeting.' She smiled and turned to Rachel. 'Isn't it tomorrow Danni's flying back home?'

'Yes. She's on an early flight.'

'You'd better go and see her, say goodbye if you're not going to be around after today. It'll be end of September before we're back together again.'

'I'll do that,' he said, turning and walking zombie-like towards Danielle's block. What would he say to her? Did she know the truth already?

His hand went to his brow and his head began to swim, his heart now starting to pound rapidly. His anger had subsided and now the numbness he'd felt earlier was replaced by pain. How could he give her up? She was his half-sister but he was hopelessly in love with her.

Chapter 25
The Present – 2008

He climbed the steps and entered the corridor, tapping gently on her door. 'Danni, it's me. We need to talk.'

She came to the door, her eyes puffy and red with crying. He went inside and closed the door behind him. 'You know don't you?'

Danielle nodded her head and kept on staring straight ahead until she knew she could speak without breaking.

'When did you find out?' James took her hands in his.

She let out a trembling breath. 'Just today when I saw your mother.'

'You recognised her?'

'I've met her once. That was maybe six weeks ago.' Danielle lifted her head and looked him directly in the eyes. 'Why didn't I put two and two together then? I was so uptight about meeting her that the surname didn't ring a bell. And if it had, I wouldn't have expected it to end like this.' She swallowed hard. 'We can't see each other again, James. It wouldn't be right.'

James stretched out his arms and gathered her in, clinging as she clung. 'I realised that the minute I discovered what had happened.'

'But when did you find out?' she murmured, pressing her face to his chest.

'Literally fifteen minutes ago. A journalist approached me and wanted to interview me.' He shook his head and pushed

Danielle to arm's length. 'I still don't really know what it's all about. You say you've met up with my mother. Did she give you a full explanation?'

'I don't really want to talk about it, James. It's so hurtful. Briefly what happened was that your mother abandoned me at the hospital when I was born. Mama went in there and took me away to France. I always thought she was my real mother, until after the operation. It was only then Papa told me the truth.' Tears began to stream down her face again. 'It was only through the search for a donor that it came to light.'

James tried to blink away his own tears as he clung to Danielle. 'I don't know how I'm going to cope without you, Danni. And what about next year? I love you with all my heart and I can't bear to see you go.'

Danielle turned her hot, damp cheek on to his shoulder. 'I know exactly how you feel, James. It's the same for me. But we have to split and start our lives afresh.' She wiped her face with the back of her hand and sat down on the bed. James sat beside her, taking her hand in his. 'I've been thinking it through whilst I've been back here, Danielle continued. One of us has to leave. When I return to Perenchies I'm going to try and transfer to one of the French universities.'

'But you can't. I'll never see you again.'

'Sorry, James. It's hard for me too. But it's the only way out. We could never be brother and sister, or even just friends, not after we've been lovers.' She hesitated and attempted to dry her eyes. 'I'd like you to leave now. I need some space, some time to myself before I pack my things ready for tomorrow.' She stood up and took his hands in hers. 'I'll never stop loving you, James whatever our relationship, although some day I would like to regard you as my brother.'

James pulled her close again and kissed her. 'There'll never be anyone else in my life if I lose you.' Tears sprang to his eyes once more and, although he tried to control his emotions, his lips began to quiver.

'Don't say that, James. Life must go on. You'll meet someone else, I'm convinced of it.'

He seemed to steel himself as he released his hands, let go of her and turned. He opened the door and walked out of her life forever.

Danielle was distraught. She couldn't eat, she couldn't sleep. Her love for James had engulfed her like a giant wave. She sat in the dark with her curtains drawn. Papa knew nothing of the revelation. And Danielle wanted to keep it that way.

But now it all made sense. James had told her about his visit to the Blood Service and, to lighten the conversation, they'd joked about it. But when he'd slipped his hand into his pocket and produced a card from his wallet she'd been staggered.

'But that's my group too,' she'd murmured almost inaudibly. 'How do you mean it's different from mine?'

'Did I catch what you said, Danni? It's your group too?'

Danielle nodded. 'That's right.'

'Isn't it amazing? I actually asked at the clinic if the blood was specifically for you, but they intimated it was for someone else.'

'Of course. I was surmising, nothing more. The fact that we have the same group doesn't mean we have exactly the same rare antigens.'

'It's obviously coincidental.'

Coincidental? Although at the time Danielle had tried to convince herself that their having the same group meant nothing, the extra components being more important, she seriously began to wonder if he had been the intended donor. It was amazing that they both had the same group. Could they possibly be compatible? Perhaps she'd never find out.

But now she knew. The donor must have been James. It couldn't have been coincidental. A rush of heat surged through her. It sounded ridiculous even to herself but the 'what if' factor kept looming before her. What if she and James really had become an item? What if they had married and had children together? James had certainly made it clear he wanted a serious relationship. And what about that night? The outcome could have been disastrous but, fortunately, nothing had come of it. It wasn't as though she was pregnant. But it had been an incestuous relationship, one she was sure neither of them would have allowed to happen had they known.

She shivered and the vacuum inside her increased. Why did she have to lose everyone she loved? She'd lost Mama and now she'd lost James too.

She frowned. She should have known right from the start that Joanna Harlow could have been James's mother. After all, the evidence would have pointed to that conclusion. They were both from Leeds. But her main focus had been to tell the woman exactly what she thought. She'd been so wrapped up in doing just that, she allowed nothing else to impinge.

But there was one question that kept on floating through her mind. *Why did the woman keep James and not me? She wanted him but she didn't want me!*

Danielle blinked the tears away. There was one thing for certain, she must get away. Although she hadn't heard from the academic board as to whether or not she needed to stay down for a year, she had managed to catch up on her studies. But that didn't mean she had to stay at Edinburgh. She would be sad to leave, but it was the only way.

When James eventually returned to Leeds he felt raw. Nothing more could touch him and have the same impact as when he met Danielle. And nothing else could hurt him.

He entered the lounge. His father was seated in an armchair and his mother on the sofa. 'I wondered how long it would be before you came back, son,' his father advanced in gentle tones.

James tried to tamp down his irritation. 'What was there to come back to? My whole world has been turned inside out. What you don't seem to understand is that Danielle and I have had a relationship since we started at university. The minute I saw her I knew she was the one for me. And then this happens. And to be told about my mother by a nosy journalist, a meddling old man, how do you think I feel?'

His mother sat up and turned to face him. 'That should never have happened. We were wrong not to confide in you, James. I can't tell you enough how sorry I am. The reporter had no right to do that. But you must hear me out. I need to tell you about the circumstances in which I left my baby, and how much I regretted it when she was taken away. It was in a moment of foolishness, a moment of instability that I left her. After a few days, when I decided I wanted her back, she'd disappeared. And I've had to suffer the guilt and the loss of her all my life.'

'I suppose it doesn't matter how I feel,' he called after them. 'I love Danielle.' His eyes filled with tears. How could it happen to him?

A horrified look came over Joanna's face and she opened her mouth to speak. But James interceded. 'But, Mum, you could have told me, then perhaps my relationship with Danielle would never have started.'

'I was so ashamed I didn't even tell your father. And I so much didn't want to hurt you, or for you to think less of me.'

'But you didn't give it a chance, did you?'

'No, I suppose I didn't.'

Wayne stood up from his chair and went over to James. 'Come on, son,' he said, slipping an arm around him. 'We're sorry to see you so broken-hearted over this, but it's for the best you split with Danielle, believe you me.' He hesitated before he continued. 'Your mother's been to see Dr Jefferson and she's explained what has happened. You can imagine she was horrified when she realised how much you and Danielle thought about each other. She could tell by the way you looked at the lass.' He turned to his wife. 'Joanna, tell James what the doctor told you.'

'Come and sit next to me, James.' She patted the seat beside her. 'I love you more than anything in the world, and naturally I was frightened you wouldn't understand if I told you about the baby. I was worried you'd begin to hate me.'

'I could never hate you, Mum, whatever you've done in the past.'

'The doctor tells me birth relatives, who don't know they are related and have never met, can spark off intense feelings when they do meet. They often have a need to feel close and intimate, without knowing why.'

'Yes, and that's exactly how Danielle and I felt about each other.' He gave a deep sigh. 'And did he give any solution, your doctor?' His voice held a note of cynicism.

'I'm sorry James, but it's all quite complicated, something I can't explain. I know it's not the answer you would like, but at least it's a start to know it's something other people have gone through.'

'But what's going to happen now? Have you made arrangements to see Danielle again?'

'I've given her my address and phone number, but I very much doubt she'll contact me. She was very angry when we met.'

'I'm not surprised. First the illness, then she needs a rare blood type, after that her mother dies. And now she discovers you didn't want her when she was born and thought fit to abandon her. How do you think she feels?' His comment held an element of derision.

Joanna started to cry. 'My poor baby. What have I done to her?' She turned to James. 'I promise, I was going to tell you.'

'Next year when Danielle and I were contemplating getting married!' He took a deep breath and shook his head. 'That's it for me. I can't take any more.' He still didn't have the full story, but what he'd heard was enough for now. He stormed off and went upstairs to his bedroom.

'Joanna don't get upset again, love,' Wayne begged as he reached out and took her hands. 'Let it rest for now. He'll come round.'

When Papa left for the office, Danielle went back in her room. And she never gave him cause to suspect anything about the discovery she'd made. James was constantly on her mind, but she tried to blot out all thoughts of him by becoming absorbed in her studies. And it was as she read through her notes, she came across a photocopy of a paper one of the students had passed on to her after a lecture by a well-known London Consultant Psychiatrist. The subject of his lecture was genetic sexual attraction – attraction between close relatives – a condition known in the profession as GSA. Danielle was curious and she read the paper avidly, disappointed she hadn't been present at the time of the lecture, although she hadn't known then that she and James were siblings. But what interested her was that some of the closely related couples interviewed were unable to stop their feelings for each other although, according to the psychiatrist, this magnet-like attraction is quite normal and there is no need for anyone to feel guilty about it. In time the relationship should settle in its proper context.

Danielle tried to digest the psychiatrist's words, telling herself that her relationship with James would eventually revert to that of brother and sister. And although she couldn't think about James without feeling sad, the psychiatrist's words provided some reassurance.

Having made a decision not to return to Edinburgh she realised her energies must now be concentrated on her plans for the future. If she could sort out a university and concentrate on her studies, hopefully it would take her mind off both Mama and James.

After a thorough trawl of the many universities offering medicine in France, Danielle finally chose Universite Pierre et Marie Curie in Paris where she applied to be interviewed. She realised it might be tricky in view of the fact that she had already completed one year of her course in Edinburgh, but she could explain that when she attended for interview.

The Head of the School of Medicine was kind to her when she explained about the death of Mama, the operation, and the fact that she'd had to catch up on her studies when she returned.

'I'm very impressed,' he told her. 'You were absent for a whole term and yet you caught up on your studies and passed the first year exams.'

'But it wasn't without hard work,' Danielle replied.

'I'm sure it wasn't. But we have two options here. The Edinburgh course and ours here in Paris are completely different. We can either place you in year two or keep you back in year one. Now I must explain that you will need to work doubly hard if you take the first option. But if you take the second it will be much more straightforward. If you opt to stay back, you will have an advantage over the other students. You will already have covered much of the work and you would most likely come out with tip-top results. According to the references from Edinburgh you were an excellent student there, and there's no reason why that level of success cannot continue.'

'I must admit I'd be more satisfied to stay back and repeat the first year. I would prefer to start afresh rather than put in lots of extra work to cover the areas we didn't study in Edinburgh during the first year.'

'I think you've made the right choice, my dear. And although you can't afford to slacken your efforts, it would give you some respite especially after the setbacks you've had during your time in Edinburgh.' He smiled benignly. 'We'll send you a formal acceptance and perhaps you would inform the department in Edinburgh accordingly. I look forward to seeing you at the start of the course. It will be a pleasure to have you with us.'

Danielle was delighted with the result of her interview. Now she could start afresh. She had promised to keep in touch with Amy and Rachel, but she had made no such arrangements with James. That would be dangerous. But perhaps in time she would get over the heartache, and she certainly hoped James would, too.

Later that day when Danielle called in the factory to tell Papa the news, she realised he'd told just about everyone in the company about her success in Edinburgh and her possible change of university. She received so many congratulatory comments from the women on the shop floor that she felt embarrassed. But perhaps they were feeling sorry for her after losing Mama, and then the operation.

'Oh, Papa. Why do you have to boast like that? They were all looking at me and commenting when I arrived.' She shook her head and frowned.

Marcel took her hands and squeezed them. 'It's not everyone who has a daughter as clever as mine,' he replied, 'I have the right to boast,' he added as his gaze switched to the door. He stood up. Pierre Clarisse was standing there.

'Pierre, so good to see you again.' He walked across the room and offered his hand. Pierre took it. 'Have you met my daughter?'

Pierre turned to face her and a smile broke out, lighting up his handsome face. 'Yes I have, but in very different circumstances. Remember, Marcel when we called to see Doctor Fry? You took me along to see Danielle.' He paused. 'You're certainly lucky to have a daughter as clever and as beautiful as Danielle.' And now his smile was brimming with sensual invitation. 'I must say, I'm looking at a different woman from the one I saw before.' He gazed unashamedly at her with eyes so liquid brown you could almost drown in them.

Danielle vaguely remembered him from when he came to the ward with Papa, but his visit had been fleeting. She gave a wide-eyed, fascinated glance and took in this tall, powerful figure. He seemed to fill the office physically with his height and with his strong, dominant presence. A pink glow began to spread from her chin to her forehead. Papa and his boastful comments! He caused her no end of embarrassment at times.

Marcel beamed. Not that he was matchmaking. He'd never dream of doing that. He knew what it was like being on the other end. But wouldn't it be wonderful if Danielle and Pierre took an interest in one another? Two very beautiful and very bright sparks together. That was a thought.

But then it occurred to him. Didn't she have someone who held a torch for her at the university? When they were alone, he must ask her what happened there.

'Pierre and I have business to discuss, cherie. Do you want to wait for me or are you anxious to get away?'

'I'd prefer to get back, Papa. I've lots to do.' She turned to Pierre. 'Nice meeting you,' she offered.

He took her hand and kissed the back of it gently. 'It was my pleasure, Danielle. Let's hope we meet again some time,' he advanced, his voice sexy, his grin pure devilment.

Danielle felt herself unaccountably disturbed both by his actions and his words, and she tried to pull herself together. She needed to get away.

It was early evening when Papa phoned. 'How about a meal at Le Bistrot Bouvier?' he suggested. 'It seems like ages since we were there together. I'm planning to finish here at seven. Would you like to come along and meet me, say about seven thirty?'

'I'd love to, Papa,' she replied as she headed towards the bathroom to take a shower. 'Give me fifteen minutes either way.'

He was sitting at his usual table when she arrived. She hurried across to greet him, bending over and giving him a hug. 'It's so good to be back together, Papa, just like old times. And when I get to Paris, I can come home regularly and see you.' And then she tried to blink away the mist before her eyes. 'The only person missing is Mama.'

'I know, treasure. It'll be a long, long time before we get used to being without her. But let's try to be positive.' He gave a faint half-smile and quickly changed the subject.

'Pierre was very impressed when he met you this afternoon. I think he was besotted the way he looked at you.'

'Papa, stop it. It's all in your head.' She laughed out loud.

'But I've seen that look before. What about the young man who came to visit you at university, the one who brought you the flowers? I seem to recall his name was James. He looked at you in exactly the same way.'

Her stomach churned. She felt a knot of guilt form in her chest. She hadn't thought about James since yesterday. That was a first and hopefully a start. And then her face lost its tension. 'It didn't work out Papa. We weren't meant for each other after all.'

The moment the words came out of her mouth, she wondered where they had come from. But she breathed a sigh of relief. That was positive thinking.